Road to Briarwood

Holly Bebernitz

For Jessica

Holly Bebernitz

Romans 12:10

Quinn Rose PRESS

Road to Briarwood is a work of fiction. Names, characters, places, and incidents are the products of the author's imagination and are used fictitiously. Any resemblance to actual events, locales, or persons, living or dead, is entirely coincidental.

Published in the United States by QuinnRose Press

ISBN: 978-0-9891721-1-0

Cover design: Michael Regina

Printed in the United States of America

www.hollybebernitz.com

Acknowledgments

Angela Bilger: for providing insight into the world of those who aspire to be professional musicians. Her detailed and patient correspondence was invaluable in creating a believable portrait of Lorna Maron.

Joan Cordell: for sharing her vast experience with musical auditions and performances and for suggesting suitable instrumental selections for the program which occurs in the story.

Jim Hamlett: for his expert advice on the staging of the fine arts festival and for his expert advice on writing in general.

Anna Harmon: for providing information about the legal matters which affect the characters.

May Leporacci: for suggesting appropriate vocal numbers for the program.

Leslie Miller: for her research on gourmet meals for formal dinners.

Michael Regina: cover artist.

Rachael Stringer: proofreading and formatting the final manuscript and preparing it for publication.

Aaron & Haley, Aidan and Allison; Paul & Heidi, Ryland and Ella; Ethan & Lindsay: in all ways, in all times, my joy.

My readers: for loving the first book enough to make me believe I could write the second.

Dedicated to the memory of John M. Dennison, longtime friend, whose faith in me never wavered, and who always encouraged me to pursue my dreams, no matter how improbable.

Chapter 1

Strangers on a Train

If only I had left Dennisonville on Saturday, I would've had time to talk to Margaret *before* the first day of faculty orientation. She would've given me a complete rundown on the new people on staff, and I would've recognized Elspeth Sherwood at once. If I'd known she was the new provost, I could've advised the janitor, Talmadge Hampton, to wait till later to change the fluorescent light. But I didn't leave Dennisonville till Sunday, and, as a result, there was no possibility my second year at Brighton Park Community College would begin any better than the first one had.

As Dr. Sherwood tapped on her gold-plated name badge and demanded through clenched teeth if I knew "who she was," I stared, bewildered, at her and wondered how, only a few minutes into the fall semester, everything had gone so wrong. Only twenty-seven hours had passed since I'd awakened in my third floor room at the Magnolia Arms and had lain in the dark, knowing once I rose, summer would end. I would leave the beautiful house to return to my musty classroom, needy students, tiny apartment, and chatty roommate, and would begin to cross autumn's thousands of days off the calendar.

Nestor Carlyle, the gardener at the Magnolia Arms, had driven me to the train station. While he parked the truck, I lugged my big black suitcase to the platform and sank down on top of it to search my purse for my ticket. When I stood, my dinosaur of a bag toppled onto the leather briefcase of the man standing next to me. Before I could splutter out an apology, the man kicked my suitcase and snatched up his briefcase, cradling it as if he were quieting a child plucked from the path of a speeding car.

"What do you think you're doing?" he asked.

"It was an accident," I said. "No harm done."

I heaved my bag upright and sized up the stranger.

If he hadn't been wearing jeans with his starched blue shirt and brown suit jacket, I would've guessed he was a stockbroker or corporation president. Any man who parted and tamed his hair so meticulously must be accustomed to dismantling financial empires and dismissing staff. He set down his briefcase a safe distance from me and cleaned his gold wire-rimmed glasses with a monogrammed handkerchief. Then he bent down to straighten the tassels on his expensive loafers, worth more, no doubt, than my entire wardrobe. At least my suitcase hadn't fallen on his foot and snagged his argyle socks.

"No harm done," he mumbled. "Easy for you to say."

"Excuse me?" I said.

He pointed at my offensive bag. "The zipper on the side compartment might've scratched this leather. Do you have any idea how much an attaché case like this costs?"

Attaché case? I thought. Who does this guy think he is—James Bond?

"I'm pretty sure I do," I said. "I offered to buy one for my father for his birthday, but he said he'd rather have a new leaf blower."

My attempt to lighten the moment failed.

The stranger sneered. "Was the general store all out of corncob pipes?"

I turned to face him. "Look, Mr.—I was sitting here minding my own business—"

Nestor joined us on the platform. I decided not to spoil my last few minutes with him by reliving what had happened, so I kept quiet. The stranger turned away.

"Thanks for staying for my birthday, Agnes," Nestor said. "You really should've gone home sooner, so you had time to rest before you go back to work tomorrow."

"I wouldn't have missed it for the world," I said. "It's not every day a guy turns 30."

Nestor pulled out his wallet and handed me a check.

"I almost forgot," he said. "Ivy Leigh wanted you to give this to Flossie—payment for the last order of pot holders."

I tucked the check inside my purse.

"Give Flossie our love," Nestor said. "Maybe she can come with you next time."

"Maybe," I said. Then, sniffling like a five-year-old on the first day of school, I stared at the ground, my shoulders rising and falling as I wept. "Thanksgiving is ages away."

Nestor pulled a paper towel from his pocket. "I knew you'd need this, so I grabbed one as we left the kitchen. These goodbyes don't get any easier, do they?"

"No. I didn't want to leave after my first two trips, and I don't want to leave now."

"Don't cry, Agnes. You're going back to Jonas and Margaret. Don't forget that."

"You're right," I said. "That does help."

Nestor lingered on the platform till time for me to leave and then hugged me so tight he lifted me up off the concrete. I buried my face in his shoulder. When I looked up, I noticed the stranger staring at me, still scowling. Unnerved by the thought of sitting near him during the long journey, I hung on Nestor's arm till the stranger entered the train and all the other passengers followed behind him. Only Nestor's urging to "get going" dislodged me from the platform.

I boarded the train at the last possible moment and slid into an aisle seat, next to a woman in a long-sleeved black pullover sweater tucked neatly into the waistband of her camel-colored slacks. Her hair, so light a shade of artificial blonde it was almost white, was teased, combed straight back, smoothed under, and held in place by a tortoise shell headband. A generous coat of powder on her face made her dark red lips look like black cherries on vanilla ice cream. Behind her narrow black-framed glasses dotted with tiny rhinestones at the corners, her pale hazel eyes glistened.

"Excuse me," I said. "Do you mind if I lean over you to wave goodbye to my friend?"

She nestled back in her seat. "Not at all. Just be careful you don't jostle Mary Smith."

"Who?" I asked.

She pointed at a potted peace lily between us on the floor.

"For my new home," she said.

"The plant is named Mary Smith?"

"All my plants have names," she said. "Don't yours?"

"No, I'm not a plant person," I said. "But my friend is—the one I want to wave to?"

"Sorry," she said. "I'd never stand in the way of a fond farewell, or sit in the way either."

I waved till Nestor spotted me and kept waving till the station faded out of sight. Then I leaned back my head and squeezed my eyes shut in a futile attempt to stop the gush of tears.

The woman patted my arm. "There's no worse feeling in the world than saying goodbye to the one you love, is there? Are you engaged?"

Eyes open, I turned to her. "Engaged?"

"Has he popped the question yet?"

"No, he hasn't popped the question," I said. "He's the gardener."

Her eyes widened. "Oh-o-oh. He feels unworthy to ask your hand in marriage."

If I'd met this lady a year earlier, I would've responded to her inquiries with chilly indifference, quieted her with an insincere smile, and kept to myself all the way to Plainview.

But since I'd met Flossie Bingham, I'd learned to regard the eccentricities of "little old ladies" as unspoken requests for companionship.

"No, he doesn't feel unworthy," I said. "He studied at Princeton."

She spread a red-checked dish towel on her lap and settled a large gray Thermos on top. "So, you're *not* a wealthy heiress hiding a forbidden love for the hired help?"

"No, I'm not an heiress," I said. "I'm a schoolteacher."

She unfolded a pink paper napkin and tucked it under her chin. "How noble of you to forsake your aristocratic roots to serve mankind. Do you like Russian tea?"

"Never tried it," I said. "And I don't have any aristocratic—"

"Then you must join me," she said. "Could you hold this while I look for the extra cup? I always bring one in case I meet a new friend."

She shifted the Thermos to my lap. Then she rifled through the contents of a large flowered canvas bag till she produced two apples.

"Hold these?" she asked.

I balanced an apple in each hand while she pulled out a box of graham crackers, set it in her own lap, and stacked three paperback romance novels on top.

The titles read: *Catherine of Fern Valley*, *Dogwood Hill*, and *Lilith's Tudor Rose Quilt*.

The reason for her wishful notions about Nestor and me became clear.

She produced a pale blue glass mug and traded me for one of the apples and the Thermos. When she untwisted the silver cap, a delectable fragrance drifted up.

"I hope you like cloves," she said. "I always add more than the recipe calls for." She poured tea in my cup. "There you are—?"

"Agnes," I said. "Agnes Quinn."

"What a lovely name. It's so important what name a person has."

4

The tea surprised me. "This is wonderful. What's in it?"

"Instant tea, powdered orange drink, lemonade mix, sugar, cinnamon, cloves."

"My friend Flossie would love this," I said. "I'll have to write down the recipe for her."

She snuggled back in her seat. "It's the perfect comfort drink. I used to make it for my daughter when she was little, but now … she doesn't much care for anything I do."

Her voice broke. She ducked her head; her chin quivered.

Relieved I hadn't refused her offer of refreshment and conversation, I squeezed her hand.

"Your daughter is fortunate to have a mother like you, Mrs.—?"

She turned toward me and smiled. "Winifred Parker-Potts. My friends call me Winnie."

"Parker's an unusual middle name," I said, hoping to distract her and cheer her up.

She placed a pink paper napkin on my knee, handed me her nearly overflowing cup, and fumbled in her bag till she found a paring knife wrapped in plastic secured by a rubber band.

"Not my middle name. It's Parker—hyphen—Potts. Two husbands. When I married Arthur, I couldn't bear to give poor old departed Vernon the heave-ho, so I kept his name, too."

Once she'd undone the rubber band, she slipped it on her wrist, and then, holding the apple in her left hand, sliced a perfect wedge with the paring knife she wielded with her right.

"Very thoughtful," I said, wincing from the perilous proximity of the knife to her thumb.

"Hyphenated names are so unique," she said. "I've often thought mine would look nice on the cover of a mystery. *The Gladiola Murders* by Winifred Parker-Potts."

"You're a writer," I said. "I should've known. You just happen to have your manuscript in your bag, don't you?"

"No, not in there," she said. "All up here." She tapped her temple. "Even if I had started writing, I'd never carry anything that valuable with me. It might get lost."

I thought of my own manuscript, *Magnolia Neighbors*, tucked away in my suitcase.

"A sensible precaution," I said.

Her mouth full of apple, Winnie asked how long I'd been teaching.

"Only a year."

She swallowed. "And how long have you been hiding your romance from your parents?"

"I told you—I'm not hiding anything," I said. "If you must know, I'm dating a lawyer named Sefton Wilkinshaw. As a matter of fact … he and I are collaborating on a book."

Even as I said these words, I still couldn't believe I was talking about myself. Though Sefton and I had been conducting a long distance romance for almost a year, I still felt I was dreaming whenever I talked about my relationship with him.

Winnie, however, was not impressed.

"Does Mr. Wilkin-whatever-his-name-is know you're in love with another man?"

"Wilkinshaw," I said, "and I'm not in love with Nestor. He's like my brother … well, not like my brother exactly. Nestor is way more impressed with me than my own brother ever—"

I halted mid-sentence when I spotted the mysterious stranger maneuvering up the aisle. In the same manner as he had on the platform, he glanced at me and frowned.

The silent but poisonous exchange was lost on Winnie, who continued her interrogation.

"If you and this lawyer are so in love, then why did *Nestor* bring you to the train station, and why were you crying?"

"Because he's my friend—one of a whole houseful of friends," I said. "This is the third time I've visited them in a year, and I *always* cry when I leave."

Winnie leaned on the armrest between our seats and cradled her chin in her hand.

"Now we're getting somewhere. Tell me about these people."

Since I never tired of talking about the Magnolia Arms, I gazed out the window and pondered where to begin—how to condense the most miraculous year of my life into a few sentences. On my first day at Brighton Park when I parked in the wrong space, I began the most important friendship of my life—got tangled up in the rescue of a failed dream—was framed for stealing—left my job and took up residence in the place I'd been dreaming of—reunited my friend Jonas with Margaret, his lost love—found a love of my own.

Not even Winnie would believe the story.

"Tell you what," I said. "Let's start with you … after I get back from the bathroom."

While we'd been philosophizing about love, I'd been preoccupied with more basic matters. Full of tea and desperate for relief, I'd delayed a trip to the bathroom for fear of encountering the stranger in the narrow aisle. When I could wait no longer, I scanned the aisle, found the way clear, and darted safely into the restroom. My return trip was less fortunate. I'd taken only three steps when my nemesis appeared at the opposite end of the car. Like gunslingers at high noon, we advanced. I spotted an empty seat and stepped aside to let him pass.

A copy of *Mumford's Guide to Civil War Reenacting* clutched in his arm, he raised one eyebrow. "That's my seat," he said.

"Did you want to sit there, lady?" asked a little boy by the window. "Please."

"Uh ... no," I said. "I'm sitting with a friend."

"When you're ready," the stranger said.

I stepped back into the aisle, and he sat down.

"No more crumbs from you," he said to the little boy. "Remember."

The child nodded and clutched a half-empty potato chip bag in his hands.

Vowing never to watch *Murder on the Orient Express* again, I walked away. The moment I returned to my seat, Winnie placed a full cup of tea in my hand.

"Now where were we?" she asked.

Too rattled to talk, I diverted her.

"You were going to tell me about your daughter," I said.

Easily sidetracked, Winnie began her tale.

"Darlinda Sue was the dearest little curly-headed thing," she said.

"Darlinda? That's an unusual name."

Winnie laughed. "I wanted to name her 'Darling,' but her father wouldn't hear of it. So we compromised."

"Probably for the best," I said.

"She stopped calling herself Darlinda after she turned twelve. That's why I was having a hard time finding her."

"She's missing?"

"Only to me," Winnie said. "She warned me if I didn't quit nagging her about her boyfriend, she'd leave home and I'd never see her again, and that's precisely what happened."

Winnie dabbed at her eyes with the pink napkin.

"How long has it been since you've seen her?" I asked.

"Years," she said. "Arthur would never let me go after her, but once he died, there was nothing to keep me from launching out on my own."

"So you're on your way to find her?"

"Yes, and this is as close as I've gotten," Winnie said. "Maplewood."

"That's only forty-five miles from where I live," I said.

She powdered her nose with a compact from her purse. "Darlinda runs a business there."

"What kind of business?"

"Entertainment," Winnie said.

Since Maplewood was hardly a bustling cultural center, I was concerned what kind of entertainment Darlinda might be engaged in.

"How did you find out she was in Maplewood?" I asked, wondering if I could empty my most recent cup of tea into Winnie's plant before she noticed.

"Darlinda had an accident while she was performing. She listed me as nearest relative on the form she filled out at the hospital. They've just contacted me about her delinquent bill."

"You're not going to Maplewood to pay her medical bills, are you?"

"Of course," Winnie said. "This is the chance I've been waiting for. It's the first time she's reached out to me. Maybe—if I help in her hour of need—I can win back her heart."

"But she didn't contact you. A collection agency did. You're not responsible for her bills—no matter what they're for."

Winnie shook her head. "You'd have to be a mother to understand."

We ate graham crackers and swapped stories for the rest of the trip. When we reached Maplewood, I held Mary Smith while Winnie gathered her belongings.

"Thank you, Agnes," she said. "When I see my Darlinda, I hope I find she's grown up to be just like you."

My heart ached as I watched Winnie, flowered bag in one hand, plant in the other, standing on the station platform to survey her surroundings. Though I'd never met the prodigal daughter, I'd already foreseen the outcome of Winnie's quest. Darlinda had listed her mother's contact information, knowing full well Winnie would be so desperate to find her she'd gladly pay the bill. I grieved for Winnie's broken heart, dreaded the disappointment she was facing, and concluded she'd be better off finding new friends than locating her errant daughter.

I moved to Winnie's seat and closed my eyes. Worried, worn out, lonely, unsettled by the stranger, I fell headlong into the recurring dream I had each time I faced a crisis. I was stranded backstage in a dark auditorium. The curtain was about to rise. I could not recall a single line of my part. The roar of the audience grew louder. My panic increased. I stepped into the spotlight.

The train stopped. I jolted awake, realized I was drooling, and pried my eyes open in time to see the sinister stranger standing in the aisle next to me.

"You might want to wake up if you're getting off here," he said. He tapped on the corner of his mouth. "You might want to wipe your mouth, too."

Mortified, I scraped my hand across my lips.

When I stepped off the train, I saw no sign of the stranger, but was relieved to see the little boy safe in the arms of a smiling woman, who was most certainly his mother.

I was even more pleased to find Muriel Porter waiting for me. I rushed toward her, dropped my bag, and hugged her.

"The wanderer is home at last," she said. "But why the tears?"

"I'm glad to see you," I said. "It was a long trip."

"You can fill me in over supper," she said. "I have a new entrée I want you to try."

Muriel owned the Drifters' Rest, famous for the best food and the best coffee in town.

"Are Margaret and Jonas meeting us for dinner?" I asked.

Muriel hesitated. "They'd planned to, but there's been a bit of an emergency."

My heart stopped. "What's wrong?"

"They've taken Flo Sloan to the doctor. She wanted to wait till you got home to tell you, but there's no need to keep the secret now. Buck and Flo are going to have a baby."

"That's wonderful," I said, "but what's the problem?"

"Flo is one of those women whose 'morning sickness' lasts most of the day," Muriel said. "She's dehydrated."

"I'll go see her tomorrow after school. A visit to the ranch would do me good."

"From what I hear you'll need *something* to cheer you up after your first day. Brighton Park is upside down since the new administrator showed up. Everybody's talking about her."

"You mean the new provost? Margaret told me she'd arrived, but nothing else."

"Elspeth Sherwood," Muriel said. "But let's not talk about her—might spoil your appetite. I want to hear all about your summer."

While I dined on chicken and spinach manicotti, Muriel quizzed me about my friends at the Magnolia Arms.

"Are Posey and Xander still together?" she asked.

"Yes. Xander's saving for a ring."

"And is Ivy Leigh well?"

I nodded. "A food critic from Raleigh gave the restaurant a stellar review. She's busier than ever."

Muriel served blueberry pie and coffee and then took me home.

Though I was fond of my roommate, Flossie Bingham, I was relieved to find a note from her saying: "Spending the night at the Sloans. They'll need help after her doctor visit." Flossie was a gentle soul, superb cook, and cared for my cat Saturn when I was away, but she rarely stopped talking. Formerly my neighbor, she'd appealed to me for help when her son Warner brought home a new wife—the owner of the motorcycle stunt show he'd joined—and insisted Flossie move out of their apartment. She'd been staying with me till she "found a new place."

I left my unopened suitcase by the door and sank down on my favorite spot on the sofa. When Saturn, ever a willing listener, leaped on my lap, I filled him in about my remarkable summer, the eventful trip home, the sinister stranger, and Winnie.

"At least I don't have to worry about seeing either of them again," I said. "And as for tomorrow … at least I'm not a first-year teacher, so I'm no longer at the bottom of the food chain. Margaret is chairman of my department. She's the best boss ever. I've made such good progress on my book, I'll be able to submit it to a publisher by December. Sefton hasn't proposed, but he hinted. If I work hard and save some money, maybe I can quit teaching after we get married and spend the rest of my life writing books."

On Monday morning I stopped at the Drifters' Rest for coffee and a bagel. Fortified, I drove to Brighton Park and entered the library where faculty orientation was held each year. I sat down at the table farthest from the lectern and watched as the faculty, clutching tattered briefcases and balancing paper plates of stale doughnuts on top of Styrofoam cups, edged toward their chairs and settled down for the long morning ahead.

We lifted our eyes to the imposing banner suspended from the ceiling and read:

Brighton Park Community College
Welcomes Dr. Elspeth Sherwood
Fall 1977

"Striving for the Superior"

The librarian, Elinor Ellershaw, sat next to me and pointed to the sign. "An unfortunate motto, don't you think?"

"What does it mean?" I asked.

"I think it's intended to be rhetorical … 'don't settle for the mediocre; strive for the superior.' But the way it's worded sounds like we're supposed to spend the year—"

"Striving for *our* superior," I said.

"That's what everyone is saying."

"Where's Margaret?" I asked. "She's usually early to these meetings."

"Probably with Lorna Maron."

"Who?"

"The new teacher in your department. First-year jitters. You remember."

I didn't mention I was having second-year jitters.

"Good morning, Miss Quinn. Did you have a nice summer?"

I looked up to find Talmadge Hampton, our janitor, at the end of our table, holding a tall aluminum stepladder at his side.

Talmadge, nicknamed "Ham," was an fixture at Brighton Park. He had aspired early to a maintenance career and practiced his craft alongside his father, Torbert, like a medieval apprentice. Ham was neither well-groomed nor well-spoken. He was, however, reliable, hard-working, and completely devoted to the teachers of Brighton Park. Only mention the wobbly leg on your desk or the squeaking hinges on your door, and the next morning you'd find your problem solved. Soft-hearted and shy, Ham rarely appeared during school hours. Attention of any kind was painful for him, so we never embarrassed him with either praise or blame.

"I had a wonderful summer, Ham," I said. "How about you?"

"Dad and I got a lot done," he said. "Excuse me." He pointed to a dark corner of the ceiling. "I got to fix that light. You know how dad likes things perfect."

As Elinor and I talked, I watched Ham cart the tall step ladder into place and position it beneath the broken light.

"Anyone else new besides Lorna?" I asked.

"Kennesaw Fleming."

"Ken-ne-what?" I asked.

"Not so loud," she said. "He may be here somewhere. 'Kennesaw.' You know, like the town in Georgia."

"No, I don't know the town in Georgia," I said. "I'm awful with geography."

"I looked it up," Elinor said. "Civil War history, the railroad. They filmed a movie there."

"Who would name their son after a town in Georgia?" I said.

"Someone did," Elinor said, "unless he changed his name himself."

"What does he teach?" I asked.

"History."

"Of course," I said. "Only a history teacher would be emotionally charged enough to change his name to a town in Georgia."

Ham removed the long fluorescent bulb, descended the ladder, and disappeared behind the wall of people.

"Tell me about this Lorna girl," I said. "What's her story?"

"If you'd come home a few days earlier," Elinor said, "you could've spent a little more time in your office and found these things out for yourself."

"If I'd come home earlier, I would've missed Nestor's birthday. Then again, I would've missed the guy on the train yesterday."

"What guy?"

I recounted the story of the toppling suitcase, trying to sneak to the bathroom, meeting the stranger in the aisle, the frightened child.

"And of all things," I said, "when he was getting off the train, he made fun of me when he caught me sleeping with my mouth open."

"I should be the last person in the world to suggest you're reading too many books," Elinor said, "but really, don't you think you're letting your imagination run away with you?"

"I'm telling you … there was something sinister about that guy," I said. "Haven't you ever met someone who made you nervous?"

"Actually, yes. Dr. Sherwood."

"What happened?"

"She and her secretary came into the library last week. She strutted around, pointing at things and commenting, while the secretary made notes on a clipboard."

"Maybe she's planning improvements," I said.

Elinor shook her head. "I've seen her type before. She'll stay long enough to prove how good she is at slashing budgets and trimming staff. Then she'll leave for a better position."

"You think she'd go after the library staff?"

"Not only the library. With her it's all about the bottom line. Mark my word."

Latecomers straggled in. The burgeoning assembly jumbled themselves into clusters of three or four, sharing photos of summer vacation, laughing, patting each other on the back.

The clamor swelled from a pulsating hum to a dull roar.

Elinor stood. "I'm going to look for Margaret. She should be here by now. Dr. Sherwood is opening this session by introducing the department chairs. If Margaret is missing—"

"I'll save two places," I said.

"Three," Elinor said. "Lorna will be with Margaret."

Since when had *Lorna* become a factor in our plans? I thought.

I scooted a book across the table to hold one place and was sliding my purse to the other, when, over the din of the crowd, I heard a shrill voice shrieking.

"You there, what do you think you're doing?" it said.

I looked up. Ham, once more at the top of the ladder, was holding the new bulb with both hands, his arms extended high over his head as he positioned the light into place.

I stood, but couldn't see through the throng of people.

Again the voice screeched. "I'll have your job for this."

Startled, Ham turned to look back over his shoulder. The bulb slipped from his right hand and swung down behind his back like a pendulum.

Without thinking, I charged through the herd of teachers, shouting as I dodged tables and bumped into chairs.

"Hey," I said, "don't yell at him. If you make him nervous—"

Ham tilted backward. The bulb slid down, balanced a moment on its end, fell forward, and shattered. Teachers scattered as the glass flew. Panicked, Ham locked his left arm around the ladder, and pulled himself in, holding on as the ladder wobbled and slammed into the reference section. Ham thudded to the floor.

By the time I pushed through the front row of onlookers, Ham was on his hands and knees, trying to stand. The coach rushed over to help and guided him toward a chair.

"Easy there, big guy," he said. "You may have broken something."

"I'm all right," Ham said. "I know how to fall."

A petite woman in a black skirt and jacket, a long white silk scarf draped over her shoulder, pranced toward Ham. She placed one hand on her tiny waist and swept the other through the air. Though her back was toward me, her voice was unmistakable.

"You shouldn't have tried to do this by yourself. Our insurance policy states—"

"That does it," I said.

As I stormed ahead, the geology teacher made a grab at my arm. "Agnes, no. That's—"

Ham caught sight of me and shook his head. "It's all right, Miss Quinn. Don't—"

I approached from behind and tugged on the woman's scarf.

"I don't know who you think you are," I said, "but around here we treat each other with respect, whether it's the janitor or—"

Dr. Elspeth Sherwood whirled around, tapped on her gold-plated name badge, and demanded through clenched teeth if I knew "who she was."

I stared, bewildered, at her and peeked at my watch.

She crossed her arms, tilted her head to one side, and looked down her perfect nose.

"I'm sorry, Miss Quinn," she said. "Am I interrupting your schedule?"

Dumbfounded by the chain of events, I couldn't make sense of what she was saying.

"What?" I asked.

"You're looking at your watch. Am I boring you?"

I fixated on a copy of *Lyrical Ballads* on the library shelf behind her. "Not yet," I said.

My reprimand concluded, I returned to my seat, my eyes riveted to the floor as I threaded my way through the stunned and silent faculty. Margaret, Elinor, and a young woman I supposed was Lorna Maron were waiting at my table.

I picked up my books. "I'm leaving," I said.

"No, you're not," Margaret said. "Sit down and be quiet."

I complied. Dr. Sherwood stepped to the lectern to introduce the department chairs.

When Margaret's name was called and she walked to the front, Elinor whispered to me, "I'm proud of you, Agnes, and so is Margaret, but we can't get on this woman's bad side. There's too much at stake."

Lorna did not look up.

When the department chairs returned to their places, Dr. Sherwood asked the new faculty members to stand when she called their names.

My arms folded, I leaned back in my chair and glanced around the room as she read the list: "Jack Arbuthnot. Robert Carlton. Claudia Craig. Kennesaw Fleming."

When Kennesaw Fleming stood, my elbow collided with Elinor's as we jabbed each other at the same time.

"That's him," she said.

"That's him," I said, "the guy on the train."

"What's the problem?" Margaret asked.

"Long story," I said.

"Can it wait? Lorna needs to listen for her name."

"Sure," I said, and kept quiet for the remainder of the session.

When Elinor suggested we all go to lunch, I bowed out.

"I have work to do," I said. "You three have a good time."

An hour later, Margaret knocked on my office door, entering before I could answer.

She sat in the chair across from my desk. "So … how are you?" she asked.

"Fine. How are you?"

She shook her head. "Don't try that with me, Agnes. We've been friends too long."

"No," I said, "I'd really like to know how you are. We haven't had a chance to talk."

She shrugged her shoulders. "We would have if—"

"I know. 'If I'd come back earlier.' Believe me, *that's* a mistake I *won't* make again."

She sighed. "You're in rough shape, aren't you?"

"Yes, I'm in rough shape. I got off to a bad start last year, and now the same thing has happened again. I can't do anything right around here."

"I wouldn't say that. If you hadn't gotten off to a 'bad start' last year, you would've never come to the Magnolia Arms. We wouldn't have met, and Jonas and I wouldn't be married."

"But you wouldn't be working for Dr. Sherwood either."

"I don't work for *her*, Agnes. I work for my students and the teachers in my department. We can deal with her, like we dealt with Olympia Pillburn, but there are *ways* of doing that."

"And yanking on her scarf is not one of them?"

I was relieved when she laughed.

"No. But I was proud of you for speaking up for Ham," she said. "Don't think I wasn't."

"Then why did you tell me sit down and be quiet?"

"Because if you'd walked out, Dr. Sherwood would've known she got the best of you."

"I guess your pal Lorna thinks I'm a first class moron," I said.

"She's not my 'pal,' Agnes. She's a broken-hearted girl who needs help."

"I didn't make a very good first impression, did I?"

"Actually, she said she admired you and is looking forward to meeting you. Do you have plans for dinner, or do you 'need to work' tonight, too?"

"I think I could take the evening off," I said. "Meet at the Drifters' Rest at six?"

That afternoon when I arrived at home, Flossie was waiting for me on the porch.

She held out her arms as I walked up the steps and hugged me a long time.

"I'm so glad you're home," she said. "And I'm sorry to spring this on you so soon, but … something's come up."

"I know," I said. "Is Flo doing better?'

"No … I mean, yes, Flo is better. I'm not talking about her. There's someone inside."

"Who?"

"A lady. I was pulling weeds out of the begonias this afternoon, when she came by and asked if I knew the people who lived in the apartment next door."

"Another bill collector looking for Warner?" I asked.

"That's what I thought at first. But when I told her I used to live there with my son till he got married, she got a funny look on her face and asked if I'd tell her his wife's name."

"Why would she want to know that?"

"She said it might be her daughter," Flossie said.

"Her daughter?"

"I only needed one look at this lady to know she couldn't possibly be the mother of a girl whose idea of fashion is a blue leotard and black leather jacket."

"You said that?"

"No, I only thought it," Flossie said. "But when I said, 'The Darla I know can't possibly be *your* daughter,' she hugged me and asked when they'd be home. It broke my heart—"

"—to tell her we haven't seen or heard from them in months," I said.

Flossie nodded. "When she started crying, I invited her inside. Can she stay with us tonight? We just can't send her away to a lonely motel room."

I took a deep breath and opened the door.

Winifred Parker-Potts sat at my kitchen table with Mary Smith at her feet.

Chapter 2

Guess Who's Coming to Dinner

Winnie jumped from her chair. "Agnes, what are you doing here?"

"I live here," I said.

"You live here with Flossie?"

"No," I said, "I don't live with her. She lives with me."

"Ever since that *Darla* woman—" Flossie said.

"Ever since Flossie's *son* made her move out," I said.

Flossie took the hint. "Yes … ever since *Warner* made me move out."

"Why don't you sit down, Winnie?" I said. "You must be exhausted."

"You look a little rough yourself, Agnes," Flossie said. "Why don't you *both* sit down, and I'll start supper?"

I sat at the table and shooed Saturn away from nibbling on Mary Smith.

"None for me," I said. "I'm meeting Jonas and Margaret at the Drifters' Rest."

"I can't stay either," Winnie said. "I'll have to find a hotel."

"Nonsense," Flossie said. "Stay here tonight. We have plenty of room."

I glanced at Flossie's rollaway bed, folded and parked in a corner of the living room.

If I didn't draw the line sometime, I'd soon be running a home for outcast mothers.

"Actually, Winnie, you might be more comfortable at—" I said.

Winnie sniffled. "Thank you. I really don't want to be alone tonight."

Flossie rummaged through the pantry. "Potatoes … a can of corn … if I'd known we were having company, I would've gone to the grocery store today."

"Don't go to any trouble," Winnie said. "Anything is fine."

Flossie opened the refrigerator. "What a relief. Carrots, a stalk of celery, and half an onion. Vegetable soup it is. And I'll make biscuits."

Winnie lifted Mary Smith onto the table and scratched behind Saturn's ear.

"I didn't think I'd see you again, Winnie," I said. "How did you end up here?"

"I went to the hospital early this morning," she said, "and got shuffled from one department to the next for most of the day. I know so little about Darlinda Sue—"

Flossie took her favorite soup pot from the cabinet. "Darlinda who?"

"Darla's real name," I said.

"I couldn't convince anyone I was her mother," Winnie said. "Finally, an orderly, who overheard me asking a nurse, took pity on me and told me where Darlinda worked."

"You didn't go there alone?" I asked.

Though Warner and Darla had moved away months ago, memories of him, scowling at me from behind his aviator glasses, still made me shudder.

Flossie spun around, a half-peeled potato in her hand. "You saw Warner?"

"I saw *someone*," Winnie said. "I took a taxi to the back of beyond, down a long dirt road, up a hill, and around a curve to an old wooden building, a tin shed, and a trailer."

"The cab driver didn't leave you there?" I asked.

"No-o-o," Winnie said. "I asked him to wait. I stood at the door of the garage and shouted till someone appeared."

"What did he look like?" Flossie asked.

"Overalls, mid-forties, bald, overweight."

Flossie resumed her peeling. "Not Warner. He has his flaws, but he has beautiful hair."

"This man said he hadn't seen Warner or Darlinda in months, but he gave me their address," Winnie said, "so I went there."

"You must've spent a fortune on cab fare today," I said.

Winnie nodded. "It was a long drive to the trailer park. When I told the manager who I was, he gave me a *terrible* tongue-lashing about what bad tenants Warner and Darlinda were."

"Poor thing," I said. "You didn't deserve that."

"It was worth it. He gave me a stack of bills forwarded from this address, so that led me here."

With amazing speed Flossie sliced carrots into a copper-bottomed pot. "And you're welcome to stay here as long as you need to."

"It might be a better idea—" I said, then stopped to consider.

The Drifters' Rest was on the first floor of a restored two-story brown brick house. Muriel lived upstairs and kept a room ready for "friends in need." Winnie could ride with me, spend the night there, and start looking for her own apartment tomorrow. But if I took Winnie now, she would join us for dinner. Lorna was already intruding on my reunion with Margaret and Jonas. A party of five was more than I could cope with, especially since, after I complained about Dr. Sherwood, I wanted to spend the rest of the evening talking about the Magnolia Arms.

"A better idea to what?" Winnie asked.

"… for me to take a bath before I go," I said. "Might perk me up. I'm pretty tired."

"Good idea," Flossie said. "That way the hot water heater will have time to fill up again. After the day Winnie had, I'm sure she'd like to relax in a nice hot tub after dinner."

I took a bath, got dressed, and was on my way to the front door when the phone rang.

"Get that, would you, Winnie?" Flossie asked. "I've got dough on my hands."

Winnie answered the phone. "Quinn residence. No, this is Winnie. No, I'm only visiting. I met Agnes on the train. Wait … here she is." Winnie gave me the phone. "Your mother."

I braced myself for the barrage of questions, beginning with, "Why didn't you call yesterday when you got home?"

I'd long since given up trying to keep my mother supplied with all the information to which she considered herself entitled. Still unreconciled to my unpredictable life, she longed for me to be like my responsible older brother Toby. My dating Sefton had provided my mother a measure of satisfaction, but my continued trips to the Magnolia Arms, as well as my friendship with "people twice my age," annoyed her. Flossie's presence in my apartment was a perpetual irritant to her. And now I must explain Winnie.

"Hello, Mom."

"Who answered the phone?" my mother asked.

"A friend I met on the train yesterday."

"You've taken in another homeless woman?"

"She's not homeless," I said. "She's looking for her daughter and—"

"So has your other roommate moved out? Prissy or Bessie or whatever her name is."

My mother was kind to animals, a wonderful cook, and a devoted wife and mother, but she'd never been able to remember names.

"You mean Flossie," I said.

Flossie called back over her shoulder. "What?"

"Nothing," I said.

"What?" my mother asked.

"Her name is Flossie, and yes, she's still here. She took care of Saturn while I was out of town this summer."

"I don't know *why* you can't spend a few days with us in the summer," Mom said.

"I told you. I'm researching my book. I have to—"

"You have no problem running off to that Petunia Inn *every other month.*"

"Magnolia Arms," I said, "and I've only been there three times."

"Why can't you find time to pick up the phone and say you've arrived home safely?"

"I'm sorry," I said. "I was—"

"Wasn't today your first day back at work? How did it go?"

I didn't even consider telling her the truth. "Wonderful. In fact, I'm on my way to have dinner with my department chairman and one of our new teachers."

My inspired approach diffused the situation.

"Department chairman?" she said. "Wait till I tell your father. Imagine that—both our children—well-respected educators, influential leaders in their schools."

"How is Toby, by the way?" I asked.

Since my mother never tired of discussing my brother's continued success, his wife's superior qualities, and the accomplishments of their three exceptional sons, our conversation ended on a pleasant note. I hung up the phone.

"Your mother sounds lovely," Winnie said. "May I ask where you keep your dishes?"

As I watched Flossie dicing celery into the simmering soup and Winnie taking bowls from the kitchen cabinet, I felt a glimmer of compassion. If they'd been my maiden aunts, I would have thought the scene idyllic.

My hand on the doorknob, I asked, "Would you like me to bring dessert home?"

Flossie's eyes twinkled. "Bread pudding, if Muriel has some. Or pie."

"Will do," I said. "Leave a pillow and blanket on the sofa for me."

"Absolutely not," Winnie said. "I'll sleep on the sofa. I'm not going to take your bed."

"We're going to stay up late and watch movies and eat popcorn," Flossie said.

I knew better. Flossie fell asleep on the sofa every night before eight.

As I drove to the Drifters' Rest, the gruesome scene with Dr. Sherwood seeped into my mind like a vengeful ghost. I wondered for the hundredth time why I could not manage to live a quiet, ordinary life like the other teachers at Brighton Park. Why did disaster keep stalking me like a bloodhound after an escaped prisoner? Had I not sacrificed my writing career to become a teacher? Had I not returned to school when I longed to stay at the Magnolia Arms? Why did my good intentions never pay off?

Muriel, looking like a seasoned governess in a black skirt and starched white blouse, greeted me at the door of the Drifters' Rest.

"This way," she said. "Margaret reserved a table for four."

I scooted into the chair in the corner. Muriel filled my water glass.

"I heard you met the new boss," she said.

"Dazzled her," I said.

This was, in part, true.

Muriel walked toward the kitchen. "I know exactly what you need."

She returned with a basket of hot yeast rolls and a small dish of butter.

I buttered a warm roll, swallowed it in three bites, closed my eyes, and relaxed for the first time since I'd left Dennisonville.

"Hello, Agnes."

I opened my eyes to find Grace Bonner, the assistant librarian at Brighton Park, standing behind the chair next to me.

Grace was one of my favorite people at Brighton Park. Shy, self-effacing, serious, she was the quintessential librarian. We had become friends and allies when we tried to prevent a conniving English teacher from replacing Elinor with another librarian. After I appointed myself amateur detective, Grace helped me investigate.

Our efforts resulted in Elinor's exoneration.

"Hello, Grace," I said. "I didn't see you today."

"I was exiled to the second floor. Dr. Sherwood has us weeding out books—"

I held up my hand. "I'm sorry, but could we not talk about her? I'm trying to talk myself into a better frame of mind before Jonas and Margaret get here."

"Of course," she said. "I heard what happened."

"Not one of my finer moments," I said. "Would you like a roll?"

She pulled out the chair and sat down.

"No, I've already eaten. I saw you sitting here alone and thought I might ask you something ... in confidence. I might not get a chance tomorrow."

"Sure," I said. "What is it?"

She bowed her head and twisted the strap of her purse. "Since I'm only the assistant librarian, I don't have much interaction with faculty. I mean— not socially."

"Everyone loves you, Grace," I said. "Surely you know that."

Her face reddened. "I don't mean that. I ... well, there are some new faculty members this year, and one of them is so handsome, and he seems to be about my age."

"Grace Bonner," I said. "Are you asking me to fix you up with one of the new teachers?"

She pushed her glasses up her nose. "He probably wouldn't take a second look at me, but I can't help wondering if—"

"If he's available?"

"Yes. I thought you could find out about him—maybe from Margaret."

"I'll ask her," I said. "Do you know his name?"

She lifted her head. "Kennesaw Fleming. Isn't that masculine and assertive?"

My mouth fell open. "I ... yes, assertive. But maybe you—"

"You think I'm right? He's around thirty?"

"Yes," I said, "maybe a little older, but Grace, I don't think—"

I was relieved to see Jonas, Margaret, and Lorna come through the door. I'd need time to think of a subtle way to discourage Grace from her romantic notions about Mr. Fleming.

"There's Margaret now," I said. Grace walked with me toward the door.

Jonas, though thirty years my senior, was one of the handsomest men I'd ever known. Tall, lean, broad-shouldered, his thinning silver hair always trimmed and styled, he smelled of wintergreen and pine.

He hugged me. "Hello, stranger," he said. "I hear you got off to a rough start ... again."

"Went all the way to the top," I said, "—insulted the boss in front of the entire faculty."

"Hello, Grace," Margaret said. "Would you like to join us?"

"I've eaten," Grace said. "I'm on my way home."

"Have you met Lorna Maron?" Margaret asked.

"Not yet." Grace extended her hand. "We're glad to have you, Lorna. I hope you'll be happy at Brighton Park."

Pale and quiet, Lorna smiled.

If she'd been wearing a bonnet and lace-trimmed shawl, I would've thought she'd recently stepped from the pages of a Jane Austen novel, the fragile anguished heroine, auburn-haired, blue-eyed, grieving over her family's woes, and lamenting her true love's being out of reach. Her pain was almost tangible, so poignant I felt wretched for resenting her.

"And you'll remember Agnes," Margaret said to Lorna.

"Yes," Lorna said. "I'm sorry you couldn't join us for lunch."

"Me too," I said.

Muriel approached our table after we were seated.

"Tonight's special is grilled flounder, scalloped potatoes, broccoli salad," she said. "Shall I bring four?"

"I'm not hungry," Lorna said. "Water is fine."

"Did Margaret forget to tell you?" Muriel asked. "On your first visit to the Drifters' Rest, it's customary to order the special. Eat what you want, and we'll send the rest home."

We all agreed to the flounder, and Muriel took the empty bread basket.

Lorna sipped her water. "This is a lovely place," she said. "Do you come here often?"

"Every day on my way to school," I said. "Once you've had Muriel's coffee, anyone else's is second best, even your own."

"Is Muriel always so … forceful?" Lorna asked.

"We've found we all do better when we take her advice," Margaret said. "If Agnes hadn't listened to her, Jonas and I wouldn't be married."

"What do you mean?" Lorna asked.

"On my first day last year," I said, "I had the nerve to park in Jonas' parking space."

"Reserved parking is available?" Lorna asked.

I laughed. "No, but Jonas had a list of unwritten rules he expected us all to live by."

Margaret reached for Jonas' hand. "He was a different man back then."

"What does that have to do with Muriel?" Lorna asked.

"She told me how to win Jonas over," I said. "Onion bagel and a jar of spicy mustard. Best advice I ever got."

"An unusual form of bribery," Lorna said.

"But absolutely true," Jonas said.

Lorna turned to Jonas. "How did that lead you to Margaret?"

Jonas unfolded his napkin and placed it in his lap. "After Agnes and I became friends, she encouraged me to talk about my past."

I laughed. "Encouraged? That's a nice way to put it. 'Wheedled' is more like it."

"Call it what you will," Jonas said. "Without Agnes, I'd never have found Margaret, much less had the nerve to ask her to marry me."

Lorna turned to Margaret. "Where did he find you?"

"At the Magnolia Arms," Margaret said. "Most beautiful house ever built."

Jonas leaned back in his chair. "The one we're living in now is pretty nice."

"He can say that," I said, "because he built *both* of them."

I reached in my purse for a photo and handed it to Lorna. Margaret leaned over to look.

She was more beautiful than when I'd first seen her a year ago at the Magnolia Arms and brought her back for a reunion with the man she had loved for thirty years. Married to Jonas since Valentine's Day, Margaret still exuded the bliss of a new bride, her gray eyes sparkling whenever she looked at him. A veteran English teacher, her personality was a comfortable mingling of firm and fragile, impenetrable and vulnerable, her heart tender, her resolve unbreakable. Though Jonas was reveling in his retirement years, Margaret had assumed the chairmanship of the English department at Brighton Park.

"When was this taken?" Margaret asked. "Everyone looks wonderful."

"Ivy Leigh asked Sefton to take it," I said. "After you left, she realized how few photos she had of her friends. She vowed never to be without pictures again."

Tears pooling in her eyes, Margaret stared at the photo of her six friends standing on the large columned porch. Jonas handed her his handkerchief.

"Is anyone related?" Lorna asked.

"No," I said, pointing to Xander and Posey, "but these two will be. They're practically engaged."

"And who is this next to you?" Lorna asked.

"Nestor Carlyle, the gardener," I said.

"Then this must be Ivy Leigh," Lorna said. "Is that her husband?"

"No," Margaret said. "That's Monty."

"He's very distinguished," Lorna said.

"British," I said. "Wears tweed jackets, walks with a cane, and has tea every afternoon."

Lorna returned the photo. "He looks like my piano teacher in college."

"You're a pianist?" I asked.

"Used to be."

"You're still a pianist, Lorna," Margaret said. "You may have lost your nerve. You didn't lose your talent."

"Tell that to the last audience I played for," Lorna said.

"What happened?" I asked.

Holding her palms face up, Lorna surveyed her hands as if they were strangers.

"Fumbled on an arpeggio," she said. "I couldn't recover. Couldn't remember what note came next. Couldn't breathe. I don't remember how I got offstage."

Muriel returned with the server, who placed a large tray on a stand. Muriel set a plate in front of each of us and stood back, arms crossed, admiring the table.

"Enjoy. And save room for dessert," she said and walked away.

"Go ahead, Lorna," I said. "What happened after you forgot what you were playing?"

Under the table Margaret mashed my toe with her foot. "How's the book coming, Agnes?" she asked, skewering a bite of potato.

I pulled my foot away and scowled at her. "Fine."

"How exciting," Lorna said. "What's your book about?"

"The Magnolia Arms," I said. "My boyfriend and I are collaborating on a two-volume history."

As a general rule, I didn't use the word "boyfriend" when describing Sefton, but the occasion warranted this bit of adolescent swank.

"Does he teach at the college?" Lorna asked.

"No," I said, my voice tinged with condescension. "He's a lawyer."

I handed Lorna a photo of Sefton and me.

"Handsome," she said. "How long have you been dating?"

"Almost a year. Are you dating anyone?"

This time Margaret jabbed my knee. "Shall we decide on dessert?" she asked.

This was the final affront. In the last thirty-six hours I'd left my friends, endured an endless train ride with a chatty companion and her potted plant, been stalked by a surly stranger, behaved like an idiot in front of my colleagues, been crowded out of my own home by two women who weren't even related to me, and now one of my dearest friends, who was supposed to make my homecoming endurable, was treating me like a red-headed stepchild.

"None for me," I said, "but I promised to bring something home for Flossie and Winnie."

"Flossie and who?" Jonas asked.

I laid my napkin on the table. "It's a long story. I just remembered I'm expecting a phone call from Sefton. I'd better get going."

"You haven't finished your dinner," Margaret said.

I picked up my plate. "I'll take it to go."

Jonas stood. "I'll walk you out."

He followed me to the counter where I drank coffee every morning. When I put down my plate, Muriel looked up.

"I need a box and the check, please," I said, "and two orders of bread pudding to go."

Muriel narrowed her eyes and spoke in a low voice. "Your friends haven't finished."

"I have," I said.

Jonas stepped beside me. "Put her meal on my check, Muriel. Dessert, too. And pour me some coffee so I can stand here and talk to Agnes without being too obvious."

Muriel filled a white ceramic mug and slid it toward him. "Be right back," she said.

Jonas poured cream in his coffee and stared into his cup as he stirred.

"I know it was hard for you to come back," he said.

I stared down at the counter. "When I was crying on Nestor's shoulder before I left, he reminded me how nice it would be to come home to you and Margaret."

"Margaret is not herself," Jonas said. "She's been taken off guard as much as you have."

I was unmoved. "By what?"

"Helping Lorna has stirred up some painful memories. Margaret is struggling."

"But she has no reason to be struggling *now*. She found you. You're married. She has a home, a job, more friends than she knows what to do with … happily ever after. The end."

Jonas shook his head. "Memories are like weeds. You mow them over and pull them up and think you're done, but the roots are still there. Let the ground warm up and—"

Muriel returned with two Drifters' Rest bags. "Here you go. I put in some of the lemon buttermilk cake you like. I hope you feel better tomorrow, Agnes. Try to get some sleep."

Jonas walked me to the door. "Do me a favor," he said. "Wave goodbye to Margaret."

I did as he asked. Margaret smiled and waved back.

At home I found Flossie and Winnie, asleep, propped up at opposite ends of the sofa, popcorn bowl empty, television on, Judy Garland singing "Have Yourself a Merry Little Christmas" at the end of *Meet Me in St. Louis*. I turned off the television, draped Flossie's magenta afghan over her, and brought a blanket from my bedroom for Winnie. When I stepped into the kitchen to put the Drifters' Rest bags in the refrigerator, I noticed Flossie had stuck a note on the door. Sefton had called, said he was meeting a client, and would call back tomorrow.

Disappointed, I locked the front door, turned out the light, and headed to my bedroom. Saturn was waiting at the foot of my bed. I sat next to him and stroked his sleek gray fur.

"I've got to do better tomorrow," I said. "I'll go straight to my office and work, invite Lorna to lunch, and write my mother a nice newsy letter. Maybe I can work on my book, too."

Saturn purred as we drifted off to sleep. He, at least, had no quarrel with me.

Clattering and clanging woke me before dawn the next morning. I walked into the kitchen and found Flossie plugging in the waffle iron. I sat at the table, set for three.

"Good morning, sleepyhead," Flossie said.

"Sleepyhead?" I said. "It's 5:30."

I leaned my elbows on the table and watched Flossie bustling at the kitchen counter. Though plump, she possessed the grace of a swan. Her Hawaiian print housecoat, a faded flurry of yellow hibiscus, pink flamingoes, and lime green palm leaves, draped her ample hips and swished and billowed as she whipped the batter with her harvest gold electric mixer. Her slate gray hair, piled Gibson-girl style on top of her head, was in its usual state of disarray, her round wire-rimmed glasses nestled in the mass of tangles, waiting to be rescued when she asked me where they were.

Winnie, in a pink bathrobe, filled my coffee cup. "Did you have a nice time last night?"

"It was all right—not really what I expected."

"The dinner was disappointing?" Winnie asked.

"Not the food," I said.

"Then—?" she asked.

"Margaret invited one of the new teachers. We couldn't talk about anything that mattered. I spent the whole evening playing nice."

Flossie set two golden waffles in front of me. "I've always been glad you were nice to me when we first met."

Winnie handed me the butter knife. "I'd love to hear the story," she said.

Flossie wiped her hands on her apron. "Agnes and I had been neighbors for several weeks before we actually met. Warner had met her and described her to me, so I knew who she was."

I bit into a waffle, light and crispy. "These are wonderful," I said.

Flossie pinched her thumb and finger together. "Added a dab of vanilla extract. As I was saying, I was at my church in Maplewood—"

"That's a long way to go to church," Winnie said.

Flossie shook her head. "I don't go there anymore. As I was saying, I was at church one Sunday and saw Agnes. I tried to get her attention to ask for a ride home."

"She whispered a little too loudly," I said, "and the rector got upset."

Winnie slid the syrup toward me. "You whispered during the sermon?"

Flossie returned to her bowl of batter. "I was trying to show her Warner's picture, so she'd know who I was, but she wouldn't look up. She was praying."

I'd never admitted to Flossie I had pretended to pray as a polite way of ignoring her.

Fearing the story would continue until lunchtime, I intervened.

"After the service I was speaking to the rector's wife," I said, "—a childhood acquaintance of mine—when Flossie joined us, and then the rector came over ..."

Flossie tapped her wooden spoon on the mixing bowl. "Waving his arms, his robe flapping behind him, told me he was *tired* of me disrupting his sermons and then Agnes—"

I dabbed a bite of waffle into a pool of syrup. "Let's just say I came to Flossie's rescue, and we went to lunch."

"We've been friends ever since," Flossie said. "Want some bacon?"

Winnie handed me a napkin. "Maybe this new teacher needs a friend as much as Flossie did—or as much as I did. Why don't you invite her to dinner? Flossie's making chicken pot pie."

Flossie brightened. "Yes. If there are four of us, we could play games afterwards."

Having received permission to invite a guest to my own home, I drove to school and started to my office, nicer than last year's, but still drab and stuffy compared to my third floor room at the Magnolia Arms. I'd always preferred to work near the windows on the second floor of the library, so I stayed in my office only when necessary, a practice I planned to continue. When I opened my door, I found a magnificent wooden roll top desk in place of the rusty metal one. Confused, I backed up and checked the name on the door.

"Hello, Miss Quinn."

I hadn't heard Tony Castarini approach.

He looked in my office. "Nice. 'Bout time they got you a new desk."

"Hello, Tony. I don't know where it came from. Wasn't there yesterday."

"Could I talk to you?" he asked.

Since the day he had stayed after class to admit he had "never seen the point of reading made-up stories," Tony Castarini had been my favorite student. When I read *Beowulf* aloud to his class, Tony, surprised he could "see the whole thing in his head," decided he would "find out where the library was." After a few months with a tutor in the resource center, he transformed into a respectable scholar. He would never have a Ph.D. after his name, but he was going to graduate, having crammed a four-year education into six. He credited me with his success.

Tony plopped down in the chair by the door. I sat near the desk, but still assuming a mistake had been made, did not touch it.

"Did you have a good summer?" I asked.

"Yes, ma'am. I took a couple of classes I needed to make up. You know how much time I wasted my first three semesters."

"But you've made up for that, haven't you?"

He nodded. "I'm going to graduate in December, thanks to you. Before you were my teacher, nobody took the time to help me."

"That's nice of you to say, Tony. I'm really—"

Fidgeting, he leaned forward and propped his elbows on his knees. "That's partly why I'm here. I've always felt I could talk to you."

"You need a job reference?"

"No. It's not that," he said, running his hand through his hair. "Let me ask you. How old do you think I am?"

I was beginning to feel uneasy about the direction of our talk, but tried to stay calm.

"I'm not sure," I said. "You've been in college for six years? About twenty-three?"

He smiled. "No. I didn't graduate from high school till I was nineteen."

"So you're closer to twenty-five?"

"Twenty-six," he said. "So you'd say I'm 'mature,' right?"

"Yes. 'Mature' is a word that would fit you."

"So … if I wanted to date someone on staff here, I could do that after I graduate, right?"

I stopped breathing. "Yes, but Tony, I—"

He leaned to one side and pulled a folded note from his back pocket. Then he returned his elbows to his knees and holding the paper with both hands, read in a trembling voice.

> *I'm like a car on a two-lane road*
> *Driving behind a truck.*
> *I want to pass and move along,*
> *But somehow I'm always stuck.*
>
> *The road I'm on will lead to you,*
> *But I am moving slow.*
> *I want to tell you how I feel.*
> *Otherwise, how will you know?*
>
> *You've won my heart by being nice*
> *And kind in every way.*
> *I've often thought I'd ask you out,*
> *But don't know what you'd say.*
>
> *Before we go our separate ways,*
> *And I leave you behind.*
> *I ask: Will you go out with me*
> *In spite of my average mind?*

Exhausted with his effort, he leaned back, the crumpled paper still in his hand. What would I say to such sincere but misdirected eloquence?

"Tony," I said, "that is a beautiful poem, but—"

He looked up. "So ... is this good enough to give to Miss Bonner?"

"Miss Bonner?"

"We're about the same age, don't you think? She can't be much older than I am."

"I ... Miss Bonner ... ?"

"I know," he said. "She's too good for me, isn't she?"

"No, I wouldn't say that."

"The whole thing started because of that paper you assigned last year. I had no idea what to do. When I got to the library, she helped me every day and never seemed to mind."

"But that's the way she is, Tony. She would've done that for anyone."

"I know. That's the point." He stood and laid the paper on the desk. "Would you look this over and correct the errors? Then I'll recopy it. Thanks, Miss Quinn. You've been a big help."

When he opened the door, I saw Torbert Hampton, Ham's father, standing in the hall.

Though he was the head of maintenance staff, I always felt compelled to stand when Mr. Hampton entered the room. Tall, gray-haired, with an imposing square jaw, thin lips, prominent nose, and intense green eyes, he would have been equally at home in a board room or throne room. Even when carting a toolbox or paint can, he carried himself with the dignity of an executive. I once told him I considered him a true Renaissance man and asked if he'd ever thought of taking up sculpting. "Strange you should ask," he had said. "I used to be a stonemason."

Mr. Hampton remained in the doorway. "Good morning," he said. "Do you like where we left the desk, or would you prefer it somewhere else? We can move it anywhere you like."

"You left this desk?"

"Ham and I moved it in last night."

"So it's not a mistake? I thought it was intended for someone more important."

"There are few people more important to us than you, Miss Quinn, especially after what you did for Ham yesterday."

"But this is such an extravagant gift. Did you bring it from your home?"

He walked to the desk and ran his hand over the wood. "I built this for my wife Rosalind. No one's used it since she died. Hampton men don't sit at desks."

"But doesn't Ham want to keep it?"

"It was his idea to give it to you," Mr. Hampton said. "He's grateful."

"We all love Ham. Anyone would've done what I did."

His eyes met mine. "But no one else did."

"I don't know what to say, except 'thank you.' I'll feel more at home in this office now."

"You're welcome," he said. "I hope you have a good year."

Satisfied the desk was indeed mine, I sat down and pulled out the drawers one by one, hoping perhaps to find a note or dried flower Mrs. Hampton might have tucked away. I stacked a few books on one corner and displayed my favorite photo of Sefton on the other. My old gray stapler and bargain store lamp looked out of place on the exquisite wood grain, so I stowed the stapler in a drawer and set the lamp by the door for the trip home. I was smoothing the wrinkles from Tony Castarini's crumpled paper when the phone rang.

When I lifted the receiver, I heard the familiar voice I most needed to hear.

"Hello, Agnes. I wish you were still here. I've got a lot of potatoes that need peeling."

"Ivy Leigh. You have no idea how glad I am to hear from you. Is anything wrong? You've never called me at school."

"Nothing wrong here," she said, "but Margaret is a mess."

"What do you mean?"

"She called me last night. We talked for over an hour. That's why I'm calling you."

"I guess she told you what a pain I've been," I said.

"No, nothing like that. I already know the whole story, so I'll come right to the point. You have to help her."

"If one more person tells me I need to help Lorna Maron, I'm going to—"

"No, not Lorna. Margaret."

"Why does everyone think something's wrong with Margaret? She has everything she's ever wanted."

Ivy Leigh sighed. "Trust me on this one, Agnes. The moment Margaret saw the first tear fall down Lorna's face, she began reliving the past she's tried thirty years to forget."

There was never any point in arguing with Ivy Leigh, so I gave in.

"I don't get it, but I'll take your word for it. I'd do anything to get back to what we call 'normal' around here. What do you want me to do?"

"When we hang up, go straight to Margaret's office. Act like nothing has happened. Tell her you want to invite Lorna for dinner tonight. And *don't* tell her I called you."

"I was going to invite her anyway," I said. "Flossie's making chicken pot pie."

"Wish I could join you," Ivy Leigh said.

"You could come this weekend."

"I'll have to—if you can't help Margaret. Now hang up and go see her."

Within five minutes I knocked on Margaret's office door.

"Hi," I said. "Sorry to bother you. Where's Lorna's office?"

When Margaret looked up from her desk, I could tell she'd been crying.

"In your old office," she said. "Was there something you wanted?"

"Flossie and Winnie want me to invite Lorna for dinner."

"Winnie? You mentioned her last night. Is she a new neighbor?"

"For now she's a guest," I said. "I'll tell you the whole story later. I promised myself I'd get some work done today."

Margaret's face relaxed into a smile. "Did Ivy Leigh call you last night?"

"No," I said. This was true.

"I'm glad you came by. I wanted to invite you to have dinner with Jonas and me this Friday. We have a surprise for you."

"I'd love to," I said.

Having followed Ivy Leigh's instructions, and thus cleared my conscience, I was strolling toward Lorna's office when I spotted Kennesaw Fleming stapling a paper to the bulletin board at the end of the hall. I slowed my pace, briefly entertaining the notion of ducking into one of the empty classrooms, but feeling ridiculous for even considering this option, I kept moving. His eyes still riveted to the paper he'd posted, he spoke as I came nearer.

"Hello, Agnes."

"Hello," I said, still walking.

"Are you interested in acting?" he asked.

I turned around. "Excuse me?"

He continued staring at the paper. "I'm starting a local branch of Civil War re-enactors. We need volunteers to play casualties."

"Not many women joined the ranks on either side," I said.

33

He turned to face me. "We're doing the first battle of Bull Run and need someone to play Judith Henry. She refused to leave her house and—"

"She was killed by a bullet meant for snipers," I said.

For the first time I was grateful my father had taken us to Civil War battlefields on our family vacations.

Kennesaw turned again to the bulletin board, stepped back, tilted his head to one side, and with his fingernails pried loose the staples one by one.

"Crooked," he said. "So will you join us for our first meeting?"

"No," I said and turned to leave.

Re-stapling the paper, he spoke louder as I walked away.

"Let me know if you change your mind," he said. "You'd be good at dying."

Chapter 3

It Happened One Night

When I arrived home that evening, I found both Flossie and Winnie attired in black satin pants and silk brocade jackets—Flossie's a glittering wine-gold design and Winnie's a shimmering silver-blue. Winnie had tamed and secured Flossie's fluffy locks into a smooth bun, adorned with a mother-of-pearl comb. The table, elegant as the hostesses, was decorated with Flossie's burnt orange placemats and a centerpiece of pine cones and walnuts encircling three antique-white pillar candles on a clear glass oval plate. The chicken pot pie waited on the stove for its grand entrance. I couldn't believe this was my apartment.

"Wow," I said. "You two look amazing … and the table …"

"We tried to tie a ribbon around Saturn's neck," Winnie said, "but he wouldn't have it."

Flossie spooned green beans into a ceramic bowl. "Winnie made the cake."

I took a pimiento-stuffed olive from the relish tray on the table. "Where did you get the beautiful outfits?" I asked.

"My second husband travelled a lot," Winnie said. "He brought them from Tokyo."

"Nice of you to share with Flossie," I said.

Flossie set the beans on the table. "Took some getting used to," she said. "But I like it."

"Hurry and change," Winnie said. "I left a kimono in your room."

"I'll change into my jeans," I said. "I don't want Lorna to feel left out."

When Lorna arrived at six, Flossie and Winnie both hugged her.

"Agnes has told us so much about you," Winnie said.

"She didn't mention how thin you are," Flossie said. "You'll take home the leftovers."

Winnie lit the candles, and we gathered around the table. Flossie, explaining the casserole dish was too hot to pass around, spooned portions of the chicken pot pie onto each plate.

"Thank you for inviting me," Lorna said. "Everything looks delicious."

"I'm always glad to meet Agnes' teacher friends," Flossie said. "I don't have much education myself, but I admire people who do—especially women."

Winnie passed the steamed rice to Lorna. "My Darlinda would've been a good teacher."

"Your daughter?" Lorna asked.

"Yes," Winnie said. "She's married to Flossie's son."

"How nice," Lorna said.

"Not really," Flossie said. "Neither of them has much of a future."

Lorna gazed at the flickering candles. "Exactly what my parents think about me."

"You?" I asked. "Don't be silly. You're every parent's dream child."

Lorna sipped her water. "You'd think so, wouldn't you? But you're wrong."

Flossie, a forkful of glazed carrots poised in midair, frowned. "That can't be true."

Winnie laid her hand on Lorna's arm. "You're so lovely and ... clean."

To our surprise, Lorna leaned her head back and laughed.

"Clean ... if only that's all it took to keep Dr. and Mrs. Maron happy."

Winnie blushed. "What I mean is the last time I saw Darlinda, she was wearing a black leather jacket, had bleached-blonde hair, and—" Winnie sniffled—"a tattoo."

Flossie, seated next to Winnie, patted her hand. "That's not all Darla's fault, dear. I'm sure my Warner has been a terrible influence on her."

Lorna looked from one to the other. "I apologize. I didn't mean to—"

"Not your fault," I said. "Winnie's been looking for her daughter a long time. When she discovered what Darla's been doing ... the outcome was different than what she'd hoped for."

"I tried so hard," Winnie said. "New white patent leather shoes every Easter." She shook her head. "Listen to me—going on nineteen to the dozen in front of our guest."

Our guest, I thought. This time yesterday *you* were a guest.

"Yes, let's cheer up," Flossie said. "Or we won't be in the mood to play Monopoly."

"Tell us, Lorna, how *did* you end up at Brighton Park?" I asked, eager to get the story without Margaret poking my knee under the table.

Lorna cut a green bean with her fork. "It's a little like your daughter's story, Winnie."

"I can't picture you in a black leather jacket," Winnie said.

"Or a blue leotard," Flossie said.

"No," Lorna said. "But I was in love with someone—"

"It's always about a man, isn't it?" Flossie said, popping a cherry tomato into her mouth.

"The most intelligent woman can be deceived when it comes to love," Winnie said.

"I'd been so sheltered at home—so focused on music, I didn't date much. When I met Nolan at college, and he was a pianist, too, I thought—"

"You could make beautiful music together," Winnie said.

"That was my dream, too," Flossie said.

My mouth dropped open. "You were a pianist? You never told me that."

She shook her head and leaned back in her chair. "Oboist. I was a performer of some repute in my community orchestra. Sometimes I soloed."

"Tell us over dessert," Winnie said, "after Lorna finishes her story."

"In the beginning everything was wonderful," Lorna said. "Nolan was so charming and attentive. I thought I'd found the man of my dreams."

"Did another girl come between you?" Winnie asked.

"No," Lorna said. "Bach did."

Flossie spooned a second helping of green beans onto Lorna's plate. "Bach?"

"And half a dozen others," Lorna said. "There's a lot more to being a musician than the occasional inspired performance in front of a grateful audience."

Flossie held a sweet pickle between her finger and thumb. "Talent, technique, and passion … you need all three to be a great musician. That's what my teacher said."

"Nolan had passion, but no finesse. He'd grown so accustomed to being told how talented he was, he couldn't adjust to being one of a dozen first-class musicians in college."

"Including you?" I asked.

Lorna shrugged her shoulders. "So people said. My friends tried to warn me about him, but I wouldn't listen. He was my first love and—"

"Love is blind," Flossie said.

"When did you realize he was wrong for you?" Winnie asked.

"At the end of our sophomore year, I won a competition Nolan and I had both entered."

Flossie nodded. "And the green-eyed monster reared its ugly head."

"If he loved you, he would've been pleased," Winnie said. "My Arthur and I entered our dogs in the same competition every year, and whenever Charlemagne won, Arthur—"

"Charlemagne?" Flossie asked.

"My Great Dane," Winnie said. "When Charlemagne won, Arthur was delighted."

Lorna moved the food around her plate, but did not eat. "I can't help wondering if we might still be together if I'd been an ordinary person rather than a musician."

"It's not your fault you worked harder than he did," Flossie said.

"Or that you're more talented," I said.

Lorna put down her fork. "He ignored me for days before he admitted the reason he was angry. I was so desperate to win him back, I actually apologized for winning the contest."

"What did he say?" I asked.

"He said, 'It's too late to change that now, isn't it?'"

From that moment I did not look at Lorna in the same way. Though she was twice as beautiful as anyone I'd ever known, and ten times as smart, her dreams had crashed and burned like anyone else's would. In her own way, Lorna was every bit as needy as Flossie or Winnie. No wonder Margaret had taken her under her wing.

"How did you end up being an English teacher?" I asked.

Lorna sipped her water. "That summer I kept hoping Nolan would call, but he never did. In the fall when we came back to school, he had another girlfriend."

"Is that when your stage fright started?" I asked.

"Not right away," Lorna said. "I tried to talk myself out of wanting him, but I couldn't. Seeing him with that other girl and enduring his silence ..."

"What did you do?" Flossie asked.

"I asked my parents if I could come home, but they wouldn't hear of it. My mother worried what her friends at the garden club would say, and my father never accepted failure."

"Did you transfer to another school?" I asked.

38

"No … but I gave up the piano. Changed my major to English. Since it was my secondary field, it didn't take me long to make up the courses I needed."

Flossie wiped her eyes. "I know what it's like to give up the instrument you love."

"It was a relief at first," Lorna said. "After that turmoil, it was wonderful to sit alone in the library with a pile of books. But my teacher was heartbroken."

"Do you know where Nolan is now?" Winnie asked.

"No," Lorna said. "But sometimes I find myself wondering."

"Take it from me," Winnie said. "It's possible to love twice. At this very moment, some handsome young man may be in your future—someone who will love you for who you are."

"You girls eat your supper now," Flossie said. "You have a busy day tomorrow."

Winnie winked at Flossie. "We do, too."

Our conversation turned to mundane topics. After pineapple upside down cake and Monopoly, Lorna went home.

"Poor Lorna," Flossie said as she wiped the kitchen counter. "Such a sweet girl. I can't imagine anyone resenting her, can you, Agnes?"

Since I'd done nothing but resent Lorna from the moment I'd seen her, I was in no position to respond.

"It was nice of you to invite her, Agnes," Winnie said. She embraced me, the wet dishcloth in her hand soaking my shirt. "Your parents must be proud of you."

The phone rang. Hoping it was Sefton, I hurried to answer.

"Hello," I said.

"Agnes?"

"Dad?" Since my father left the weekly telephone calls to my mother, I was worried.

"I wanted to talk to you while your mother was gone to the store," he said.

"Is something wrong?" I asked.

"Nothing's wrong," he said. "She's going through a hard time right now, and I thought you should know. She misses you and your brother and would appreciate a little of your time."

"If it's about this summer—I already explained that. I'm working on my book and …"

"I know about your book, Aggie, and I'm happy you have a young man, but that doesn't stop your mom from wanting you here." He breathed in. "I'm sending you a check tomorrow."

"What for?"

"To buy a plane ticket so you can come home for Labor Day. You'll have the day off, won't you?"

"Yes, but, that's only a week away, and I have so much to do before—"

"I know when it is. If your mom could see you for a couple of days, it would help her and help me, too. Will you do this for me?"

"Sure, Dad," I said. "I hate for you to spend that much money."

"It will be worth every penny. Let me know when your flight will arrive."

I agreed to his plan and hung up the phone.

"Is something wrong at home?" Flossie asked.

"My dad wants me to come home for Labor Day. He says my mom misses me."

"You must go," Winnie said. "We can move the cookout to the following week."

"Cookout?"

"Flossie and I thought we might buy a barbecue grill so we could eat outside on these crisp fall evenings."

The phone rang again. Still hopeful, I answered.

"Hello," Sefton said. "You okay?"

"You have no idea how glad I am to hear from you."

I slid down the wall and sat on the floor with my knees tucked under my chin.

"I'm sorry I didn't get to talk to you last night," he said. "Did you have a nice trip home?"

"Actually, no. I met a stranger on the train who—"

"Is that Sefton?" Flossie called from the sink.

"Yes," I said.

"Tell him I said hello."

"Me, too," Winnie said. "Only tell him who I am first."

They giggled like school girls.

"Was that Flossie?" Sefton asked.

"Yes … and Winnie."

"Winnie?"

"The ride home was eventful," I said.

Over the clattering of dishes and sloshing of dish water, I related the story of meeting Kennesaw Fleming and Winnie. When I related my encounter with Dr. Sherwood, Sefton laughed—not the reaction I'd hoped for. By the time I got to Tony Castarini and the desk Mr. Hampton had given me, the man I loved was stifling a yawn.

"Should I save the rest till later?" I asked. "You sound tired."

He yawned again. "Sorry. It's been a rough couple of days."

I felt like a balloon with a slow leak. "I'll tell you the rest tomorrow night."

"Not sure I will be able to call again this week," he said. "We have a lawyer flying in from Boise."

I failed at disguising my disappointment. "Okay."

"Sorry, Aggie," he said. "But we talked about this before I left Dennisonville. I'm still the new guy in the office. I have to prove myself."

"I know. But the summer was so wonderful, and I miss you—"

"You'll be all right. You're strong."

"Could we at least talk about our project for a minute? I'm wondering if the chapter—"

"Don't take this the wrong way," he said. "But writing is a sideline for both of us. We have to get back to the real world. There's plenty of time to finish the story."

He sounded too much like a smug, condescending older brother.

"I'll try to remember," I said.

"I'll call next Saturday … or Sunday. It depends."

"I won't be here. My dad wants me to fly home for a couple of days."

He failed at disguising his relief.

"The next week then," he said. "Good night, Aggie. Sweet dreams."

By the time I hung up the phone, Flossie and Winnie had finished the dishes and relocated to the living room.

Flossie patted the sofa. "Join us."

"No, thanks. It's been a long day. I'm going to bed."

Saturn was already snuggled between my two roommates. I scooped him up to take him to bed, but he leaped from my arms and dove back into his place.

Even my cat had abandoned me.

My suitcase, still unpacked, sprawled on the floor like a slain dragon, harmless, but impossible to ignore. I took out a blouse to wear the next day, returned the photo of my three nephews to the nightstand, lifted out my

manuscript, *Magnolia Neighbors,* and sank down on the bed to thumb
through the pages. After several tries at novel writing, I had redirected my
energy to a history of the Magnolia Arms and was pleased with the result.
This narrative, populated with believable characters engaged in an intricate
plot, had more twists and turns than a back country road.

I changed into my favorite threadbare pajamas and slipped into bed.
How strange, I thought, to be "home," and yet feel so out of place. Haunted
by Lorna's story, I only half slept. I rose early and tiptoed from the apartment
before Flossie and Winnie woke, stopped by the Drifters' Rest for coffee,
reported to Muriel I'd made a friend of Lorna, and ordered a turkey sandwich
to go. Once at school, I cloistered myself in my office, determined to
reconcile myself to the grim academic responsibilities which lay before me.

My expectations, as usual, were unmet. Kennesaw Fleming dropped by
to ask if I'd reconsidered going to the re-enactors' meeting. Tony Castarini
returned to find out if I'd talked to Grace, who in turn came by to see if I'd
learned anything about Kennesaw Fleming. Margaret looked in after lunch to
tell me Lorna had come to her office "smiling for the first time" since she'd
met her and then reminded me about dinner Friday evening. In spite of the
interruptions, I was satisfied I'd made a successful, though reluctant, shift
into real life, until Elinor arrived to share the recent news.

"About what?" I asked.

She tilted her head and pursed her lips. "Dr. Sherwood's new assistant."

"Who cares? Once classes begin, the administration will ignore us, and
we can go back to flying under the radar."

"You won't be flying under the radar for long," Elinor said. "Remember
last year when the home ec teacher left to have her baby and your friend,
Sharon ..." Her voice trailed off.

"No," I said. "Not that."

She nodded. "I overheard some teachers discussing it, so I made a few
inquiries. Dr. Sherwood hired her this morning."

I sank back in my chair. "Wh—why? How?"

"Your guess is as good as mine. She'll be here on Friday." Elinor looked
worried. "Are you all right?"

"Other than feeling like I've been kicked in the stomach," I said.

What a dismal prospect—my longtime nemesis, Sharon Merriman-
Cheswick was not only to be an employee, but an *administrator* with power
to lord it over me.

Sharon and I had been neighbors growing up. In spite of our escalating abhorrence for each other, our mothers remained best friends. Not long after I started teaching at Brighton Park, my mother informed me Sharon had married an Episcopalian rector and moved to Maplewood, forty-five miles away, and had urged me to visit Sharon's church in order to reconnect with her. I obliged to keep peace. The meeting might have occurred without incident if only Flossie Bingham hadn't been a factor, but when Sharon and her husband ridiculed Flossie, I responded by embarrassing Sharon in front of their parishioners.

Neither Sharon, *her* mother, nor *my* mother had ever forgiven me. Flossie had been devoted to me ever since, a relationship which in itself had proven challenging.

Grateful there were no dinner plans to face, I drove home to discover a barbecue grill on my front porch and a decrepit grandfather clock in my living room.

"What's all this?" I asked the two bright-eyed ladies who greeted me.

"We found an estate sale," Winnie said. "Wait till you see the bargains we snatched up."

In addition to the tall clock, my already small, cramped apartment was crammed with two wooden chairs, a cardboard box stuffed with quilting squares, a stack of mildewed books—all "first editions" according to Winnie—a samovar, two matryoshka dolls, several yards of burlap, and a red-roofed doghouse with "Watson" painted over the doorway. Speechless, I sank onto the sofa and stared around me.

"One burger or two?" Flossie asked. "Or do you prefer ribs?"

"Ribs?"

"For the barbecue, of course. No need to wait till the weekend, is there?"

"No," I said. "No need to wait. How in the world did you move all this stuff in here?"

"The man in charge of the sale was so kind. He drove us back here in his truck."

So eager to get rid of all the junk you took off his hands, I thought.

"But the clock," I said. "How … ?"

"Winnie and I sat in the back and steadied it. The clock bonged a good deal of the time I can tell you, but we made it."

"But *why*?"

"Why did the clock bong?"

"No. Why did you buy all this stuff?"

Flossie stood in front of me. "Don't take this the wrong way, dear, but as much as I've enjoyed our friendship, one really needs friends one's own age, don't you agree?"

My eyes wide and mouth gaping open, I nodded.

"I hope you won't be upset," she said, "but Winnie and I have started apartment hunting."

I hoped my enthusiasm was not too apparent. "Any luck?"

"Not yet, which brings me to the favor I need to ask. May we drop you off at school, so we can use your car to widen our search? Our progress is hampered by riding the city bus."

"You don't drive," I said.

"Winnie does."

"Do you know your way around town?"

"We can get by."

The first hopeful news since I'd left Dennisonville made me reckless. I agreed.

The next morning the three of us piled into my car and drove to Brighton Park. Flossie handed me a sack lunch and wished me a good day.

"Be careful," I said.

By noon my phone was ringing.

"Agnes," Flossie said. "We need help. We've had an accident."

My heart pounded. "Are you all right?"

"We're not hurt, but Winnie's in a bit of a pickle."

"Was the accident her fault?"

"Not exactly. We were looking for Meadowlark Estates. When I saw the street number on a sign, I yelled, 'There it is.' Winnie slammed on the brakes, and the car behind us—"

"Rear-ended you?" I asked.

"Yes. The man was *very* upset."

"And that's the trouble Winnie's in?"

"Not only that. The police officer took one look at Winnie's driver's license and informed her it was expired. She's going to get a ticket for sure—maybe more."

"Where are you? Will I be able to drive the car home?"

"No, the car will have to be towed. I didn't get everything the man said, but there was something about the bumper assembly, trunk lid, floor pan. But don't worry. We'll pay for it."

I hurried to the library to ask Elinor if I could borrow her car. She handed me the keys.

"I'll have Ryder pick me up after school," she said. "We'll come by your apartment and get the car."

Seconds after I'd hurried to the parking lot and slipped into the driver's seat, there was a tap on the window. I looked up at Kennesaw Fleming. He motioned for me to open the window. I did—about an inch.

He leaned over to speak through the narrow opening. "Isn't this the librarian's car?"

"Yes. What business is it of yours?" I turned the key in the ignition.

His beard, scruffy and black, had grown for several days, making him even more menacing.

"She's a nice lady," he said. "I thought I should look out for her. You never know who might be cruising around the parking lot looking for cars to steal."

Unnerved, I jammed the car into what I thought was reverse and revved the engine. "Elinor doesn't need *you* to look out for her. She has a husband. Now, if you'll excuse me. I have an emergency to take care of." Stuck in neutral, I went nowhere. The engine whined; I put the car in gear.

I backed out and raced from the parking lot with the image of Kennesaw Fleming, watching as I drove away, shrinking in my rearview mirror.

After I brought Flossie and Winnie home, I spent the afternoon trying to calm Winnie, getting instructions from the insurance company, and securing a rental car. The day's mail contained not only a letter from my father with a check for my airline ticket, but also a letter from my mother explaining she was turning my room into a guest room and would be sending my books and papers one box at a time. She "advised" me to make room for them. Puzzled at her snippy message, I concluded my father was keeping my visit a surprise.

On Friday, looking forward to the evening with Jonas and Margaret, I drove to their new home. I'd seen the house in its initial stages of construction a year ago when Jonas began building. But while I'd been away, Margaret had sent no photos, explaining Jonas wanted the finished product to be a surprise. When I saw a sign reading "Grinstead Manor," I left the main road and followed the driveway to the two-story gray stone house graced with gables and arched windows. Margaret opened the door before I could ring the doorbell. I stepped inside.

Across the spacious, high-ceilinged room a row of tall windows looked out on the wooded backyard. In the living room, two gray-and-white striped chairs and a gray sofa were arranged around a square coffee table. A photo of the Magnolia Arms and Margaret and Jonas' wedding photo were featured on the mantel of the fireplace. To my right, a half wall separated the living room from the kitchen, pale yellow, lined with glass-fronted cabinets. Rows of blue Italian dishes, clear glasses, and delicate china cups lined the shelves. In an open dining area, a long table was set for three.

"Was it Jonas' idea to have the living room and kitchen all one open space?" I asked.

She walked toward the kitchen. "Did you ever see Jonas' apartment?"

"No, only his office."

"His apartment wasn't much bigger," she said. "He vowed never to live in a cramped place again."

I gazed up at the high ceiling. "No worries about that. I feel like I'm in a cathedral."

"Wait till you see the second floor," Margaret said.

She led me upstairs and opened the first door on the right. We entered a cozy room, furnished with a double bed, dark green overstuffed chair, and a writing desk. Margaret pointed to the large window which offered the same view of the majestic oaks behind the house.

"Jonas remembered how much you like windows," she said.

"The window is for me?"

Teacher-like, she crossed her arms. "This is your study. We expect you to finish your book here."

I sank onto the edge of the bed, folded my hands in my lap, and stared at the floor.

"Are you all right?" she asked. "We thought you'd be pleased."

"I am. Your home is so beautiful … it almost makes me forget about the mess I'm in."

"Anything like the mess you were in when I first met you?"

I couldn't help laughing. "It's way worse than that."

Jonas called from downstairs. "What's a fella gotta do to get something to eat around here?"

She stood. "We'll talk about it over dinner. And you need to catch me up on Monty. You left the other night before I could ask how his book is coming."

Montague St. James, a kind-hearted, gracious gentleman, was the first resident I'd met at the Magnolia Arms. He had found me in front of the house and invited me to dinner. The next morning, when he discovered I was a "fellow author," he wasted no time soliciting my advice. Sensitive to the dreams of other writers, I wouldn't have objected to reading an occasional paragraph or offering a stronger verb or noun, but Monty's expansive prose and sprawling epic rambled on page after page. Reading his tedious and lackluster narrative was a full-time job in itself.

"You'd think," I told Margaret and Jonas over dinner, "in all his years as a bailiff, he would have acquired a stockpile of fascinating stories, but the *way* he words things …"

Margaret shook her head. "He can never come straight to the point."

"Or realize nobody cares what the mother of the defendant was wearing," I said.

"Is he close to finishing?" Jonas asked.

"His parting words," I said, "were he intends to finish by the time I come for Thanksgiving, so I can give the story one more read before he sends it to a publisher."

"Oh, dear," Margaret said. "That's a grim prospect, isn't it?"

"Less grim than my other prospects," I said, spilling out the story of my crowded apartment, shopping roommates, Sefton's disinterest, Sharon's arrival, and my trip home.

"And on top of all that," I said, "Winnie wrecked my car today."

Jonas cleared his throat, turned to Margaret, and they both laughed.

"See?" he said to Margaret, "I told you things have a way of working out."

"Working out?" I asked. "Did you understand what I said? My car is *wrecked*. It was *used* when my parents bought it. If it can't be repaired, I'll have to take on a car payment and—"

Still laughing, Jonas stood and picked up his plate. "You're not going to need to buy another car, Agnes. The house isn't the only surprise we've been keeping from you."

"Come on," Margaret said. "We'll have dessert when we come back."

"Where are we going?" I asked.

Jonas' eyes were dancing. "To the garage." We walked through the front door to the driveway. "Wait here. Close your eyes and no peeking."

Margaret stood next to me, holding my hand. I heard the garage door open and Jonas' footsteps. Then I heard a door shut, an engine roar to life, and tires rolling on the pavement.

"Open your eyes," Margaret said.

47

Jonas was behind the wheel of his white pick-up, the same truck he'd been driving a year ago when he pulled in next to me in the parking lot of Brighton Park and scolded me for taking his parking place. I'd snapped back at him and jerked my car into the next space—he'd walked away in the rain. I'd turned to stare at this very truck, wondering what the fuss was about, when I glimpsed for the first time the faded logo of the Magnolia Arms and tried to make sense of the broken black lines and green specks.

Now—here I was—standing in the driveway of Jonas and Margaret's new home, gaping at the truck, which had intersected their lives with mine. The logo, a stately magnolia tree in full bloom, gleaming in the faded radiance of the evening sun, was restored to the door. The words "Magnolia Arms" were printed in firm black letters beneath the image.

Jonas beamed. "There's another one exactly like it on the other side. What do you think?"

I ran my finger over the painting. "It's … wonderful. Better than I imagined."

"You can thank Ivy Leigh," Margaret said. "She rummaged through dozens of photos before she found an old picture of the truck. She said to tell you 'you owe her.'"

"Why do I owe her?"

Jonas stepped out of the truck. "Because I'm giving the truck to you." He took my hand, turned it palm up, and dropped in the keys.

"Me? Why?"

"I told you," he said. "Without you, Margaret and I would still be acting like fools, sitting alone in empty rooms, miles apart, dreaming of what might have been."

"So you see why Jonas laughed about your car," Margaret said. "I told him you couldn't afford insurance on two vehicles. Now you won't have to worry about fixing your car."

"Get in," Jonas said. "Take it for a spin. You, too, Megs. I'll do the dishes."

Margaret and I, windows down, drove along the country roads, leaving the friction and fractures of our hectic week behind. Longtime, comfortable friends, we felt no need to chatter. We knew each other's histories well; we had no need to ask what the other was thinking. We rode in silence on the wildflower-lined road, each born along the current of our own thoughts, trying to make sense of the baffling nature of life and love.

At last Margaret broke the silence.

"What do you think of your study?" she asked.

"It's the second most beautiful room I've ever seen."

"I told Jonas no matter how we decorated the room, you'd never love anyplace like your room at the Magnolia Arms."

"Do you miss *your* room?" I asked.

Margaret turned away. "How did you guess?"

"Because I'm homesick and I only spent a summer there. You lived there for thirty years. And Ivy Leigh is your best friend. You must miss her, no matter how happy you are with Jonas."

Looking out the window, she spoke in a calm, deliberate voice. "When I got off the train last October and saw Jonas waiting for me, I thought nothing could ever be wrong again."

"I'll never forget it. It was like a movie—only better."

"Those first few days ... the sad, wasted years fell away. The love I thought I'd forgotten was still there ... only stronger. The old pain was back."

"Pain?"

"That terrifying feeling of knowing someone has entered your life and transformed you into someone you never dreamed you could be."

"Makes you wonder why people *want* to fall in love, doesn't it?"

She turned to me. "It's been wonderful, Agnes—being with Jonas. He's still the man I fell in love with, but I've fallen in love all over again with the man he is now."

"I love seeing you together," I said. "Almost brought me to tears during dinner."

"Me, too," she said. "For the last several dinners ... ever since Lorna arrived."

"Why does everyone keep saying that?" I asked. "What's she got to do with anything?"

Margaret shook her head. "It took me by surprise, too. But the emptiness in her voice, the loneliness in her eyes ... brought back all my memories. I don't know what to do with them."

She bowed her head, sighing, struggling to keep tears from falling.

"I've felt that way before," I said, though I wasn't sure I had.

"When I look at Jonas and see how happy he is, I can't forgive myself for hurting him. If only I'd let him explain about Olympia, we might've had a lifetime together instead of—"

"Have you told him how you feel?"

She nodded. "Yes. He says he doesn't blame me—that we were both young and headstrong and that we have to start from where we are."

"Sounds like good advice to me."

We drifted into silence again, drove back and finished the evening with coffee and simple, pleasant conversation. When I left, Jonas instructed me to turn in my rental car and said he would drive my truck to my apartment in the morning. Margaret promised she'd soon be herself again. They invited me to spend the weekend following my trip home. I drove to my apartment. Hoping to sneak in and go to sleep without any further conversation, I put my hand on the doorknob. Flossie, beaming, cracked the door and stood there, blocking my view into the living room.

"You can't believe everything that's happened since you left," she said.

"I was only gone four hours." I pushed on the door, but could not budge her.

"First, let me tell you *our* news," Flossie said.

The longer she delayed, the jitterier I felt. "What is it?"

"We saw a commercial on television. The Motorcycle Stunt Show—the one Warner and Darla are in—is coming to Maplewood, and Winnie and I are going."

"Imagine that," I said, not at all enthused. "You'll *both* get to see your children."

"The only thing is … it's next weekend, when you'll be away."

"Sorry to miss the reunion," I said, sorrier to miss a weekend alone in my apartment.

"And now for *your* news," Flossie said. "Winnie and I aren't the only ones to be reunited with our families." She flung open the door. "Tah-dah."

There stood Winnie, smiling, with her arm around my brother Toby.

Chapter 4

The Grand Hotel

Flossie bumped my shoulder with hers. "Don't just stand there. Give your brother a hug."

Winnie dabbed at her eyes. "Goodness. What's the matter with me? I'm so weepy."

"What's wrong, Aggie?" Toby asked. "You look like you've never seen me before."

I *hadn't* seen him since Christmas a year ago, and I'd *never* seen him sporting a thick moustache and shaggy hair hanging over his ears and collar.

He looked like Mark Twain.

"I wasn't expecting you," I said, "… that's all."

But since you're here, I thought, can you sign my copy of *Life on the Mississippi*?

Even more confounding—Toby *hugged* me. I hadn't felt such genuine affection from him since he scooped me up after a bike crash when I was six.

"Come to the table," Flossie said, "and talk to Toby while he finishes his sandwich. We all ran for the door the moment we heard your car."

Dumfounded, I watched as Flossie led Toby to the kitchen. Winnie slipped her arm through mine and whispered. "Isn't this heartwarming? I love a happy reunion."

"Are you hungry, Aggie? Toby asked.

"No," I said. "I've had more than enough."

Flossie poured milk in Toby's empty glass, said she would leave us alone so we could "catch up on family business," and winked at me before she left.

As Toby wolfed down his sandwich, I tilted my head and narrowed my eyes to make sense of what I was seeing. I'd never known him to be anything but impeccably dressed and groomed. And I hadn't seen him in gym shorts since his failed attempt at track when he was 15.

He gulped the glass of milk, wiped his mouth with the back of his hand, and leaned back in his chair.

"Those gals are gems," he said. "I didn't know you had *two* roommates. Last time I heard you had only one."

"Winnie's visiting," I said. "And they're looking for an apartment."

"So … you probably won't be able to put me up for awhile."

"Put you up? Aren't you supposed to be running the math department at your school?"

He pushed away from the table and propped his arm on the back of his chair. "Supposed to be. I don't know what's happened to me, Aggie. I've lost my edge."

"Your edge?"

"I used to love going to work, and now I can hardly force myself to get out of bed. I know you can't understand. You've never lived under the kind of pressure I do."

My insides smoldered, but I remained calm. "How would you *possibly* know how I live? You've only called me once since I've been here."

A statistic I hadn't realized I'd kept track of till that very moment.

"That can't be right," he said.

"It *is* right," I said. "The only things I know about you are what Mom tells me." I pushed the napkin holder toward him. "Wipe the milk off your moustache."

He ignored the napkins and swiped his lip with his hand. "What do you want to know?"

"First of all, why are you *here*?"

He leaned into the table. "I need help, and I can't ask Mom and Dad."

"You need *my* help," I said, as skeptical as a mother catching her child in a lie. "When I needed *your* help a year ago, you told me to 'spare you my theatrics.' Remember?"

Unruffled, he pursed his lips. "You mean when you got fired?"

"I was railroaded," I said.

Flossie returned to the kitchen. "Sorry to interrupt. I moved the rollaway bed to your room, Agnes. Winnie and I will move in there, so you and Toby can finish talking and—"

I held up my hand. "I'm done talking."

Flossie irritated me further by kissing Toby on the cheek. "Don't worry, dear. Everything will look brighter in the morning. I put a sleeping bag on the floor and a nice fluffy pillow."

He took her hand. "Thank you. And thanks for the sandwich."

Late that night, too frustrated to sleep, I stared at the living room ceiling while Toby snored and mumbled. I tried to remember the last time he had been "brotherly," but my memory, like a scratchy record on a gramophone, refused to squeak out anything but discord and static—sticking, unsticking, hitting the final groove only to repeat again. Eight years older than I, Toby should have been my champion, my fan, an ardent supporter. Instead, he had devoted his life to lecturing me about my faults and prophesying how my shortcomings would eventually result in our parents' broken hearts.

But here he was—truant from his job, absent from his family, presuming on my mercy and the safety of my home.

Desperate for sleep, I plundered in the kitchen cabinet for a bottle of aspirin, downed three, and shuffled back to the sofa. Near dawn, I drifted off, only to be awakened by laughter from the kitchen. I blinked my eyes at the faint light filtering through the Venetian blinds and stumbled to the bathroom to be first in line for a hot shower. Then I sneaked into my bedroom, locked the door, and plopped down on the bed. I couldn't bear being trapped in my over-populated apartment all day, but I was too tired to plan my escape.

Flossie tapped on the door. "Agnes, are you all right?"

"Yes, I'm getting dressed."

She spoke through the door. "We're ready to go. Would you like us to wait for you?"

I opened the door. "Go where?"

"Toby needs some clothes, so we offered to take him shopping. Want to come?"

"You can't take the rental car," I said. "I have to return it today."

"We're going to take the bus. Toby said he's never ridden a city bus before."

My sagging spirits lifted. They might be gone for hours.

"Good idea," I said, raising my voice. "Maybe he can get a haircut while you're out."

Toby called from the living room. "I heard that."

"Thanks, Flossie," I said. "You three go ahead and have a good time."

"We'll stop by the grocery store on the way home," she said. "We'll need more food now that we have another mouth to feed."

I followed her to the living room.

"Sure you won't come with us, Aggie?" Toby asked.

"I'm sure. "One question, Toby. Does Janette know where you are?"

He hung his head. "No. We had another argument before I left. I said I needed some time alone and didn't know when I'd be back. I told her not to worry."

"Do Mom and Dad know where you are?"

He smirked in the old familiar way. "That's two questions."

Flossie took his arm. "Come on. No more arguing. We'll miss the bus."

"We'll be home before dark," Winnie said, and they were gone.

I went straight to the phone, looking forward to the first time I would play the role of the sensible sister reporting my brother's foolishness to our parents, instead of the other way around.

But when my mother, panic in her voice, answered the phone, my euphoria evaporated.

"Hello? Hello? Janette, is that you?" she asked.

"No, it's Agnes."

"Oh … Agnes. I can't talk right now. I'm expecting a call."

"Is it about Toby?" I asked.

"What makes you say that?"

"Because I know he ran away from home yesterday."

She bristled. "Who told you that?"

"No one *told* me. He showed up at my house looking like a bum."

She screamed to my father. "Stuart. Stuart. Toby is with Agnes. He's with Agnes." She laughed and cried and gasped for breath, then spoke to me again. "Let me talk to him."

"He's not here," I said. "Flossie and Winnie took him shopping."

Her tone froze solid. "What's my son doing with *them*?"

"He showed up in gym shorts and a sweatshirt—didn't bring a change of clothes."

"That doesn't sound like Toby."

"And it looks like he hasn't had a haircut in weeks. Why didn't you tell me he was having a mid-life crisis?"

The volcano erupted.

"I don't know," she said. "Maybe because you're never *home* to answer the phone and when you *are*, you can't talk because there's so much *racket* from those people you live with."

"Whoa. What brought that on?"

Silence. "I can't talk about this right now. I have to call Janette."

Click.

I thought about calling back to talk to my father, but decided to let the hot coals I'd ignited burn down to embers.

The phone rang again. When I heard Jonas' voice, I breathed a sigh of relief.

"Good morning," he said. "Have you taken back the rental car yet?"

"No … I got off to a slow start."

"Good. I'll be right there with the truck. I'll follow you to the rental car place, and then you can bring me home. How's that sound?"

"Perfect."

No one could come up with a solution to a crisis better than Jonas. I'd tell him about Toby, he'd tell me what to do, and one problem would be solved.

Once we dropped off the car, Jonas handed me the keys to the truck. On our way back, I told him about Toby's arrival.

"As if I didn't have enough trouble," I said, "now I have to deal with my brother."

"And you resent that?" Jonas asked.

"Yes, I resent it. My whole life all he's ever done is tell me to grow up."

He pointed to my foot. "Ease up on the gas pedal there, kiddo. You're going to have to get used to a bigger engine. How long is Toby planning to stay?"

I eased my foot off the accelerator. "He wants me to 'put him up for awhile.'"

"Doesn't he have a job?"

"Yes, he's the chairman of the math department, which he never lets anyone forget."

"Have you *asked* him why he's here?"

"All he said was he's lost his edge," I said.

"And he's how old?"

"Thirty-two."

"Hmm," Jonas said. "Sounds like he's feeling his mortality."

"What's that supposed to mean?"

Jonas put his arm on the back of the seat. "Some men get to a certain age, feel like half their life is behind them, and wonder what they have to show for it."

"He's got a lot to show for it," I said. "A good job, a beautiful wife, three sons."

"But he may think he's missed something, and he'll never have a chance to get it back."

"You mean, like climbing Mount Everest or something?"

"Could be. Or he could just want to find out what it's like to do something reckless. I never met him, so I couldn't say for sure."

"I can't imagine that happening to Toby. It never happened to my dad. Did *you* ever feel that way?"

"No. I was so busy trying to keep memories of Margaret at bay, I didn't dare stop working." He turned to me. "Can I give you some advice?"

"I wish you would."

"Take him someplace quiet and talk to him. Find out what's wrong. Maybe you can use the opportunity to build a relationship with him."

"It's too late for that."

"You don't know that. Instead of remembering yourself as the little sister he shoved aside, think of yourself as the friend he turned to when he needed help."

When we pulled into the driveway, the front door burst open. Margaret rushed toward us. Jonas opened his door and hopped out before the truck rolled to a stop.

Margaret fell into his arms. I turned off the engine and hurried to join them.

Jonas held her close. "Megs, what in the world is the matter?"

She lifted her tear-stained face. "It's Monty."

My heart sank. "Monty? What happened?"

"He was helping Nestor in the backyard ... got his feet tangled in the garden hose ... fell and broke his hip."

"Poor thing," I said. "Is he going to be all right?"

She shook her head and turned to Jonas. "He's going to need surgery. I have to go. Monty is one of my oldest friends. Besides, Ivy Leigh will need me."

Jonas cradled her face in his hands. "I'll come with you."

She sniffled. "What about the workmen coming this week?"

"Agnes can housesit and keep an eye on things. But what about your classes?"

Margaret wiped her eyes. "I've already called Dr. Spradley. He said he'd be glad to come out of retirement for a week."

Jonas turned to me. "Can you take us to the train station in the morning, Agnes?"

"Of course."

He put his arm around Margaret.

"Bring Toby with you," he said. "After you drop us off, you can come back here and have that long talk."

The next morning, I stood on the porch with Winnie and Flossie while Toby put our suitcases in the back of my truck.

Winnie gave me a quick peck on the cheek. "Maybe we can visit in a few days. I'd love to see that house. It sounds so beautiful."

Flossie was silent.

"Something wrong?" I asked.

She took my hand between hers. "If it weren't for you, I wouldn't have a roof over my head, so ... I probably shouldn't say this."

"What?"

She squeezed my hand. "You've been given a rare gift, and you don't even know it."

In all the months I'd known Flossie, this was the first time I'd seen her face clouded with anger and her voice on the verge of scolding.

"What do you mean?"

"You haven't said a kind word to your brother since he's been here. You didn't even *pretend* to be glad to see him."

I looked over my shoulder to be sure Toby was out of earshot. "I'm sorry you're upset, but you don't the whole story."

"I know my son has hurt me *way* more than your brother has hurt you, but I'd give *anything* if Warner would walk in and ask to stay awhile."

Images of Warner and Darla crowding in on top of everyone else made me shudder.

"Good point," I said. "I'll try to do better."

"Do you *mean* that or are you just saying that to get me to be quiet?"

Flossie had always been hard to fool.

I hugged her. "I mean it. Jonas already said the same thing."

"Good," she said. "You might not get another opportunity like this. Don't mess it up."

Promising to reform, I walked toward the truck. Toby was waiting on the driver's side.

"Mind if I drive?" he asked. "This is a classic."

"Sorry. I haven't called the insurance company yet."

He opened my door. "Dad would be proud to hear you talk like that."

"I've been paying my own insurance for a long time, Toby. I know what to do."

In reality, it was Jonas who had reminded me to call the insurance company, but Toby didn't need to know.

We drove in silence. When we reached the center of town, Toby rolled down his window.

"This is a nice place to live, Aggie. I see why you like it here. I'm looking forward to seeing your school on Monday."

I turned to him. "You want to go to *work* with me?"

"Sure. I can hang out in your office while you're teaching. Then I can meet your friends."

"What about *your* job?"

He rested his arm in the open window. "I have ten days of sick leave, and I intend to use every one of them."

I clamped both hands on the steering wheel. "What's gotten into you? Are you on some kind of voyage of self-awareness? I don't know if you noticed, but the '60's are over."

He was unfazed. "Voyage of self-awareness. I like that. And in case you don't remember, Mom and Dad refused to let me participate in the '60's."

Jonas was waiting outside when we arrived. Toby carried our bags to the porch. After brief introductions, Jonas, Margaret, and I left for the station. Toby stayed behind. When I returned, I was happy I couldn't find him anywhere. I carried my suitcase upstairs to my room and closed the door behind me. Sitting at the desk, I stared out at the morning sun cresting the tall oaks, pouring into the half-tame, half-wild backyard. I rolled a clean sheet of paper into the typewriter and resumed my story where I'd left off the week before.

The picture perfect flower girl, Olympia McBain, her light brown hair curled into ringlets, glided up the aisle ahead of her father's bride. Her pink taffeta dress swished, her white patent leather shoes clicked on the stone floor, but not a single petal dropped from her hand. When she arrived at the front of the chapel, she deposited her basket, still full, at her father's feet and took her place beside her brother Bentley who was folding paper airplanes on the front row. Her father scowled at them, and then beamed at his bride, escorted by her melancholy son.

The front door slammed.

"Aggie," Toby called. "Hey, Aggie, what's for lunch?"

I came downstairs and found him, cross-legged on the floor, watching TV. His hair, windblown, stood out in all directions.

"Where were you?" I asked, heading toward the kitchen.

He pulled off his sweatshirt and tossed it on the sofa. "Exploring the property. What were you doing? Nosing around?"

"If you must know, I was writing."

He hopped up and followed me. "You're still writing? I thought you gave that up in college. Are you finally finishing that bunny rabbit story you started in second grade?"

Should I resent his condescension or be pleased he remembered?

I held out a jar of pickles. "The history of the Magnolia Arms. Open this."

He took the jar. "The history of *what?*"

"The Magnolia Arms … the house Jonas built, where I met Margaret last year."

He unscrewed the lid, pulled out a pickle with his fingers, and bit it in half, smacking. "You used to yell at me for eating out of the jar," I said.

He gulped down the pickle and leaned against the counter. "You *were* a pretty annoying kid. Can I help you do anything?"

"Take that loaf of bread to the table … and the tomato."

I opened the refrigerator and found sliced ham, cheese, mayonnaise, and lettuce.

He leaned over my shoulder. "Is there any mustard?"

"No plain mustard. Jonas only eats spicy."

He nudged the refrigerator door closed with his elbow and came to the table. "You eat with them enough to know those kinds of details?"

"No. They're still newlyweds. I don't want to intrude."

"Newlyweds? At their age? How long have they been married?"

I smeared mayonnaise on a slice of bread. "It's a long story. You'd be bored."

He pulled out his chair. "That was the old Toby. I'm a great listener now."

Toby listened with polite attention, leaving his sandwich uneaten. By the time I finished, he had propped both elbows on the table and rested his chin in his hands.

"I'd forgotten what a great storyteller you are—made me remember how Mom used to make you recite poetry when company came for dinner."

I groaned. "I was fourteen before I finally had enough nerve to refuse."

He stood, clasping his hands to his chest. "Still the maiden, clinging firmly, quivering lip and fair face white, stilled her frightened heart's wild throbbing: 'Curfew shall not ring tonight!'"

"Stop it," I said, giggling in spite of myself. "You did your fair share of saxophone solos. I never understood why Mom asked you to play. You had absolutely no talent."

He raked his hands through his bristly hair. "She didn't want to show partiality. Everyone knew you were her favorite."

My mouth fell open. "You can't be serious. You've always been the fair-haired boy."

"Me?"

"You have no idea how many times Mom has asked why I can't be more like you ... or like Sharon."

He sat down. "Sharon? She still brings her up?"

"Yeah. And to make matters worse, Sharon is the new assistant provost at my school."

He reached for the loaf of bread and twisted it closed. "So your charmed life has finally taken a detour."

Taking his plate, I stacked it on top of mine and started toward the sink. "Charmed? Where did you get that idea?"

"Flossie. She told me about your exciting life and all your friends—the lady who runs the restaurant, the rich lady who owns the mansion, the people at that inn."

I took two coffee mugs from the cabinet. "I wouldn't argue about my friends being remarkable, but *my* life ... exciting? Not at Brighton Park. Want some coffee?"

Before I realized what had happened, Toby rushed across the room and wrapped his arms around me, his moustache scraping my ear.

As if comforting a child, I patted his shoulder and stood back. "Don't you think it's time you told me what's wrong?"

"Could we take a walk? Maybe I can tell you if I don't have to look you in the eye."

I turned on the coffee pot and followed Toby through the back door. We stepped off the back porch and started toward the woods at the edge of the property. Following the makeshift path Jonas had begun clearing, we pushed back branches and stepped over piles of leaves. Like an intrepid explorer, Toby led the way, calling over his shoulder as he blazed the trail.

"Like our old camping days, Aggie. Remember how much fun we had?"

Fun? My memory was of my careworn mother, up to her elbows in Thermoses and plastic dishes at our campsite. When she spotted Toby and Dad shouldering backpacks, she would call out, "Take Agnes with you," whereupon Toby would complain that I would only slow them down and my dad would beckon me to follow, warning me about poisonous snakes.

"Yeah, I remember," I said. "Do you take your boys camping?"

"No. About as adventurous as I get is taking them to the park ... once in awhile."

"Then why aren't you home doing that today?"

Toby tugged on a wisteria vine hanging low over the path.

"Janette says until I 'stop acting like a child,' the boys are better off without me. She said she doesn't know who I am anymore. I'm not sure I do either."

Clever rejoinders sprang up in my mind like mushrooms after a rainstorm, but with Jonas' words echoing in one ear, and Flossie's in the other, I thought twice.

"Jonas says you're feeling your mortality," I said.

He frowned. "You *talked* to him about me?"

"I had to explain why you were here."

"Great," he said. "One more person who thinks I'm a lunatic."

"He thinks no such thing. He told me to invite you here, so we could talk. He said I should forget you're my brother and treat you like a friend. That's what I'm trying to do."

He bowed his head. "I shouldn't burden you with my problems."

"What problems? You've succeeded at everything you've ever tried."

He kept walking. "Lots of people have 'succeeded at everything they've tried,' but *they* end up with condos in Florida and friends to play golf with."

"You don't play golf," I said.

"That's the whole point."

"The whole point of what?"

He whirled to face me. "I don't want to get to the end of my life and realize I never took time to do the things other people do."

Startled at his sincerity, I softened my tone. "But what more could you want? You have a good job, a beautiful wife, three cute kids—"

"Four," he said.

"Four?"

"Janette's pregnant ... *again*."

I grabbed his arm. "That's great. I bet Mom and Dad are thrilled."

"Wish I was."

"You're not?"

"It costs money to raise kids—especially if they're gifted. Janette wants to put William in a private school. Lewis already takes piano lessons. Alfred David is only three, but—"

When Toby said my youngest nephew's name, I winced. Poor little guy—saddled with an unfortunate pairing of his great grandfathers' names, always used together.

"You're not in financial trouble, are you?" I asked.

"We're doing all right, but by the time this baby graduates from high school, I'll be 50. There won't be any time left to do the things I want to do."

"What is it you want to do ... exactly?"

He shrugged his shoulders. "I don't know. Backpack across Europe, sail to the Galapagos, visit Machu Picchu, Kuala Lumpur."

"I didn't think ... math teachers went in for that sort of thing."

He brushed leaves from an old log and sat down. "Max Roby does."

"Who?"

"New teacher at my school. Came last year. Teaches geometry."

I sat next to him. "And frequents the Galapagos?"

He nodded, approving, as if I had successfully explained the Theory of Relativity.

"Yes. Math teacher like me, except that everyone likes *him*."

"Everyone likes you," I said, though I had no idea whether anyone did.

"No, they don't. My students think I'm too strict, and the teachers in my department think I'm hard to get along with."

"But nobody says those things about Max?"

"Now you understand."

I didn't, but had somehow stumbled onto the reason my sensible brother had slid headlong into a morass of self-doubt. I listened without interrupting.

At first he had reveled in his status as the "youngest department chair in his high school's history" and was not "all that surprised" when his colleagues treated him with polite indifference.

"It's the price you pay for being a whiz kid," he said. "I've paid it all my life."

Once Max Roby arrived, however, the tectonic plates of Toby's world began to shift.

Intelligent *and* personable, Max disproved Toby's theory that it had to be "lonely at the top."

He drew on the ground with a stick. "The final straw was when I walked into the teachers' lounge where Max was showing slides of his trip to the Himalayas."

"If you're short on money," I said, "I wouldn't recommend—"

He snapped the stick in half. "That's not it. Everyone had brought their lunch, but no one had invited me."

"Maybe they thought you had a class or something."

"No. They didn't want me there. And later I overheard Max saying the principal has invited him and his wife to their mountain house for Labor Day weekend."

"And that's what shoved you over the edge?"

"Wouldn't *you* be upset if your boss had never invited you on a trip like that?"

My blood ran cold. A weekend with Elspeth Sherwood? What could be worse?

When we reached the house, I poured the coffee and found a box of Drifters' Rest apple turnovers in the pantry. As Toby munched and brushed flakes of pastry from his moustache, I tried to comfort him with tales of Trixie Thorpe and Mavis Applewhite, the teachers who had taken an instant dislike to me the year before.

We moved to the living room. Toby asked about the Magnolia Arms. Convinced his interest was genuine, I brought my manuscript from upstairs and read the first chapter of *Magnolia Neighbors* to him.

Spellbound, he asked for another chapter.

I laid the story in his lap. "Can't. Busy day tomorrow. You're welcome to read it."

I said good night and went to bed, hoping Toby would read late into the night and be too tired to wake early the next morning.

No such luck. I woke to the smell of bacon and coffee.

Toby, beaming over his largesse, was in the kitchen when I came downstairs.

He kissed me on the cheek. "Good morning. I remembered you like a big breakfast."

Toby had at least tried to tame his hair. Sitting across the table, I watched him shovel a forkful of scrambled eggs into his mouth.

A stray bit of yolk dangled from the edge of his moustache.

"Do you think Jonas would mind if I borrowed a tie?" he asked. "I want to create a good impression. You've probably told all your friends your brother is a teacher, too."

In fact, till Toby arrived, I'd never discussed him with *anyone*, except to answer the occasional question about how many siblings I had.

On the way to Brighton Park, I went over my Monday schedule and suggested Toby might prefer visiting the library to sitting in my office.

He straightened his borrowed tie. "You know best."

I introduced him to Elinor, who offered to give him a personal tour after her morning staff meeting. With Toby in Elinor's safekeeping, I entered my classroom with a clear conscience, proud of myself for behaving exactly as Jonas and Flossie had advised.

My foray into the world of literature and grammar cleared the cobwebs from my mind. I headed back to the library, hoping to find Toby cheered up after spending time with Elinor. Not only did she have a good and gentle heart, but she also had decades of experience dealing with teachers. Maybe she had given Toby a few hints about getting along with his coworkers.

Lost in thought, I was startled when someone tapped my shoulder.

"Excuse me," a student said. "Is your name Quinn?"

"Yes."

He pointed over his shoulder. "That lady back there told me to get your attention."

I peered through the throng of students.

Sharon Merriman-Cheswick, clipboard in hand, was prancing toward me, her platinum blonde hair glistening in the morning sun.

She started talking before she reached me. "You're *impossible* to find."

Bustling students turned to look and moved on.

Wide-eyed, I tried an innocent grin. "They say the safest place to hide is in a crowd."

"What?"

"Something I heard in an old movie once." I pinched her sleeve between my fingers. "This is a beautiful blouse. Silk?"

Peeved, she pulled away. "Yes. And dry-clean only."

"Sorry." She knew I did not mean it. "What do you need?"

She straightened her turquoise-framed glasses. "Where's your friend?"

"Which friend?"

"Mrs. Grinstead."

I turned and started toward the library at a brisk pace.

Several inches shorter than I and teetering in high heels, Sharon struggled to keep up.

"Do you need something from her?" I asked.

"I'm the assistant provost," as if this explained everything.

I slowed, laying a friendly hand on her shoulder. "How's that going, by the way?"

"Fine. Who's substituting in Margaret's classes?"

"I don't know," I said, though I did. "Anything else?"

She fell behind again as I resumed my speed. "Who did you take to the library?"

Turning around, I walked backward, still talking. "You're joking, right?"

She pointed with her pencil. "Watch where you're going."

"What?"

Strong hands clamped onto my arms as I collided with Archie Tillman, the center on the basketball team.

"Whoa," he said. "You okay?" He steadied me till I regained my balance.

"Sorry, Archie," I said.

He winked. "Anytime."

Sharon caught up to me. "That's what you get for trying to be cute."

Biting my lip, I tried to regain my dignity.

"Margaret has gone to visit a sick friend. Dr. Spradley is filling in. The man I took to the library is my brother Toby."

I stopped myself from adding, 'you *moron.*'

She hugged her clipboard to her chest. "You can't be serious. He looks like a bum."

My face grew hot. "Toby is the head of the math department at his school ... unlike *your* brother Roger, who has *never* had a job. By the way, is he out of prison yet?"

Her eyes blazed. "You listen to me, Agnes—"

"No. You listen to me. The last woman who tried to get the best of me is teaching seventh grade English across town. Remember that."

"Is that supposed to be a threat?"

"Nope," I said. "Just a reminder. I'm not the scared little kid who used to live across the street from you. I'm a *teacher.* I was here before you got here, and I'll be here after you're gone."

I walked away without looking back.

When I reached the library, I found Elinor enjoying a cup of tea in her office.

"Where's Toby?" I asked. "Exploring the math section?"

"No. He's not here. Ham came by to fix the sink in the girls' bathroom. When I introduced him to Toby, he invited him to see their workshop."

"That'll be good for Toby," I said. "Spending time with men like that."

Eating a quiet lunch in my office, I congratulated myself on being a good sister.

Toby was spending the day with some of the finest people I knew.

After my afternoon class, I walked back to my office.

The day was done, and nothing had gone wrong.

Until I opened my office door ... and found Toby and Kennesaw Fleming kneeling on the floor, a United States map spread out between them.

His index finger poised over Georgia, Toby looked up.

"Hey, Aggie. When Ham brought me to your office, your friend Kennesaw was waiting in the hall. Did you know he's a Civil War re-enactor?"

"How did you two get in here?"

"Ham let us in," Toby said. "I told him I couldn't leave without letting you know."

Stepping over the map, I walked to my desk. "Leave? Aren't you staying till Saturday?"

Kennesaw folded the map and returned it to his "attaché case," the infamous piece of luggage my suitcase had toppled on when we met at the Dennisonville train station.

Toby stood. "I meant 'leave' to have dinner at the Hamptons' house."

I fixed my eyes on Kennesaw. "And what are you doing here?"

He squared his shoulders. "I was hoping you'd reconsidered the re-enactors' meeting. When you weren't here, I invited your brother."

"I told you I'm not interested. And neither is my brother. He's only visiting."

Kennesaw opened the door. "I thought if Toby wanted to try out a meeting, he could find a local group when he goes home. Not everyone is as unimaginative as you."

Toby laughed. "Unimaginative? She's been making up stories since she was three."

"My mistake," Kennesaw said. "Nice meeting you, Toby. Have a good time at the Hamptons. See you later, Agnes."

Kennesaw closed the door behind him.

I pushed my chair under the desk. "Ready to go?"

Toby picked up my book bag. "I'll walk you to the truck. I'm meeting Ham there."

When we reached my truck, Toby opened the door. I got in and rolled down the window.

"I like it here, Aggie. I'm going to fill out an application tomorrow. A fresh start is just what I need, don't you think."

I was glad I was sitting down. "Don't … don't you think you should discuss this with Janette first? What about *her* job?"

"She's a nurse. She can get a job anywhere. Just think—you and me on the same faculty together. They might write an article about us for the school newspaper."

Ham showed up in time to spare me from banging my head on the steering wheel.

Relieved to return to Jonas and Margaret's house, I ate a sandwich on the patio and spent the rest of the evening writing.

On the drive to school the next morning, I crafted a speech to deliver to Toby, citing half a dozen good reasons he should go home and stay where he was.

Head down, mumbling to myself as I walked to my office—"Think of the boys' leaving their friends and their school"—I almost bumped into Mr. Hampton waiting by my door.

"Good morning," he said.

Startled, I looked up. His olive green uniform was starched and pressed as usual.

"Mr. Hampton. I'm glad you came by. I wanted to thank you for entertaining Toby. Is he spending the day with you again?"

He shook his head. "No. He's on his way home. He asked me to tell you."

This was too good to be true. "You mean … *his* home?"

Mr. Hampton pointed to the door. "Could we talk in private?"

I fumbled in my purse for my keys. "Sure. Did he take a train?"

"No. Come inside. I'll explain."

He pulled out my chair. "Still enjoying the desk?"

"Yes, but how in the world did you talk Toby into going home?"

He moved a chair closer to my desk and sat down.

"Don't think of me as some kind of hero. I'm afraid I resorted to lying to help your brother. I'm here to confess that."

"I've … told an occasional lie myself," I said, which was true.

"Not like this one." He breathed deeply and settled back to tell his story. "Toby found our home very comfortable. It didn't take much to persuade him to confide his troubles."

"You mean about his school?"

He nodded. "I'm a simple man, and I've always been kind of a loner. I don't understand the need for approval, but it's important to Toby … what other people think."

"Always has been."

He rested his hands on the chair arms. "There was no point trying to reason with him. That wasn't my concern. My concern was the good wife he left behind worrying about him."

"You've got that right. Janette is a wonderful person."

His expression grew stern. "When I thought of her at home alone with those three little boys, worrying about her husband … I decided a wake-up call was in order. That's when I lied."

"About what?"

"While Ham was in the kitchen doing dishes, I told Toby it was my wife's birthday and I hadn't had time to visit the cemetery. I asked him to go with me."

"It wasn't her birthday?"

"No. It was last week. That's what gave me the idea. As we drove to the cemetery, I told Toby about Rosalind and how much I'd give for one more day with her."

"What did he say?"

"Nothing. He stayed in the car while I stood at the grave. Good thing, too. I hadn't thought to stop and buy flowers. And it gave me a chance to apologize to Rosalind for lying."

"I'm sure she understood," I said. "So … that's when Toby decided to go home?"

"It might have been, but he was still worried about facing the people at work." He stroked his chin. "So I thought up a lie for that, too."

"For where he'd been all this time?"

He nodded. "It came to me in a flash. I told him to tell his friends he'd taken a weekend trip to buy a car."

"You sold him a car?"

"I *loaned* him a car."

"Won't that inconvenience you? How will you get to work? Ride with Ham?"

He laughed. "Besides our trucks, Ham and I own five classic cars. Toby took a liking to the '55 Thunderbird. I told him to drive it to work and invite his friends to the parking lot."

I couldn't help smiling. "What color is it?"

He stood. "Baby blue. Now that I've cleared my conscience, I'll be on my way. You let me know how Toby gets on, would you? And tell him he's always welcome in my home."

"I will. Thank you, Mr. Hampton."

He paused at the door. "Toby asked me to thank you and tell you goodbye. And there's one more thing."

"What is it?"

"He said yesterday, when Mr. Fleming opened his briefcase to take out the map, Toby saw several photos of Mrs. Ellershaw and her husband."

"Elinor and Ryder? Why would Kennesaw—?" Wait. Toby's never met Ryder. How did he know who he was?"

"Recognized him from the photo he saw in Elinor's office. When Toby asked Fleming about the photos, he got flustered and mumbled something about writing an article about Ryder."

"What kind of article?"

"He wouldn't say. Toby was convinced he made it up. He said what bothered him most was the photos appeared to be taken without the Ellershaws' knowledge."

"I don't like this one bit. We'd better keep an eye on Kennesaw Fleming."

"Already am," Mr. Hampton said.

Chapter 5

Random Harvest

After the good news about Toby, I breezed through Tuesday, dodging everyone except students, eating lunch alone in my office, and leaving campus after my 3:00 class. I considered dropping by my apartment to brag to Flossie about my success with Toby, but opted out of a lengthy conversation and drove back to the Grinstead home to eat supper while I worked on my latest chapter. Though pleased the book was almost finished, I dreaded saying goodbye to the heroine Julia Bridger, whose life had intersected with mine while I was still in college.

I had met Julia's son, Jameson Bridger, four years earlier at the end of my sophomore year, on the day Xander Plumley professed his love for me. Enamored with someone else, impossibly out of reach, I had refused to listen to Xander's attempts to reason with me. Exhausted by my stubbornness, he finally blurted out, "You've been looking love in the face for two years and haven't recognized it." His statement stunned me; my response deflated him. He left me on the sidewalk by the Stanton-Giles University bookstore. I sank down on a bench.

Jameson Bridger, a distinguished elderly gentleman, asked if he could join me. He introduced himself and asked the way to library. As we walked, he told me about his mother, Julia Bridger, a desperate young widow, who had married a callous man, Leo McBain. "She wanted to provide security for me," Mr. Bridger said, "and be a mother to Leo's children." She had discerned Leo's intention—to seize her first husband's inheritance—too late. Despite Leo's badgering, she had clung to Jameson's legacy. That inheritance, I discovered later, was the very property on which the Magnolia Arms had been built.

At 17, fed up with the McBains and determined to find a means of supporting his mother himself, Jameson left home. But Julia, broken by years of misery with Leo, mourned her son's absence. Her health failed. When Jameson received word she had been hospitalized, he hurried home. He argued with Leo, struck him, and was ordered to leave. Julia Bridger died without seeing her son again. Jameson quit college, worked, and prospered; his wealth eventually exceeding his stepfather's. Glad to leave the past behind and possessing extensive landholdings, he gave no thought to the Dennisonville property.

After Julia's death, Leo, an accomplished architect, joined the faculty at Ridgeland Architectural College, where he mentored a promising student named Jonas Grinstead. By then Leo's dissolute son, Bentley, had exhausted his father's patience. Leo disinherited him and made Jonas co-owner of the Bridger property—a grand gesture which precluded Jonas from rebuffing daughter Olympia's relentless pursuit of him. Relieved to move to Dennisonville to build his dream house, Jonas was exasperated when letters from Olympia began to arrive. He discarded them unopened—an action he would have taken even if he were not already in love with Margaret Hawthorne.

Olympia, not to be ignored, proceeded to Dennisonville. When she lied to Margaret about her "understanding" with Jonas and claimed they were to be married "once Jonas finished his house," Margaret believed her. Previously wounded by a former lover, Margaret refused to hear Jonas' side of the story. His dreams in tatters, Jonas abandoned the Magnolia Arms and left for Brighton Park where he nursed his broken heart and lived a safe, solitary, predictable life for thirty years. His cherished routine might never have altered except for two events: the death of Leo McBain and my arrival at Brighton Park.

When Leo McBain's death left Olympia in control of his estate, her first order of business was to exact revenge on the man who had rejected her. She hired a private investigator to find Jonas and hound him into relinquishing his claim on the property. At first, Jonas ignored her threats, but when he survived a heart attack, he resolved to stop avoiding Olympia and to save his house. He sent me to investigate her claim the house was "worthless." I moved into the Magnolia Arms, became acquainted with the residents, and began to piece together the true story.

A few days after I arrived, Ivy Leigh mentioned Leo McBain. When I realized who he was, I began haunting the library and courthouse in search of the one man who could help us—Jameson Bridger. I found his address and wrote to him. Not only did he remember me, but he came to the Magnolia Arms, accompanied by his brilliant young attorney, Sefton Wilkinshaw, to investigate Olympia's legal right to the house. Jonas and Margaret had their long-postponed happy ending. Sefton and I had our promising beginning. Jameson Bridger thanked me for making it possible for him to "come home."

"I'd given up silencing my ghosts," he told me. "I've always regretted my mother died without knowing my father's legacy was safe from the McBains. Your diligence made her wish possible. She would've been grateful ... so am I."

This sentiment sealed my decision to give up novel writing to focus on this true story.

Sefton and I had amassed so much material, we agreed to compile our findings and publish them. Our initial plan was for Sefton to begin with the original purchase of the property by Jameson's grandfather and conclude with the death of Jameson's father. I would continue with Jonas' building the Magnolia Arms. We made progress while working together, but when we parted, Sefton turned his attention to his first passion—law—and he kept delegating more of his assignment to me. The last time I had seen his manuscript, *Briarwood Manor*, he hadn't even introduced Leo McBain into the story.

If Sefton had been an ordinary man, I would have rebuked him for his indifference. But since I did not want to risk losing him, I remained unflappable, no matter how halfhearted he became. Perhaps his concrete legal mind prevented the characters from becoming as real to him as they were to me. I often wondered if I should be writing the book with Nestor, who never tired of discussing it with me. Nestor had been so taken with Julia Bridger, he created a hybrid rose he named for her.

Lost in thought, I jumped when the phone rang and was glad to hear Margaret's voice.

"I hope I haven't called too late, Agnes," she said.

"No," I said. "I'm awake. I'm writing."

"Good to hear. Before I forget ... Jonas wants to know how your brother is."

"Much better. He went home."

"How did you talk him into that?"

"I didn't," I said. "Mr. Hampton did."

"Mr. Hampton?"

"Long story. I'll tell you when you come back."

"That's why I'm calling," she said. "We're coming home tomorrow."

"Monty's improving?"

"Yes, the surgery was a success. He's moving to rehab soon."

"How long before he can come home?" I asked.

"We all discussed it last night. He can't come back here—not for awhile. He won't be able to climb the stairs, and there's no room available for him on the first floor."

"I hadn't thought about that," I said.

"When the doctor says Monty can travel, Jonas will bring him to Plainview to recuperate."

"But you have stairs, too," I said, "and he can't stay with me. I—"

Margaret laughed. "Don't worry, Agnes. We called Charlotte. She's invited Monty to stay at her house as long as necessary. She's even going to hire a private nurse."

Charlotte Wrayburn was the wealthiest woman in town—maybe the state. Her home, comfortable, though palatial, had been a refuge for Jonas after he left the Magnolia Arms. When he arrived in Plainview, heartbroken and alone, Charlotte and her husband offered to let him live in the apartment over their garage in exchange for his service as their handyman. They had remained friends. When Charlotte learned of Jonas and Margaret's engagement, she insisted on hosting the wedding. That's when she met Monty. At the reception they continued to waltz together long after the rest of us had worn ourselves out.

I straightened the desk and went to bed. The next morning, I left a pair of pajamas in the dresser and a change of clothes in the closet, put my suitcase in the truck, and returned to school. When I walked to my office after class, I found Kennesaw Fleming waiting at my door. He was holding a bouquet of white daisies and red chrysanthemums. My stomach churned.

He held out a small card. "I was at the admin building and saw these flowers sitting on the information desk. When I saw your name on the envelope, I thought I'd bring them to you."

I took the card, unlocked the door, set down my books, and reached for the vase.

He ignored my gesture and carried the flowers to the desk. "I'll set them here. Okay?"

"Fine," I said, remaining by the open door.

"Did your brother come with you today?"

"No."

He pulled a pamphlet from his inside coat pocket and laid it next to the flowers. "I brought him some information on re-enactors. "Could you give it to him?"

"Maybe," I said.

"Are you always so mysterious?" he asked.

"No."

He laughed. "So I'm to remain in suspense as to who sent the flowers?"

"It looks that way."

He walked toward me and paused at the door. "Have a good trip."

I closed the door and leaned against it. Kennesaw Fleming had dogged my steps since I left Dennisonville. Was there no way to avoid him? And how did he know I was travelling this weekend? Toby must have told him. Sighing, I gazed at the bouquet. The only time Sefton had sent flowers, and they had to be delivered by Kennesaw Fleming. I took the card from the envelope and read: *For the best sister-in-law ever. Thanks for sending Toby home. Love, Janette. P.S. If this baby is a girl, we're naming her for you.*

Not from Sefton after all.

At the end of the day, flowers in hand, I returned home. Flossie and Winnie, bubblier than usual, welcomed me with a barbecue.

Flossie hugged me. "I'm so proud of you, Agnes. Toby called to let us know he arrived safely at home. You've done a wonderful thing for your brother."

I kept quiet about Toby's trip to the cemetery with Mr. Hampton.

Winnie set the flowers on the table. "I hope these will still be fresh on Saturday. We're planning to invite Warner and Darlinda here after the motorcycle show."

"I wish you could go with us this weekend, Agnes," Flossie said.

"I'd love for you to meet Darlinda," Winnie said.

My head began to swim. Flossie, Winnie, and their wayward children all piled into my apartment this weekend—with no one to supervise?

"I'm not trying to rain on your parade," I said, "but I think you need a pass to get backstage at those kinds of events."

Flossie took a bowl of potato salad from the refrigerator. "This is the closest I've come to seeing my Warner since he left, and *no one* is going to—"

Winnie gasped. Flossie and I looked up.

"What's the matter?" I asked.

Winnie, beaming, pointed to her peace lily by the living room window. "Look. Mary Smith is blooming for the first time since I left home to look for Darlinda. It's a sign."

How could I tell these two hopeful mothers their children were not welcome in my home? I tried to assure myself two little old ladies could not force their way through the raucous crowd at a motorcycle show, but I could not dismiss the possibility. If they did and brought their delinquent kids back here, Warner could hotwire my truck and ride into the sunset with Darla.

I asked Jonas to keep the truck at his house while I was gone. He agreed and offered to drive me to the airport and then take the truck home. I was glad for the chance to talk to him.

We left Plainview and took the highway to the Charlotte airport.

"Did you enjoy your trip?" I asked.

"We did, though it's always bittersweet to be there."

"For you or for Margaret?"

"Both. I know she misses her old home and her friends. For me … the house feels familiar, and yet it's so different from what I envisioned when I designed and built it."

"Is that difficult for you—your dream house not being yours?"

He smiled a sweet, sad smile. "The dream of living there with Margaret and our children hounded me so relentlessly, I forced myself to stop thinking about it years ago."

I hated the pain in his eyes. "They would have been gorgeous, intelligent kids," I said.

"Stubborn is more like it."

"Only if they had been boys."

He laughed. "Surely you've noticed Margaret is a *little* strong-willed herself. Are you excited about going home?"

"I wish I were. I'm only going because my father asked me to. My mother is still disappointed I didn't come home this summer. I'm hoping she'll be pleased I rescued Toby."

"Margaret said it was Mr. Hampton who persuaded him to go home."

"It was, but my parents don't know that. I don't think Toby told them, since he didn't even tell his wife. She sent flowers to thank me for helping him."

"That's nice," he said.

"I guess so."

"You didn't like them?"

"I assumed they were from Sefton, so I was disappointed."

Jonas paused. "Sefton doesn't seem like the kind of man to send flowers for no reason."

I bristled. "What do you mean by that?"

"Only an observation. He didn't strike me as the sentimental type. Of course, I was only with him a couple of days last Christmas when he brought Jameson to the Magnolia Arms."

I knew Jonas was right about Sefton, but didn't want to admit it to myself.

When we arrived at the airport, Jonas stopped at the curb and lifted my suitcase out of the truck. "I hope you have a good time." He kissed me on the cheek. "Margaret and I will meet you at the airport on Monday."

The flight was uneventful. I didn't meet a single mysterious stranger and sat next to a businessman whose silence made it clear he wanted to be left alone. I was happy to comply.

My dad, looking tired, met me. When we arrived at home, he told me to wait on the porch while he went in the house. I heard him call to my mother.

"Betty? You'll never guess who I ran into."

My mom came from the kitchen. I stepped into the living room. If I had expected a warm welcome, I would have been disappointed. She appeared confused, thinner than the last time I had seen her, and had dark circles under her eyes. She looked as if she had been crying.

"Hi, Mom," I said.

She looked at my dad and then at me. "Agnes … what are you doing here?"

"We wanted to surprise you," I said as I put my arms around her.

She was trembling. "I wish I'd known you were coming. I'd have gone to the store."

Dad set down my suitcase. "Aggie has a long weekend, and I thought we could spend some time together."

"Long weekend?" my mother asked.

"Labor Day," I said.

"Give me the car keys, Stuart," she said, "and I'll go to the store."

"We'll go in the morning," Dad said.

My heart ached for my dad. His big moment had not gone as he planned. I worried he had asked me to come home to give me bad news in person.

When I came downstairs the next morning, I found him lingering over his morning coffee and the crossword puzzle.

I poured a bowl of corn flakes. "Where's Mom? I was hoping for pancakes."

"At the store," he said. "She left at 7:00. Couldn't rest till she'd done the shopping."

I refilled his cup and sat at the table. "I'm sorry the surprise didn't go like you'd hoped."

He wrote a few letters in his puzzle and laid down the paper. "It's not your fault."

"Is she *still* not over Toby? I know it was a shock, since he's always been the—"

"She might've been all right," he said, "if it hadn't been for the car Toby drove home."

"The car? Didn't Toby explain? He didn't buy it. My friend loaned it to him."

"It doesn't matter how he got it. The point is … he loves it. He's talking about taking the boys to a classic car show next weekend."

"That's good. It'll give him something to do besides work. Make him more human."

Dad took off his glasses and laid them on the table. "Remember when we all got food poisoning at the church picnic and how we've never eaten deviled eggs since?"

The memory still made me shudder. "Yes."

"Your mom has the same dislike for Fords. Someone we knew in high school … had one. A hot rod. Convertible."

"So?

Mom pulled into the driveway and honked the horn. Dad looked out the kitchen window. "Come help me with the groceries," he said. "We don't have much time to talk."

My mother, toting a grocery bag, opened the back door. "Can you bring in the rest, Stu?" She placed the bag on the counter. "I thought we'd make your favorite cake, Agnes."

This, I knew, was her way of apologizing for her lackluster welcome the night before.

"I'd love that," I said. "I'll go help Dad."

I joined my dad at the car. He placed a bag in each of my arms.

"Tell me," I said, "why is the car such a big deal?"

He lowered his voice. "Your mother will have to tell you. I've already made up some story about needing to go to the hardware store. See if you can get her to talk while I'm gone."

I had never seen my dad so rattled.

After we brought in the last bag, he picked up his car keys, said he had some errands to run, gave us each a peck on the cheek, and hurried out.

Mom busied herself with the groceries and made small talk, asking about my flight, my first week of school, and my cat, whom she loved.

"Did you have breakfast?" she asked. "I could scramble some eggs."

"No, thanks. I ate cereal. Have you talked to Toby since he got home?"

She slid a can of green beans onto the pantry shelf. "Yes. Did he call you?"

"No. Janette sent me flowers, though. Wasn't that nice?"

She closed the pantry door and took a dishcloth from the towel drawer. "Flowers?"

"To thank me for helping Toby."

She approached the table and wiped it with the cloth. "I haven't seen Toby since … his … trouble. Does he seem different to you?"

"Yes. I hardly recognized him."

Her face blanched white; she sank onto a chair. "What does he look like?"

Startled at her reaction, I downplayed the Mark Twain similarities.

"His hair's a little longer, and he's grown a moustache," I said.

"What about his sideburns?"

"I didn't pay much attention," I said, without mentioning I couldn't see them because his hair hung down so long over his ears.

As she talked, she continued wiping the table, though it was clean.

"Your friend who gave Toby this car … is he a shady-type character?" she asked.

"Mr. Hampton? He's the kindest, most noble man I've ever known."

She frowned. "Toby said he's the maintenance man."

"He is, but that has nothing to do with his character. Why are you worried?"

She gave the table another swipe, left the dishcloth in a heap, and walked toward the sink.

"I knew a man once," she said, "who owned a car like that, and he …"

She leaned both hands on the sink and began to sob. I rushed to her and guided her to the table. She held her face in both hands, gasping, sniffling, gulping in air. Helpless, I filled a glass with water, set it in front of her, and waited. After a few minutes, she wiped her face with the dishcloth and sank back in her chair.

"You must think I've lost my mind," she said.

"No," I said. "But I would like to know what this is all about. Can you tell me?"

"I honestly thought I could get through my whole life without the past catching up with me, but no matter what I do ..."

"You can't possibly have a *past*," I said. "You and dad live the most ..." I almost said 'boring' ... "stable lives of anyone I've ever known."

If she heard me, she gave no indication. "I know you must have wondered sometimes why I was so hard on you, why I lectured you about your poor decisions and silly ideas."

"You said it was your job as a mother."

Again she ignored me. "Parents can't help wanting their children to avoid the same mistakes they made."

"I didn't think you and dad had *ever* made any mistakes."

Her eyes flashed. "Your *dad* never made any mistakes. I made enough for both of us."

"Please tell me what's wrong," I said. "You're worrying me."

She drew in a deep breath and sighed. "You know your dad and I grew up on the same street and went all through school together."

"Yes, and Grampa Delaney," I said, imitating my grandfather's many retellings of the legend, "'saw Stuart's potential from the very beginning and hired him to work in the store ... '"

"' ... when he was only twelve,'" my mother repeated with me. We both smiled.

"What you *don't* know," she said, "is there was another boy named Russ Wilcox. He had the most gorgeous strawberry blonde hair. I loved him from the moment I laid eyes on him."

Since neither of my parents had ever been nostalgic about their younger years, I was not surprised to learn they had an old friend they had never mentioned.

"Did he love you?" I asked.

"No. I wasn't his type. He loved my best friend, Miranda Hillingdon."

"Let me guess," I said. "Cute blonde? Petite? Big blue eyes?"

"No. Dark hair and green eyes. Cheerleader. The four of us went everywhere together."

"You and dad and Miranda and Russ?"

She took a sip of water. "Yes. I loved Russ so much I was willing to settle for being in the same car with him, even if he was in the backseat with Miranda."

"That's the saddest thing I ever heard," I said. "But you must've wised up. Otherwise you wouldn't have married Dad. Did Russ marry Miranda?"

She ran the dishcloth across the table again. "No. Our senior year a new boy moved to town. He was handsomer than Russ and a better athlete. Miranda fell for him. Russ was furious."

"And you were thrilled?"

"I was. With Miranda out of his reach, I thought I might have a chance to win Russ over. I was ecstatic when he asked me to the homecoming dance. It was our first official date."

"Miranda went with her new boyfriend?"

"*And* she was homecoming queen, of course."

"So … Russ invited you to the dance so he could keep an eye on Miranda."

She grimaced. "Exactly what your dad said, but I wouldn't listen. My dream had come true. I didn't care how. I had Russ's arms around me. We were whirling across the floor."

"Where was Dad?"

Fresh tears sprang to her eyes. Her voice quivered. "Standing by the wall—watching."

I reached for her glass. "More water?"

She nodded. When I stepped away, she began to speak, a flood of words pouring out, pent up memories spilling onto the kitchen table. I remained behind her, listening to her faraway, unfamiliar voice. The white enamel kitchen walls faded into a gymnasium, basketball hoops suspended over dancers, tables of red punch and homemade cookies lined up beneath the scoreboard; my mother, young and dreamy, resting her head on Russ Wilcox's shoulder; his head jerking left and right as he searched for Miranda; my father, plain and sturdy, in a blue suit borrowed from his father, leaning against the wall.

I tiptoed back to the table. My mother, fixated on the past, scarcely knew I was there.

By Christmas, Miranda announced her engagement. Russ was frantic. My mother, still hopeful, tried to reason with him. My father tried to reason with my mother. When Miranda announced a June wedding, so she could accompany her future husband to college, Russ flew into a rage. By now my grandparents, who had never liked Russ, arrogant and conceited as he was, began to forbid my mother from seeing him till he "calmed down." My mother was desperate, and Russ was not about to be humiliated again.

"One day we were driving in his car," she said. "He was fuming about Miranda as usual, and suddenly he said, 'I'm not going to let it happen.'"

"Let what happen?" I asked.

"He said he'd 'show her.' He wasn't going to let her get married before he did."

The room went white; I gripped the edge of the table. "What?"

"We skipped school that Thursday … went to the courthouse, got a marriage license …"

"You were too young," I said.

"We lied about our ages."

"You *married* Russ Wilcox?"

"It wasn't the wedding I'd always dreamed of," she said.

"You eloped?"

She nodded. "We drove to a discount motel in Savannah for our honeymoon."

"Did you tell your parents?" I asked.

"Russ didn't want me to, but I couldn't let them worry."

"What did they say?"

"Daddy said we couldn't live with them. Mama wanted to know if I could still graduate, because she'd planned a big party."

"So what happened to Russ?" I asked. "Did he slam his hot rod into a telephone pole, or did Grampa kill him?"

"Nothing that simple," she said. "The week before Miranda's wedding, her fiancé called it off … said he didn't want to be saddled with a wife while he was in college."

I shook my head. "So Russ left *you* to go back to *her*."

"He did, but she wouldn't have him. My parents were relieved and wasted no time having our marriage declared void."

"Void?"

"Since we were underage and hadn't gotten our parents' consent, the marriage wasn't legal. So I went back to the courthouse—with my parents— and the whole thing was over."

"What a story," I said. "But *how* did you end up with Dad?"

"My father asked him to marry me."

"That was drastic. Did Grampa not trust you to make your own decisions anymore?"

"No, that's not the reason," she said.

"Then what was it?"

"I was pregnant … with Toby."

Chapter 6

The Lost Weekend

By the time my dad arrived at noon with three take-out chicken dinners from Bob's Pancake World, my mom, exhausted from crying and talking, had gone upstairs for a nap. Dad, wearing the same blue plaid flannel shirt he had worn every Saturday for the last four years, set the containers on the table. He leaned against the kitchen counter, pulled a black comb from his front shirt pocket, smoothed his wavy salt-and-pepper hair, and turned to me.

"So … what do you think?" he asked.

I hugged him. "I've never been prouder to be your daughter."

He heaved a sigh. "We always meant to tell you and Toby the truth, but we kept putting it off till it was too late."

"No blame from me," I said, taking the dinners from the plastic bag. "It must have been an impossible decision."

He washed his hands in the kitchen sink. "How's your mother?"

"Taking a nap."

We sat on the yellow vinyl chairs with chrome legs at the yellow Formica dinette table and opened our Styrofoam containers—past and present converging over chicken and biscuits.

"Now you know why your mother has always doted on Toby," he said. "She's never stopped worrying someday Toby would turn out like Russ—in spite of all our best efforts."

I slid a pat of butter into a biscuit. "That's why she was so upset about the car."

He sipped sweet tea from his plastic cup. "I thought she would faint."

"Surely she didn't think Toby was going to give up teaching to open a garage. That's not even rational."

He rested his elbows on the table. "Keeping a secret like that muddles your thinking. It took a toll on her. Sometimes I wished we could blurt everything out and be done with it."

"And Russ never knew Toby was his son?"

"No," he said. "That's why your Grampa Delaney asked me to marry your mom. They wanted to be rid of Russ once and for all."

"And you were okay with being 'Plan B'?"

"I'd been in love with your mom since I was fifteen."

"How did you put up with her throwing herself at Russ?"

"I knew one day he'd break her heart. I wanted to be the one to pick up the pieces."

"But how did you manage to keep the whole thing quiet?" I asked.

"It wasn't as hard as you might think. When Miranda left for college, Russ joined the Army. Your mom and I had a quiet wedding in the pastor's office and moved away."

"Whose idea was that?"

"Your Grampa Delaney's. He didn't want anyone counting days and calculating dates once the baby was born."

"What did *your* parents say?"

"I never told them. If they figured it out, they didn't say anything. I don't think they wanted to know. That's how we dealt with things in those days."

"How many people know?" I asked.

"You're the sixth."

I counted on my fingers. "Mom's parents, you and Mom, and me. That's five. Who's the other one?"

He wiped his mouth with a napkin. "Jewel Merriman. That's the reason she and your mother were inseparable."

Jewel Merriman, Sharon Merriman-Cheswick's mother, had been my mother's closest friend since before I was born. One of my most vivid childhood memories was wandering into the kitchen to find my mother and Jewel talking in low tones and then shooing me out.

I stabbed a bite of chicken with my fork and waved it through the air. "That makes perfect sense. Mom would've needed an ally … a kindred spirit."

Dad closed the lid on his dinner. "More kindred than you know."

"What do you mean?"

He looked over his shoulder and back at me. "Did you wonder why Doc Merriman left home last year after decades of putting up with his annoying wife and those awful kids?"

84

I shrugged my shoulders. "I thought he was worn out from listening to Jewel whine."

He lowered his voice and leaned in. "Listening to Jewel whine about Sharon's *father*."

"You mean Doc Merriman *wasn't* Sharon's *father*?"

"Nope. Sharon's real father took off when she was a baby." He tossed his napkin on the table. "That nearsighted little weasel couldn't have fathered such a gorgeous girl."

I had never seen this side of my father. He had always been quiet and reserved, speaking his mind only when he was angry. Now that we had breached the wall of secrecy between us, I discovered we were more alike than I had imagined. While Mom napped, I made another pot of coffee and preheated the oven for the chocolate cake. While I cracked eggs, Dad cracked jokes; poured out his heart while I poured the batter into pans. I had never felt closer to him than on that undisturbed Saturday afternoon.

For the rest of the day we treated Mom as if she were recovering from injuries sustained in a car wreck. We spoke in quiet tones, listened when she wanted to talk, kept quiet when she started crying again, each of us trying to adjust to the new reality we were sharing. For the first time I felt like my parents' friend, a confidant they trusted and respected. Though I had a thousand questions and a thousand pieces to fit into some sort of coherent whole, I refrained from hammering them with questions I was dying to ask.

The weekend passed quietly by. On Sunday night when I was packing to go home, my mother knocked on my bedroom door, asked to come in, and sat on the edge of my bed.

She picked up a pair of socks and handed them to me. "I've always wondered what you'd think if you ever found out my secret. Are you disappointed in me?"

I sat next to her. "Not in the least. You're a wonderful wife and mother. Nothing will ever change my mind about that. I'm sorry you've carried this around so long by yourself."

"It hasn't been easy," she said. "I thought I could finally stop worrying, but now there's one more challenge to face."

"What do you mean?"

"The new baby. Every time Janette has given birth, I've been terrified the baby would have red hair like Russ. Red hair is an excessive gene. It can show up anywhere."

"I think the word is 'recessive,'" I said. "The boys all have dark hair. Chances are this baby will, too. Try not to worry."

She hugged me. "I'm so happy you have someone like Sefton. He'll never break your heart the way Russ broke mine."

When we said goodbye Monday morning, Mom asked if I intended to tell Toby what I had found out.

"Your secret is safe with me," I said.

Promising to come home for Christmas, I boarded the plane, sat by the window, and stared at the billowing clouds as we flew toward Charlotte. I felt like a doomed character in a Greek tragedy. Only days after I had bonded with my brother for the first time, I discovered we had different fathers. And even worse, I possessed a dreadful secret I could hold over Sharon's head. Chastising myself for entertaining such a notion, I dozed off, only to dream I sauntered into her office the next morning and said, "Sharon, guess what I found out over the weekend?"

Margaret and Jonas met me at the airport. Margaret and I climbed into the truck while Jonas put my suitcase in the back.

"Jonas wanted you to have your truck for tomorrow," Margaret said, "so I followed him in my car to your apartment."

"I'm glad you both came," I said. "It's good to see you."

"You look tired," she said. "Did the weekend go well? Was your Mom surprised?"

"So surprised she didn't know what to say."

"Your dad must be great at keeping secrets," Margaret said.

"You have no idea."

Jonas climbed into the truck. "Did you get any writing done while you were home?"

"No. I … hadn't been home in such a long time, I spent all the time I could with them."

Margaret patted my knee. "I'm sure they loved having you all to themselves for awhile."

When we reached my apartment, Jonas got out and carried my suitcase to the door.

"Would you like to come in?" I asked Margaret. "I could make some coffee."

"No, thanks," she said. "I have a few more things to do before tomorrow."

Jonas returned to the truck and handed me the keys. "You okay, kiddo? You were awful quiet on the way home."

"I'm just tired," I said. "Whirlwind trip."

I was surprised to find the apartment empty and dark. "Hello," I said. "Anyone here?"

Saturn bounded from my bedroom and leaped onto the back of the sofa. When I scooped him up, he rubbed his face against my chin and purred.

"This is nice," I said. "You haven't been this glad to see me since Flossie moved in."

Thinking Flossie might have left a message on the refrigerator door, I carried Saturn into the kitchen. He leaped out of my arms and skittered toward his food bowl. Empty. So was his water dish. I filled both and continued to look around the kitchen. There was no note anywhere. The flowers Winnie hoped would "stay fresh" had showered petals onto the table. I inspected the living room. Mary Smith's leaves drooped over the sides of the container. The single white bloom Winnie believed to be a sign of good things had shriveled and turned brown.

Fighting a surge of panic, I tried to remain calm and think. Flossie and Winnie were going to the motorcycle show on Saturday night, find their children, and bring them here. Maybe that's what happened. They were all out shopping or eating. But the empty pet dishes and wilted plants were signs no one had been here in days. Flossie would never leave Saturn uncared for. If I called the police and said, 'My friends went to visit their children. I think they've been kidnapped,' would anyone take me seriously?

The phone rang. I lunged for it, half-expecting an emergency room nurse to tell me Flossie and Winnie had been in an accident.

"Hello?" I said, breathless.

"Hi, Aggie, have a nice trip?" Toby asked.

I gasped into the phone. "Flossie and Winnie are missing."

"Missing? That's not likely, is it?"

"I came in a few minutes ago. It looks like they haven't been home for days. They went to see their rotten kids, and I'm afraid—"

"Whoa. Hold on a minute," he said. "Start from the beginning."

I explained Flossie and Winnie's weekend plans. "They were going to bring Warner and Darla home with them, but no one has been here. Should I call the police?"

"Maybe the reunion went well enough the four of them went on a trip together."

"Flossie would never do something like that without asking someone to feed the cat."

"I didn't think about that," Toby said. "Give them one more night to come home and then call the police in the morning if they haven't."

"I feel so guilty," I said, "for being irritated with them. They wrecked my car and hauled all this junk in here. But if something happens to them … I'll …"

"You've got nothing to feel guilty about," Toby said. "You should hear the way those two talk about you. They think you hung the moon."

I sniffled and blew my nose. "I'm sorry I'm acting like this. Why did you call?"

"I wondered what Mom and Dad said about me … while you were home. Are they mad?"

"No, they're not mad. They're happy you went home to your family."

He sighed. "That's a relief. Would you like to come see us this weekend and go to the car show with me and the boys?"

"Thanks for the offer, but I can't take a trip two weekends in a row. Were the boys excited about the Thunderbird?"

"Yes. So is Janette. She got a babysitter so we could drive it on a date. How cute is that?"

An image of my dreamy-eyed mother cuddled up next to Russ Wilcox in his Ford hot rod flashed into my mind.

"That's great, Toby. Keep romance alive."

"Speaking of romance, have you heard from Sefton?"

"No, he's like on some kind of probation—at least in his own mind. I have to schedule the times I call him. He doesn't like to be taken by surprise … that legal mind of his.

"At least he'll make a good living when you get married. Try to get some sleep. Call when the girls come home, okay?"

I slept on the sofa, so I would hear Flossie and Winnie if they came home. Saturn snuggled next to me and purred till I went to sleep. When we woke in a still empty apartment, I called the police. The officer who took the report asked if I suspected an accident or foul play and then asked when I would be home so an officer could investigate. I told him around four o'clock, left a note in case Flossie and Winnie came home while I was gone, and went to school.

As I walked to my office after morning classes, I heard Grace Bonner call my name.

I turned around. Clutching a piece of paper in her hand, she hurried to catch up with me.

"I found this on my desk this morning," she said. "I don't know what to do."

Tony Castarini had delivered his poem to the woman he loved.

"He didn't sign it?" I asked.

"You know who sent this?"

"I do."

"It wasn't Kennesaw, was it?" she asked, her eyes sparkling.

"Good heavens, no," I said. "He would never write a note like that, and if he did—"

She folded the paper. "You're right. He's too educated to write like this, isn't he?"

"Not only too educated," I said. "He's not sensitive enough to—"

Two men in suits approached us. I assumed they were detectives who had come to take my statement. The taller man, distinguished, with a face cold and chiseled enough to be poised on Mount Rushmore, spoke first.

"Are you Agnes Quinn?" he asked.

"I am. Are you with the police?"

The shorter man, thin and pale in a gray seersucker suit and red bow tie, raised one eyebrow.

"No, we're not policemen. I'm Dr. Morton Penrose, and this is …"

The tall man interrupted. "We need to speak to you"—he glanced at Grace—"in private."

Blushing, Grace walked away. I led the men to my office, invited them in, and sat behind my desk. Instead of accepting my invitation to be seated, they stood in front of me. Though the tall man produced a business card, I did not read his name, dazzled as I was by his diamond ring and monogrammed shirt cuffs. He laid the card on the desk.

"My name is Dr. Charles Maron. I believe you know my daughter, Lorna."

"Lorna's father," I said. "It's nice to meet—"

"We've just left her classroom," he said. "She refused to speak to us. I spoke to …" He turned to Dr. Penrose. "What was her name?"

Dr. Penrose flipped through the pages of a small spiral notepad. "Grinstead."

"Mrs. Grinstead told us you were Lorna's friend," Dr. Maron said.

"I am."

"Good. Maybe she'll listen to someone her own age who can reason with her about giving up this Peace Corps mentality to resume her studies."

Dr. Penrose pushed his round glasses up his nose. "What Dr. Maron is trying to say is …"

"I'm not *trying* to say anything," Dr. Maron said. "I've invested a fortune in Lorna's future, and I have no intention of keeping quiet while she—"

"Please understand, Miss Quinn," Dr. Penrose said. "Lorna is a virtuoso. The loss of her talent to the music profession … to the world … would be unspeakable."

"So you are—?" I asked.

"Her teacher," he said. "Rather … I was."

"She told me how upset you were when she gave up the piano."

"Did she mention how upset *I* was?" Dr. Maron asked.

I shot him my sternest teacher stare. "No. Only that you don't accept failure."

"I don't appreciate your tone, young woman," he said. "I'm not on trial here."

Dr. Penrose took a handkerchief from his pocket and cleaned his glasses. "You'll have to excuse us. We are both concerned for Lorna, and if we sound—"

"I don't need to be excused," Dr. Maron said, tapping on my desk. "I will not apologize for trying to stop my daughter from wasting her talent in this backwater clapboard schoolhouse."

Standing, I shoved back my chair. "This school is well-respected throughout the state."

Dr. Penrose straightened his bow tie. "We intend no offense, Miss Quinn. As a teacher, I have high regard for my colleagues no matter what their discipline or—"

Dr. Maron waved his hand. "Spare me the sermon about the dignity of the profession. I'm merely saying this is not the place for a Maron."

I walked toward the door and opened it. "Don't you think that's for her to decide?"

"This is getting us nowhere," Dr. Maron said and brushed past me into the hall.

Laying his card on my desk, Dr. Penrose walked toward me. "This has not gone at all like I'd hoped." He stopped at the door. "I apologize for Dr. Maron. He's not accustomed—"

"To being resisted?" I asked.

He stepped into the hall and turned to face me. "As a favor to a fellow educator, would you do one thing for me?"

"If I can."

"Ask Lorna to play for you. If you heard her perform even once, you'd understand. Please … help her."

By the time he finished, his eyes were red, glistening with reluctant tears. "I'll try," I said.

Still worried about Flossie and Winnie, I muddled through the day, lecturing on "auto-pilot" as all teachers learn to do. Eager to meet with the police, I hurried to the parking lot after my last class, crafting my statement as I went. 'Mrs. Bingham and Mrs. Parker-Potts are elderly women' I would say. 'A visit with their own children may seem like a harmless way to spend an evening, but—'

Margaret, waiting by my truck, interrupted my practice.

"Why didn't you tell me Flossie had been missing since Saturday?" she asked.

"I didn't know till I went into the apartment last night. I thought they might come home by morning. I would've told you today, but I've had a lot of interruptions—"

She held out a piece of paper. "Flossie's been trying to call your office all afternoon. When she couldn't reach you, she called the library. Elinor took a message."

I glanced at the paper. "Whose number is this?"

"A gas station on the other side of Maplewood. Use the phone in Elinor's office."

We walked toward the library.

"Are they all right?" I asked.

"Flossie said they're hungry and tired and Winnie sprained her ankle, but not to worry."

Elinor and Margaret lingered in the office as I dialed the number. The station owner answered and put Flossie on the phone.

"Flossie," I said, "are you all right? What happened? Did you find Warner?"

"I'm fine," she said, "but Winnie is in pitiful shape. We may need to take her to the doctor tomorrow."

"You mean for her ankle?"

"Not only that. I'll tell you later. Wait a minute." Her voice became muffled as she put her hand over the receiver. She spoke again. "Winnie said to tell you we're sorry to be a bother."

"It's no bother. Put the owner on the phone, so he can give me directions."

As I neared the gas station, I found Flossie waving and pointing to a parking place on the side of the building. I was barely out of the truck before she hurried toward me, buried her head in my shoulder, and sobbed. Her hair, wilder than usual, smelled of smoke. Her clothes were tattered and dirty. Her face was scraped from her eyebrow to her chin, and she had deep scratches on her left arm.

She pulled back. "I shouldn't hug you. I'll get blood on your clothes.

"Don't worry," I said. "I'm just glad you're safe."

"You'll have to help me with Winnie."

Looking worse than Flossie, Winnie was resting on an old wooden bench by the door of the station. Her head bowed, she was embracing her shoe like a child hugging a teddy bear. She did not look up as we approached.

I knelt in front of her. "Winnie? Flossie said you hurt your foot. We're going to help you into the truck. Can you stand?"

Lifting her head, she held out her hand and laid it against my cheek.

"Every moment we were in that dreadful place," she said, "all I could think was how unkind my own daughter was and how kind you are ... I wished I had thanked you more often."

"It's all right, Winnie," I said.

"You're a dear girl, the best friend I've ever had ... well, besides Flossie. If it hadn't been for her, I'd have given up, but she made me keep walking."

Flossie put her hand under Winnie's elbow. "Enough of that, old girl. Come on now."

We eased Winnie into the truck. She slid to the middle, leaned her head back, and fell asleep before I could pull onto the highway.

"What happened?" I asked. "Did you go the motorcycle show?"

"We did. We were so happy to be on our way. It was a long ride, but it didn't seem like it. We were so excited about surprising our kids."

"You were able to get backstage after all?" I asked.

"Yes. The funny thing is the rest of the people in the show treated us like royalty. Warner and Darla are very popular in their own ... circles."

"Were they glad to see you?"

"Not at first," she said. "They seemed irritated. But when we invited them to supper, they changed out of their theatrical clothes and seemed to be in a better frame of mind."

"Where did you go for dinner?"

"Someplace Darla said she'd always wanted to go. Very pricey. Winnie fit right in, but I felt like a duck out of water."

"Fish," I said.

"Yes, they had fish. In fact, Warner ordered lobster ... and steak."

"Doesn't sound like someplace Warner would want to go," I said. "He's such a …" I started to say 'thug,' but not wanting to wound her further, let the sentence hang in mid-air.

She turned to me. "There's no need to mince words, Agnes. I've been thoroughly undeceived about my son. Do you have a tissue? Mine were in my purse."

"Your purse," I said. "Did we leave it at the gas station?"

"No. Warner stole it *and* Winnie's, too. Or maybe Darla took Winnie's. I don't know."

"They stole your purses?"

"Yes, and everything in them. They've probably drained us dry by now."

Staring at her, I nearly ran off the road. "When did this happen?"

She gazed at the road as she relived the scene. "We had such a good time at dinner—talking over old times. Then we told them we were looking for an apartment."

"Did they seem interested?"

"They were interested, all right," she said. "Asked us a zillion questions about how we were going to afford it. That should have been a warning, but I ignored it."

"You and Winnie paid for the meal?" I asked.

"Winnie did. She said it felt good to be needed. We were thrilled when they asked us to spend the night. I had filled Saturn's dish before we left, so I thought he'd be okay. Is he?"

I nodded. "It didn't hurt him to skip a couple of meals. Did Winnie pay for a hotel, too?"

Winnie groaned and half opened her eyes. "Are we there yet?"

"Not yet," I said. "Want to stop and get something to eat?"

"No, no," she said. "I'm not properly dressed." Her head slipped over on my shoulder, and she dozed off again.

"We didn't stay at a hotel," Flossie said. "They *told* us they had a friend who had a 'guesthouse' where we could stay. They stopped to buy groceries, the liars …"

"There was no guesthouse?"

"No. Unless you want to call it a guesthouse for bums. Drove us ninety minutes out of town and into the woods. Way back up a dirt road. When we got inside, there were no beds."

"What did you do?"

"I asked what in the name of Ned we were doing there. Warner said their show business lives kept them surrounded with people, and they liked the 'cabin' for peace and quiet."

"It went from being a guesthouse to a cabin?"

"More like a shack. I told him *we* didn't need peace and quiet, and they should take us back to town so we could catch the bus. They said it was too far. They'd take us in the morning."

"You must have been miserable," I said. "Did you sleep at all?"

"Darla built a fire in the fireplace, and Warner spread two old blankets on the floor. Winnie didn't want to lie down on them at first, but sometime after midnight, we dozed off."

"Where did Warner and Darla sleep?"

"They *didn't*. The last thing I remember was them arguing over some card game they were playing. When I woke up in the morning, they were gone and so were all our belongings."

"I'm sorry, Flossie," I said. "You must be devastated."

She slapped the dashboard. Winnie jerked, but didn't wake up. "I'm not as devastated as I am disgusted and just plain mad. We could've been killed. Did they never stop to think of *that*?"

"What do you mean 'killed'?"

"When we found they were gone, I wanted to start home right away. Winnie wouldn't hear of it—insisted they had only gone for a walk."

"How sad," I said.

"How pathetic you mean," Flossie said. "And then Winnie searched high and low for cleaning supplies, so we could spruce up the 'cabin' before they came back."

"You cleaned the place?"

"Prairie woman style with a scrub brush. By the time I convinced Winnie they weren't coming back, it was late afternoon. We couldn't have made it to the main road before dark."

"You spent another night there?"

"We managed to keep the fire going and found an old skillet under the sink. We ate beans and potatoes like a couple of broken-down cow pokes on the rawhide trail."

"How awful."

"It got worse," she said. "We started out as soon as the sun rose. But neither one of us has any sense of direction and we had ridden there in the dark, so we had no idea which way to go."

"How did you decide?"

"I knew Plainview was west of Maplewood, so we went opposite of the rising sun. We were no Lewis and Clark—I can tell you that."

"They had a guide," I said.

"I wish we had. We would've been all right if it hadn't been for that gully. It was deep and there was no way around it, so we decided to sled down.

"No wonder you look so beat up."

"We sat on our coats and tried to slide, but I went head over heels, and when Winnie tried to stop herself from slamming into me, she jammed her foot into a rock."

"That would slow you down even further … helping her walk."

"If it hadn't been for that old railroad bed, we'd probably still be wandering around. But we started following it, thinking we'd wind up near a town somewhere."

"That was smart," I said.

"It led us to a main road. We were hobbling along when a truck driver stopped and asked if we needed help. I told him we'd been robbed and were trying to get home. He gave us a ride."

"Bless him," I said. "Just in time."

"The gas station owner was nice, too," she said. "Gave us water and candy bars and potato chips. Pretty sad when total strangers are nicer than your own son."

We arrived at home. Flossie and I helped Winnie inside. While they cleaned up, I called the police, who said they would arrive later in the evening to write a report. While we waited, enjoying canned soup and saltines, Flossie asked about my trip. I described the weekend as the "best time I'd ever had with my parents." We settled Winnie on the sofa, propped her foot on a pillow on the coffee table, and applied an ice pack. Flossie sat on the opposite end. With Saturn curled up between them, we waited for the police to arrive.

I was pouring water on Mary Smith when the phone rang.

"Hello," Sefton said. "How is your week going?"

"Better now that you've called. I can't tell you how happy I am to hear your voice."

"How was the trip home?"

"Good," I said. "Mom was happy to see me."

Sefton should have been the one person I could confide in about Toby, but I couldn't bring myself to tell him.

"I've got good news," he said.

"The firm gave you an office with a window?"

"Not yet," he said. "It's not about work ... well, sort of. I'm going to a conference in Charlotte in a couple of weeks, and I thought I'd stay over a few days and come see you."

"That's the first good news I've had in a long time," I said.

The rest of the week followed a more conventional pattern. Winnie, still limping, refused to go to the doctor, but proceeded straight to the bank to close her account, nearly empty from Darla's thieving. Then she insisted on a trip to the hairdresser. Flossie, after pressing charges against Warner and Darla, bounced back, finding comfort in her familiar routines of cooking and cleaning. The apartment began to look better every day. The piles of "acquisitions" were disappearing. Even the grandfather clock was gone.

I assumed they were sprucing up the place for Sefton's visit.

I was wrong.

Chapter 7

And Then There Were None

By the following week, Flossie was trumpeting her opinions of Warner either to me or talking to herself over a sink full of soapy water in the kitchen. Disinfected and exposed to love, her wounded heart was healing.

Winnie, however, had suffered one too many cruelties from Darlinda, the adorable child she had once outfitted in taffeta and ribbons. Nursing her bruised ankle and her memories, she withdrew further every day.

The cat, sensing Winnie's sorrow, was always in her shadow.

Bearing my parents' secret was as irksome as breaking in a pair of shoes a half size too small. I was as grieved for my mother's broken heart as if she had been cast off, newlywed and pregnant, only yesterday.

No matter where I looked, I could find no one whose heart did not hide some secret sorrow: Lorna, crippled by memories of a man who had never deserved her; Dr. Penrose, whose prodigy was teaching grammar; Margaret, who still bore the guilt of empty years she might have filled with Jonas.

So in spite of Flossie and Winnie's safe return, a respectable insurance check for my totaled car, and the promise of Sefton's arrival, a gray sadness, larger than any I had ever known, settled over me.

I would have sunk further into melancholy if Margaret had not summoned me to a meeting in the library. Assuming Elspeth had dreamed up another new requirement to foist upon the already overworked faculty, I grabbed a pen and notepad and arrived on time.

Elinor met me at the door. "My office. Have a seat."

Entering, I found three chairs gathered around a small round table holding three mugs.

"Coffee or tea?" Margaret asked.

"Coffee," I said.

Elinor slid a box labeled 'Drifters' Rest' toward me. "Special order. Picked them up this morning. Oatmeal or snickerdoodles?"

"Two of each," I said, laughing. "Where's everybody else?"

"No one else was invited," Margaret said.

"Why are we here?"

"You," Margaret said. "We want to know what's wrong."

"Nothing," I said. "What makes you say that?"

"You haven't been the same since your trip to see your parents," she said. "Both Jonas and I noticed when we drove you home from the airport."

Elinor's face was etched with worry. "Is one of your parents sick?"

"No, they're fine … relatively speaking."

"Relatively speaking?" Margaret asked.

Sighing, I scrunched my eyes closed. If anyone could be trusted, it was these two.

I looked from one to the other. "This has to stay between us. I promised my mother."

"Nothing will go beyond this room," Margaret said. "You know that."

"Okay," I said. "Here goes seven and eight."

"Seven and eight?" Elinor asked.

"You're the seventh and eighth people to know about my brother," I said. "Half-brother."

Elinor spoke first after I told the story. "No wonder you've been so distracted."

"How do you feel about this?" Margaret asked.

"At first," I said, "I was glad my parents felt they could confide in me, but the more I thought about it—"

There was a gentle knock at the door. Grace Bonner peeked in.

"Sorry to disturb you," she said. "But I have to talk to Agnes. It's an emergency."

By the time I stepped into the hallway, she was near weeping.

"What's wrong?" I asked.

Her voice trembled. "Kennesaw and Lorna just came into the library *together*."

"*That's* the emergency?" I asked.

She pouted. "It's an emergency to me."

"I'm sure there's nothing to it. They probably bumped into each other in the hall and walked in at the same time. Last week I ran into Coach Brimble in the hall, and we came in—"

She shook her head. "No. No. They're friendly. I can tell."

"Lorna's friendly to everybody. I promise you she's not interested in dating anyone right now, and if she were, it would *not* be Kennesaw Fleming."

She took a step back. "What do you mean by that?"

Her peevishness surprised me.

I weighed my words. "They're from different worlds. She's cultured and refined. He's ... well, you've seen him since he started growing that beard."

Arms crossed, she scowled. "Yes, I've seen him. What are you saying?"

"He's looks like Jubal Early."

"Who?"

"The Confederate general. All I'm saying is Lorna isn't over the guy she loved in college, and if she were to fall in love, it would *not* be with a Civil War re-enactor."

She stiffened. "Re-enacting is a perfectly respectable hobby. Not everyone can have a boyfriend who's a *lawyer*. Some men have more ordinary interests."

"I didn't mean to offend you, Grace. I'm only saying Kennesaw is not Lorna's type and never will be. For starters, she could *never* take him home to meet her parents."

This misguided attempt at logic only made the situation worse.

Grace squared her shoulders. "I, for one, would be proud to take him home to meet my parents."

"I'm sure you would. But Lorna's father is a snob. Remember the day you asked me about the poem? He interrupted us and sent you away when he wanted to speak to me alone."

She nodded. "I remember. By the way, you never told me who wrote that poem."

I had not exactly been *dodging* Grace since she asked about her secret admirer, but I hadn't sought her out either. This was not the ideal time to reveal Big Tony's identity.

"I didn't? I guess we never got back together after Dr. Maron interrupted us. And—"

"Quit stalling."

"Tony Castarini," I said.

"Who?"

"You know ... the student you helped with his research paper last year."

"I help lots of students," she said.

"Tony is … the … swarthy guy with wavy hair. He wrote his paper on the Globe Theater."

Grace put her hand over her eyes. "Not *him*. My first love note and it's from a man half my age, slow, and overweight?"

"First, he's only three years younger than you, and he may not be smart, but he has a good heart, and he's not *that* overweight. He can't help it if his family owns an Italian restaurant."

Grace turned to go. "It's okay, Agnes. You can stop trying to convince the homely girl she should be grateful *anyone* noticed her. Now, if you'll excuse me, I have work to do."

Her 'work,' I suspected, was keeping an eye on Kennesaw and Lorna.

"Is she all right?" Elinor asked when I returned.

"No," I said. "I never thought I'd see the day I'd offend Grace Bonner, but somehow I ended up stepping on her toes."

"You can't expect a woman in love to behave rationally," Elinor said. "Not even a librarian."

"You've noticed she's interested in Kennesaw?" I asked.

"Who hasn't?" Margaret said.

I plopped down onto my chair. "That's a relief, because I think I was just fired as her confidant. It's just as well. It would be nice to have one less heartsick woman to tend."

"Are Flossie and Winnie doing any better?" Margaret asked.

"Flossie is," I said, "but Winnie is so depressed I think she might need professional help."

"Any news about Warner and Darla?" Elinor asked.

"Not yet. I'm not sure what will happen if the police catch them. Flossie said she's through giving Warner second chances, but it would destroy Winnie if Darla went to jail."

"If that happens, we'll have to think of some way to help her," Margaret said.

"Everything would've been fine if they hadn't gone to that stupid motorcycle show," I said. "What kind of blind devotion sends mothers after kids who want nothing to do with them?"

"I can't answer that," Elinor said. "I've never been a mother, but I've watched Ryder grieve for his children ever since I've known him. The longing never leaves him."

Ryder Ellershaw, Elinor's husband, was a Korean War veteran. Prior to his military service, he had been a happily married man, the father of a young son and infant daughter. When he returned, scarred, limping, with a patch over one eye, his wife refused to stand by him while he recovered. While he was still in rehab, she disappeared with the children. The next time Ryder heard from her was when the divorce papers arrived. Disabled, with his fitness to provide for a family still in question, he could not fight her. He had never seen his children again.

"Maybe Ryder's the one to help Winnie," I said. "Could we get them together?"

"Would Winnie come if we invited all of you to dinner?" Elinor asked.

Margaret's eyes sparkled. "I've got a better idea. Let's have a party."

"What for?" I asked.

"The best reason," she said. "To cheer everyone up. Monty will be here next weekend. We could have a welcome party for him. Winnie won't suspect a thing when we invite her."

"Next weekend?" I asked. "Sefton will be here, too."

"We should invite Grace," Elinor said. "Maybe it will take her mind off Kennesaw."

"And Lorna," Margaret said.

Inspired, we scheduled an impromptu planning meeting at the Drifters' Rest and called our respective homes to say we wouldn't be there for dinner. The first order of business was to enlist Muriel to cater. She agreed, stating she would have menu suggestions by the time we finished our dessert. Since Monty would be recuperating at Charlotte's house, we decided that was the ideal place to host the event. I called Charlotte from Muriel's office. Charlotte was delighted, adding it had been "entirely too long" since we had all been together.

"Should I hire musicians?" Charlotte asked.

"Actually," I said, "a pianist has joined our faculty. I've heard she's extraordinary."

"Wonderful. The Steinway has been sadly neglected since my granddaughter got married and moved away. She was the only one who played it."

"I'll talk to Lorna," I said.

Though my mind had become so crowded with other people's problems I'd considered putting a *Standing Room Only* sign on my forehead, I had not forgotten my promise to Dr. Penrose. His concern for Lorna, unlike the

glaring self interest of Dr. Maron, still haunted me. On the way home, I began
thinking of how to coax Lorna back to the keyboard

When I arrived at my apartment, I found Flossie sitting on the top step.

"What are you doing out here?" I asked.

Smiling, she patted the place next to her. I sat down.

"We were going to tell you over dinner," she said, "but you sounded so
happy when you called earlier, I didn't want to spoil your evening by asking
you to change your plans."

"What's the matter?"

"Winnie wants to go home," she said.

"You mean … to her own house?"

Flossie nodded. "The only reason she left was to find Darla, and now
that she's found her, there's no reason to stay away any longer."

"I'm sorry, Flossie. I know you'll miss her."

She paused. "I'm going with her. I can't let her go alone. You understand."

"I do," I said. "She's in no shape to make the trip by herself. When will
you be back?"

"I'm not coming back. I know now there will never be a place for me in
Warner's life. Time to move on."

I slipped my arm around her shoulders. "Not till after the party."

Margaret, Elinor, and I set to work planning and issuing invitations.

Insisting on a formal occasion, Charlotte ordered fresh flowers for all
her downstairs rooms and specified silver and china would be used on the
table. Muriel drafted her cook Annabelle to manage the Drifters' Rest on the
day of the party so she could begin preparations at Charlotte's house after
breakfast. When Winnie, who had not ventured out since the day she closed
her bank account, learned a farewell party was to be given in her honor, she
agreed to shop for a dress.

When everything was finalized, I called Sefton. I couldn't wait to tell him
about our plans. His reaction deflated me.

"I'll be tired after the conference and the long drive," he said. "I won't be
in any mood to socialize. Couldn't we just have dinner by ourselves?"

"We won't stay long," I said, certain he would feel better once he
surrounded himself with my friends.

Margaret called Monty.

"He was quiet for a long time," she reported, "and then said we would
find him 'changed.' I think the fall may have broken more than his hip."

Grace Bonner declined, confiding she had sworn off "couples' events" years ago.

"It's not a couples' event," I said. "Ryder and Elinor and Jonas and Margaret will be the only couples there. The rest of us are single."

"You'll have Sefton," she said.

"We're still single … for now, anyway. Please come, Grace. It will cheer you up."

"The only thing that would cheer me up," she said, "was if Kennesaw had been invited and was going to pick me up on his way there. *Was* he … included on the guest list?"

"No. He doesn't know any of our friends—"

She walked away before I could finish.

Only Lorna—who might prove equally resistant—was yet to be invited.

I dropped by Margaret's office to ask her opinion of Lorna's father and Dr. Penrose.

She winced. "So they came looking for you. I felt guilty about giving your name to Dr. Maron, but at the time—"

"I don't mind. What I mean is, I didn't mind meeting Lorna's teacher. In fact, I promised him I'd try to persuade Lorna to start playing the piano again."

"Let me guess," she said. "You have a plan."

"Do you still sing?" I asked.

"All the time … but not in public."

"You wouldn't mind performing for our friends, would you?"

"No. In fact, I asked Ivy Leigh to make sure Monty brings his accordion with him."

"Will your secretary let me have a look at Lorna's class schedule?" I asked.

After I discovered Lorna and I were both free on Wednesday afternoons, I started toward the maintenance building. I'd need an ally.

I knocked on the door as I opened it. "Hello, Ham."

Ham bumped into a stool in his rush to the door. "Hello, Miss Quinn. What are you doing here? Is there a problem?"

"No. Everything's fine. I need your help."

"What do you need?" he asked.

"A piano."

"You want us to move one into your office? I don't think there's room."

"No, I'm trying to arrange a private recital. Have you met Miss Maron?"

He blushed. "Not yet, but I've seen her … from a distance."

I explained my plan to Ham. "Is there a room on campus where Miss Maron could practice—somewhere she won't be disturbed?"

He nodded. "I know the perfect place—in the fine arts building. A room no one uses anymore since we built the new wing with the practice rooms."

On Wednesday afternoon I tucked a songbook into my book bag and made my way to Lorna's classroom. She was grading papers; a tape player blared Beethoven's Ninth.

"Hello, Lorna," I said. "I see you're settling into the life of a teacher."

She looked up. "I am. And it agrees with me ... the lack of pressure ... the solitude."

"Those are plusses," I said, "but sometimes company is nice. Don't you agree?"

She turned down the volume on the final movement. "Depends on the company."

"We're having a dinner party. Margaret, Elinor, their husbands, Flossie, Winnie. Sefton will be here. You know almost all the guests except for Monty and Charlotte."

"You've mentioned Monty. But who's Charlotte?"

Setting my book bag on the floor, I sat at a desk on the front row. "Loveliest, most cultured lady in town. Probably a lot like the people you grew up with."

"Not necessarily a selling point," she said.

"Trust me. I wouldn't introduce you to anyone who would make you uncomfortable."

She hesitated. "Flossie and Winnie will be there? Should I have my kimono cleaned?"

I laughed. "No, Charlotte has specified a formal occasion. An official welcome for Monty, who's coming here to recuperate from a fall. And to say goodbye to Flossie and Winnie."

"They're leaving?"

I brought her up to date on the disastrous attempt to reunite with their children.

"I'd love to come," she said. "Give me directions to the house."

I stood to go. "There's one more thing. Margaret has probably never mentioned it, but she has a wonderful voice. She wants to welcome Monty by singing some of his favorite songs."

Lorna tapped her red pen on the desk. "And you want me to play for her?"

When I couldn't interpret the expression on her face, I changed my approach.

"No," I said. "You're not the only teacher around here with hidden talent."

"Oh?"

I picked up my bag and started to the door. "Walk with me, and I'll tell you the story."

"Where are we going?"

"To practice," I said.

As we headed toward the fine arts building, I told Lorna about the talent show at the Magnolia Arms and how I'd accompanied the performers.

"I didn't know you played," she said.

"Enough to get by. As pianists go, I'm about a C+."

"You want me to give you a lesson?"

"Margaret wants to sing 'Let My Song Fill Your Heart.' Do you know it?"

"One of my teacher's favorites," she said. "I played it for him all the time."

"Could you help me with it?"

As agreed, we met Ham, who guided us to Rehearsal Hall. The room, deserted and dark, had a wonderful musty smell. We waited by the door till Ham made his way down the aisle and slipped behind the curtain. When a single spot illuminated the piano, we walked toward the front and onto the stage. I sat down and made a pretense at playing Margaret's song, fumbling on purpose. I had hoped Lorna would interrupt and nudge me off the bench. When she didn't, I kept going. Either she didn't suspect my tactics or was too polite to stop me.

I blundered to a halt. My hands still on the keyboard, I looked up. "What do you think?"

"Have you never heard this piece before? The rhythm isn't all that difficult."

"Maybe if I could hear it once," I said, "… played correctly."

She sat down, flexed her fingers over the keyboard, rippled through arpeggios and scales, and then, like sunrise after a storm, music streamed into the dim and silent auditorium. Dr. Penrose had not exaggerated—Lorna had a rare gift, *was* a rare gift. At first, she feigned reading the music, playing by the book. But then it was as if some dam broke within her, and the song poured forth, surged, flowed, slowed, ceased, the last note as poignant as the first. Her hands slipped into her lap. Neither of us spoke. From the far corner of the stage, Ham applauded.

"I don't know how you manage to stay away from the piano," I said. "It's part of you."

She stared at the keys like long lost friends. "It's like riding a bicycle. You never forget."

"That was no bike ride," I said. "That was ..."

"Poetry," Ham said, approaching us. "Anytime you want to come here to play the piano, Miss Maron, all you have to do is ask. I'll make sure you're not disturbed."

"Thank you, Ham," she said.

His eyes widened. "You ... you know my name?"

"I remember you from the first day of school—in the library, when you fell ..."

"When you were changing the light bulb," I said.

He ran his fingers through his hair. "Oh, that." He looked up. "Miss Maron, I wonder if you know a song called 'Widmung'? My mother used to play it, and I haven't—"

Lorna turned back to the keyboard and began to play again. Though I had no idea what the composer had intended to convey, somehow I knew this was a story about the triumph of love. From the corner of my eye I saw Ham take a handkerchief from his pocket. I glanced at him and saw in his face the same little boy he had once been, resting his hand on the side of the piano as his mother played. Grief flickered across his rugged face. He bore her absence as sweet pain.

When Lorna finished, Ham cleared his throat and stuffed his handkerchief in his pocket. "I don't know how to thank you. For a minute there I was back home."

"It's one of my favorites, too," Lorna said.

"You're good, too, Miss Quinn," he said. "Course, not as good as Miss Maron."

I seized the moment. "He's right, Lorna. It's silly for me to accompany Margaret, when you'll be at the party and can play for her yourself. Would you?"

We started down the steps.

"Wasn't that the plan all along?" she asked. "I'm sure my father didn't leave here without trying to enlist someone in his cause."

"I don't care about him," I said. "But Dr. Penrose ..."

"Hurting him is my worse regret," Lorna said. "He had such high hopes for me."

106

"If you'll play at the party, I'll write and tell him the news."

"And if I hadn't agreed?" she asked.

"I would've asked you to coach me," I said.

"I can still do that, Agnes, if you'd like. You have potential."

"Potential to do what?" I asked.

"Be a good accompany-ist," Ham said. "Accompan ... I'm never sure what the word is."

Busy planning the party, I stopped brooding about Russ Wilcox. Flossie was cooking every day, cramming my freezer with casserole dishes sealed with aluminum foil. Grace continued to keep her distance. When Tony Castarini asked what she had thought of his poem, I said she found it "sensitive." Lorna's vacant expression softened into the shadow of a smile, the result, no doubt, of her afternoon sessions at Rehearsal Hall. Ham, true to his word, escorted her. I considered writing to Dr. Penrose, but decided to wait till I'd heard Lorna play for an audience.

Sefton called only once during his conference at Raleigh. As usual, he was in a hurry. I contented myself with the knowledge he would soon arrive, and we could try to revive the satisfying relationship we'd enjoyed at the Magnolia Arms. I vowed not to discuss the book. After all, I'd had little time to work on my own chapters. As much as I regretted the wretched circumstances which would send Winnie away empty-handed and broken-hearted, I couldn't help looking forward to long evenings at the typewriter in the privacy of my home.

On the morning of the party, I woke early and sprang out of bed. After breakfast we gave the apartment a final cleaning and then I took a shower and washed my hair. I could not wait to wear the outfits I'd bought for the weekend: a navy blue dress for the party, and khaki pants and a red paisley blouse for running around town with Sefton. Like a teenage girl waiting for her prom date, I hovered around the window most of the morning.

"You'll wear yourself out, Agnes," Flossie said. "A watched pot never boils."

Sefton arrived at noon. I hurried out the moment I saw his car in the parking lot. He still had one foot in the car when I wrapped my arms around him. Struggling to regain his balance, he stumbled backward against the car when I leaned in to kiss him.

"Take it easy," he said. "People are watching."

I stood back while I straightened his clothes and then hugged him again. "Sorry. I've dreamed of this moment for so long."

He kissed me on the forehead. "It's only been a few weeks."

"Seems like a year to me," I said.

Hand in hand, we walked into the apartment.

Flossie introduced Sefton to Winnie.

"Agnes *said* you were handsome," Winnie said, "but seeing is believing."

Sefton laughed. "I'm not sure I look that good. Not after the week I've had."

"We'll soon have you back to your old self," Flossie said. "Come to the table. I've made egg salad sandwiches. No dessert … since we'll be eating so well at dinner tonight."

"I'll wash my hands," he said, "and I need to make a quick phone call. I'll pay for it."

Like a faded painting in the hands of a restorer, Flossie and Winnie brightened as they lavished their love on Sefton. I had forgotten how their pleasure in simple things like tea and flowers and crafts and chores and chatter had made the apartment pulsate with their joy of living. Content Sefton was within arm's reach, I kept quiet, relishing the scene. He laughed; I reached for his hand. He drew my hand to his lips, kissed it.

The weekend was going to be everything I'd hoped for.

Flossie stood to clear the table. "Why don't you take a nap, Sefton? You must be tired."

He thanked her for the idea, walked toward my bedroom, and closed the door.

"You, too, Winnie," Flossie said. "This will be your first night out since your accident."

Winnie scooped up Saturn and headed to the living room. Flossie put her finger to her lips and motioned me to follow her.

She raised her voice. "Come on, Agnes. I want to collect a few leaves as keepsakes."

We stepped onto the front porch and sat on the step.

"This is an important night for you, Agnes," she said. "That's why I want to give you some advice."

"Don't overeat?" I asked. "Don't worry. My dress is a perfect fit. I'm not about to—"

She shook her head. "Don't expect more from Sefton than he's able to give. He's not like you. He's not reliving your summer memories of long lazy days with nothing to do. Don't—"

The door flew open behind us.

"I'm too excited to take a nap," Winnie said. "Could you come inside? I need your help."

When we entered the living room, Winnie pointed to her fake alligator suitcase by the wall and asked me to lift it onto the sofa.

She undid the clasps and brought out a shoebox. "Here, Agnes, see if these will fit."

I opened the box and took out a pink patent leather high heel. "I appreciate the offer, Winnie, but my dress is blue. Besides, your foot is two sizes smaller than mine."

She sat on the sofa. "Not you. Me. Ever since I heard about the party, I've been wondering if the swelling in my foot has gone down enough for me to wear these shoes."

I knelt on the floor and took off Winnie's slipper. She was as pleased as Cinderella when her injured foot slipped into the shoe.

She lifted her foot and turned it side to side. "What do you know about that? It's a sign."

I didn't mention she had said the same thing when Mary Smith bloomed the day before the motorcycle show … and the kidnapping.

Winnie tootled off to the bathroom, returned with her make-up bag and hairbrush, and organized a makeshift beauty parlor on the kitchen table.

Flossie donned a long-sleeved lavender dress with pearl buttons on the cuffs. Winnie and I persuaded her not to wear a hat. Instead, Winnie styled Flossie's hair into a sensible bun accented with a purple silk flower—much too large. After Winnie did her own hair, she pointed out my hair could use some attention. I declined her offer.

Our commotion woke up Sefton. He took a shower while I got dressed, and then Flossie, Winnie, and I waited in the living room while he got ready in my room. He emerged wearing gray pants and a light blue shirt.

My stomach churned. "I thought I told you it was formal."

"Formal? You mean black tie?" he asked.

"No … just a suit."

"I've worn a suit every day for the past week. I thought when I got here I could relax."

Flossie stepped forward. "Maybe just a tie would do, dear."

Frowning, he returned to my room and re-emerged, tying a tie as he walked to the door.

"Let's take my car," he said. "We won't all fit into your truck."

We drove toward Charlotte's house. I knew if we had been alone, Sefton would have clammed up, but Flossie and Winnie drew him into their conversation until he mellowed. Half sick, I stared out my window. The evening had been tarnished before it began.

When we arrived at Charlotte's house, I asked Sefton to help Winnie.

Before he could turn off the car, I opened my door and started toward the house. I hoped the walk to the door would allow me time to get hold of myself and swallow the lump in my throat. When they joined me on the porch, I rang the bell.

"Prepare to be welcomed by an honest-to-goodness butler," I said.

The door swung open. A tall, lanky guy in a dark blue suit and red plaid vest bowed low.

"Welcome, ladies and gent," he said. "We're fresh out of caviar, but there's plenty of pigs-in-a-blanket." He stood upright, grabbed my hand, pulled me in, swept me up in his arms, and twirled me around.

"Nestor," I said. "Why didn't you tell me you were coming?"

He set me down. "Wanted to surprise you."

Before I could introduce Flossie and Winnie, he held out his hand. "You must be Flossie." He hugged her like an old friend and then took Winnie's hand. "And you're Winnie. Agnes says you love plants. Are you a rosarian?"

Winnie was charmed. "Not professionally."

He offered an arm to each of them. "Let me escort you ladies through the garden." He called over his shoulder as they walked away. "Hello, Sefton. Good to see you again. Monty's in the library, Agnes."

Taking Sefton's hand, I started toward the library. "Sorry about the suit business," I said.

He shook his head. "Don't worry about it."

Monty was resting in one of two wingback chairs across from the long leather sofa.

I kissed him on the cheek. "How's my fellow author?"

"Haven't done much writing since my accident," he said. "I brought the memoir with me. Hope to get some work done while I recuperate."

I had learned about Monty's memoir—a comprehensive review of his career as a county court bailiff—on my first day at the Magnolia Arms. Even Nestor, the kindest and most patient of men, had tired of proofreading the manuscript. When Nestor's glasses had broken (by accident, he solemnly avowed), he chose not to replace them, rather than decline Monty's daily requests for editing. It had fallen to me "as a fellow wordsmith" to peruse

Monty's elaborate prose. Though he had scant hope of being published, not one of us would tell him.

"You remember Sefton, don't you?" I asked Monty.

Monty extended his hand. "I do. How are you, young man, and how is Mr. Bridger?"

"I'm fine, but Mr. Bridger is ill. Got the flu and had to be hospitalized with pneumonia."

"What?" I asked. "Why didn't you tell me?"

"I'm sure Sefton didn't want to worry you," Monty said.

"Is he going to be all right?" I asked.

Sefton was dismissive. "He's nearly eighty. It will take some time."

"I wish you'd told me," I said. "You know how important he is to me."

Monty intervened. "I say, Agnes, Muriel mentioned canapés. Could you bring us some?"

Glad to have an excuse to walk away, I left for the kitchen.

Muriel, in spite of having cooked and prepared food since morning, looked as if she had just stepped from the dining room of the Waldorf Astoria. When she had found time to redo her hair and change into a stiff formal white apron I could not imagine, but she was legendary for doing the impossible and making it look effortless.

"What's wrong with you?" she asked, swatting my hand as I reached for a stuffed mushroom.

"Nothing. What could possibly be wrong?"

"You look like someone just stole your puppy. Have you seen Monty?" she asked.

"I did. He sent me for appetizers."

She pointed over her shoulder at two young men preparing food. "Monty knows I hired servers. Why did he send you?"

I swallowed the mushroom and licked my fingers. "He was trying to prevent a scene."

"A scene? You don't have 'a scene' this early in the evening. Those come later."

"Just let me take the trays," I said. "It will help me make a graceful entrance."

She pointed to the silver trays. "Take those. Then I'll send in the drinks."

I picked up the trays. "What are these?"

"Potato nests with sour cream and smoked salmon. I never serve wimpy hors d'oeuvres to men."

As I was returning to the library, I spotted Charlotte gliding down the stairs like a classic film star. She was wearing a navy blue tea-length dress with a long floral silk scarf draped over one shoulder. She waved. Trays in hand, I met her at the bottom of the stairs.

"I see we had the same idea," she said. "Navy blue is so versatile."

"I was thinking more along the lines of 'budget.' And I didn't think to buy accessories."

She kissed me on the cheek. "No matter. Your smile is enough. Is your young man here?"

"He is," I said. We walked to the library together. I set a tray on each end table.

Nestor, Flossie, and Winnie had come in from the garden. Flossie had taken the other wingback chair, and Winnie, sitting at one end of the sofa, was staring around the room, enraptured. I introduced them to Charlotte as Nestor and Sefton helped themselves to the hors d'oeuvres.

The doorbell rang. Ryder and Elinor joined us in the library. Charlotte, their long-time friend, embraced each of them, and then introduced them to Winnie.

"I'm happy to meet you, Winnie," Elinor said. "I'm sorry you're leaving so soon."

Ryder, informed about Winnie's heartache, sat next to her, and introduced himself.

I had never told Winnie the chain of events that had made me Ryder's friend instead of his adversary. Only a year before, I had rushed into the Drifters' Rest to get Muriel's help with a problem. Ryder, at that time still unbalanced about his missing wife and children and protective of Muriel, had resented my bothering her. In the heat of the moment, he heaved a bud vase at me. Though his aim was faulty, I tripped. The fall resulted in a concussion and black eye, but for Muriel's sake, I did not press charges. Ryder had been grateful.

The doorbell sounded again. Jonas and Margaret had arrived. The moment Nestor spotted Margaret, he hurried across the room to hug her.

"Nestor," she said. "We didn't know you were coming."

He grinned at me. "I couldn't very well let Monty have my two best girls all to himself."

Margaret knelt by Monty's chair.

"I'm so glad you're here," she said. "Are you feeling better?"

"I am now," Monty said.

When Margaret stood, I grabbed her arm and guided her to the potato nests.

"Did you know Mr. Bridger was in the hospital?" I asked.

"No," she said. "When did you find out?"

"Just now. Sefton has apparently known for awhile. Why didn't he tell me?"

"I'm sure he had a good reason," Margaret said.

"Why is everyone so certain Sefton has a *good reason* for—?"

Elinor approached us. "Monty wants another canapé."

Lorna arrived last. When the butler escorted her into the library, Ryder stood. Sefton gazed at her and jabbed Nestor's elbow. Winnie gasped.

It was a scene straight out of a fairy tale—the exquisite princess in a shimmering gown arriving at the castle to greet her adoring subjects.

At least that's how it seemed. Her dress was actually pale yellow and didn't shimmer, but she was so stunning I suddenly felt like a scullery maid.

Apparently the only one capable of breaking the spell she had cast over the room, I walked toward her.

"Good to see you, Lorna," I said. "Let me introduce you to Charlotte."

Charlotte took her hand. "I'm glad you could join us. My Steinway has been lonely."

Lorna said she hoped Monty healed quickly and told Winnie and Flossie she was sorry they were leaving when she had so little time to get to know them. The men had gathered around us. Lorna greeted Jonas and shook hands with Ryder. Sefton extended his hand to Lorna.

"I'm Sefton Wilkinshaw," he said.

"Agnes has told me all about you," Lorna said. "You're a lucky man."

I pulled Nestor forward. "And this is Nestor."

"The gardener," Lorna said. "Agnes didn't tell me you'd be here."

Nestor put his arm around my waist. "It's not easy to surprise this girl, but I try."

When Muriel announced dinner was served, we entered the dining room.

Jonas seated Charlotte at the head of the table and took his place at the other end. Sefton helped Monty into the chair on Charlotte's left. Margaret sat next to Monty with Elinor, Lorna, and Nestor on her left. Flossie was delighted to be on Charlotte's right. Ryder sat between Flossie and Winnie, a circumstance pre-arranged so he and Winnie could talk about their absent children.

I sat next to Jonas with Sefton on my left. At last Sefton and I were side by side in the setting I had dreamed of.

Nestor, directly across from me, caught my eye. "Like old times, isn't it, Agnes? Me and you and Monty and Margaret at the same table together?"

Jonas put his napkin in his lap. "How did I manage to be lucky enough to have a good-looking girl on either side of me?"

"I was thinking the same thing about being surrounded by three handsome men," I said.

"Three?" Nestor asked. "Since when have you thought of me as handsome?"

"There's a first time for everything," Sefton said. "And I won't argue with you about beautiful girls, Jonas."

My heart fluttered. It was the nicest thing Sefton had said to me since he arrived.

The dining room was resplendent. Crystal and sterling silver were arranged on a gleaming white linen tablecloth. Large clear vases of purple irises and white daisies adorned the dining table and sideboard. As servers entered, the room filled with an almost tangible aroma. One by one they set prepared plates in front of us while Muriel narrated.

"New York strip steak with grilled mushrooms and asparagus, crisp potato galette, and braised red cabbage."

"This is amazing," Sefton said. "I haven't eaten like this since my last trip to New York."

"You should visit the Magnolia Arms more often, Sefton," Nestor said. "You'd be surprised at what Ivy Leigh is serving in our restaurant now."

"I'd love to meet her sometime," Lorna said. "I feel like I know her."

Nestor turned to Lorna. "You should come, too, Lorna. I'm sure Agnes wouldn't mind if you stayed in her room."

He raised his eyebrows at me, because he knew I *would* mind.

Sefton unfolded his napkin. "Might not be the sort of place you're used to, Lorna. Lots of stair climbing and being thrown together with random guests and the household staff."

"Household staff?" Nestor said.

Sefton leaned on the table. "Sorry, I didn't mean—"

Trapped in the awkward moment, we turned our attention to our plates. Nestor, head down, grew silent, a sign he was irritated. Sefton cut his steak and asked Lorna where she had gone to college. Jonas knocked my knee under the table. I looked up; he winked. I gazed at the other end of the table. Flossie's purple flower bobbed as she shared a story with Charlotte. Ryder was speaking low to Winnie. Margaret, laughing, laid her hand on Elinor's arm.

I pictured myself dragging my chair to their end of the table and squeezing in between Monty and Margaret.

Nestor was wrong. It wasn't like "old times" at all, but somehow we rallied.

When Jonas discovered Nestor was staying till Monday, he invited him to visit their home and see the new landscaping. Their conversation turned to trees and perennials. Our attention to dinner led Lorna and Sefton to friendly exchanges about their favorite restaurants in Boston. Dessert generated the usual banter about regrets we 'hadn't saved room' and vows to return to sensible eating tomorrow. After the meal, Charlotte sent for Muriel, whom we applauded. She informed us coffee and tea would be served in the conservatory.

As everyone stood, I edged around them to reach Charlotte. I whispered to her.

"You mean the living room, don't you? Isn't Margaret going to sing? What about—?"

Her eyes twinkling, she put her finger to her lips. "I had the piano moved. You'll see."

The conservatory, a spacious room with a high-pitched glass roof and three walls made of windows stretching to the ceiling, extended into Charlotte's backyard and offered a breathtaking view year-round. I had spent entire afternoons there as raindrops cascaded from a stormy sky or golden autumn leaves, shaken by a bracing wind, swirled around me.

But I'd never been in the conservatory at night.

Though last in the line of guests, I could hear Flossie, who entered first.

"Oh, my. Oh, my. I've never seen anything like this."

"It's … gorgeous," Winnie said.

The others didn't speak at all. I understood why when I reached the door.

Leafy green ferns and half a dozen vases of irises and daisies lined the walls. Tall white candles in silver candlesticks or candelabras illuminated the room. Outside thousands of tiny white lights adorned the majestic trees. Flossie and Winnie sank onto white cushions in brown wicker chairs. Ryder, Elinor, and Jonas sat on the wicker sofa near the doorway. Nestor helped Monty ease into a rocking chair and then stood beside him. Wanting to be near the trees, I sat in the window seat. Sefton sat next to me. Charlotte guided Lorna to the piano bench. Margaret stood near her.

Charlotte addressed us.

"I'm so glad to have all of you here again. We haven't been together since Jonas and Margaret's wedding. I only wish the rest of the Magnolia Arms' contingent could be with us."

Monty lifted his cup. "Hear. Hear."

"I'd like to welcome Sefton for the first time," Charlotte said, turning to Sefton. "May this be the first of many visits."

Sefton nodded.

"It is also my pleasure to welcome Winnie for the first time. Though she and Flossie are leaving in the morning, I hope we can expect them back."

"You can," Flossie said. "We intend to do a lot of travelling in the future."

"We'd like to give a special welcome to Lorna and thank her for agreeing to play for us. Now she and Margaret would like to present a musical gift to Monty."

Once Lorna lifted her hands to the keyboard and Margaret began to sing, my disillusionment with the flawed evening evaporated. Their song extracted me from the foggy world where I played the roles of insecure girlfriend, struggling author, and hard-working teacher. In this place, this never-to-be-replicated moment, I was part of a remarkable circle of friends, whose hearts, invested in each other's welfare, were bound together. I looked from face to face to face. Each of these people, broken-hearted, had sought a place of solitude only to find their pain could be healed only in a relationship.

Everyone except Sefton, whose life had been one unbroken string of successes.

Charlotte stood next to Monty with her hand on his shoulder. Ryder reached for Elinor's hand. Jonas' eyes were riveted on Margaret. Everyone else, Nestor and Sefton included, was glued to Lorna. Who could blame them? She was brilliant, passionate, expressive ... lovely. We applauded when they finished. To my astonishment, Lorna asked if there were any requests. Flossie suggested we were in the perfect setting for Moonlight Sonata. Margaret took her place next to Jonas. Lorna played. The candles flickered. The lights outside twinkled. I should have been supremely happy.

But I wasn't.

Sefton never once put his arm around me or even turned to smile.

The requests turned to show tunes, and the mood changed. I took the opportunity to slip out of the conservatory. On my way to the kitchen for a glass of water, I stopped at the great gold-framed mirror in the foyer and stared. My eyes looked tired. My dress no longer seemed "perfect." My thick, naturally curly hair had flopped down over my right eyebrow, while Lorna, even after a long week and performing half a dozen songs, still looked radiant. I tilted my head and narrowed my eyes at my reflection.

"Are you thinking of travelling through the looking glass?"

Nestor appeared behind me.

Turning from the mirror, I looked over his shoulder into the conservatory. "Nah, I was just wondering if blue is my color."

"Looks good to me," he said. "I'm glad you came out here. I was afraid I might not get a chance to talk to you before I leave."

"I heard you tell Jonas you were staying till Monday," I said.

"Yeah, but I knew you'd spend the day with Sefton tomorrow, and I'll be at Jonas and Margaret's house. On Monday morning you'll be at work when I get on the train."

"Want to walk in the garden?" I asked. "No one will miss us."

We entered the garden and followed the stone path, the stars and lights shimmering over our heads.

"I have good news and bad news," Nestor said. "Which do you want first?"

"Bad news? Besides Monty? Is someone else hurt?"

"Everyone is fine, except the new guy who just arrived—your friend from college, Chester Cranston."

"Chester? Last I heard he was in the Amazon rain forest."

"He had to come home," Nestor said. "Yellow fever."

"Yellow fever? I thought we eradicated that."

"Not in South America. When Xander found out how sick Chester was, he asked Ivy Leigh if we could invite him to the Magnolia Arms."

"She agreed, of course."

"Once he was no longer contagious. He's staying in Monty's room."

"Chester was such a good friend," I said. "You know he's the one who helped me rescue Saturn? Actually, I helped *him*. I'll send a note for him. Now what's the good news?"

"Come to the kitchen, and I'll show you."

When we came into the kitchen, Nestor walked toward the round table in the bay window. Beaming, he lifted a magazine from a stack of half a dozen and handed it to me.

There on the cover of *Our State*, the magazine of choice for North Carolina residents, was Nestor Carlyle on the lawn of the Magnolia Arms.

My mouth fell open. "This is amazing."

"There's an article inside, not only about the landscaping, but about my greenhouse, our orchids, and the Julia Bridger Rose. *And* I'm going to be interviewed on WRAL."

I flipped through the pages. "Does Jonas know?"

"Not yet. I'm going to show him tomorrow when I visit them."

I embraced Nestor. "I never knew a celebrity before."

"Hardly that, but I'm going to send a copy to my old professor at Princeton to show him there's life after grad school."

Flossie appeared at the kitchen door. "There you are. Winnie and I want to go home and get some sleep. Early day tomorrow. Jonas and Margaret are going to take us."

"No need for that," I said. "I'll be right with you."

She shook her head. "No. This way you and Sefton can have some time alone. Winnie and I have been conniving all day. Good night, Nestor."

Nestor and I followed her from the kitchen and said goodnight to everyone. Monty asked when I would be back for a writing session. After Ryder and Elinor left, Flossie and Winnie thanked Lorna for playing and followed Jonas and Margaret to their car. Sefton asked Lorna and Nestor if they would like to go somewhere for coffee. "Tired after a busy week," they both declined. Sefton shook Nestor's hand and apologized again.

"Sorry about the 'household staff' comment," Sefton said.

"Don't give it another thought," Nestor said. "Good night, Agnes."

When Charlotte said goodbye, she took off her scarf and draped it around my neck. "Thank you for arranging this evening."

"Thank you, Charlotte. I'll treasure this always."

Sefton and I drove into the dark night.

He stared at the road. "Nice party. The meal was delicious."

"Muriel never disappoints."

Silence perched between us like a vulture ready to pick my bones clean.

"Will you miss Flossie and Winnie?" he asked.

"I don't know. I've gotten used to having them around. It will be nice not to be so crowded and to be able to talk to you without being interrupted."

He sighed. "Yeah ... about that. I don't think I'll be calling much for awhile."

Frowning, I turned to face him. "Calling *much*? I can count on one hand the times I've talked to you in the last month. How much longer do you need to 'prove yourself' to your firm?"

He gripped the steering wheel. "Look, Agnes, there's no easy way to say this. The only reason I came this weekend was to say I don't think things are going to work out between us."

And there it was … the plain excruciating truth.

"Is that the reason you wanted us to 'eat alone' tonight, so you could say that?" I asked.

He shrugged his shoulders. "Yeah."

"I don't understand. Everything was fine when we said goodbye at the end of summer. What did I do to mess things up?"

"Everything was not 'fine' at the end of the summer. No one messed anything up. We're different people than we were a year ago."

"I don't feel different."

"That's my point. You're content exactly as you are, but I'm not. I don't want the same things now that I did when we first met. I live in a world with a lot of demands and you …"

"I *what*?"

"You're not cut out for it."

I tied Charlotte's scarf in a knot. "I could learn. It's not like I'm some backwoods girl fresh off the farm."

"I didn't say you were." He paused. "You're going to make a wonderful wife for someone, but it isn't me."

"So that's it? Just like that?"

"I'm sorry, Agnes. We're just not a good fit for each other."

"You never intended to help me write that book, did you?"

"I did at first, but like I said, I have different priorities now. I brought the chapters with me. Tomorrow we can spend a few hours working on it before I have to go."

"I have to take Flossie and Winnie to the train station in the morning."

"Then meet me at the Drifters' Rest after you drop them off. I'll treat you to breakfast. We'll spend a couple of hours together, and then I'll head out."

When we stepped onto the front porch, Sefton took me by the shoulders, leaned in, and kissed me on the cheek. I unlocked the door.

"Take my room," I said. "I'll sleep in the living room so we don't wake you when we leave for the train station. We'll be up way before dawn."

"All right," he said. "I'm glad you're taking this so well. You're so emotional, I didn't think you would."

Flossie had arranged a pillow and sleeping bag on the floor. I lay on my back, tears dripping into my ears as I stared at the ceiling. Comforted by Flossie's snoring, I fell asleep.

During the ride to the station the next morning, I gave no hint anything had gone wrong. We kept our goodbyes light-hearted and brief, promised to write often and call once a week. Flossie urged me to "come straight home after school" for awhile, since Saturn would have to adjust to being alone all day. Winnie gave instructions about caring for Mary Smith, whom she had left behind as a gift.

When I arrived at the Drifters' Rest, Muriel handed me a note from Sefton.

Chapter 8

A Song to Remember

Sinking onto a stool at the counter, I read my name, penned no doubt with the Cross pen Sefton had specified for his Christmas gift. Till now I had admired his handwriting as firm and distinctive. Today I found it pretentious. He had underscored my name with a short curved diagonal line on the front and written his initials, SRW, on the flap of the envelope. Muriel offered to get the letter opener from her office.

"Don't bother," I said. "I'll toss this in the trash on my way out."

She waved a twenty dollar bill. "He told me why he was meeting you here—left this for your breakfast, told me to keep the change … the louse. To think he ate *my* food only last night."

"Just coffee," I said, pointing to the twenty. "Donate that to the animal shelter."

For reasons I did not myself understand, I did not rip into the envelope. As if handling a sacred relic, I slid my finger under the flap and along the edge, unfolded the letter, and read:

Agnes, Forgive me for not waiting. Saying goodbye last night was difficult enough. Repeating the process today would have done neither of us any good. I left the manuscript on your kitchen table. It's for the best I didn't contribute any more to the story than I did. I don't have the sensitive soul of a writer. You do. All the best, S.

When Muriel returned with coffee and two waffles, I handed her the note.

"Throw this away for me," I said.

She tucked the letter into her apron pocket and left me alone while I ate. Head down, I cried over my waffles. Muriel refilled my cup three times and refused money when I tried to pay.

"Drop by on your way to school tomorrow," she said. "I'm trying a new scone recipe, and I'll need your opinion."

Hoping cool air would help me concentrate enough to drive home without running over a curb, I got into my truck and rolled down the window. The day, surprisingly beautiful, mocked my sadness.

When I arrived at my apartment, Margaret hopped out of her car and hurried to me. There was no need to ask why she was there. Muriel had called to tell her about Sefton.

She put her arms around me. "I'm so sorry, Agnes."

"What's wrong with me?" I asked, laying my head on her shoulder.

"Nothing's *wrong* with *you*," she said, guiding me to her car. "You're coming with me."

I swiped my hand under my nose. "I promised Flossie I wouldn't leave Saturn alone."

Instead of pointing out the absurdity of this, she walked with me to my door. "We'll feed the cat and talk for awhile. Then you're spending the rest of the day with us. Jonas insists."

"All right," I said. "But don't tell Flossie."

As we entered Margaret's house, she asked if I wanted to rest in my room. When I said I didn't want to be alone, we walked through the living room and into the backyard where we found Jonas, Nestor, and Mr. Hampton.

Jonas motioned me to join them. "Over here, Agnes. We need your advice."

Mr. Hampton, a fully-equipped tool belt around his waist, waved and smiled.

Nestor called to me. "Agnes, would you tell Jonas he's got plenty of room back here for a greenhouse? He wants to build a pergola instead. We've been arguing since I got here."

I knew perfectly well they had *not* been arguing and did *not* need my advice. This was their gentlemanly way of making me comfortable … no explanations necessary.

"What's a pergola?" I asked.

The morning passed quietly. Consoled in the company of my friends, I watched absent-mindedly as the men swapped opinions about lumber, stain, and waterproofing, and measured the area where they would build. Nestor and I reminisced about the herbs Ivy Leigh grew on the screened porch of the Magnolia Arms. We ate lunch on paper plates on a red-and-white checked tablecloth on the patio table. When we finished, Margaret cleared the dishes as Jonas and Nestor returned to the yard. Mr. Hampton stayed behind. When I stood, he asked if he could speak to me for a moment.

"Of course," I said.

"First," he said, "I wanted to ask about your brother. Is he doing well?"

"He is. His boys love the car."

He nodded. "Glad to hear it. I also wanted to say I'm sorry about the disappointment you've suffered. No lady should be treated that way, especially not a nice lady like you."

"Not the first time I've had a goodbye letter from someone who'd already left. Probably won't be the last." Assuming this was all he had to say, I reached for his glass. "More tea?"

"There's one more thing," he said. "Ham says you play the piano."

I sat down again. "Well enough to get by."

"Ham is trying to work up the courage to ask you to accompany him."

I couldn't imagine Ham willing to face an audience for any reason. "Does he sing?" I asked.

"No. He whistles."

"Whistles? Where would he do that?"

"The whistlers' competition in Louisburg," he said. "He enters every year. Last time the recording he used malfunctioned, and he couldn't keep going. He's afraid the same thing will happen this year."

Standing, I gathered the remaining plates and cups. "So he wants to be accompanied by a musician who won't malfunction? I'm not sure I can guarantee that."

He stood and strapped on his tool belt.

"If you would practice with him a few times," he said, "you could decide if it's something you're able to do. He's been looking for an accompanist a long time."

How could I refuse Mr. Hampton? Or Ham?

"I'll try," I said.

"Thank you. Ham will come by your office sometime this week. I didn't expect to have a chance to talk to you first. Please don't let on you already know."

Still avoiding the subject of my wounded heart, Jonas and Nestor drove me home late that afternoon. When we turned the corner at the end of my street, Jonas cleared his throat.

"Will you be all right by yourself?" he asked. "Losing someone you love makes it impossible to sleep."

"I'm tired," I said. "I probably won't have a problem."

He pulled in next to my truck. "Is there *anything* I can do for you?"

"Actually, yes. Sefton left before I could find out what hospital Mr. Bridger is in."

"I'll find out," Jonas said.

Jonas waited in the car while Nestor walked me to the door.

"Bye, Agnes," he said, holding me. "We're one month closer to Thanksgiving."

"It can't come soon enough. Oh, wait." I entered my apartment and returned with the letter I'd written to Chester. "Give Chester my love," I said. "And everyone else, too."

I said goodbye, closed the door behind me, and surveyed my silent and unspoiled surroundings. No suitcases lined the walls. The rollaway bed was not tucked into the corner. Flossie's knitting basket was absent from the end of the sofa. The bounty from estate sales and yard sales was gone. The room was so perfectly empty, I felt like I'd returned from a funeral. The only visible reminders of my guests were the magenta afghan Flossie had knitted, Mary Smith, and the abandoned manuscript. When the cat rubbed against my leg, I picked him up and walked toward the kitchen.

"Not a word to Flossie," I said. "If she finds out I left you alone all day, I'll never hear the end of it."

My first solitary evening in over a year was a tailor-made opportunity to write, but I couldn't persuade myself to go near the typewriter. Though still an amateur, I had reached one indisputable conclusion about writing. Perhaps the "great" authors did their best work while sunk in despair, soothing their agony with opium or alcohol, but we ordinary mortals needed equanimity and peace of mind. I picked up Sefton's manuscript and sat on the sofa. Saturn wasted no time hopping onto my lap. Before I finished the first page, the phone rang. Flossie and Winnie had arrived at their home.

Passing the receiver back and forth between them, Flossie began with how much they had enjoyed the trip. Winnie said travelling was much nicer with a friend.

"You remember how much fun we had on *our* trip, Agnes," Winnie said.

They'd passed the miles planning how they would redecorate Winnie's house.

"We thought we might adopt a cat, maybe two," Flossie said. "How's Saturn?"

"Right here in my lap," I said.

"Is Sefton still there?"

"No. He left earlier than he had planned. Wanted to get back to work."

"I don't suppose Nestor is there, is he?"

"No. Why do you ask?"

"I wanted to ask his advice about Winnie's yard. It's a terrible mess."

Monday and Tuesday were blissfully dull. I slipped back into my routine and hoped my days would be as well-ordered and cemented as bricks in a retaining wall. Lorna was right—the life of a teacher, if well maintained, was one of manageable pressure and welcome solitude after the day was over. Seventy-two hours after my too-good-to-be-true boyfriend had jettisoned me from his life, I eased into a tolerable melancholy. I'd been through this before and would undoubtedly go through it again. Not yet thirty, I felt I'd arrived at, as Wordsworth wrote, the "years that bring the philosophic mind."

On Wednesday Ham dropped by to offer me the position of accompanist. He described the three events in the competition.

"I haven't decided if I'll enter the allied arts event," he said, "but for classical I want to do Liebestraum and for popular 'I Could Have Danced All Night' from—"

"*My Fair Lady*," I said. "What does 'allied arts' mean?"

"You do something else while you whistle ... wear a full costume, if you want ..."

I pictured myself juggling while Ham whistled "Flight of the Bumblebee."

"You wouldn't want me on stage for that, would you?" I asked. This was a deal breaker.

"We won't worry about that one. But what about the other songs? Do you think you could play them with me?"

"Depends on the arrangement," I said, "and I'd have to practice ... a long time."

He lifted the key ring from his belt. "I can let you into Rehearsal Hall any day you want."

"Except Wednesdays," I said. "Is Miss Maron still practicing at the same time?"

"She is. I tell you, Miss Quinn, I've never in my whole life heard anyone play like she does. To think ... people would pay all kinds of money to hear her, and I listen for free."

"Why don't you ask her to accompany you?"

"I couldn't do that. The audience would have their eyes on her, not me. No one would hear a note I whistled. Plus, I don't know her well enough to ask *her* to travel to Louisburg."

Yeah, I thought, no one would be distracted by plain old Agnes plunking out a tune.

The next day I found tattered sheet music stacked on my desk. On the cover of each selection "Rosalind Hampton" was written in a delicate hand in the lower right-hand corner.

Burdened with the irreplaceable nature of Mrs. Hampton's music, I started toward the library, the nearest place I could make copies. In no mood for another scowl from Grace, I hoped to slip past the checkout desk without her noticing me. Relieved to discover she was not there, I strolled past the biography section and turned the corner. To my astonishment, Grace, leaning against one of the copiers, was staring up into Kennesaw Fleming's eyes. Clearly, he was saying something which pleased her. She was a rosy shade of red. I inched back. His eyes still riveted on Grace, he spoke.

"Need to use the copier, Agnes?"

The stack of papers Grace was holding slid down and scattered. Kennesaw stooped to help her. I side-stepped the mess and raised the lid on the other copier.

Grace, on hands and knees, said nothing. Kennesaw stood and looked over my shoulder.

"Aren't you violating copyright laws?" he asked.

"No," I said. "I'm going to use these pages for practicing. After the performance I'll throw them away."

"Practicing for what?" he asked.

"Carnegie Hall. Sorry you missed the party, Grace," I said, though I wasn't.

"Elinor told us it was lovely," Grace said.

"Us?" I asked.

She tapped her straightened papers on the copier lid. "Mr. Fleming came by to …"

"To ask if the library had the *Official Records of the War of the Rebellion*," he said.

"No library should be without it," I said.

Fuming, I started to my office and spotted Sharon Merriman-Cheswick too late to avoid her.

"Agnes," she said. "How nice. You've saved me a trip to your office. Dr. Sherwood needs to see you this afternoon." She looked at her clipboard. "You're free at 3:00."

"What now?" I asked.

"We have an assignment for you," she said.

"I can't take on another assignment of *any* kind for *any* reason."

She stiffened. "Neither the assignment nor appointment with Dr. Sherwood is optional."

At 3:00 Dr. Sherwood's careworn secretary offered me a glass of water and showed me into the inner office.

Dr. Sherwood, speaking into the phone, was perched behind a massive mahogany desk at which an average-sized man would have appeared appropriate. Elspeth, delicate and diminutive, looked more like a child playing school. I gazed at the sheer white curtains and dark green drapes at her windows, diplomas lining the walls, and French provincial chairs. I couldn't decide if I had been summoned to Citizen Robespierre or Barbie. Sharon, seated across from Elspeth's desk, turned to greet me. Binder in her lap, glasses perched on the end of her nose, she patted the arm of the chair next to her.

The seat of the chair, stiff and uncomfortable, barely yielded to my weight as I sat. Resting my elbow on the arm of the chair, I tried to appear at ease, but doubted I was succeeding.

Dr. Sherwood hung up the phone and addressed me.

"Are you having a good semester so far?" she asked.

"Yes," I said to her insincere pleasantry.

Turning sideways, she propped her elbow on her desk. "Sharon said your brother came to visit you."

"He did."

Undaunted by my sullen replies, Elspeth pressed on. "You've had other visitors, too."

"No," I said.

Sharon lost her patience. "Dr. *Maron*? And Dr. *Penrose*?"

"So?" I asked.

Elspeth interrupted. "Dr. Maron requested a conference with me before he left town."

"Does he want a job?" I asked.

"No," Elspeth said. "But he does have a job for us. He's offered to finance one of my building projects in return for our help."

"Curious," I said. "He told *me* he doesn't want Lorna wasting her talent in this 'backwater clapboard schoolhouse.'"

Sharon gripped the arms of her chair. "He did not. Dr. Maron is a consummate educator. He would *never* say such a thing. You're exaggerating."

"I have no reason to exaggerate," I said. "And what does *any* of this have to do with me?"

Elspeth stood, walked to the front of her desk, and leaned against it. Embarrassed at my sturdy size 9½ shoes next to her tiny high heels, I pulled my feet under my chair.

"I want a concert hall, Agnes," Elspeth said. "We had one at my former school. I want one here. It will set us apart from other schools of our size. Dr. Maron has agreed to finance it."

"Concert hall," I said. "We have a perfectly good auditorium."

"No," she said. "I want a performance venue with a more intimate setting, a smaller seating capacity, and state-of-the-art acoustics. I want to leave my mark on this campus."

You've already left your mark, I thought, concert hall or not.

"But why are you telling *me* all this?" I asked. "I teach English."

Leaning in, she placed her hands on my shoulders. I shuddered.

"Because *you* are the linchpin to the entire operation," she said.

"Me? What can I do?"

"Persuade Lorna Maron to participate in the music festival we're planning," Sharon said.

Elspeth stood back. "Dr. Maron is convinced if we can get Lorna back on stage, her passion for music will be rekindled. He wants us to feature Lorna as the principal performer."

"We know you two are friends," Sharon said. "You'll have more influence with her than either of us. Dr. Maron thinks so, too."

"It was his idea to approach you," Elspeth said.

I shook my head. "He left my office in a huff. He wouldn't ask me for a favor."

Elspeth returned to her chair, leaned back, and pressed her fingertips together.

"Isn't marriage in your near future?" she asked.

My mouth dropped open. How did *she* know about Sefton?

"What does that have to do with anything?" I asked, offering no further information.

"We thought you might enjoy a vacation *after* the festival," Elspeth said. "To visit your fiancé and plan your wedding. Would you like that?"

"You're trying to bribe me?" I asked.

"Not a bribe," Elspeth said. "An incentive. We'll pay for the trip and cover your classes."

Gripping both chair arms, I leaned forward. "We don't have the right to ask Lorna to take on a project like this. She's a brand new teacher with a full schedule."

Elspeth gave a scarcely perceptible nod at the binder in her cohort's lap. Sharon flipped open the cover, pulled out a newspaper article, and unfurled the page like a sheriff displaying a "Wanted" poster to a posse. Suspended from her manicured nails was my story, "Trevorode's Quest," first place winner of the Pulaski prize sponsored annually by the *Dennisonville Chronicle.* A year ago I had entered the contest at Margaret's urging, intending to donate the $500 prize toward paying off the debts of the Magnolia Arms. Astonished when I won, I'd been happy to present the money to Ivy Leigh.

This scenario unhinged me, not only because I had never fully reconciled myself to turning my unfinished novel, *Trevorode the Defender,* into a short story about time travel, but also because I was growing increasingly disturbed by how much these two knew about me.

If their intention had been to knock me off balance, they had succeeded.

I snatched the paper from Sharon. "Where did you get this?"

"*The Dennisonville Chronicle*, of course," Sharon said. "Public record."

"I had no idea you were an author," Elspeth said. "Are you working on a book now?"

"Yes."

"Do you have a publisher in mind?"

"No."

Again she nodded to Sharon, who handed me a business card from the inside pocket of her binder.

Elspeth indicated the card. "My brother-in-law, Daniel Ogden, is a publisher. When you've finished your book, I could put your manuscript into his hands myself; if, that is—"

"If I use my influence with Lorna."

Tilting her head, she raised her eyebrows and smiled. "Everyone wins."

Sharon closed her binder and folded her hands on top.

"When is the festival?" I asked.

"January," Sharon said, like a spider to a fly.

"You should at least notify the music faculty," I said. "They'll want some input."

"Leave them to me," Elspeth said. "I know how to deal with artistic temperaments."

Feeling like Benedict Arnold, I went straight to Margaret's office to confess. When I discovered she had left for the day, I drove to their house and rang the doorbell. No answer. I opened the gate and found Jonas working in the backyard. He didn't seem surprised to see me.

"Margaret's getting take-out from the Drifters' Rest," he said. "She knew you'd be here."

"How?"

"Elspeth talked to her before she called you in."

I sank down on a pile of 2 x 4's. "Since when have I become the most influential person at Brighton Park?"

He shrugged his shoulders. "We all have our gifts. Hand me the Phillips head screwdriver, would you?"

Twenty minutes later Margaret appeared at the back door and called us to supper. Over barbecued chicken sandwiches on French buns, we talked about parental expectations, Machiavellian politics, loyalty, and destiny. Margaret admitted Elspeth had been to see her to discuss how "Agnes might help the situation." I was relieved neither Margaret nor Jonas reproached me for allowing Elspeth to lure me into her scheme with the promise of a publisher.

"As much as we might hate to admit it," Margaret said, "Elspeth does have connections. She moves in circles you and I will never break into."

"It still bothers me she and Sharon know so much about me," I said.

"Don't your mother and Sharon's mother still talk every day?" Margaret asked.

"Of course," I said. "If I hadn't been so rattled, I would've thought of that."

Jonas spooned the last bit of coleslaw onto his plate. "I think you girls are skirting the main issue."

"Really?" Margaret said. "What's that?"

"What's best for Lorna," he said.

"Exactly," I said. "As much as I'd like a shortcut to a publisher, I have no right to ..."

Jonas shook his head. "When Lorna performed at the party, she had the whole room in the palm of her hand. She must get back to the piano."

"For the sake of the world," I said. "That's how Dr. Penrose put it."

"He was right," Jonas said. "Besides that, you'd be doing Lorna a favor. You of all people should realize that. Margaret and I wouldn't be together now if it hadn't been for your—"

"Soft heart," Margaret said.

"I was going to say 'hard head,'" Jonas said. "Once you set your mind to something—"

"Okay, okay," I said, laughing. "I get it. You're giving me permission to interfere. I hate to eat and run, but I promised Flossie I wouldn't leave Saturn alone too long."

"I know he misses them," Margaret said.

"Me, too," I said, "in a strange sort of way. But I need the time alone to write. Now that I've taken on Sefton's half of the project, I'm further behind than ever."

"Hand me the chapters as you finish them," Margaret said. "I'll edit as you go."

We said good night, and Jonas walked me to the door. "I've been saving the bad news till last. Mr. Bridger is in Duke Hospital—not doing well. If you want to see him …"

"You think I should I go right away?"

He handed me an envelope. "Bought you a train ticket. Round trip on Saturday."

Knowing better than to argue, I thanked him.

"There's cab fare in there, too, and money for lunch and dinner. Margaret will check on the cat. Maybe the trip will do you good, put some distance between you and your troubles."

Arriving at the station before dawn, I boarded the train and took a window seat. Though I had brought Sefton's manuscript with me, I left it in my tote bag and thinking about everything and nothing at all, stared out as trees, ramshackle barns, and a few cows raced past the window.

When we reached the station, I took a cab to the hospital and found the information desk.

"Jameson Bridger," I said to the receptionist.

She searched her list. "Family?"

"No."

"Mr. Bridger is in ICU. No one but family is allowed to see him."

My heart sank. "I've come a long way. Could I at least leave a note?"

She directed me to the ICU waiting room, where quiet, frightened people were gathered. On the sofa a middle-aged couple, holding hands, whispered. A young woman, head bowed, twisted a man's handkerchief in her hands. A solitary man with short gray hair tapped his fingers on the arm of his chair. I sat at a table by the window and wrote to Mr. Bridger, apologized for not staying in touch, explained I hadn't known he was ill, thanked him again for saving the Magnolia Arms, told him I'd enjoyed working on the story, and promised to honor his mother's memory.

When a nurse entered, I hurried to her.

"Could you deliver this to Jameson Bridger?"

She tucked the note into her pocket. "He won't be able to read it."

"Could you read it to him? It's important."

"I'll take care of it." She scanned the room. "Miss Chandler?"

The young woman and the nurse disappeared behind the door.

Feeling helpless, I returned to the information desk. My scheduled departure was hours away—I'd need someplace to pass the time. The receptionist recommended a nearby deli. I sat at a table and wiped away tears with a paper napkin. Though I had known Mr. Bridger only a few years and had never spent much time with him, I considered him one of the most important people in my life. Now I was going to lose him. My irritation with Sefton resurfaced. Why hadn't he told me Mr. Bridger was ill? I might have had one last conversation with him.

"Excuse me. Miss?"

Looking up, I recognized the gray-haired man from the waiting room.

"Yes," I said.

He spoke in such a low voice, I struggled to hear him.

"I couldn't help overhearing when you asked to see Jameson," he said.

"Are you a friend of Mr. Bridger's?"

"No, I'm his brother ... his ... stepbrother."

As awestruck as if I'd met a celebrity, I reached for his hand.

"You're Bentley McBain?"

He drew back. "You know my name?"

"Know your name? I feel like I know *you*."

"You do? How?"

"From Jameson," I said, "... and Jonas. I'm Agnes Quinn."

"Agnes? Jameson told me about you. You're the writer."

The server returned with my order. Seeing Bentley, she asked if she should bring another menu.

"Can you stay a few minutes?" I asked Bentley.

He hesitated. "I guess so, if you're sure it's all right with you."

"Of course. I'd love to talk to you."

He sat down across the table from me. "Me? Why?"

"Because I'm writing about your family, and you're part of the story."

"The part everyone would like to forget," he said.

"That was a long time ago."

"Not so long," he said. "I was paroled only last month."

"We all have baggage, Bentley."

He unwrapped his silverware. "I have enough for a moving van."

"Less than your sister," I said. "If she had walked in, I would've hidden behind a menu. I'd never ask her to sit down with me."

He smiled. "You've met her."

"Three times. And each meeting is seared into my memory."

"In that case," he said, "I'll stay on the basis of common ground."

Over a hamburger, Bentley told a heart-wrenching tale of being in and out of trouble and jail for most of his adult life. He had kept up with his family by reading newspapers. Since both Olympia and Jameson were prominent social figures, Bentley followed their activities with minimal effort. When his father Leo died, Bentley had hoped there might be some mention of his name in the obituary, but it was omitted.

"It was as if I'd never been born," he said. "It's bad enough to be an outcast of society, but when your own family doesn't acknowledge you, you feel invisible."

"I'm sorry, Bentley," I said. "No one deserves that."

"What I worried about most was what I'd do when I got out. I'm too old to live by my wits and con people out of their money like I used to."

Our server returned with the check. Eager for Bentley to finish his story, I invited him to take a walk with me. We wandered aimlessly up one block and down the next, pausing at last to rest on a park bench by a fountain. I could hardly believe I was sitting next to the reckless young gambler and thief with whom my research had made me familiar. Worn out by years of suffering and lack of loving human contact, he was a pitiable figure, nothing like his arrogant sister Olympia.

"When I was paroled a month ago," he said, "I had nowhere to go. Since my sister and I had made Jameson's life miserable, I assumed there was no way he'd help me."

"So you tried Olympia first?"

"Thought I had no choice. I hoped she might at least pay me to disappear."

"But she wouldn't even do that?" I asked.

"Her butler turned me away at the front door, so I sneaked around to the back door. The maid, bless her heart, fed me and told me Jameson would help me—said he had a good heart."

"I'm not surprised Olympia's staff had better manners than she did," I said.

"I spent what little money I had on bus fare to Jameson's house. He not only let me in—he welcomed me like his brother."

"That's how he is," I said.

"That's because of Julia—his mother."

"I know Julia well," I said. "At least I feel like I do."

"She tried to be a good mother to me and Olympia, but all we did was make her life miserable. Of all the rotten things I've done—and I've done plenty—that is my worst regret."

"How long were you with Jameson before he got sick?"

"A little over a week. It's the only thing I've ever done right in my whole pathetic life—find Jameson in time to make amends before it was too late."

"I'm glad you got to talk to him," I said. "I didn't know he was sick."

"I've never seen anyone go down so fast. First, it was the flu, then pneumonia, and now … they're not certain he'll recover. He said I was his brother so they'd let me stay with him."

Overcome, he bowed his head. I slipped my arm around his shoulders.

"If you hadn't been here," I said, "my trip would've been wasted."

He lifted his tear-stained face. "The nurse had sent me to the waiting room while the doctor examined Jameson. When I heard you ask about him, I decided to follow you."

"Why?"

"I wanted to tell you … I'll read your letter to him." He stood. "I should get back now."

"And I have to get to the train station." I scribbled my phone number on a scrap of paper. "Please call me with any news."

He promised and started back toward the hospital. As I watched, he paused, turned, and waved. Bound by our mutual love for Jameson, Bentley and I had become instant friends.

The first thing I did when I arrived at home was call Jonas.

"I thought I'd never hear of him again," Jonas said. "Give him my number if he calls."

"I didn't think you were that close."

"Hardly know him. But I've always felt guilty his father cast him aside in favor of me. If he's just gotten out of prison, he'll need a hand, and I intend to give it to him."

Exhausted, I sank onto the sofa, grateful there was nothing to prevent me from drifting off to sleep … nothing except the incessant ringing of the phone.

Charlotte called to invite me to lunch and to spend the afternoon with Monty.

"He's spending too much time alone," she said. "Until he's well enough to get out of the house, I'm scheduling visits from friends. He's anxious about his book."

I'm anxious about my own book, I thought, but agreed to come.

Half an hour later the police called to report Warner and Darla had been arrested. I gave them Winnie's home number and wondered if the news would do more harm than good.

Shortly before midnight, Bentley called.

"He's gone, Agnes," he said.

"I'm sorry. Did he suffer?"

"No, it was peaceful. I told him we had lunch together and read him your letter."

"Do you think he understood?"

"I can't be sure," Bentley said. "But the nurse seemed to think so."

"Thanks for calling. I told Jonas I met you. He asked me to give you his number."

"Jonas wants to hear from *me*?"

"That's what he said."

The next day I went to Charlotte's house. My plan was to take Sefton's manuscript with me and work alongside Monty as he polished his own paragraphs. As an afterthought, I brought Ham's music. Charlotte wouldn't mind if I practiced on her piano. Over lunch I told Charlotte and Monty about my trip to Durham and my disappointment at not being able to speak to Jameson. Charlotte, who had been the first person to tell me the story of Bentley McBain, was eager to hear every detail of our meeting. Monty was interested only in the crimes Bentley had committed.

"You can ask him yourself," I said. "I have a feeling Jonas is going to invite him here."

"Capital," Monty said. "Imagine if he and I could collaborate on a book about crime and punishment. I could write about the court, and he could contribute the seamier side of prison life."

"Indeed," I said, glancing at Charlotte, who shook her head, warning me not to object.

She asked if Monty would like to join us in the conservatory while I practiced.

He declined, citing a need to concentrate on the Adams' case.

After we left the room, Charlotte squeezed my arm.

"That's the most animated I've seen Monty since the night of the party. If Bentley does arrive, we'll have to get those two together."

"I'm not sure that would be best for Bentley," I said. "Reliving his prison life."

She opened the conservatory door. "We'll see. My piano has been getting quite a workout since the party."

"It has?"

"Lorna's been here three times. She said performing that night made her remember why she loves the piano—she said she felt like she'd come home."

As I left Charlotte's house, I was relieved I could face Lorna with a clear conscience. I hadn't sold her out after all. There would be no argument to concoct about her debt to humanity, no sermon to deliver about the sin of burying her talent. Her grateful audience had reminded her why she loved her instrument. The festival would be the impetus she needed—a non-threatening venue with other musicians sharing their abilities for a noble purpose.

The phone was ringing as I walked into my apartment.

"Hello," I said.

A quavering duet sang into my ear. "Rock-a-bye, baby, on the treetop."

"Flossie?" I asked. "Is that you?"

"Me, too," Winnie said.

They had the receiver between them.

"We have the best news," Flossie said. "Warner and Darla have been arrested."

"I'm glad you think it's good news," I said. "When the police called last night and I gave them your number, I was worried how you'd react."

"We feel fine," Flossie said.

"Are you getting any of your money back?"

"Something better than money."

"What?" I asked.

"We gave you a clue. Didn't you get it?"

"No."

"We'll try again."

They joined their voices in another chorus of "Rock-a-Bye, Baby."

"Would one of you tell me?" I asked.

"Darlinda's going to have a baby," Winnie said.

"That's not all," Flossie said. "They're giving the baby to us."

Chapter 9

Great Expectations

With the disappointments of recent weeks behind me, I drove to school with a renewed sense of purpose. Flossie and Winnie no longer needed me. My mother was on the mend. Dr. Sherwood and Sharon, satisfied they had bested me, might leave me alone for awhile. Lorna was shaking off her painful memories. Now that Grace Bonner had snagged Kennesaw Fleming, perhaps she would be her old self again. Best of all, I could stop worrying about measuring up to Sefton's expectations. I'd known all along our relationship was a dream. Waking up was a welcome relief.

On Monday I called Buck Sloan to ask if I could bring Lorna to his ranch to go horseback riding. Sloan's Canyon was the perfect setting for telling Lorna about the festival. When Buck said we were welcome, I telephoned Lorna on Tuesday. On Wednesday I told my parents about Sefton. My mother was heartsick; my father said I was better off without him. On Thursday I sent for Tony Castarini to inform him Grace Bonner was dating a teacher. Noble in defeat, Tony said it never would've worked anyway, since Miss Bonner "knew nothing about the restaurant business."

On Friday I woke up with the flu.

After I called Margaret to tell her I wouldn't be at school, I put on my coat over my pajamas, wrapped up in two blankets, and lay shivering on the sofa all morning. At noon I woke up sweating, changed pajamas, and laid the damp ones out to dry. My head pounded. My throat was raw. I coughed till my sides ached. I swallowed my last two aspirin, guzzled water, and yearned for chicken soup. But too sick to move, I could only lie on my back and doze off and on, conjuring up frightful, fantastic dreams about piano recitals and prisons.

Waking up in the dark, I stared at the clock on the living room wall. Was it 7:15 or 2:35? And what was that ringing? Saturn tumbled to the floor when I threw off the blankets and staggered to the door to tell the intruder to go away. Struggling with the lock, I opened the door. Darkness. Nobody there. The ringing would not stop. The phone? Lifting the receiver, I leaned against the wall and slid to the floor.

"'Lo."

"Agnes?"

"Mmmm."

"This is Margaret. Are you all right?"

"Ah-ohn-no."

"Have you eaten?"

"Throat … hurts," I said.

"I'm on the way. Unlock your door."

"I did. Doorbell ringing."

The next thing I remember, Margaret was helping me up off the kitchen floor. At least I thought it was Margaret. She had on a surgical mask.

"Margaret?" I asked.

"It's me. I borrowed some masks from Muriel's sister, Dolly."

"The nurse?"

"Yes, the nurse."

With Margaret's arm around me, I trudged to the bathroom. She steadied me against the sink and turned on the bath water.

"We have to get your fever down," she said. "The water will be cool, but you have to sit in it. Don't get your head wet. You'll get a chill. I'll warm the soup."

I sank into the bathtub. A few minutes later I heard Margaret tap on the bathroom door.

"Time to get out," she said. "I've laid some clean pajamas by the door."

By the time I stumbled back to the living room, Margaret had moved the blankets to one end of the sofa and placed a bowl of soup on the coffee table.

"I haven't felt this bad since I had my tonsils out when I was seven," I said.

"You and a hundred other people. They're calling it an epidemic."

"I was supposed to go riding with Lorna tomorrow."

"I'll call her. You can reschedule."

Achy and weak, I blubbered. "Why did this happen to me? I'm not a bad person. I try to help people. I take in stray animals. All I want to do is write a book. Is that too much to ask?"

Margaret reached over and patted my knee. "I'd hug you, Agnes, but I can't get sick."

"I don't want you to," I said, wailing. "I wouldn't wish this on my worst enemy."

"You don't have to. Sharon came down with the flu yesterday."

Near delirious, I jabbered on. "I want to go home."

"I can call your mother. I'm sure she'd come and stay till you're well."

"No. I want to go home to the Magnolia Arms where I belong. I need to be in the town where Jameson grew up and Julia loved him in those far off happy years."

"Beautiful. Let me get a pen, so I can write it down. You won't remember you said it."

Leaning over the bowl of soup, I lifted the spoon and took aim at the swirling carrots. "You mean I write better when I'm dying with consumption?"

"You don't have consumption," Margaret said. "And you're not dying."

"Jameson got the flu, and *he* died," I said, tears dripping into the chicken soup.

"He was an elderly man with a bad heart." Searching in my desk drawer, she called over her shoulder. "Ivy Leigh is coming."

"Ivy Leigh? Why?"

"Muriel is sick, too, and most of her staff. She called Ivy Leigh to fill in till she's well."

"You don't think this is consumption?" I asked, lying down again.

Margaret covered me with a blanket. "No, it's not consumption. I'm going to take your key so I can get in if you need me. I'll lock the door."

"Thank you," I said and fell asleep.

When I woke up, the sun was shining and Nestor was standing over me.

"You're awake," he said. "Can I get you anything?"

"Nestor?" I asked, reaching out my hand. "Is it really you?"

"It is," he said, wiping my forehead with a damp washcloth. "I came with Ivy Leigh. We got in early this morning. Margaret let me in."

Still racked with fever, I started crying again. "Will you take me home?"

"You are home."

"I mean the Magnolia Arms."

He brushed my hair from my forehead. "Next month," he said. "Ivy Leigh is already planning Thanksgiving dinner."

"Next month? It's July," I said.

"It's October," he said. "Let me help you sit up. I made some toast. And you can drink some apple juice."

"I love apple juice."

"I know," Nestor said.

For the next 48 hours I hovered between life and death—at least that's how I felt. Nestor helped me back and forth between the bathroom and the sofa, fluffed my pillows, arranged my blankets, held a glass while I sipped through a straw. When I called for him at night, he would bound up from a sleeping bag on the floor or lean forward from a chair beside the sofa. Visitors came and went. Nestor would answer the door, mumble phrases, rustle paper bags, rattle pots and pans in the kitchen. Once I thought I heard him typing.

Sometime before dawn on Monday, my fever broke. I woke up soaking wet, struggled onto one elbow, and spotted Nestor across the living room. Curled up on his side, he was facing the wall and snoring softly. I almost called to him, but decided to let him sleep. I found clean folded pajamas on my bed and took them to the bathroom with me. I took a shower, washed my hair, and let the warm water run over my stiff shoulders. When I came out of the bathroom, I smelled coffee.

"Good morning," I said, easing into a kitchen chair.

Toast popped up in the toaster. Nestor put it on a plate, set it in front of me, and shoved a jar of apricot preserves in my direction.

"One egg or two?" he asked.

"One. Anything happen in the world since I've been in a coma?"

He broke an egg into a bowl and whisked it. "Your college cancelled classes today."

"Things *must* be bad."

"They said this will be known as The Great Flu Epidemic of 1977."

"Anything else?" I asked. "Were you talking on the phone, or did I dream that?"

The egg sizzled when he poured it into the skillet. "If you mean last night, that would have been Jonas. He wanted me to tell you Bentley McBain is on his way here."

"He didn't waste any time, did he?"

"Bentley or Jonas?"

"Neither."

Whether I was suffering from the aftereffects of fever or because I'd never seen Nestor in my kitchen, he didn't look the way I remembered him.

His black hair, usually cut short, had grown out and curled over the edge of his collar. His shoulders looked broader, and he was wearing a new shirt.

"Have you been working out?" I asked. "Your shoulders—"

"Comes from lifting all those flower pots."

"You were lifting flower pots a year ago, but your shoulders weren't so—"

He scraped the egg onto a plate. "Okay, you caught me. I've been working out. Xander wanted to look good for his wedding, and Chester is in such bad health, we all joined a gym."

"You look great," I said. "And it's good to see you. We didn't have much time to talk when you were here for the party."

He set the plate in front of me. "You were busy playing hostess." He paused. "I haven't had a chance to tell you I'm sorry about what Sefton did to you."

I shrugged my shoulders. "I knew it would never work. He was too good for me."

"You've got that backwards. *You're* too good for *him*. I always thought that."

"You're only saying that because you love me," I said.

"I'm saying it because it's true. Finish your breakfast."

Better, but far from well, I lounged all morning on the sofa with Saturn snuggled by my feet. Elinor arrived at noon with groceries and a stack of books. While Nestor put the food away, Elinor brought me up on the news, listing which of the faculty had gotten sick and which had escaped.

"Poor Grace," she said. "We had her and Kennesaw over to dinner on Friday night, but she got so feverish, he had to take her home early."

Though hoarse, I squeaked out my objection.

"You let Kennesaw into your *house*?"

Elinor held up her hand. "Margaret said you'd be upset, but I have to be supportive of Grace. We've worked together for years. If something comes of the relationship—"

"Relationship?"

Nestor came from the kitchen. "What's wrong?"

"Elinor invited Kennesaw Fleming to her house," I said.

"Kenne-who?" he asked.

"Kennesaw Fleming. A new teacher at our school. He's been stalking Elinor."

Elinor leaned forward. "Stalking? What do you mean by that?"

I blew my nose. "Remember when Flossie and Winnie had their wreck, and you loaned me your car?"

"Yes."

"Kennesaw was waiting in the parking lot. He *knew* which car was yours."

"That's not unusual," she said, "to know what kind of car a co-worker drives."

I dismissed her explanation. "And when Toby was here, Kennesaw gave him a brochure on the re-enactors' group. When he opened his briefcase, Toby saw pictures of you and Ryder."

Now Elinor turned pale. "What kind of pictures?"

"Taken in different places ... obviously without your knowledge, Toby said."

"Why didn't you tell me?" she asked.

"I should have, but everything's been so crazy. Flossie and Winnie went missing and then Monty came and then Sefton threw me on the trash heap."

The surge of emotion brought more tears and a coughing fit.

Nestor went to the kitchen for a glass of water.

"I'm sorry, Agnes," Elinor said. "I didn't mean to upset you. I'm just nervous about what this all means. It's one thing to have Kennesaw in my office, but my *house*. If I'd known—"

"If it makes you feel better," I said, "Mr. Hampton has been keeping an eye on—"

Laying her hand on her lips, she stifled a cry. "Oh, no."

"What's wrong?" I asked.

"Ryder's pocket watch is missing—the one that belonged to his father. He kept it in a box in his desk drawer in the den. He thought he misplaced it, but ... do you think Kennesaw took it?"

"I wouldn't be surprised," I said.

She stood. "Maybe I should tell Ryder about the photos."

"Not yet," I said. "No need to upset him till we figure out what Kennesaw is up to."

"How can we do that?" Elinor asked.

"If I didn't have to go home," Nestor said, "I'd befriend this Fleming guy and find out what he's up to."

"That's what we need," I said. "A spy."

When Elinor left, Nestor walked her to her car and then rejoined me in the living room.

"How is she?" I asked.

He sat across from me. "Worried."

I leaned back my head and put my hands over my face. "How do I manage to create a mess wherever I go?"

"This isn't your fault," he said.

"I should've told her about the photos. I don't know why I didn't."

"There's nothing you can do about it now, and it's not going to do you any good to get upset just when you've started to feel better. Want to watch a little TV?"

"Not now. My eyes hurt."

He stood and started toward my desk. "How about if I read to you?"

"Perfect," I said, stretching out again, eyes closed. "See what Elinor brought."

I heard Nestor walk to his chair. He rustled through pages and began to read:

Her fears forgotten, Julia sat on her cloak on the barn floor and watched Eliot work. As he fashioned the wood, he told of sunshine and blue skies, vines on white walls, roses by the front door of his childhood home. She breathed in the sweet, clean cedar fragrance and wished time would stand still. She had met Eliot only seven days ago, when he had knocked on the door of her aunt's home and asked for work. And yet, the thought of his being drawn back to the open road broke her heart. She longed for him to stay.

Opening my eyes, I gazed at Nestor. "*What* are you reading?"

"Chapter One of *Briarwood Manor*—'The Journey of Eliot Bridger.'"

I sat up. "I'm sorry … what?"

"Eliot Bridger—Julia Bridger's husband … Jameson Bridger's father?"

"Yes, I know who Eliot Bridger is. I don't remember seeing that in Sefton's manuscript. It doesn't sound like his writing."

"It's … not. In his papers there was a letter from Julia to her mother. Eliot had been hired to do some work, and Julia fell in love with him the moment she saw him."

"And what about the barn … and the cedar wood?"

"Julia's aunt left a cedar chest to Julia in her will. Stands to reason it had sentimental value. I put two and two together. It's possible."

"The Journey of Eliot Bridger?"

"Sefton didn't use chapter titles, but I think they add a nice touch," he said.

"You're an amazing man," I said.

"You're an amazing woman. But I don't think you need constant attention any longer. Why don't you get in your own bed and close the door so I can clean up in here?"

"May I take the manuscript with me?"

He put the pages back in order and handed them to me.

"It's your book," he said.

"How many pages did you write?" I asked.

"Twenty or so. Just fiddling around with a few ideas."

"A few ideas? I haven't written that much … or that well … in a week."

He took my hands and pulled me up. "You'll do better once you're well. You'll see."

Closing the door of my room behind me, I settled on my bed and hoped I could get through all twenty pages before I nodded off. No need to worry. Nestor's storytelling was spellbinding—a seamless combination of technique and passion, pathos and craft.

He had reached back in time, taken Julia Bridger's hand, and drawn her into the present.

Energized, I threw back the covers and opened my door. With his manuscript in my hand, I started toward the kitchen, but stopped when I heard Nestor talking on the phone.

"No, I haven't told her … she's still not well. Yes, I'm sure it can't be tonight … No, she hasn't brought it up … yeah, I know …"

So this was why he sent me to my room, I thought. He wanted to make a phone call. But who was he talking about? And what did he need to tell me?

I cleared my throat as I walked to the kitchen.

Hearing me, he spoke louder into the phone. "Okay, I'll tell her you called."

"Who was that?" I asked after he hung up.

For the first time since I'd known him, Nestor blushed.

"Xander. He called to … see if … to give me a message for Ivy Leigh. She told him to call me if he needed anything. Said she'd be too busy to talk while she was at the Drifters' Rest."

Still light-headed, I sat at the table. "So you were talking about Muriel?"

He straightened the salt and pepper shakers on the table. "Muriel?"

"You said, 'she's still not well.' You were talking about Muriel?"

"Oh, yeah … Muriel," he said, walking to the sink. "Need some water?"

"No, thanks." I laid the pages on the table. "You've missed your calling."

He took a glass from the drainer and wiped it with a towel. "Should've been a butler?"

"No. A novelist."

"Oh, that. Well, remember I once wrote a dissertation … learned a lot about syntax while I cranked that out."

I shook my head. "That may be true, but what you've written here came from someplace deeper than an intellectual grasp of the English language."

He filled the glass with water. "I've always been interested in this story. You know that."

Resting my elbows on the table, I said, "I have a publisher."

"You do? How did you find one?"

Nestor sat across from me, and we talked like we used to at the end of the day when we had finished the chores Ivy Leigh had assigned. Our conversation was effortless, nothing like the measured words and abridged stories I told Sefton when he allowed me a few moments of his time. After an hour, Nestor suggested we sit on the sofa where I'd be more comfortable. We moved to the living room. He spread Flossie's afghan over my legs. I told him the whole story of Sefton, holding back nothing, allowing my frustration to take center stage.

An hour and a half later, Nestor asked if I would like to get some coffee. I put on a sweater over my pajamas and handed him the keys to my truck. As we drove, I told him about my mother's marriage to Russ Wilcox, that Toby was not my father's son, and how my childhood now made sense in a sad sort of way. He pulled into the drive-thru at Wholly Donuts and ordered coffee. On the way home, I shared my disappointment about not being able to talk to Jameson before he died and about meeting Bentley.

"And now Bentley is on his way here," I said. "What would Olympia think?"

That night it began to rain. Nestor judged it "good sleeping weather" and ordered me to bed early. Gazing at the ceiling, I listened to the water pelting the windows and roof and was utterly content. Being sick had forced me to focus on nothing but my own health and had reset my emotional equilibrium. All my problems seemed more manageable. Or maybe I felt better because I'd confided in someone I trusted. I fell asleep and woke late in the night to the sound of typing. Must be dreaming about finishing my book, I thought, and closed my eyes.

When I got up the next morning, I found Nestor packing his clothes.

"You're leaving?" I asked.

"Leaving here. So are you. We're going to spend the day at Jonas and Margaret's house. I thought it would be nice for you to have a change of scenery."

"Good idea. Let me feed Saturn, and I'll—"

He zipped his suitcase. "Already done. I told Jonas we'd be there as early as we could. He wants me to help him with his pergola before I go. You can spend some time with Bentley."

"I hate to miss seeing Ivy Leigh before you leave."

He put his suitcase by the door. "No worries. Margaret's picking her up from the Drifters' Rest so we can have dinner together before Jonas takes us to the train station."

"I wish you could stay a little longer."

"It's like Joe Gargery said, 'Life is made of ever so many partings welded together.'"

This was one of the things I loved most about Nestor. He was never without an appropriate literary reference.

Dressed in comfortable clothes, I climbed into the passenger seat of my truck. Kindred spirits, Nestor and I had always been at ease with silence. As we drove toward Jonas and Margaret's house, I peeked at him from the corner of my eye. It seemed like yesterday Ivy Leigh had sent him and Monty to pick me up at the Whispering Pines Motor Lodge and chauffeur me to the Magnolia Arms. How had this lanky gardener with the prickly sense of humor ended up being my closest friend?

Jonas welcomed us at his front door.

"You look a little puny, kiddo," he said.

Bentley appeared behind Jonas. "Hello, Agnes."

I extended my hand. "Hello, Bentley. This is my friend Nestor."

"You two make yourselves at home," Jonas said. "Nestor and I are going to get to work."

As if we had finished our conversation in the park only hours before, Bentley and I settled in the living room to chat like comfortable old chums.

"Thanks for giving me Jonas' number," Bentley said. "I couldn't believe he wanted me to contact him."

"He was glad to be able to help you. Have you made any plans yet?"

"We talked about it last night. Margaret is going to ask her friend Muriel if I could work in the kitchen at her restaurant. I haven't done much honest work in my lifetime."

"Maybe you could go to school. Have you ever thought about that?"

"Jonas suggested that, too," he said, "but I don't think I'm college material."

"You won't know till you try. You could start with an evening class." Bentley smiled. "Jameson was right about you."

"Me? What did he say?"

"He said you were one of the kindest people he had ever met."

"The feeling was mutual," I said. "I admired him more than I can say."

"He said the same thing about you."

"No kidding?"

"He said helping you get the best of Olympia was one of the most rewarding moments of his life. He said you'd be glad to tell me the whole story if I asked. Would you?"

I began with meeting Wilkie Brooker, the private investigator Olympia hired to find Jonas, and proceeded to my first unpleasant encounter with her in the dining room of the Magnolia Arms. Bentley applauded when I recounted how I pounded on Olympia's car window the day she arrived to lay claim to the house.

"You should have seen Ivy Leigh," I said, "when she approached your sister and said, 'Why do you want my home?' Every bit of color drained from Olympia's face."

He sank back into the sofa. "Is that scene going in the book?"

"I'm a long way from writing that chapter. I had a co-author who was supposed to write the first volume, but he bailed out on me. Now I have to write his part before I can write mine."

"And what does that cover?"

"The first volume begins with Jameson's grandfather purchasing the property and goes through your father's financing Jonas' building the Magnolia Arms."

"So you will write about Julia marrying my father?"

"Yes. And I hope you'll let me take advantage of your experiences. I know Jameson's side of the story, but your perspective would be a great addition to the book."

A faint smile softened his face. "I can do better than that. Be right back."

Bentley hurried from the room. When he returned, he handed me a tattered envelope.

"This is my most cherished possession," he said. "I want you to have it."

The envelope was addressed to Bentley. The return address was Julia Bridger's.

"Julia wrote to you after your father sent you away?" I asked.

He nodded. "She's the only person who stayed in contact with me."

Though I was itching to open the envelope, I held it out to him. "I can't keep this. It's priceless."

Hands behind his back, he said, "Please take it. It will help you tell Julia's story. I never returned her love. At least I can honor her memory. Keep it till your book is finished."

The front door swung open. Ivy Leigh and Margaret had arrived. I hurried to greet Ivy Leigh, but instead of hugging me, she pulled back.

"You know I love you, Agnes, but I've managed to keep free of the flu all week, and I don't intend to get it tonight. I have my own restaurant to run— at least for now."

Margaret slapped her on the arm. "I thought I told you to break it to her gradually."

Ivy Leigh started toward the living room, talking over her shoulder as she walked.

"There's no sense in dragging out the story," she said. "We'll get the news out of the way and then have a good visit till Nestor and I have to go."

"I do *not* want to be around for this conversation," Margaret said. "I'm going upstairs to change clothes. Call me when you're done."

Ivy Leigh walked straight to Bentley, who stood to greet her.

"You must be Bentley," she said, extending her hand. "I'm Ivy Leigh Ransom."

"I've heard a lot about you," he said. "I'm honored to meet the woman who got the best of my sister. If you ladies will excuse me, I'll see if I can help Jonas, so you two can catch up."

Directing me to a chair, Ivy Leigh sat on the sofa. Even dressed in a sensible black skirt, white blouse, and apron tied snug around her waist, she was regal. Slim and attractive, she looked ten years younger than fifty-five. "Heart of gold, backbone of steel," Monty had described her, and he was right.

"What are you grinning at?" she asked.

"It's good to see you," I said.

"Good to see you, too. Are you feeling better?"

"Still worn out, but I think one more good night's sleep will help."

"And are you feeling better about Sefton?"

"I'm trying. Nestor said he didn't deserve me."

She folded her arms. "He didn't. We all thought that."

"I wish someone had told *me*."

"You know perfectly well you wouldn't have listened. You had to find out for yourself."

"Speaking of finding out for myself, what do you mean you 'have your own restaurant to run *for now*'? You're not thinking of closing the restaurant? Nestor said it was doing well."

"I'm *not* closing it. But being at the Drifters' Rest has made me realize we can do so much more, and I've taken it as far as it can go."

"You can't expect the two places to be the same," I said. "Muriel's place is open all day. Your restaurant is open only for dinner."

Eyes sparkling, she leaned forward. "But what if we *did* serve three meals a day? We'd be like the Drifters' Rest—buzzing with excitement—never the same day twice."

"You sound like you're going to miss being here."

She leaned back. "I am. And that's why Muriel and I are going to switch places."

"You mean you'd move here, and she'd move to the Magnolia Arms?"

"Precisely. With her expertise she can transform our restaurant into a first class dining establishment."

"But Muriel can't do all the cooking herself."

Ivy Leigh was unruffled by my objections. "I've been teaching Posey."

"Posey would give up teaching voice lessons to be a cook?"

"I won't know till I ask her. But she did say she doesn't want to teach after she and Xander get married."

"But who will manage the Magnolia Arms and take care of the residents and guests?"

"Nestor, of course," she said. He knows the place as well as I do."

"But who will do the gardening?"

"Nestor has trained Xander. You know that."

"But Xander is finishing his degree in chemistry," I said.

"Gardening is the perfect work for someone who's cooped up inside a classroom all day."

"But when I think of the Magnolia Arms, I think of *you*. You're the heart of it. How can you think of leaving? You've lived there over thirty years."

In spite of her fear of contagion, she reached over and grabbed my hand.

"You know it's never been the same for me since my husband Marshall died. I miss Margaret every day. And now Monty is gone, too."

"But Monty is coming back, isn't he?" I asked.

"Maybe, but that's not the point. I'll always love that house and the people I've met there. Nestor and Xander and Posey."

"And me?"

"Of course you," she said, "because in some ways you love that house more than the rest of us put together, though I've never understood why."

"It's my destiny," I said.

"Yes, 'destiny.' I used to think it was a silly idea, but now I know differently. Your coming to the Magnolia Arms brought us all together. I'd never have known Muriel otherwise."

"And she wouldn't be thinking of moving there."

Ivy Leigh pointed out the window. "The same thing goes for those three. If you hadn't found Jameson Bridger, Bentley would've had no one to turn to. Now he'll have a home."

It was still too much to process. I rubbed my forehead. "You won't leave before Thanksgiving? I've been looking forward to it for so long."

"No. We decided to make the switch after the New Year."

Margaret came downstairs. "Are you two finished?"

"She took it surprisingly well," Ivy Leigh said. "Shall we get started on dinner?"

Ivy Leigh, adamant about my infectious state, insisted I stay out of the kitchen, but Margaret allowed me to sit on the opposite side of the counter. Only after I promised to keep my breathing shallow did Ivy Leigh relent. Laughing, the two women ordered each other around the kitchen, bossing and being bossed as only lifelong friends are comfortable doing. Over my shoulder I looked out the window into the backyard where Nestor and Jonas worked while Bentley looked on, making occasional comments.

Ivy Leigh was right. What would have become of Bentley if I hadn't stuck my nose into Jonas Grinstead's past?

Lost in reflection, I didn't hear Ivy Leigh saying my name.

"Agnes. Agnes," she said, shaking her head. "Still a daydreamer, I see."

"I'm sorry," I said. "Still a little fuzzy. What did you say?"

"I said I hear you're taking up the piano again."

"Yes. Our friend Ham is going to be in a whistling competition, and he asked me to accompany him."

"And when is this competition?" she asked.

"In the spring."

She winked at Margaret. "How fortunate." She feigned interest in the tomato she was dicing. "You can take advantage of some expert coaching when you come for Thanksgiving."

"How's that?" I asked.

Margaret grimaced; Ivy Leigh could barely keep from laughing.

"An old friend of yours wrote to ask if we had room for him for a few weeks," she said. "He's a bit run down and needs a quiet place to recuperate."

"An old friend?"

Ivy Leigh tilted the cutting board over the salad bowl. Tomatoes cascaded in.

"Maybe you'll remember if I tell you he was particularly fond of chicken Paprikash."

"Oliver?" I asked. "He wants to come back?"

Dr. Oliver Martin Farrell was perhaps the most memorable, though not the most likable, of the Magnolia Arms' residents. A young pianist of some renown, he had chosen to live there in order to enjoy the seclusion he needed to practice the piano. Because he paid twice the usual rent in order to have his privacy assured and personality tolerated, Ivy Leigh had bowed to his numerous and capricious demands. Though the rest of the household was accustomed to his acerbic ways, I was not and promptly got on his wrong side within an hour of my arrival.

"We haven't told him *anything* yet," Ivy Leigh said. "We only said he could stay for as long as he needed, but could not have his old room back."

Dinner that night was as bittersweet as any gathering of close friends soon to be parted. Though I knew we would be reunited in a few weeks, I still dreaded saying goodbye and decided to go home right after supper rather than prolonging the inevitable. Ivy Leigh still refused to hug me, but kissed her index finger and patted it on my cheek.

"Goodbye for now," she said. "Come a few days early so you can help me with dinner."

Margaret and Jonas urged me to stay at home one more day and rest.

"I'll walk you out," Nestor said.

Bentley stepped out on the porch with us. When he asked if I remembered the letter, I opened my purse and produced it.

"I'll make a copy," I said, "and then send this home with Margaret. Or maybe you could visit the school. You'll want to meet Elinor. And you've been invited to meet Monty, too."

"Margaret mentioned him," Bentley said. "The retired bailiff? It would be nice to meet one of those when I'm not sitting with a defense attorney." Laughing, he entered the house.

Nestor walked with me and opened the truck door. "What's this letter Bentley was talking about?"

"It's from Julia. He said it would help with the story."

"You sure you're okay to drive?" he asked, closing my door.

"I'm sure. Not light-headed at all."

He shook his head. "I mean you're not going to read while you drive, are you?"

"No," I said. "I don't know what it says, but I intend to savor every word. I'm staying home tomorrow. Will you call me in the morning and let me know you arrived safely?"

"I will," he said. "Now go straight home and get into bed."

Though I considered parking under a streetlight to read Julia's letter, I drove home, fed the cat, changed into my pajamas, and climbed into bed.

It was just as well I had planned to stay home another day; there was no going to sleep after reading the letter.

The next morning Nestor called as he had promised. I couldn't wait to tell him he was right about Eliot Bridger and the cedar chest.

"Now all we have to do," I said, "is find Millie Hubbard."

Chapter 10

Shadow of a Doubt

"I was right about the cedar chest?" Nestor asked. "Me and my keen powers of deduction. But who's Millie Hubbard?"

"Julia's youngest sister," I said. "She has the cedar chest—*had* the cedar chest."

"That was in the letter Bentley gave you?"

"It must have been one of the last things Julia wrote before she died. Leo had already sent Jameson away. Julia didn't want to die without *someone* knowing where her possessions were."

"But why would she tell Bentley of all people?"

"She couldn't tell Leo," I said. "Olympia wouldn't care and couldn't be trusted."

"Could you start at the beginning? You lost me."

"Leo was threatened by Julia's love for Eliot. He insisted she leave her belongings behind when she married him. She couldn't part with the cedar chest, so she gave it to her sister."

"But would her sister still be alive?"

"Julia was sixteen when Millie was born. She'd be in her eighties, but *lots* of people are."

"You honestly think you can find her?" he asked.

"I found Jameson, didn't I?"

"You had a little more to go on."

"We have something now. When Julie wrote to Bentley, Millie was newly married and had moved to Greenwood Road in Littleton. She might still be there."

"You can't be serious," he said. "People don't live in the same house for sixty years."

"My grandparents have. Littleton isn't that far from you. If Millie still has that cedar chest … imagine what's in it. A journal, letters? Think what it would add to our book."

He paused. "I'll drive over Saturday morning."

When I had not heard from Nestor by Saturday evening, I could stand the suspense no longer and called the Magnolia Arms.

"Nestor's not back yet, Agnes," Ivy Leigh said. "Littleton is too far to make a one-day trip. I told him to spend the night and start back tomorrow."

"Have you heard from him?" I asked.

"He called when he arrived, but nothing since. Everything okay there?"

"I'm cautiously optimistic. Are you still planning to move here in January?"

"More convinced than ever."

When Nestor hadn't called by Sunday night, I assumed the visit had gone so well he stayed another day. I went to bed. With Saturn purring by my side, I closed my eyes and pictured Nestor in Millie Hubbard's attic, dusting off Julia's cedar chest, poring over photos, journeying backward in time to Briarwood Manor. Millie wouldn't part with the cedar chest, of course, but she would pack everything in a box and watch from the porch as Nestor put the box in his truck. Waving, she would call, "Say hello to Agnes," as he backed out of the driveway.

When Nestor returned to the Magnolia Arms, he would store Julia's mementos in my room. When I arrived for Thanksgiving, Ivy Leigh would insist I go straight upstairs to begin my work. By nightfall I'd still be sifting through Julia's keepsakes, turning pages in her diary, unfolding yellowed newspaper clippings. Maybe Julia had saved a lock of Jameson's hair. I'd bring the box home with me on the train and spend solitary evenings writing, editing, and proofreading. I'd finish the book; Elspeth would recommend it to the publisher. Dozing off, I could almost feel the pages in my hand.

My first day back at school my students greeted me as conquering hero. After we shared flu stories with each other, we returned to the business of education as if the whole ill-fated epidemic had never happened. When I arrived at my office, I called Buck Sloan to ask if we could reschedule the visit to Sloan's Canyon for Saturday and then confirmed the plan with Lorna. Returning home triumphant but exhausted, I was shaking cat food into Saturn's bowl when the phone rang. Flossie needed Sefton's telephone number.

"He's the only lawyer we know," she said. "We want to get our ducks in a row before the baby comes."

"I can give you his number, Flossie," I said, "but before you talk to him, you should probably know he and I aren't together anymore, so don't mention my name."

"When did this happen?"

"A few days ago."

She held the receiver away from her mouth. "Winnie, you were right."

"Right about what?" I asked.

"Winnie said the reason we hadn't heard from you was that you broke up with Sefton and didn't know how to tell us."

"I didn't break up with Sefton. He broke up with me. And the reason I didn't call is because I had the flu."

"I knew this would happen," she said.

"Knew I'd get the flu?"

"No, knew your life would fall apart when we left. You need someone to look after you."

"My life hasn't fallen apart," I said. "I'm over the flu and better off without Sefton. Everyone says so."

"Who's everyone?"

"Nestor for one. He came to take care of me while I was sick."

Receiver at arm's length again: "Winnie. You were right. Nestor loves Agnes."

"Hold on a minute," I said. "Nestor doesn't love me. Not in the way Winnie thinks."

"Sefton wouldn't talk to you when you were *well*," Flossie said. "And yet Nestor came *all the way* from Dennisonville to risk catching the flu. If that isn't love, what is?"

Even from a distance, I could not argue with her simple brutal logic.

"I can't talk right now," I said. "Gotta pen? I'll give you Sefton's number."

Later that night Margaret called to let me know she was bringing Bentley to school.

"I'll bring him to your first class," she said. "After that would you take him to the administration building? I've scheduled a tour of the campus for him."

"Glad to. Anything else?"

"Yes. Join us for lunch. Muriel's reserving a table for three."

Bentley McBain sat on the front row of my classroom. As I observed him, pen in hand, scribbling notes about "The Pardoner's Tale" in a spiral notebook, I could hardly concentrate on my lecture. Though still reticent, Bentley was a different man; his face less haggard, his eyes more vibrant. The obstreperous boy, who had refused Julia's love and made her life miserable, was determined to take advantage of his second chance. I wished she could see him now. I wished *Olympia* could see him now.

We met Margaret at noon and rode in her car to the Drifters' Rest. After Muriel seated us, Bentley gazed around the room, as captivated as if he were dining at Buckingham Palace.

"What do you think of Brighton Park?" I asked him.

"I think it's the most wonderful place I've ever seen," he said.

"Wonderful? That's not a word I would use to—" I said. Margaret zeroed in on me with a warning look. I changed course. "You must be excited about enrolling. Did you apply?"

"Bentley is going to enroll for the spring term," Margaret said. "I suggested your remedial English class."

I raised my water glass in a toast. "Congratulations. I bet you'll be a first-rate scholar."

"Don't look now," Margaret said, "but Grace and Kennesaw just came in."

"What is it with him?" I said. "Everywhere I go, he's one step behind me."

Bentley pushed back from the table. "You want me to have a word with him?"

Margaret reached for Bentley's hand. "No. That won't be necessary."

Kennesaw spotted us and spoke to the hostess, who led them to the table next to ours.

"Isn't this nice—" Kennesaw pulled out Grace's chair—"running into you like this?"

Grace, expressionless, did not share his opinion.

"Hello, Grace," Margaret said.

Kennesaw held out his hand to Bentley. "We haven't met. I'm Kennesaw Fleming. I teach with Margaret and Agnes."

Bentley stood and shook hands. "Bentley McBain."

"And how do you know Margaret and—?"

"He's an old family friend," Margaret said. "Recently relocated. Jonas and I are helping him get settled."

"Are you applying for a position at the college?" Kennesaw asked.

"I'm thinking about it," Bentley said.

"If you're going back to the college after lunch," Kennesaw said, "I'd love to talk to you about my re-enactors' group. You bear a striking resemblance to John Breckenridge."

Grace spoke up. "I only have an hour for lunch."

Kennesaw chuckled. "Excuse me. The little lady gets impatient when I don't pay her enough attention. I'll look for you back at the campus, Bentley."

Convinced Kennesaw was trying to overhear us, Margaret, Bentley, and I formed an unspoken pact to engage in meaningless conversation. I shuddered as I watched Kennesaw, knife in one hand and fork in the other, attack his food; his thick, black beard brushing the top of his tie as he leaned over his plate. Grace did her best to interest him in what she was saying, but Kennesaw ignored her. She touched his hand; he pulled away. She caught me staring and dropped her eyes. My heart ached for her. Couldn't she see he was the wrong man for her?

Worn out from a full day of work, I should have slept well on Friday night, but didn't. Though I had been concocting plans for days, I still could not settle on the right approach for telling Lorna about the festival. I had come up with three strategies, imagined every possible objection, and fashioned counterarguments for each. I was still shot through with guilt for snaring Lorna in her father's scheme. How would she react if she discovered Dr. Sherwood had persuaded me to cooperate by bribing me with the promise of a publisher?

Beyond that, was breaking the news to Lorna in the great outdoors really the best idea? What if she was the timid, delicate type who was skittish around animals? My whole scheme might backfire before Buck got the horses saddled.

On Saturday morning Lorna met me at my apartment. As we drove to Sloan's Canyon, I told her how I had become acquainted with Buck Sloan and his aunt Geneva Gilbey.

"I always ride Geneva's palomino Buttercup," I said. "But there's another gentle horse, a pinto named Franklin. Buck recommends him for beginning riders."

"No need," Lorna said. "I started riding when I was four. We had our own stables."

"How nice," I said, half-relieved, half-jealous.

Buck welcomed us. "I hope you ladies came hungry. My wife's been in the kitchen since just after sunup."

"She's over her morning sickness?" I asked.

Buck grinned. "Yep. She's blossoming. I put the crib together yesterday."

After breakfast Buck took us to the stable, saddled the horses, and led them outside. In one smooth motion, Lorna grasped the saddle horn and, without putting her foot in the stirrup, swung herself onto Franklin.

Did she have to be beautiful, talented, *and athletic*?

I mounted Buttercup, and we set off at a gentle trot.

Without warning, Lorna said, "Race ya," and urged Franklin into a full gallop. Laughing, she waved as her auburn hair streamed out behind her.

So this was what she was like before her father and Nolan sapped her vitality.

After an hour we stopped to rest under a giant oak. While the horses grazed, Lorna and I quizzed each other about our childhoods and families. Lorna had lived a life I could only imagine.

"Is there anything you can't do?" I asked. "Do you sing and play the harmonica, too?"

She chuckled. "I sing, but no, I've never tried the harmonica. I used to ride all the time, but once I started playing the piano, everything else took a back seat. Do you ride often?"

"Not as often as I'd like. If I have free time, I like to spend it at the typewriter."

A slight smile on her face, she plucked a wildflower from the grass. "I *used* to feel that way about the piano. Now I wonder what I missed out on because I was always practicing."

Great, I thought. While Lorna's picking dandelions and reveling in the simple pleasures of life, I'm on the verge of lecturing her about artistic integrity and her obligation to humanity. Hoping to appear casual, I walked to Buttercup and stroked her mane as I spoke.

My back to Lorna, I said, "You must miss performing *sometimes.* I'm no expert on music, but I've never heard anyone play like you … except maybe Oliver, but his—"

"Oliver?"

"Oliver Martin Farrell. The only *serious* musician I've known till—"

"You *know* Oliver Farrell?" she asked.

Her abrupt change in tone made me turn to face her.

"Yes. He was living at the Magnolia Arms when I first arrived. He left before I did, but Ivy Leigh says he's coming back for Thanksgiving."

She hopped up and brushed the grass from her pants. "You're going there for Thanksgiving, too, aren't you?"

"Yes, but—"

Rushing to me, she grabbed my arm. "Could I go with you?"

"I guess so—"

Her eyes gleaming, she brought her hands to her face. "This is amazing. Do you think you could talk Oliver into helping me?"

"Help you do what?"

"Get ready for the festival," she said, grasping Franklin's reins.

"I don't know … Wait. You *know* about the festival?"

She swung into the saddle. "Arley Mayhew told me. Which way are we going?"

Mounting Buttercup, I pointed toward a distant ridge.

"The *biology* teacher told you about the music festival?" I asked. "How did *he* find out?"

"From Wanetta Haverford," she said, pressing her feet into Franklin's sides.

More confused by the moment, I nudged Buttercup, and we walked alongside.

"The choral director?"

Lorna stifled a laugh. "When Wanetta told Arley about the festival, he got *very* excited. Wanted to know if *non*-music faculty could audition. He's a bassoonist."

"You can't be serious."

"I *am* serious. Wanetta said he'd have to ask you."

"Me?"

"Word's gotten around you're in charge," she said, still grinning.

"*What?*"

"When he couldn't find *you*, he came looking for me. Thought I might know since I'm to be the *principal performer*. You can imagine how surprised I was."

"I guess all his happened while I was out with the flu," I said.

A variable I hadn't factored in.

"I couldn't ask you what was going on," she said, "so I called Margaret."

Sighing, I shook my head. "I'm sorry, Lorna. All this time I've been planning the perfect way to tell you, and as usual I've bungled everything. Are you upset?"

"No. I shouldn't have strung you along, Agnes, but you're so creative, I wanted to see what you'd say. Please forgive me. I enjoyed this entirely too much."

"I'm just glad you're okay with the plan."

"The concert hall will be good for the school," she said. "I'm glad I can help."

"So … you know about the deal your father made with Dr. Sherwood?"

"*And* that they asked you to talk to me, since we're friends. I gotta hand it to my father. No one can come up with a plan and manipulate people into buying in better than he can."

"I can't tell you how relieved I am," I said. "If there's anything I can do to help …"

"You mean besides introducing me to Oliver?"

"Yeah, about that. He really doesn't like me, so it might be better if you arrived unannounced and let Ivy Leigh introduce you. Anything else?"

"Yes. Tell Dr. Sherwood I won't be in the festival unless you are, too."

"*What?*"

"If I go to the trouble to prepare for a concert, I'm not going to risk another attack of stage fright. I'll need a friend backstage with me."

"I'm not a professional musician."

"You're going to accompany Ham, aren't you?"

"Yes, but only because the last time he performed, he lost his nerve and couldn't keep going. He needs moral support."

"So do I," she said. "And if *you're* on the program, they'll have to hold auditions for any non-music faculty who want to participate. Music is for everyone. People forget that."

"Dr. Sherwood isn't going to like it," I said. "Your dad won't either. They wanted to showcase your talent and help you remember how glorious life is in the spotlight."

She pulled back on Franklin's bridle and halted. I did the same with Buttercup.

"Do you want to know *why* I'm willing to get on stage again?" she asked.

"Why?"

"Because the night of the dinner party, when I performed in that beautiful room and saw the looks on the people's faces, I remembered *why* I love playing the piano."

"Practice makes perfect?" I asked.

"Nothing that prosaic. When I give someone a song, it becomes part of their life. Even after the music stops, they can relive the performance in their memory whenever they want."

"I feel that way about stories, too, though I've yet to prove it with one of my own."

"You will," she said. "I'm sure of it." She gathered the reins and turned Franklin toward the house. "Ready to go back?"

On Monday morning I was back in Dr. Sherwood's office delivering Lorna's stipulations.

Elspeth bit her pencil. "I should've known better than to trust *you* with talking to Lorna."

"Not my fault," I said. "She knew all along what we were up to. What do I tell her?"

"Tell her we'll hold auditions in two weeks," Elspeth said. "I'll call Dr. Maron. Can you really play the piano?"

"I can," I said, thinking she was impressed.

"Good. Then you can give lessons to save enough money to publish your silly book."

"Wait a minute," I said. "We had an agreement. I used my influence to get Lorna to be in the festival, and she's *going* to be in it. I upheld my end of the bargain."

"She had already decided," Elspeth said. "You said so yourself. So you did nothing."

"But I did what you asked. There's going to be a festival, and Lorna is going to play."

"The festival was *supposed* to be a concert featuring a world class pianist, not an amateur hour with a scrawny biology teacher playing 'Danny Boy' on the bassoon."

"It was Lorna's idea," I said. "Not mine."

"I'm not interested in *Lorna's* ideas," she said. "Or *yours*." She picked up the phone and dialed. "Sharon, get Dr. Maron on the phone and come show Agnes out."

"Never mind. I know the way out," I said, brushing past Sharon as she entered.

Tears stinging my eyes, I tore through the reception area outside Elspeth's office.

When I stepped into the hall, I heard my name. I turned around. Bentley was following me.

He took my arm. "Here now. What's the matter?"

Without thinking, I fell into his arms and cried.

"She makes me so mad," I said.

He handed me a handkerchief from his jacket pocket. "It must have been bad if you prefer the company of an ex-con to your boss."

I couldn't help laughing. "You have a good heart, Bentley, which is more than I can say for some people. What are you doing here anyway?"

"Looking for you. Margaret said you had an appointment with Dr. Sherwood and told me where her office was. Is there someplace we can talk?"

Bentley walked me to my office. When I opened the door, he walked straight to my desk.

"This is stunning," he said, running his hand over the wood. "Where did you get it?"

"Some friends gave it to me."

"I did some carpentry while I was in prison. Very therapeutic. I need some advice, Agnes, and you're the only person I can ask."

"You may be sorry you asked, Bentley. I'm on a losing streak right now."

"You don't know what a losing streak is," he said. "I used to lie awake at night worrying what would happen to me once I got out of prison."

It was the wrong time to quip, 'I wonder the same thing about myself,' so I said, "Must have been terrifying."

"To be my age and have no skills and no hope … I still can't believe I've ended up here with the first real friends I've ever had."

"And you haven't even met all of them yet," I said.

"That's what I want to talk to you about. Jonas and Margaret have been wonderful, but I don't want to presume on them any longer. They may be my age, but they're still newlyweds."

"True."

"Can you think of someplace I can stay till I can afford a place of my own? I couldn't pay rent yet, but I could mow the lawn or clean house."

"I think I know exactly the place. Come with me to my next class, and then I'll take you to the maintenance office and introduce you to the Hamptons."

Mr. Hampton was as gracious to Bentley as I knew he would be, offering their spare bedroom to him at no charge.

"Truth is," Mr. Hampton said, "Ham and I could use a little company. We've heard each other's stories a thousand times, and our daily lives aren't all that interesting."

"I should probably tell you," Bentley said, "I just got out of prison."

Mr. Hampton held up his hand. "Any friend of Agnes' is a friend of mine. Her good opinion is sufficient. If you'll meet me here at 5:00, I'll drive you to our house."

"Now that that's taken care of, how about some lunch?" I asked Bentley.

"Not today," he said. "Too much to do. I'll take the bus back to Jonas and Margaret's house and pack my things."

Helping Bentley kept my mind off Elspeth's treachery for most of the day. But as I drove home that evening, my frustration overtook me. As much as I hated to admit it, Dr. Sherwood was right. I hadn't talked Lorna into anything. She had not only decided on her own to do something selfless for the school, but had also managed to get the upper hand with both Dr. Sherwood and her father. The girl I had judged as helpless and delicate had a mind of her own.

The first thing I did when I got home was call Nestor. Maybe *he* had good news.

"How was Littleton?" I asked. "Does Millie still live at the same address?"

"She does."

"See there? I told you eighty wasn't so old."

"You've got that right," Nestor said. "She's on a six-week European tour."

My heart sank. "When did she leave?"

"Last week."

"Who told you?"

"Her nephew. He's house sitting while she's away."

"Did he know if she still has the cedar chest?" I asked.

"He said he *thinks* he's seen it in the attic, but he's not sure."

"And he wouldn't let you look?"

"He said he didn't know me from 'Adam's off ox' and wasn't about to let me rummage through his 'auntie's' things."

"Did you tell him about the letter?" I asked.

"I did, but he said even if I had the letter with me, Millie was the only one who could authenticate Julia's handwriting and till then the attic would remain closed."

"Why did you stay an extra day?"

"I thought if he got to know me over breakfast, I could convince him I was sincere. But it didn't work. I'm sorry, Agnes. I thought I could pull it off."

"So … you didn't call Sunday night because you didn't want to talk about it," I said.

"I can stand to disappoint a lot of people, Agnes, but not you."

"Six weeks," I said. "Thanksgiving will have come and gone by then. I was hoping to bring everything back with me after my visit."

"Whatever you do," Nestor said, "bring that letter with you when you come. I'll go back to Littleton and talk to Millie after her nephew leaves."

Nestor apologized one more time, and we hung up. Before I had time to plummet into despair, the phone rang again.

"Hello, Agnes, this is Charlotte. I'm sorry to call this late, but your phone's been busy."

"Not a problem. Everything all right?"

"Yes, Monty improves a little each day. We tried a few dance steps last night, and he's playing the accordion again."

"I need to see him," I said. "But I've been so busy."

"That's what I want to talk to you about. Has that man Bentley arrived?"

"Yes. He's been looking for a job and a place to live. He's starting school in the spring."

"Do you think he'd have time to meet Monty now?"

I called the Hamptons to arrange a visit on Sunday afternoon. When Ham offered to drive Bentley to Charlotte's house, I suggested he join us so we could have our first practice.

"Me? Go to the Wrayburn house?" Ham asked.

"The more the merrier," I said. "I'll pick you up at 2:00."

When I arrived at the Hampton home, I honked the horn; Bentley and Ham came out of the house. Ham had slicked his hair to one side and starched and ironed a white shirt with such rigor the creases in the long sleeves could have cut paper. A maroon paisley tie, adorned with a wide silver tie clip, completed the effect. Bentley, whose gray hair was too short to tame, had still applied hair cream and forced the few strands in front to stand at attention. Also outfitted in a white shirt, Bentley had opted for a blue-and-white-checked bow tie.

Ham opened the passenger door. They hesitated, unsure who should sit in the middle.

I patted the seat. "Hop in, Bentley."

Bentley obliged, and Ham, looking relieved, closed the door.

"If I'd known you two were going formal, I would have dressed more stylishly," I said.

"Did you remember the music?" Ham asked.

I pointed to the music on the dashboard. "I may need to warm up awhile," I said, not mentioning I'd made no preparation other than making copies of the selections.

"That's okay," Ham said. "I'd love to look around the grounds awhile." Ham nudged Bentley with his elbow. "Go ahead. Tell her."

Bentley reddened. "I thought we'd talk about it on the way *home*."

"No sense putting it off," Ham said. "She's going to say yes."

Bentley paused. "I've been trying to think of a way to repay you for your kindness."

"There's no need, Bentley," I said. "Everyone deserves a—"

"Let him finish," Ham said. "You'll love his idea."

"I've been trying to think of a gift I could afford," Bentley said, "and then I remembered how that Kennesaw guy follows you around all the time. I can put a stop to that."

Concerned Bentley might be reminiscing about tactics learned in prison, I said, "It might be my imagination … but I am worried about those photos and Ryder's missing watch."

"Would you like to know for sure what he's up to?" Bentley asked.

"I guess so … but how can you—?"

"Fleming doesn't know I have any particular connection to you," Bentley said. "I could join his re-enactors' group and spend some time with him. Maybe he'd confide in me."

"How 'bout that?" Ham said. "It's brilliant. We planned it last night."

I couldn't argue. "It would help me to stop worrying," I said. "Elinor, too."

"Leave him to me," Bentley said.

Charlotte welcomed Bentley and Ham and showed us into the library where Monty was waiting, pen in hand, with his manuscript and notes spread out on the round table in the corner.

Monty's eyes lit up when he saw me. "Agnes. It's been far too long."

I kissed him on the cheek. "Hello, Monty. I want you to meet some friends of mine. This is Bentley McBain and Talmadge Hampton."

Monty reached out his hand. "Honored. Won't you sit down?"

Bentley joined Monty at the table.

"Is it all right if I practice the piano, Charlotte?" I asked. "Maybe you could take Ham on a tour of the garden. He'd love to see it."

"A good idea," she said. "Come along, Mr. Hampton."

"Everyone calls me Ham," he said.

When I entered the conservatory, an unexpected rush of melancholy overwhelmed me. As my gaze fell on the place Sefton and I had sat on the night of the party, the pain of losing him came back sharper than before. I sat at the piano and tried to play. Only a few measures into Liebestraum, I realized I was in way over my head. Even if I found a simpler arrangement, I'd have to practice endlessly. As I waded through the notes, one at a time, I began to craft gentle ways of telling Ham I'd made a mistake.

Ham tapped at the conservatory door. I glanced at my watch. I'd been bumbling around almost an hour and a half.

"Ready to practice?" Ham asked.

"I haven't quite worked out all the notes yet. Could we start with a piece I already know, so I can get some idea of what to expect?"

"How about 'The Star-Spangled Banner?'" he asked.

"I'd need the music."

"Seventy-Six Trombones?"

"No," I said.

After four more suggestions, we agreed on "Für Elise."

"That's a nice one," he said. "It's the song my mom was playing when I realized I could whistle more than 'Oh! Susanna.'"

Now there's a song I could play, I thought. I sounded the first note, and Ham began to whistle, his tone so lyrical and clear, it was like raindrops crystallizing in the air before they floated to the floor. He had an inexhaustible supply of air and a staggering range. Lost in the moment, I pictured Ham in a tuxedo, posed in front of an orchestra, whistling "O Solo Mio" to a silent and enraptured audience. My hands slid to my lap.

"Don't you know the rest?" Ham asked.

Dazed, I looked up. "I used to. I can't remember now. That … that was beautiful, Ham."

"Comes natural," he said. "Actually, I've improved since I've been listening to Miss Maron practice every week. I want to do with my whistling what she does with the piano."

"A lofty goal," I said.

"Don't tell her I said that, okay?" he said. "She doesn't know I stay backstage after I unlock Rehearsal Hall for her, but I can't make myself leave, even when she's playing scales."

We found Monty and Bentley still busy at work, jotting down notes, rifling through papers and books, firing questions and responses at each other. Officer of the Court and The Accused no longer, they were working shoulder to shoulder sharing their courtroom experience.

"No one hates to interrupt a writer more than I do," I said, "but I have papers to grade before tomorrow morning. I need to get home."

"You'll have to visit our home sometime, Mr. Monty," Ham said. "My dad would love to meet you."

"Capital," Monty said. "Next Saturday? Charlotte's chauffeur can drive me over."

The following weeks were surprisingly peaceful. Along with my fellow teachers I settled into the predictable routine of a Monday through Friday life, lectures, faculty meetings, and grading and returning papers. I seldom saw Margaret or Elinor. Lorna, I supposed, was still practicing in Rehearsal Hall and organizing the festival. Occasionally, I saw Bentley coming and going from the maintenance office. Late one afternoon, I saw him and Kennesaw walking into the room where the re-enactors met. I noticed Bentley was also growing a beard. He was following through with his plan.

I tried to maintain a rigid schedule and hurried home every day after school to work on my book. It was just as well Nestor hadn't secured the contents of the cedar chest. There was more than enough to read in Sefton's abandoned notes. But no matter how engrossed I became in my work, the obligation to practice the piano never left me. Liebestraum continued to elude me, and I was worried I'd also have to prepare a piece for the festival auditions unless Lorna could somehow get me out it.

One week before festival tryouts I was hurrying to my truck when an imposing voice called my name. Before I could stop, Althea Creighton, drama teacher, overtook me and clutched my elbow with fearsome strength. We had never been introduced, but when I turned to face her and she locked me in her piercing green eyes, I understood at once why her students called her Dragon Lady. Her face etched with delicate lines, her long dyed-black hair pulled back in a ponytail, she was a walking portrait of faded grandeur and former roles for which she had once been perfect.

"What are you? A phantom teacher?" she asked. "I've been trying to catch you for days."

With mock dignity, I straightened my sweater. "I'm here."

"Did it never occur to you there are fine arts *other than* singing and piano playing?"

Baffled, but in no mood for a lecture, I took my life in my hands. "Like sculpting?"

My feigned stupidity achieved the desired effect. She drew herself up to her full height. Jaw jutting forward, she fairly snorted.

"No. Not like sculpting. Like acting."

"Or writing," I said.

"Writing is not a fine art."

"Shakespeare would argue."

"It's not a *performing* art," she said.

"Again … Shakespeare would—"

She dropped her mammoth striped tote bag, which teetered and fell on its side. Two yellow pencils and a silver lipstick tube rolled across the sidewalk.

"I will not argue semantics with you," she said. "I merely want to know *why*—after I've pleaded with the administration for *years* about a fine arts festival—all of a sudden *you*—"

"Fine arts festival?" I asked.

"*Yes*. Other community colleges have them. My alma mater had one. I don't know why we can't do the same here. And now I hear there's to be a *music* festival, and I want to know—"

"Why are you telling me all this?" I asked.

She folded her arms. "Because *you're* in charge. I don't know what kind of pull you have with Dr. Sherwood or how you talked her into scheduling auditions with *no* thought of—"

"Why does everyone think I'm in charge?" I asked. "I'm only doing what I'm told."

Grabbing the handles of her bag, she looped them over her shoulder. "All I'm saying is it's an insult to have your talent consistently overlooked and underrated."

I retrieved her pencils and lipstick. "I know what you mean. I'll talk to Lorna."

"You mean Dr. Sherwood."

"She's not holding the reins on this one," I said.

When I approached Lorna about adding drama to the festival program, she, being the democrat she was, agreed at once.

"What about Dr. Sherwood?" I asked.

"Leave her to me," Lorna said.

Auditions for the Brighton Park Fine Arts Festival were scheduled for the evening of November 4. The news that *all* faculty members were welcome had raced through the halls like a prairie fire. Whether they came to audition because they believed in the worthy cause or because they wanted to share their talent with a waiting world, I could not guess. But when Lorna and I arrived at the auditorium, at least three dozen eager performers were waiting. Lorna had invited Wanetta Haverford, choral director; Violet Pate, piano teacher; and Nat Thurlow, percussion teacher, to serve with her as judges.

Though I recognized names and faces among the hopeful participants, I had no idea so many teachers, possessing skills of varying use and appeal, walked the halls of Brighton Park every day. Cringing, I sat in the dark auditorium and watched a frightful display of juggling, ventriloquism, and autoharp playing, before any customary talent like singing or dancing appeared. When finally Rosie Creswell, the volleyball coach, stepped forward with her clarinet to play "If Ever I Would Leave You," it seemed even the walls breathed a sigh of relief.

Tillie Jenkins, interior design instructor, attempted "The Laughing Song" from Die Fledermaus. Admiring her zeal, we were grateful when, mercifully, she concluded. Hugh Galbraith, fellow English teacher, outfitted in a 19th century British regimental uniform, expounded "Gunga Din" with such verve he left us speechless. Representing the philosophy department, Liam Harding and Stella Wagner portrayed such a convincing Johnny and Katie from "A Tree Grows in Brooklyn," we stood and applauded. Althea Creighton, their coach, had proven her point. But Arley Mayhew, who played the Weber Concerto for the bassoon, upstaged even them. Not even Elspeth Sherwood could dispute his talent.

Truly there is no business like show business.

I never asked how Lorna explained my being on the program, but there was no backlash when she posted the list of performers. Relieved to have the initial phase of the festival accomplished, I dared to hope everyone would finally acknowledge Lorna as the one "in charge" and would direct any further questions to her. I could coast through the days remaining till Thanksgiving and then pack my manuscript and music and retire to the Magnolia Arms where I could spend leisurely hours at the typewriter in my cozy room and practice on the grand piano in the parlor.

The morning after the auditions a note signed "B.Mc" slid under my office door.

Planning trip with KF. Symposium at Rappahannock Station battlefield. Progress.

Two weeks before Thanksgiving I initiated my official countdown by calling Ivy Leigh to ask if I could bring a friend. When I related Lorna's request to practice with Oliver, Ivy Leigh agreed she should be the one to tell Oliver that Lorna was coming.

"Can you be here by Tuesday?" she asked.

"I'm leaving here on Monday night," I said. "I got a substitute for my Tuesday classes."

"Perfect. See you then."

The Friday before Thanksgiving, I breezed into the English department office to check my mailbox. In Lorna's box, directly above mine, an envelope addressed with bold black print caught my eye. Glancing over my shoulder like a shoplifter, I eased out the envelope. There in Sefton's dramatic script was Lorna's name underscored with a short curved diagonal line and the school address underneath. I slipped the envelope back into place and, head spinning, sank onto a chair. So this was why Sefton had left early that Sunday. After meeting Lorna, he had skipped breakfast with me to be with her.

This was why Lorna was cheerful and effervescent—it wasn't the festival. She was in love with Sefton, the boyfriend who had fallen for *her* when he had come to visit *me.*

Margaret entered the office. "What are you doing here?" she asked.

Squinting my eyes, I looked up. "Checking my mail. Why do you ask?"

"I thought you might like to be on time for your next class."

Jumping up, I hurried to the door. "Remember you're taking me to the train station on Monday."

Gloomy and crestfallen, I spent the entire weekend alone. All the progress I had made since Sefton's betrayal, all the joy I had felt over Julia's letter, all the relief I had experienced once the fine arts festival was underway, evaporated when I saw that letter from Sefton. Once again the beautiful girl had won out. Why had I believed for an instant this time would be different? Why couldn't I have discovered the letter *before* I promised Lorna she could spend Thanksgiving with me? There would be no way to avoid her while we were staying in the same house.

Nestor called Sunday night. "I probably don't need to remind you to bring Julia's letter."

"Already in my suitcase," I said.

"I can't wait to see you. Ivy Leigh said Lorna's coming, too."

"Yes, wonderful Lorna Maron is coming, too."

My sarcasm went unnoticed.

"Hope she's good at peeling apples," Nestor said. "Ivy Leigh's outdoing herself this year. I don't know how we're going to pull off all the plans she's made. We'll have a full house."

On our way to the train station Monday evening, Margaret noticed I didn't seem as happy as she "would have thought."

"Tired," I said. "It's been a *long* semester."

"You'll feel better once you're at the Magnolia Arms," she said.

When I stepped off the train in Dennisonville, Nestor swept me up in his arms, more muscular than a few weeks before. Dressed in khakis and a green plaid shirt, he looked like a model for a tourist brochure.

"You're a sight for sore eyes," he said, lifting my bag. "Wait till you see all we've done to the house."

As Nestor drove, I closed my eyes and pictured Ivy Leigh standing on the porch. She would welcome me. I would greet Posey, Xander, and Chester. We would gather around the kitchen table. After breakfast, Ivy Leigh would send me upstairs to unpack. I would climb the dear familiar stairs, open the door to my room, stand at the window, stare out at the street, and whisper to myself, 'I'm really here.' Inspired, I would sit at the typewriter. Words would flow from my fingers like cherry blossoms in a stiff spring breeze. I'd still be sitting there when …

"Are you awake?" Nestor asked as he exited the truck. "We're here."

No pilgrim catching sight of a towering cathedral could have been more awestruck than I.

Pausing to savor the moment, I gazed at the house, remembering the first time I had admired the high-pitched gray shingled roof, tall windows, and gables. Below the cupola was my third-floor room, the one Ivy Leigh had promised always to keep available for me.

Nestor walked around the truck and opened my door.

"Aren't we going through the kitchen?" I asked.

"Not today," he said, pointing to the front door, adorned with an enormous fall wreath.

He lingered behind as I walked up the four wide steps of the columned porch and reached for the doorknob. The door swung open.

"Surprise."

Flossie bounded out and squeezed me, her tousled hair obscuring my right eye. Her glasses grazed my shoulder as they tumbled from the top of her head.

Winnie, close behind, grabbed me from the other side and kissed my cheek. "Welcome. Welcome. Welcome."

Jumbled, we entered the house.

"I didn't know you were coming," I said, almost dizzy with confusion.

"We wanted to surprise you," Flossie said.

"Been planning it forever," Winnie said.

"Hello, Agnes."

Chester Cranston, or at least a faint version of the spunky college friend I had once known, held out a frail hand.

I ignored his hand and put my arms around him. "Chester. It's good to see you."

"How's Saturn?" he asked.

"He still lets me live with him," I said. "Where are Xander and Posey?"

"Doing chores for Ivy Leigh," he said. "They'll be back soon."

I heard Rachmaninov drifting in from the parlor. "Oliver's already here?" I asked.

Chester nodded. "We should go into the kitchen before we all get in trouble."

When Ivy Leigh stepped out of the kitchen into the hall, I rushed toward her.

Hugging me, she whispered, "I know this isn't what you expected, but everything's going to be fine. You'll see." And then aloud, "You look tired, Agnes. Come have some breakfast."

Ivy Leigh took my hand and led me to the kitchen. The retinue followed. There was hardly room to stand. Chester pulled out a chair for me. I took my usual place at the table.

Flossie patted my shoulder on her way to the sink. "You probably haven't had a decent meal since we moved away."

"I'm still eating the meals you left in the freezer," I said.

"Marvelous," Winnie said, tying on an apron. "How's Mary Smith?"

"Thriving," I said.

Which is more than I can say for myself at the moment, I thought.

Nestor straggled in from the hall and approached Ivy Leigh. "Ready for the list." She pointed to a bulletin board, newly installed. "Over there."

The phone rang. Flossie, nearest, picked up the receiver. "Magnolia Arms. Flossie Bingham speaking."

Retrieving the list, Nestor started to the back door. "Get some rest, Agnes. We have a big day ahead."

"Muffin or scrambled eggs?" Winnie asked, handing me a cup of coffee.

Though the parlor door was closed, I could still hear Oliver pounding out octaves.

Ivy Leigh called over her shoulder. "We saved the cherry strudel for Agnes. Don't you remember?"

Nestor opened the back door.

Flossie spoke into the phone. "Yes, Agnes is here. May I ask who's calling?"

"So you're teaching English now," Chester said. "Do you like it?"

Through the open back door, Mendel, Xander's dog, loped in and ran straight toward me. Tail wagging, he planted wet paws on my leg.

Chester took him by the collar. "Come on, puppy. I'll give you some breakfast."

"Sorry," Nestor said. "Mendel's as glad to see you as the rest of us."

"You'll have to speak up," Flossie told the caller. "I can hardly hear you. Did you say Bentley? Like the *car*?"

Balancing a spoonful of hot apple cider, Winnie crossed the kitchen. "Taste this, Agnes."

Before I could refuse, she touched the spoon to my lips. I had no choice but to inhale. The steaming liquid scalded the roof of my mouth and singed my throat as it trickled down. "Agnes," Flossie said. "It's for you. A man named Bentley. I don't remember him."

I left the table and reached for the phone. "He came after you left." I put the receiver to my ear and moved as far away from the crowd as the cord would reach. "Hello."

"Agnes?" Bentley asked. "I got your number from Margaret. I wanted to call right away."

I pressed my finger into my other ear to drown out the noise. "Anything wrong?"

"No, nothing's wrong," he said. "Can you hear me? I have to talk fast before Kennesaw comes back from the gift shop."

"Where are you?"

"Remington, Virginia," he said. "At the symposium. This is the first chance I've had to call."

"You found out something?"

"Yes. I know why Kennesaw came to Brighton Park."

My heart pounded. "You do? Why?"

"Kennesaw Fleming isn't his real name. It's John Ellershaw. He's Ryder's son."

Chapter 11

Lost Horizon

As transfixed as a tenderfoot facing a herd of spooked cattle, I braced myself against the kitchen counter and tried to rein in the thoughts stampeding through my mind.

The photo on Elinor's desk of young Ryder, his wife, and children … was it *possible* the little boy in jeans and a striped shirt grew into the man we knew as Kennesaw Fleming?

"Agnes? Are you still there?" Bentley asked.

"What's wrong, Agnes?" Flossie asked. "You're white as a sheet. You better sit down."

"Have you told anyone else?" I asked Bentley.

"You're the first," he said, his voice shrinking to a whisper. "He's coming back. I have to hang up now."

The phone went silent.

Flossie shook my arm. "Agnes. What's wrong? Has something happened?"

"No. No," I said, rubbing my forehead. "I didn't get much sleep on the train, and it's a little warm in here. I think I'll sit on the porch for awhile."

"Good idea," she said. "I'll have Winnie bring you a glass of water. Can't stop my kneading right now."

I stepped out onto the spacious screened porch where Ivy Leigh grew herbs in enormous clay pots and hung dried flowers from the cedar rafters. Sitting on the end of the long wooden bench, I gazed at the backyard.

Piecing together Kennesaw's story required no conscious mental exercise; all the pieces, as if magnetized, snapped into place and connected.

Kennesaw Fleming … rather, John Ellershaw, had come to Brighton Park to find his father. He had befriended Elinor as the shortest route to Ryder. He had sized me up as Elinor's friend, and when I proved inscrutable, he had turned to Grace as the means of gaining entrance to the Ellershaw home. The photos Toby had seen in his briefcase now made perfect sense. And maybe the Civil War role-playing was only a good excuse to grow a beard to disguise any trace of the little boy Kennesaw had once been.

But why hadn't Kennesaw been honest about his purpose?

And how had Bentley pried the real purpose out of him?

The back door opened. A glass of water in her hand, Ivy Leigh walked toward me.

"Is there something I can help with?" she asked, setting the glass on the table.

I pointed to the screened door which led to the driveway. "For the first time since I walked through that door, I wish I was home instead of here."

"Tell me," she said, sitting next to me.

After I reviewed the story, Ivy Leigh assured me Ryder and Elinor would be in good hands with Margaret and Jonas.

"It's Grace I feel sorry for," Ivy Leigh said. "She'll know that guy only used her to get close to Ryder. But nothing can be done about that now. Come inside. You shouldn't be alone."

I followed her into the kitchen.

"Feeling better?" Winnie asked.

"I think so," I said. "Where's Chester?"

"In Xander's room in the basement," Ivy Leigh said. "The doctor has ordered him to rest twice a day."

"He's a nice boy," Flossie said, dusting her face with flour as she brushed away a wisp of gray hair. "You can imagine how delighted we were to meet the person who saved Saturn."

"I thought Chester was staying in Monty's room," I said.

"He was," Winnie said, pouring hot water from the kettle. "But when Oliver arrived—"

"Chester *volunteered* to room with Xander," Ivy Leigh said, "till after the holidays."

"So Oliver hasn't changed?" I asked.

"No, I haven't," Oliver said from the doorway.

As dark and brooding as I remembered, Oliver Martin Farrell had appeared in the kitchen door. With one sleeve rolled up and the other unbuttoned, drooping over his hand, he looked like he had been wrestling the piano rather than playing it. His thick black hair, glistening with perspiration, brushed the top of his eyebrows. Since we had gotten off on the wrong foot when we met and had never gotten back in step, I did not respond to Oliver. Out of respect for Ivy Leigh, he and I tolerated each other with mutual indifference, keeping our interactions civil, though chilly.

Winnie scurried to the table and pulled out a chair.

"Sit here, Oliver," she said. "I've just made a fresh pot of tea. Lemon?"

He nodded. "Are there any scones left?"

Flossie retrieved an aluminum foil covered plate from the top of the refrigerator. "Did you want preserves with these?"

I bit my lip and kept quiet.

"More tea, Agnes?" Winnie asked.

"I had coffee," I said, "but no, I don't want anything. Do you need my help, Ivy Leigh?"

"No," she said. "Why don't you go unpack? Brush off the typewriter."

"We'll catch up on the news over lunch," Flossie said.

"Not much to say," I said.

"Still," Winnie said, "I'd like to catch up on all the old friends I miss."

Old friends? I thought. You only knew them a few weeks.

"And I'll need to know who this Bentley fellow is," Flossie said.

When I walked past Oliver, he surprised me by grabbing my hand.

"Ivy Leigh told me you know Lorna Maron," he said. "Is that true?"

Incredulous, I glanced down at my hand in Oliver's.

"It is," I said.

"And she's really teaching English?" he asked.

"She is."

He released my hand. "I'd heard she had a nervous breakdown, but I didn't believe it."

Jarred by the first glimmer of human kindness he had ever shown, I met his eyes.

"I'm not sure I'd call it a nervous breakdown," I said. "She's better now. In fact, she's organizing a fine arts festival for our school. She's going to be the featured performer."

"Have you heard her play?" he asked.

"Many times." I glanced at Ivy Leigh, who nodded her head, giving me the go ahead. "You should have seen her face when she found out I knew *you*."

He bolted up from the table with such force he toppled his chair. This time he grasped both my hands. "She knows who I am? When will she be here?"

"She didn't tell me."

"Wednesday," Ivy Leigh said over her shoulder.

I thought Oliver was going to faint.

Finding my suitcase in the hall, I lifted it and started up the stairs, a thousand memories stepping on my heels as I ascended. When I reached the second floor, I knocked on the door of Margaret's old room and looked in. Flossie's knitting bag, Winnie's kimonos, and an odd assortment of shoes had taken up residence. I decided against peeking into Monty's old room. Somehow Oliver would know. At the end of the hall, Posey's door was decorated with a new fall wreath. I wondered which room she and Xander would occupy after their wedding. Would they stay here?

When I reached the third floor, I stopped at the study on the left and laid my hand on the door. Though I knew Monty was miles away, I could almost hear him reading aloud the most recent chapter of his memoir. When I had been writing in my room five steps away, I used to dread hearing this door creak open, knowing Monty was on his way with another request for "a better way" to structure a particular phrase. A strange sense of loss overcame me—so sharp it made me linger at the study to mourn Monty's absence.

I approached my room, turned the doorknob, and entered. At last … *something* about the Magnolia Arms was exactly as I had left it. Comforted by the feeling of home, I breathed in the best of all smells—sheets and towels which had been washed and hung outside to dry—only yesterday, I guessed. Except for a vase of sunflowers on the dresser, everything in the room was blessedly the same. A hopeful stack of paper, waiting to be added to my book, rested by the typewriter on the roll top desk. I walked to the arched window and looked out.

Though the Magnolia Arms now stood in place of Briarwood Manor, the home Eliot Bridger had built, I was still standing on the very property where Julia had once lived, where Jameson had played in the front yard, where neighbors had strolled by in the evening and remarked they had 'never known a family as happy as the Bridgers.' I studied the yard and wondered if Julia had planted roses by the path leading to the porch, and if Eliot, coming home after work, had impulsively plucked a bloom to present to her when she welcomed him home.

Absorbed in this blissful thought, I leaned my head against the window and pictured a handsome man in a bowler hat, tapping his cane as he hurried along the path. When I spotted an actual man approaching, I blinked my eyes and wondered if I had dozed off and dreamed. Looking closer, I realized at once I was awake. This diminutive fellow in a gray seersucker suit and red bow tie was no apparition from the past. Dr. Morton Penrose was climbing the steps to the porch of the Magnolia Arms.

How many pianists did one house need?

Sitting at the desk, I buried my face in my hands. What was Dr. Penrose doing here? Did he want a firsthand report on Lorna? Whatever the reason, he was one unexpected guest too many. Maybe, I thought, I could pretend to have the flu again, stay in my room for a few days, and slip quietly out of town on a midnight train. I could say I didn't *really* know the neighbor I'd trusted to check on Saturn every day. Or maybe I could say my brother had arrived unexpectedly again. Or maybe ... A knock interrupted my escape planning.

"Agnes," Ivy Leigh said. "There's someone here to see you."

"I have a headache," I said.

"No, you don't. Open this door."

I complied. "Who is it?"

She held out a business card. "Dr. Penrose. Said he got our address from Margaret."

"Did you know he was coming?" I asked.

"No. Margaret probably assumed he would write first, but I won't know till I ask."

"*Where* are we going to put everybody"? I asked.

"Let me worry about that. You come down and welcome Dr. Penrose. He's a mess."

Like an obedient child, I followed Ivy Leigh downstairs. When we reached the first floor, she approached Dr. Penrose, fidgeting by the front desk.

"Here's Agnes," she said. "If you'll excuse me, I have a telephone call to make. I'll leave you two to get reacquainted." She retreated to her office.

"Dr. Penrose," I said. "What are you doing ... ?"

Rushing to me, he gripped my hand in both of his. "Miss Quinn. I hope you'll forgive me."

"Forgive you for what?"

"Being so impulsive—not like me at all. But Dr. Maron has been so stingy with information about Lorna. I called your school to speak to you, but when you'd already left—"

"You talked to Margaret instead?"

Still holding my hand, he nodded. "She gave me this address. Told me Lorna would be here. I was going to write, then I decided to call, and eventually I threw caution to the wind—"

"And hopped on a midnight train?" I asked, still envisioning my own getaway plans.

"Is she here?"

"Not yet," I said. "Come with me. You look like you could use some breakfast."

Dr. Penrose followed me to the kitchen. When Flossie caught sight of him, she wiped her hands on her apron. Winnie, seeing him, smoothed their hair. Oliver, dabbing preserves onto the last scone, did not look up.

"Another guest?" Winnie asked.

"This is Lorna's teacher, Dr. Penrose," I said.

"Morton," he said, extending his hand.

Straining to swallow, Oliver pushed back from the table.

"Dr. Penrose?" he asked, gulping.

"Dr. Farrell?" Morton said. "I … never dreamed. I thought you were touring—"

"You know each other?" I asked.

"Have mutual friends, of course," Dr. Penrose said.

Oliver grabbed a dishtowel from the counter and wiped the table. "Please sit down."

"I *am* tired," Morton said, removing his coat and revealing his bony shoulders.

"A pleasure to meet you," Winnie said, taking his hand. "I'm a friend of Lorna's."

Flossie edged in. "Me, too."

"Coffee or tea?" Winnie asked.

"Tea," Morton said. "Two sugars."

"I'll leave you four to get acquainted," I said, backing toward the door into the hall.

"Where do you think you're going?" asked a familiar voice.

My longtime friend, Xander Plumley, had blocked my exit. I turned around.

"We've been waiting for you," he said, hugging me.

Posey Devoe, his fiancée, pushed in to embrace me from the other side.

"It's good to see you, Agnes," she said. "It's not the same around here without you."

I was amazed at my friends' transformation. When I had met Posey a year ago, her fine brown hair was frayed and droopy. Today she sported a modern cut, stylish and flattering. She had replaced her narrow black-framed glasses, perpetually perched on the end of her nose, with contacts. I remembered Xander, a college chemistry major, often wearing the same shirt several days in a row and never combing his hair. Today he had on creased khaki pants and a blue oxford shirt—tucked in. Like Nestor, his shoulders were broader. Wonderful, I thought, how love alters unlikely candidates.

"You two look great," I said. "Being engaged agrees with you." I lifted a sleeve of the dark blue suit draped over Xander's arm. "Is this your wedding suit?"

"Yes," Posey said at the same time Xander said no.

"What I meant," Xander said, "is I rented it."

They exchanged glances.

"Yes, rented," Posey said.

"Early," I said. "The wedding's not till February." I tapped the cut glass crystal vase Posey was holding. "And is this a wedding gift?"

"No," she said. "I brought it for Ivy Leigh to approve for the table … for Thanksgiving."

"Pretty," I said.

Posey glanced at her watch. "Is Oliver finished practicing?"

"Yes," I said. "He's entertaining a dignitary in the kitchen."

"Then let's go in the parlor," Posey said, "and catch up."

"Be right with you," Xander said, "after I hang up … this … my … suit."

Posey handed the vase to Xander. "Take this to Ivy Leigh. Let me know what she says."

"Will do," Xander said.

Posey and I stepped across the hall into the parlor. I was relieved to find the room unchanged—the usual avalanche of sheet music strewn on the floor around the grand piano; the chessboard on the marble coffee table still beckoning the next two contestants; the worn brocade sofa still piled high with comfortably worn throw pillows; and the massive burgundy wingback chairs still facing the bay window. I sank down on the sofa, hugged one of the pillows, and leaned back.

"Close the door, Posey, so we won't be bothered," I said.

She sat next to me. "Still tired from your trip?"

"Not so much from the trip as all the confusion I found when I got here."

"Aren't you glad to be back?"

"I was till I found out half the population of North Carolina arrived before I did."

"You mean Flossie and Winnie? They were so excited about surprising you."

"I was surprised all right," I said.

She patted my knee. "I know how you like your peace and quiet. Don't worry. Space will free up when Xander and I leave to spend Thanksgiving with his family."

Sitting up, I faced her. "You are? Xander and his father have reconciled?"

"Yes, as soon as he was convinced Xander would graduate from college. The whole family's going to be home. Yolanda and her husband, Zane and his girlfriend."

"Zane has a girlfriend?"

"Since August," she said.

My life had intersected with the Plumleys when Xander and I became friends in college. When I discovered Xander was the eldest of triplets and his father was an author and lecturer, I concluded they were above commonplace people—an opinion I changed soon after one phone conversation with Dr. Plumley. Xander had experienced a personal crisis and abandoned college to backpack across Europe. Though Dr. Plumley refused to search, Yolanda and Zane were unwilling to give up. After they received a postcard from Xander, asking them to contact me, Zane arrived at my house to ask for my help.

When Xander found his way home from Australia, he came looking for me and ended up at the Magnolia Arms, where he met Posey and fell in love.

Xander joined us in the parlor and sat next to Posey. "Who's that man in the kitchen?"

"Dr. Morton Penrose," I said. "Famous piano teacher."

"First time Oliver has smiled since he's been here," Xander said.

"Wait till *Lorna Maron* gets here tomorrow," I said, sneering. "He'll be beaming."

"Whoa," Xander said. "What brought that on?"

"You don't like Lorna?" Posey asked. "Ivy Leigh said she was your friend."

"She was … till I found a letter from Sefton in her mailbox at school."

"You mean *before* he broke up with you?" Xander asked.

"No, afterward, and how did you know he broke up with me?" I asked.

"Nestor told us the whole story," Posey said. "He's been worried about you."

"I felt better about losing Sefton till I saw that letter. He had agreed to meet me before he left town, but he stood me up. When I saw that letter, I knew the reason."

"Which was?" Xander asked.

"He *must* have met Lorna instead of me. What other explanation can there be?"

"Have you *asked* her if they met?" Xander asked.

"No. I've been avoiding her."

"You'll *have* to talk to her once she gets here," Posey said. "The house isn't that big."

"There may be a logical explanation," Xander said. "You should find out. You don't want that weighing on your mind … not with all the plans we've made for the weekend."

"And what does it matter, anyway?" Posey asked. "Sefton's not your boyfriend anymore. He can date who he wants. By the way, did you bring a nice dress with you?"

"By the way?" I asked. "What does a nice dress have to do with Sefton?"

Xander nudged Posey. "Ivy Leigh wants to go to church on Sunday morning."

I still didn't understand how we had transitioned from Lorna's treachery to church attendance, but Posey had never been the most straightforward thinker.

"Yes, I brought a dress," I said. "Same one I wore to the dinner party— the one I should've never invited Lorna to."

"That's a relief," Posey said. "I should've told you to bring a dress, but I forgot."

Why Posey should feel responsible for my wardrobe I had no idea, but the subject remained unexplored when Oliver opened the parlor door.

"Would you mind talking somewhere else?" he asked. "Dr. Penrose and I need to use the piano."

The three of us, accustomed to Oliver's demands, stood and walked to the door.

"Help yourself," I said, as we left.

We closed the door. Oliver began to play.

For the next five days someone would be at the piano almost continuously.

Including me.

I walked with Posey to her room on the second floor.

"Have you and Xander thought about what you'll do after you get married?" I asked.

"Haven't decided yet. A lot will depend on what happens this weekend. What I mean is … we're thinking of moving closer to the Plumleys. Depends on where Xander can get a job."

"I can't imagine your not being here when I come to visit," I said.

She hugged me. "You'll find someone else to help with the cooking. It won't be hard."

"What?"

"I've said too much," she said. "I need to finish packing. See you at dinner."

She disappeared inside her room.

Returning to my room, I unpacked and put away my clothes. Then I pulled my manuscript from my book bag, sat cross-legged on the bed, and spread out the formidable pile of unfinished work. In this same room I had hoped to finish my first book *Trevorode the Defender*. But when the *Dennisonville Chronicle* promised a cash prize for the best science fiction story, I reduced eleven carefully crafted chapters to a simple seven-page narrative in one night's work. Though my contest winnings paid for plumbing repairs, I had never fully reconciled myself to leaving my original story uncompleted.

Three months ago, I had left this room and returned to my job, determined to be a good teacher and to prepare myself to become a good wife. I had ended up with two roommates instead of one and two new teachers in my school, who had complicated my life beyond measure. For weeks I had looked forward to returning to the Magnolia Arms, knowing once I arrived, I would have time to write. And when the day at last had come, I found my beautiful house occupied by the same people who had interrupted my progress for weeks.

As bewildered as Michelangelo, contemplating the half-finished Sistine Chapel ceiling, I lay back and considered the possibility Julia Bridger might suffer the same fate as Trevorode.

After all, Sefton had been a dream too good to be true; maybe the book was, too.

Sitting up, I scraped the papers together with grim resignation.

The corner of an envelope jutted out from the stack.

I pulled out Julia's letter to Bentley, unfolded the page and read:

Your father and Jameson had an awful row and Jameson has been banned from visiting me. Since I am in the hospital at present, I have no way to contact him. In fact, I do not even know where he is. Your father refuses to talk to me about him, and I need not tell you your sister Olympia cares little for me or my son. I fear I may not leave the hospital. This is why I am appealing to you. I have no one to turn to but you. I pray you will take my request to heart.

"I have no one to turn to but you."

In that moment I felt as if Julia had written this letter to me—a conviction so poignant I held my breath.

Fond as I was of Trevorode, he was a fictional character. Julia Bridger was not. She had held this paper in her hands. Her pen had formed these words; her heart had framed this request. Afraid of her husband Leo, she had appealed to Bentley, who, by his own admission, had made her life miserable. She never knew the memory of her love had sustained Bentley through his years in prison. She never knew the confidence she placed in him had yielded the result she hoped for. He had remembered and had committed this letter—her sacred trust—to me.

I could not fail Bentley, whose only hope of repaying Julia for her kindness was to give her legacy a wide audience.

There was a knock at my door.

"Agnes," Xander said. "Chester wants to know if you'd like to take a walk with him."

"Yes. Tell him I'll be right down."

I put on my shoes, grabbed my jacket, and hurried downstairs. Maybe a walk would clear my head and help me think.

Chester, waiting by the front door, turned when he heard me.

"I'm glad you want to go. It will be like the old days, when we walked to the science building after lunch. Remember?"

I nodded. "It's hard to forget the building where I failed so many tests."

"Wait till I go to the kitchen," he said. "Winnie insisted I take a Thermos of Russian tea."

Russian tea—the reminder put me back on the train with Winnie, toting Mary Smith on her quest to find Darla. Regretting my lukewarm greeting to her, I said, "Let me get it."

I started down the hall and spotted Winnie, her head pressed against the closed French doors of the parlor. Oliver was playing the Grieg piano concerto he had performed at the talent show last year.

When I touched her shoulder, she gasped, bringing her hand to her heart.

"Agnes," she said. "You startled me. I was quite in another world. Listen … I haven't heard anything like this since the night of the party when Lorna played."

"Oliver's very gifted," I said.

As if in a cathedral, she whispered. "I wish my Darlinda could've married someone like him. Can you imagine if Oliver had been my son-in-law instead of Warner?"

"That would have been an improvement," I said, "but Oliver spends a lot of time touring. You probably wouldn't have seen him much, even if he had married Darla."

The idea was absurd, but seemed to bring Winnie comfort, so I played along.

"Do you think Morton travels a lot?" she asked.

"I wouldn't think so. He's a teacher. Probably stays close to home except when searching for Lorna."

She beamed. "I can't wait for their reunion tomorrow. She doesn't know he's here."

"I'm sure everyone will be happy to see her," I said. "Chester said you made some tea for him to take on his walk?"

Winnie came back to earth. "Chester. I wouldn't have minded if Darlinda had married *him*."

I followed Winnie into the kitchen where Flossie was chopping celery.

"Agnes," Flossie said. "Everything unpacked?"

"Yes. I'm going to take a walk with Chester."

Flossie scraped the celery off the cutting board into a mixing bowl. "*We* need to find time to catch up, too. This Bentley fellow …"

I put my arm around her shoulder. "We'll talk after dinner tonight."

Chester and I, Mendel prancing between us, stepped off the porch and onto the leaf-covered sidewalk of Belmont Drive. Latticed clouds glistened against a cobalt blue sky. The autumn air was cool and invigorating. I slowed to keep pace with Chester, who walked more leisurely than I remembered. Whether he was still recovering from his illness or had vowed to slow down and savor life I did not ask. Chester, a shy, brainy physicist, had always marched to the beat of his own drummer and forged his own path. It was one of the things I liked best about him.

"I'm glad you're here, Agnes," he said. "It gives me a chance to thank you."

"Thank me for what?"

"If it hadn't been for you, I would've never come to the Magnolia Arms."

"I guess that's true. I never thought about it."

"Xander and I talk about it all the time ... how the day you met Jameson Bridger he offered Xander a job, and Xander left after that. It was the butterfly effect."

"A sad day," I said, hoping to deflect him from pondering the space-time continuum.

"And if Xander hadn't left, he wouldn't have ended up here, and he wouldn't have invited me and *this* is where I've been getting well. It couldn't have happened anyplace else."

"It's an extraordinary house," I said.

He stopped and faced me. "It's not the house, Agnes. It's the people."

"You're right," I said, certain Julia would've said the same about Briarwood Manor.

Staring ahead, Chester resumed his pace. "You know ... Nestor's been a major factor in my recovery. He prodded me when I wanted to sleep all day or take shortcuts on my exercise."

"He told me you guys joined the gym to help Xander look good for his wedding."

"Yeah. The wedding ... I guess it was best things didn't work out between you and Xander. But you learned from the experience. You did learn something, right?"

Since I had relived the incident many times, I had no trouble quoting what Xander said on that unforgettable day when he told me he loved me and I was floored.

"Yes. I'd been 'looking love in the face for two years and hadn't recognized it,'" I said.

Chester nodded. "I'm glad you remember. Once more around the block?"

When we returned, we found Flossie and Winnie on the porch swing. Winnie held her finger to her lips so we wouldn't wake Flossie, whose hands rested on the pile of blue yarn in her lap. Morton and Oliver were still sequestered in the parlor. Chopin, I thought, as we passed by. Posey and Xander were helping Ivy Leigh in the kitchen.

"Nestor's not back yet?" I asked.

"No," Ivy Leigh said, searching the pantry. "There's a lot to do before Friday."

"Friday? You mean Thursday, don't you? Thanksgiving?"

She closed the pantry door. "Yes … but the dining room has been reserved for a private party on Friday, and he … they … have a lot of specific requests."

I snatched a pumpkin cookie from the cooling rack on the counter.

"That's new, isn't it? Letting private parties reserve the dining room?" I asked.

"Yes, but it's a special occasion for an old friend, so I agreed."

"Anyone I know?" I asked.

"You don't know that many people in Dennisonville," she said.

"True," I said, puzzled at her curt response.

"But that's three days away," she said, "and we need to concentrate on tonight's menu. Why don't you go upstairs and rest? We'll need your help serving—expecting a full house."

After a quiet afternoon, I donned my uniform, a black skirt and white blouse, and went down to the kitchen for my apron. Unseen, I stood in the doorway, watching my friends, marveling at their ability to anticipate each other's movements as they worked in unison. The kitchen was a delectable fusion of smells. It took only one sniff to recognize the scent of Ivy Leigh's secret seasoning on the standing rib roast. Potatoes, soon to be mashed and drizzled with butter, boiled on the stove. Ivy Leigh's carrot cakes lined the counter. Coffee brewed; apple cider simmered.

A stranger watching would have found it hard to believe the Magnolia Arms restaurant had been open for business only a year. Begun as an effort to raise money to pay delinquent property taxes, the restaurant, in Ivy Leigh's hands, had prospered. Dining there was now by "reservation only." Unseen, I slipped away to peek into the dining room. The original chairs, purchased from estate sales or thrift stores, had been replaced by matching chairs—sleek, black, and elegant. The raspberry pink walls and wide white enamel molding shimmered from the flickering of pillar candles on the tables.

"Better than you remember?" a voice said.

Turning around, I saw Nestor, also outfitted in his server uniform. I approached him and straightened his black bow tie.

"Elegant," I said.

"Me or the dining room?"

"Both," I said, and we laughed.

He took my hand. "Come on. Door opens in fifteen minutes."

Ivy Leigh, gorgeous in royal blue, seated the guests with her usual style. Nestor and Xander, academics of the first order, handled their trays like seasoned servers, charming the diners with witty conversation and sincere compliments. Posey, once mousy and insecure, glided through the room like a countess. Since Ivy Leigh drafted me to serve every time I visited, I hoisted my tray and kept pace with the best of them. Other than Oliver and Morton, speaking in low tones about mystical musical matters at Oliver's usual table, the rest of the crowd were locals from Dennisonville and neighboring towns.

Chester remained in the kitchen keeping an eye on Flossie and Winnie, who had been honored by Ivy Leigh's request for help.

For the first time since I had arrived, I felt like I was home, back in the surroundings I loved, where life made sense and moved at the pace I liked— until Chester appeared, panicked, and motioned for me to follow him. I handed my water pitcher to Posey and hurried down the hall. I found Chester in the kitchen, kneeling over Flossie, who was lying on the floor, whimpering. Winnie was mopping up water with a dishtowel. Steam rose from puddles on the floor.

"What happened?" I asked, though I knew at once.

"Flossie tried to pick up that pot of boiling water. It slipped. She tried to keep it from falling …" Winnie said, her voice trembling.

"Help me, Agnes," Chester said. "We need to get some cold water on these burns."

We helped Flossie into a chair. I rushed to the dining room and whispered to Ivy Leigh. She found Nestor, spoke to him, and then followed me, closing the dining room door behind us.

"We'll take her to my bathroom," Ivy Leigh said, "and put her in the tub."

Chester and I helped Flossie up and supported her as we slipped past the dining room. Ivy Leigh rushed ahead of us and began filling the tub with cool water.

"Get Winnie," Ivy Leigh said. "She can help me get Flossie into the tub. You two get back to the kitchen and clean up the mess."

The guests never knew about the disaster.

After dinner we cleaned up and gathered at the kitchen table, waiting for Ivy Leigh to bring word about Flossie.

"It's my fault," Chester said. "I should've paid attention to what Flossie was doing."

"Flossie doesn't let anyone tell her what to do," I said. "Don't blame yourself."

Ivy Leigh returned to the kitchen. "Her right leg got the worst of it. She refuses to let me call the doctor tonight, so we'll let her rest and decide what to do tomorrow."

"How's Winnie?" I asked.

"Rising to the occasion. She insists on staying with Flossie. Dr. Penrose, I was going to let you have my room tonight, but now—"

Nestor spoke up. "He can have my room. I'll move into the basement with Chester and Xander."

"Thank you," Ivy Leigh said. "And now I'd like to suggest we all go to our rooms and get some sleep. There's a lot to do tomorrow to get ready for Thanksgiving."

Exhausted, I slept well till dawn. When I opened my eyes, I was comforted to realize I was in my room at the Magnolia Arms. I took a shower, dressed, and headed downstairs. Instead of going to the kitchen where Ivy Leigh was already at work, I tapped on the door of her room and slipped in. Winnie, her head drooped on her shoulder, was sound asleep in a chair. Flossie whispered my name when she saw me and patted the side of the bed. Careful not to jostle her leg, I eased down and took her hand.

"Did you sleep at all?" I asked.

She pointed to her foot elevated on a turquoise pillow. "Better than you might think. "Winnie kept cold compresses on my leg half the night. Then Ivy Leigh came in and took over."

"I should have taken a shift," I said.

"No. You had a long trip yesterday."

"Can I get you anything?"

"Ivy Leigh is fixing my breakfast. You could help her. When does Lorna arrive?"

I started toward the door. Lorna's arrival was the last thing I wanted to talk about.

"Don't know," I said. "Be right back."

By the time I returned with the tray, Winnie had awakened and was standing at the foot of her patient's bed. When I placed the tray in front of Flossie, she attended her breakfast with her usual gusto.

I turned to Winnie. "Ivy Leigh wants you to eat, too. I'll stay here till you come back."

Glancing in the mirror, Winnie straightened her collar and left the room.

Flossie, a forkful of scrambled eggs in her right hand and a slice of bacon in her left, said, "Now, tell me about Bentley."

The story was a good distraction for both of us.

"So," she said, laying her napkin on her plate, "Ryder has his son back. We must tell Winnie. It will give her hope."

Ivy Leigh knocked on the door. "Let's check on your foot to see if I need to call the doctor. Agnes, will you take this tray to the kitchen?"

As I stepped into the hall, the doorbell rang. I set the tray on the table in the foyer and opened the door. Lorna Maron had arrived.

Even after being on a train all night, she was radiant. Smiling, she hugged me.

"I haven't seen you in a long time," she said. "Where have you been hiding?"

"Had a lot to do to get ready to leave school," I said. "Come in. Everyone is—"

Morton Penrose, in red plaid pajamas, brown paisley robe, and leather bedroom slippers, came puttering toward us. He smoothed his thin hair with one hand as he struggled to put on his glasses with the other.

"Lorna? Is it really you?" he asked.

She held out her hand. "Dr. Penrose. What are you doing here?"

"Looking for you," I said.

Morton pulled a hankie from his pocket and blew his nose.

Ivy Leigh came from Flossie's room the same time Winnie wandered from the kitchen.

Both women embraced Lorna and escorted her to breakfast. I followed with the tray and headed to the sink to wash dishes so I could avoid all the adoration heaped on our new guest. Ivy Leigh introduced Posey to Lorna, and everyone gathered around the table.

Nestor and Xander came up from the basement.

"Someone should wake up Oliver," Nestor said. "He's missing all the fun."

"I'll get him," I said, grateful for a good excuse to leave the group.

Climbing the stairs to Monty's room, I knocked on Oliver's door.

"Who is it?" he asked, sounding like Papa Bear addressing Goldilocks.

"Agnes."

"Have you forgotten I sleep till 8:15?"

"No. I just thought you might like to come down and meet Lorna Maron."

I heard him lumber to the door. He threw it open. "She's here?"

"Yes," I said, blinking at his untamed hair and wide eyes.

"Tell her … tell them … I'll be down in 45 minutes. She's not going anywhere, is she?"

I raised my eyebrows. "I heard Ivy Leigh mention something about the grocery store."

He slammed the door. I congratulated myself on my quick thinking.

Standing there, I contemplated my next move. I could go *upstairs*, make my bed, write letters, create any number of plausible explanations for being absent from the assembled guests. But Ivy Leigh would see through any excuse. No. I had to go back and at least *act* like I was glad to see Lorna. By the time I rejoined the group, Chester had come from his room and Morton had donned brown corduroy pants and a gray and blue argyle sweater. Winnie was refilling Lorna's cup. Xander and Posey sat across from her. Nestor, watching, leaned against the sink.

Winnie held up the teapot. "Tea, Agnes?"

"No, thanks," I said. "I need coffee and lots of it."

I took my favorite mug from the cabinet, filled it, and stood next to Nestor.

"Heartwarming, isn't it?" he asked. "Look at Morton. He's in heaven."

"Why aren't you over there with the rest of them?" I asked.

"I want a good view of Oliver's face when he walks in. I've never seen him off-balance."

"Lorna has that effect on people," I said. "Kinda makes me—"

"Could I have your attention, please?" Ivy Leigh said. "I'd like to talk about the schedule for today."

Silenced, everyone turned to face her. She lifted a steno pad from the counter and flipped through the pages.

"I'm speaking to my staff, of course, as I go over most of these items. But one matter does involve Lorna and Dr. Penrose—"

"Morton … please," Dr. Penrose said.

Ivy Leigh nodded. "One matter concerns Lorna and Morton. Last year's Thanksgiving dinner went so well we haven't made many changes. However, I want all of us to—"

When we heard footsteps on the stairs, we couldn't help turning our attention to the door. Even Ivy Leigh stopped talking to watch Dr. Oliver Martin Farrell, in dark blue pants and a pale yellow shirt, ease around the door frame like a child trying to catch Santa Claus filling his stocking.

Shocked by our silence, he paused, his hand resting on the doorframe. He scanned the people at the table. When his eye fell on Lorna, his face reddened, and he drew in his breath. Posey couldn't help snickering. When Xander poked her, she clamped her fingers over her lips.

Nestor cleared his throat, set his coffee mug on the counter, and sauntered to Oliver.

"Oliver, allow me to introduce Lorna Maron," Nestor said. "She arrived this morning."

Lorna stood and approached Oliver, who seemed unable to move.

She held out her hand. "Dr. Farrell. I've been an admirer of yours for a long time."

He took her hand in both of his. "Lorna," he said, almost singing. "I … I …"

Xander stood and pulled out a chair. "Sit here, Oliver."

Oliver sat. Posey slid a glass of orange juice toward him. He sipped.

"As I was saying," Ivy Leigh said, "we have a variable in our routine this year. I don't want Flossie left alone today, so I've made a schedule."

Along with the preparations for Thanksgiving dinner, Ivy Leigh had coordinated shifts for each of us to sit with Flossie. No one objected.

"We'll have a light supper tonight: quiche and fresh fruit. And then Nestor and Xander will help Flossie into the parlor for a brief concert. You wouldn't object, would you, Lorna?"

"Of course not," Lorna said. "I'll be happy to play for her."

"Does she enjoy Liszt?" Morton asked.

"I'll play, too," Oliver said.

We all turned to stare at him. At the talent show the year before, I had resorted to bribery to persuade him to play.

"I'll sing," Posey said. "Flossie loves the song I sang at Margaret's wedding."

"Well, then, it's all settled," Ivy Leigh said. "We'll start in the—"

The phone rang. Nestor answered it and held out the receiver to me. "Margaret."

"Use the phone in my office," Ivy Leigh said.

I hurried down the hall, closed the office door behind me, and sat at the desk.

"Hello," I said.

"Hello, Agnes," Margaret said. "How is everyone?"

"Everyone's fine except for Flossie," I said. "Wait. You don't know she's here—"

"I knew she was coming," Margaret said.

"Of course, you did. I should've known you'd be in on it."

"What happened?"

I described Flossie's accident.

"Give her my love," Margaret said. She paused. "I suppose you know why I'm calling."

"Bentley told you who Kennesaw Fleming is."

"Yesterday afternoon," she said. "Jonas and I talked half the night. We decided it would be wrong to keep the truth from Ryder. He's suffered so many years."

"I agree."

"We met him and Elinor for breakfast this morning at the Drifters' Rest. Then Ryder went straight to Brighton Park to find Kennesaw … uh … his son."

"Ryder's there now?"

"Don't worry. Jonas went with him."

I leaned my head on my hand. "How's Elinor?"

"Confused. Happy. Worried. Waiting in her office for Ryder."

"I had theories about Kennesaw," I said, "but not this. I don't know what to think."

"*You* don't know what to think? What about *Grace*? She and Kennesaw were supposed to leave this afternoon to spend Thanksgiving with her parents."

"Ivy Leigh thinks Grace will *know* she was used," I said. "Will you call back later after you find out how the reunion went?"

"Of course. Is Lorna there yet?"

"Yes. Already making new conquests."

"What do you mean?"

"Oliver is bedazzled," I said.

"*That* I would like to see."

By the time I left the office, the house was bustling. Chester was dusting everything in sight. Xander and Nestor were moving the round tables to the sides of the dining room so we could set up the long family style table for Thanksgiving. As I passed the parlor, I heard Lorna playing "Widmung"—a warm-up perhaps for more demanding pieces. The melody made me think of Ham. I reprimanded myself for not practicing Liebestraum and vowed to ask

Lorna … or Morton … for help. I would be foolish not to take advantage of their expertise while we were here together.

Later that morning a doctor arrived to examine Flossie's burns. Ivy Leigh and I waited in the hall.

"I didn't know there was a doctor anywhere who would still make house calls," I said.

"I'm waiving the reservation fee for his 25th wedding anniversary party in June," she said. "And promised him the evening and the menu of his choice."

After the doctor commended us for our quick thinking and continued care of Flossie, he ate breakfast in the kitchen and told us there was nothing he would do which we were not already doing. He told us to keep up the good work and call if there were any change.

The remainder of the day passed quietly. We followed Ivy Leigh's schedule to the letter, helping with the cooking or decorating and taking turns sitting with Flossie, who played chess with Nestor, checkers with Xander, and gin rummy with Ivy Leigh. After lunch and a nap, Flossie asked for her knitting. I pulled a chair next to the bed and read aloud "The Mysterious Affair at Styles." Engrossed in the story, I had not noticed Flossie was sniffling. When I looked up, I saw her wipe her eyes with the hem of the sheet.

"Poirot solves the case, Flossie. No one gets away with murder when he's involved."

"It's not that," she said. "I was thinking of little Maggie or Fletcher."

I handed her a Kleenex from the box on the nightstand. "Who?"

"Maggie or Fletcher. The names we chose for Darla's baby. Magnolia, if it's a girl, and Fletcher … after Warner's father, if it's a boy."

"Your grandchild," I said. "Is that who the blanket's for?" I pointed to her knitting.

"Yes, the pink one with rosettes at the corner is at home."

"But why are you crying? I thought you and Winnie were happy about taking the baby."

"Because of that," she said, pointing to her injured foot. "What if I had slipped and spilled a pot of boiling water where Maggie or Fletcher were playing on *our* kitchen floor?"

"In the first place," I said, closing the book, "your kitchen doesn't have restaurant size pots and pans. You won't be lifting heavy pots in your own home."

She sniffed. "I guess not."

"And in the second place, the baby wouldn't be playing on the floor while you were cooking. You'd have him … or her … in a high chair."

"We already bought one," she said.

"And in the third place, you'll get used to making accommodations for a baby. The same way you adjusted to being a mom, you'll adjust to being a grandma."

"I'll have better sense this time," she said, "than I did with Warner."

"And you'll have Winnie to help."

"I hope so," she said.

"What do you mean? Of course you will."

Flossie recommenced her knitting. "She's quite smitten with that piano player."

"Oliver?" I asked.

"No, silly, the other one. Mort."

After dinner Xander and Nestor helped Flossie into a straight back chair and with great ceremony transported her down the hall.

"I feel like a pharaoh's daughter," she said, giggling.

We congregated in the parlor where Ivy Leigh had arranged autumn desserts on a table by the wall. After we helped ourselves to pumpkin bread, pear-apple pie, or maple cheesecake, we settled down to await the virtuosos. Flossie and Winnie nestled into the wingback chairs. With Ivy Leigh between us, Posey and I took the sofa. Xander put a chair next to Posey. Nestor sat on a chair next to me. Chester eased down onto a throw pillow on the floor between Ivy Leigh and me and leaned against the sofa. Chairs for the performers were situated near the piano.

The parlor doors swung open. The musicians entered. Chester shouted "Bravo" as the rest of us applauded. Lorna announced a Chopin Polonaise and began. As the music enveloped us, I scanned the room, taking pleasure in the joy of my friends. Ivy Leigh squeezed my hand. Xander slipped his arm around Posey to draw her closer into the sublime moment they were sharing. Chester leaned forward, resting his elbows on his knees. Winnie and Flossie were riveted to Lorna, looking away only to glance at each other and smile. Nestor nudged my elbow. When I turned to him, he winked.

"Better than the night at Charlotte's house," he said.

"You mean the music?" I asked.

"That, too," he said. "Look at Oliver."

Oliver wore the dazed expression of a sailor who, after months of starving at sea, had been cast ashore into a tropical paradise.

Lorna and the night and the music.

Morton followed with Mozart's Turkish March, Oliver with Rachmaninoff's Prelude in G, Lorna with Brahms' Intermezzo in C-Sharp Minor. Lorna took a bow and returned to the piano, dumbfounding us when she played "Chopsticks." After a few measures Morton bounded up, demanded that she stop, and then took her place to play the piece correctly. Lorna, feigning confusion, sat next to him, and joined him with dazzling accompaniment. The performance was staged, of course, and achieved the intended effect. After our standing ovation, Lorna and Oliver concluded with a heart-stopping duet of "Stars and Stripes Forever."

After more applause, Morton escorted Posey to the piano. While he played "The Anniversary Waltz," Posey sang in her frail soprano voice. One by one the audience stood. Bowing to Winnie, Xander offered his hand. He did not resist when she laid her head on his shoulder. Ivy Leigh tapped Chester on the arm. While he insisted he could not dance, she placed his left hand on her waist and took his right hand in hers, leading him across the floor with grace and ease. Hesitating, Oliver approached Lorna. With proper form and several inches between them, they danced divinely.

Besides Flossie, Nestor and I were the only ones still seated.

"Shall we dance?" Nestor asked. "Chester took my usual partner."

"Never thought I'd see the day Ivy Leigh would throw you over for another man," I said.

We stood. Morton played another verse. Posey sang. Nestor drew me close to him.

"You're awfully quiet," he said. "What are you thinking?"

"Sefton never asked me to dance."

"Didn't know what he was missing," Nestor said.

After Ivy Leigh thanked our musicians for a perfect evening, Xander and Nestor carried Flossie back to her room with Winnie trailing behind. Chester began putting the parlor back in order. Lorna, Morton, and Oliver retreated to the sofa to critique each other's performances perhaps. Posey and I ferried the food and dishes to the kitchen. Once the dessert table was cleared, I asked Ivy Leigh if she needed anything else.

"Help me move my things to Margaret's room?" she asked.

I followed her to her own room and waited till she gathered what she needed. She handed me her clothes, and we walked up the stairs together. While she hung her clothes in the closet, I moved Flossie's and Winnie's things off the bed.

"At least you'll have a spot to lie down," I said. "Sweet dreams."

She sat on the bed. "I'm proud of you for helping Flossie today. I know you didn't expect to have to tend to them while you were here, but you've been patient with both of them."

"I keep hoping I'll grow up to be like you and Margaret someday."

When we heard Lorna and Posey coming up the stairs, we met them in the hall to say good night. Ivy Leigh returned downstairs. Posey showed Lorna the way to her room.

As I started to the third floor, Lorna called my name and with a stack of music still in her arms, walked toward me.

"This night was even better than our dinner party, wasn't it?" she asked.

"You made Flossie very happy," I said. "*Everyone*, for that matter. I'm surprised Oliver was able to perform."

"What do you mean?"

"Come on, Lorna. Oliver can't take his eyes off you."

"Really?"

"Don't act like you didn't notice," I said. "You must be used to it by now."

"You mean Nolan?" she asked. "You know how that ended up."

"And Sefton," I said.

"Sefton?"

"Yes, Sefton. If he's going to keep writing to you, you should give him your home address."

"*Keep* writing?" she asked.

"I saw the letter in your mailbox at school. I know Sefton's handwriting when I see it."

She flipped through the pages of her music and produced an envelope.

"You mean this letter?"

I couldn't believe she had the nerve to bring it with her, much less wave it in my face.

"Yes," I said. "That letter."

"I've been keeping it for you," she said. "I know what it is to waste tears on a man who doesn't deserve them. I thought if you weren't over Sefton yet, this would help."

"You lost me."

"Hours after he broke up with you, he wrote to say how much he enjoyed meeting me and asked if I were interested in—"

Starting up the stairs, I said, "I'm not up to this tonight."

She grabbed my arm. "It's not important what *he* said. You only need to know he doesn't deserve you. I told him so when I answered him and told him not to contact me again."

"You didn't have breakfast with him before he left town?"

"Breakfast?"

"He was supposed to meet me, but he didn't show up. When I saw the letter … I put two and two together."

"No, I didn't meet him. I'd never do that to you. I promise you I haven't seen Sefton since the night of the party, and I never will. I don't need *another* man like Nolan in my life."

"Sefton is like Nolan?" I asked.

"You're lucky to be rid of him," she said. "I brought your music for the festival. Want to practice tomorrow after dinner?"

"I'd like that," I said. "I'm sorry, Lorna. I—"

She held up her hand. "Don't give it another thought. Loving the wrong man makes the best of us irrational. Good night."

Safe in my room, I sank onto my bed. Forty-eight hours had passed since my arrival, and still the visit I had dreamed of was out of reach. Maybe—now that all the surprises were behind us—we could settle in and relax, make the most of the next three days. The house was full; we had no room for another guest. I reviewed: Flossie and Winnie were in Ivy Leigh's room, Morton in Nestor's room, Oliver in Monty's room. Ivy Leigh had moved to Margaret's room, Lorna was in Posey's room. Every room was accounted for. Satisfied, I slept.

On Thanksgiving morning I woke to the sound of Nestor's truck. I looked out my window and watched as he drove away, taking Xander and Posey to the train station. I slipped downstairs early to have breakfast before anyone else woke up. When I came into the kitchen, Ivy Leigh, sitting alone at the table, looked up from her crossword puzzle.

"You're up early," she said. "Worried you wouldn't get a muffin?"

"Actually," I said, "I thought I'd take my coffee upstairs and try to work awhile."

The doorbell rang.

Ivy Leigh laid her pencil on the table. "Must be Ida Willingale. She never remembers to buy sage for her dressing."

"Stay there," I said. "I'll get the door. Want me to bring her in here?"

She stepped to the pantry. "No. She'll wake the whole house. Tell her I'll be right there."

Before I could walk down the hall, the doorbell rang again. Quickening my pace, I called out as I reached for the door and opened it.

"Just a minute. Ivy Leigh will … . What are *you* doing here?"

"You were right about Kennesaw," Grace Bonner said. "I shouldn't have trusted him."

Chapter 12

Holiday Inn

If Ida Willingale, the neighbor two houses down, had not marched up the porch steps, peered around Grace Bonner, and said, "I need to speak to Ivy Leigh, please," I might have stood there dumbfounded till the sun came up.

Blinking my eyes, I leaned to the left, peeking at Ida. "Be right back," I said.

"Couldn't I come in?" Grace Bonner asked. "It's cold."

"No, not you," I said, taking her arm. "Come in, but be quiet."

"I beg your pardon," Ida said briskly. Despite the early hour, she had already brushed and slicked back her thin gray hair into a tight bun.

"Not you," I said. "I'll be right back with the sage."

"And what makes you think I came for sage?" Ida asked, insulted.

"Ivy Leigh is getting it," I said.

"Ivy Leigh?" Grace asked.

"The only person who can straighten out this mess," I said.

"Mess?" Ida asked. "Well, I never. That's a fine way to speak to your neighbor."

"Not you," I said.

If Ivy Leigh, sage in hand, had not appeared behind me, Ida might have stormed away, never to ask for sage or anything else again.

"Hello, Ida," Ivy Leigh said, holding out the sage. "How's the turkey coming?"

Neutralized, Ida side-stepped Grace and took the sage. "Should be ready by 1:00."

"Have you heard from Bernard?" Ivy Leigh asked, giving the name the British pronunciation, Burr-nerd, careful not to insult Ida further.

"Got in last night," Ida said. "Sleeping like a baby in his old room."

"Save me a piece of mincemeat pie," Ivy Leigh said. "I had no time to make one."

A brilliant diplomatic stroke. Ivy Leigh *hated* mincemeat.

With a final scowl at me, Ida stepped off the porch.

Ivy Leigh held out her hand to Grace. "I'm Ivy Leigh Ransom. You must be Grace."

"Grace Bonner," the newcomer said.

"Welcome to the Magnolia Arms. Leave your suitcase here and come to the kitchen. You must be hungry."

Baffled, I stood in the foyer and watched Grace and Ivy Leigh stroll down the hall.

My journey into the world of Julia Bridger had been waylaid ... again.

Winnie, bleary-eyed, peeked out Ivy Leigh's bedroom door.

"Is something wrong? Who's here?" she asked.

"Grace Bonner, the assistant librarian ... believe it or not."

"The one who's in love with Kennesaw What's-his-name?"

"You've never met even met her," I said. "How did you know that?"

"Everyone knows that," she said, closing the door.

Entering the kitchen, I saw Morton Penrose, bathrobe-clad, sitting next to Grace.

"There, there," he said, patting her hand. "You mustn't take on so. You're safe now."

"Safe?" I asked. "Did Kennesaw hurt you?"

Grace turned on me with the ferocity of a Chihuahua guarding a bone.

"Hurt me? Hurt me? The first time in my life I was taking a man home to meet my family, and he cancelled our trip at the last minute and made me look like a fool? Yes, he *hurt* me."

Ivy Leigh set a bowl of oatmeal in front of Grace. "I'm sorry, Grace. Eat your breakfast and tell us all about it."

"Don't we need to get the turkey in the oven?" I asked, rolling my eyes.

Ivy Leigh shot me a warning glance. "It's been in the oven for 45 minutes. *Oatmeal?*"

This, I knew, was her way of telling me to 'straighten up and sit down.'

"Toast," I said.

She nodded at an empty chair. I sat.

"Sleep well?" Morton asked.

"Dandy," I said.

"Good. Oliver and I worked out a schedule, so we can all take turns at the piano today. We'll get started on your festival piece. Lorna said you also need some help with Liebestraum."

Ivy Leigh set the toast in front of me. "Jam?" she asked.

Already in one, I thought.

Grace propped her elbows on the table and cried into her oatmeal.

"It wasn't supposed to be this way," she said. "I was supposed to be eating breakfast in my own house this morning. My grandparents were coming to meet Kennesaw. My cousins ..."

"So why did you come *here*?" I asked.

"Ma ... Margaret told me to come," Grace said, sobbing.

Ivy Leigh filled Grace's teacup. "Why don't you start at the beginning? We've been wondering how everyone is. *Haven't we, Agnes?*"

"Always best to start at the beginning," Morton said. "Who's Kennesaw?"

Grace put down her spoon. "A new teacher at our school. I fell for him the moment I saw him. I was so happy when he showed an interest in me. But I should've listened to Agnes."

"Agnes?" Morton asked, tucking a napkin under his chin.

"She saw through him from the beginning," Grace said.

Was this her feeble attempt at an apology?

"Agnes is a keen judge of character," Morton said. "She pegged Dr. Maron the minute she met him. You should've heard her sparring with him. Did I tell you that story, Ivy Leigh?"

"Not yet," Ivy Leigh said. "Let Grace tell her story first. How about some eggs?"

"Two, scrambled," he said.

"After a few dates," Grace said, "I was brave enough to invite Kennesaw to my house for Thanksgiving. I'd never brought a man home to meet my parents before and ... and ..."

Again she gave way to weeping.

Chester entered the kitchen. "What's going on? I heard crying. Is someone hurt?"

"Don't say 'hurt,'" I advised.

"Who's this?" he asked.

"Grace Bonner," I said. "A friend from school."

Grace looked up. "You still call me your friend after the way I've treated you?"

"Of course," I said. "We can't be faulted for how we act when we're in love."

Ivy Leigh winked at me. "Coffee, Chester?"

Chester joined us at the table. "Any friend of Agnes is a friend of mine. I'm Chester."

Grace sniffled. "Who?"

"Chester Cranston," I said. "A friend from college. Go on with your story."

Or we'll be here all day, I thought.

Grace blew her nose. "I was thrilled when Kennesaw agreed to spend the holidays with me, even when he said we'd have to start back on Friday morning."

"Who's Kennesaw?" Chester asked, reaching for the sugar bowl.

"Grace's boyfriend," I said.

Grace wailed. "He *was* my boyfriend … or I thought he was. I'm such a foo … foo-ool."

Determined to keep her on track, I asked, "So you were supposed to arrive at your parents' house last night?"

"Uh-huh. I brought my bags to work with me so we could leave after Kennesaw's last class, but I knew something was wrong as soon as I got to the library yesterday. Elinor was *late*."

"Intriguing," Morton said. "I think nothing of it when a musician is late."

"Then Margaret and Jonas came into the library with Ryder and Elinor," Grace said. "We all went into Elinor's office. She asked if I knew where Kennesaw's first class was."

"And Jonas and Ryder left to find him," I said, prodding her along.

Grace laid the soggy napkin on the table. "How did you know?"

"Margaret called yesterday, but that's as far as she got. Go on."

"Elinor was white as a sheet," Grace said. "She kept trying to talk, but couldn't manage to put two words together. Finally, Margaret said they had bad news, and I'd better sit down."

"Good morning," Nestor said, coming through the back door. "Has anyone fed Mendel?"

"I did," Ivy Leigh said. She pointed to the table. "This is Grace Bonner."

Nestor walked over and held out his hand. "Nestor Carlyle. Sorry my hands are cold."

"Cold hands. Warm heart," Morton said.

"Kennesaw's hands were always warm," Grace said. "I should've known."

Nestor turned to me. "Isn't he the guy who was taking pictures of—?"

I shook my head at him. He took the hint. The schoolteacher in me took over.

"Kennesaw Fleming is really John Ellershaw," I said. "Ryder's son. When Ryder came home from Korea injured and disabled, his wife bailed out on him and took the kids with her."

"If she really loved him, she would have stayed," Chester said.

"Ryder hadn't seen his kids since they were small," I said. "He grieved for years."

"I wonder why he never looked for them," Morton said.

"He tried," I said. "He assumed his first wife lied to their kids about him, or they would've tried to contact *him*."

Morton raised his eyebrows. "Maybe she said Ryder left *them*."

"That's what Muriel always thought," I said.

"Muriel?" Morton asked.

"A friend of mine," I said. "For whatever reason, Kennesaw … John … came to Brighton Park to find his father, but he didn't tell anyone who he really was."

Winnie, a pink satin scarf tied around her head, appeared next. "Flossie's awake."

"How is she?" Chester asked.

"Hungry," Winnie said. "Good morning, Morton."

Standing, Morton removed the napkin from under his chin. "Good morning, Winifred."

"Have some tea, Winnie," Ivy Leigh said. "I'll have Flossie's tray ready in a minute. Have you met Grace?"

"No," Winnie said, "but I've heard of her." She tied her bathrobe sash into a bow. "I'm afraid I'm not creating a very good first impression."

"Nonsense," Morton said, reddening. "Morning becomes you."

Desperate to move on, I turned to Grace. "So Margaret told you who Kennesaw was …"

"If I hadn't been sitting down, I would have fainted," she said. "The three of us waited for an hour. At last Jonas, Ryder, and Kennesaw came into the office, but no one said anything."

That would be nice, I thought.

"Agnes told us about Kennesaw," Winnie said. "A thoroughly disagreeable man."

"Jonas asked me to leave with him and Margaret," Grace said. "Kennesaw was going to call his sister so she could talk to Ryder. Elinor told me to take the rest of the day off."

"The reunion must've gone well, if Kennesaw wanted to call his sister," Chester said.

"It went *well*, all right," Grace said. "Elinor called later and said she had a huge favor to ask, and she wouldn't dream of asking if we hadn't been friends so many years."

"They wanted Kennesaw to have Thanksgiving with them," Winnie said, sighing.

"Not only that," Grace said. "Caroline, Ryder's daughter, was so happy to find her father she wanted to cancel her plans and bring *her* family to spend Thanksgiving with him."

Winnie sniffled. "That's marvelous. If my Darlinda did something like that ..."

Morton handed her a napkin.

"Of course, I couldn't say no," Grace said. "It meant too much to Ryder. Elinor felt obligated to ask me to join them, but I *couldn't*. Intrude on a moment that personal?"

Lorna, in jeans and a pale green blouse, entered the kitchen.

"Good morning," she said. "I hope everyone ... Grace ... what are you doing here? I thought you and Kennesaw were going to spend Thanksgiving at—"

"He's at Ryder and Elinor's," I said. "With his sister."

"Sister?" Lorna said. "But what's he doing at—?"

"Later," I said.

Ivy Leigh laid her hand on Grace's shoulder. "I admire you for putting Ryder's happiness above your own."

"We all do," Morton said, nodding and applauding.

"Margaret said the same thing," Grace said. "But I couldn't stay *there*, and I couldn't go *home*. Tell my parents the man I was bringing to meet them was an impostor?"

"Not an impostor exactly," Winnie said. "More like ... an actor."

"So Margaret sent you here," I said.

Grace nodded. "She said it was the perfect place for someone in my circumstances."

"Same thing Xander said when he invited *me* here," Chester said.

Ivy Leigh finished Flossie's tray and handed it to Winnie. Morton stood.

"Let me carry that for you, Winifred," he said.

Giggling, she yielded the tray, and they disappeared down the hall.

"All right if Grace stays in your room, Lorna?" Ivy Leigh asked.

"Of course," Lorna said.

"Where's your bag, Grace?" Chester asked. "I'll take it upstairs."

Grace stood. "By the front door."

"Follow me," Chester said.

He greeted Oliver, as well-dressed as the day before, standing in the hall.

"Hurry back, Chester," Ivy Leigh said. "You'll have to fill in for Xander today."

"Who was that woman?" Oliver asked.

Lorna pulled out the chair next to her. "Sit down. I'll tell you the whole story."

"I'll be in the greenhouse," Nestor said and left through the back door.

I turned to Ivy Leigh. "Need some help?"

She laughed. "I was about to ask you the same thing."

Despite a frenzied beginning, the day settled into a quiet and orderly routine. After a brief visit with Flossie, Morton returned to his room to dress and then joined Lorna and Oliver in the parlor. Winnie requested the parlor door remain open so she could hear the piano while she helped Ivy Leigh in the kitchen. I set up the ironing board in the foyer and ironed tablecloths while Chester ferried the china and silverware from the kitchen. Grateful to be occupied with a task as mundane as ironing, I let my mind wander to Thanksgiving celebrations elsewhere.

My brother and his family were with my parents. Did my mother feel better since she had shared her secret, or was she still thinking of Russ Wilcox today? Had Ryder's daughter arrived? Grace said Ryder's daughter was bringing her family. Was Ryder a grandfather? Had Elinor found time to prepare a meal for four … or more? Where was Bentley on his first Thanksgiving after prison? Sharing a meal with the Hamptons? What about Monty, who last year had said grace over the very tablecloth I was ironing? Were he and Charlotte dining alone at her table which seated twelve?

"Need some help with that?"

Flossie, outfitted in brown polyester pants and sweater appliquéd with pumpkins, had slipped a clean white sock on her burned foot and ventured into the hallway.

"No," I said. "It's a one-woman job, but I think Ivy Leigh needs some help with the beans."

I called for Chester. Flossie slipped one arm around his shoulder and the other around mine. We made our way to the kitchen where she received a hero's welcome. After we eased her into a chair, I lifted her foot onto a throw pillow on another chair.

Ivy Leigh set a bowl of unsnapped beans in Flossie's lap.

Grace, rested and in clean clothes, returned to the kitchen and offered to help.

Dinner was ready by noon.

Nestor conveyed the turkey to the center of the table. Chester escorted Flossie and seated her at the end of the table so she could keep her foot on a chair. Morton followed with sweet potato soufflé, Grace with cornbread dressing, and Lorna with cranberry-orange relish. Oliver surprised us all by offering to carry the green bean casserole. Winnie, wearing the same dress she had worn to Charlotte's dinner party, brought the broccoli salad. I remained with Ivy Leigh in the kitchen, waiting for her lighter-than-air yeast rolls to achieve the perfect shade of golden brown before we presented them.

Once the rolls were in a basket and covered with a cloth, Ivy Leigh and I strolled to the dining room. She paused outside the door.

"Look at what you've done, Agnes," she said.

"Anyone can iron a tablecloth."

"Not *that*. Look at *them*."

On the right side of the table, Grace was absorbed in a story Chester was telling; Winnie, seated between Morton and Flossie, smiled at one friend and then the other. Seated across from Winnie and Morton, Lorna and Oliver stared into each other's eyes. Clearly, they were not discussing Mozart. Nestor, waiting to seat Ivy Leigh, stood by her chair at the head of the table.

"Quite an assortment of people," I said.

Ivy Leigh turned to me. "And if you hadn't taken this 'assortment of people' into your heart, where would they be today?"

"I ... I don't know ... I never ..."

Nestor spotted us.

"Ladies and gentlemen," he said with his usual flair, "the author of our feast."

Everyone except Flossie stood. Ivy Leigh took her place at the head of the table.

Nestor prayed for friends present, friends absent, our feast, and everyone else's.

Grace only sniffed once.

Nowhere could there have been a happier group than ours. Though the couples in the budding stages of romance could not stop gazing at each other, none of them excluded the rest of us from their company. Grace, in particular, appeared to be enjoying a miraculous recovery. In the weeks she had dated Kennesaw, I had never seen her look at him the way she was looking at Chester.

We had almost finished when the phone rang. Nestor answered and returned to the table.

"Margaret," he said.

"Can I go first?" I asked Ivy Leigh.

"Go on," she said. "Just remember there will be dishes to do."

Rushing to Ivy Leigh's office, I snatched up the phone.

"Margaret?"

"Hello, Agnes. Are you as happy as I am?"

"We got off to a rough start, but we rallied. I shouldn't expect anyone *else*, should I?"

She laughed. "No. Grace is the only person I sent. How is she?"

"I've never seen her happier. How are things there?"

"Peaceful. We invited Bentley and the Hamptons. Ham wanted to tour the property, so all the men went outside till the dinner is ready."

"Have you talked to Elinor?"

"Early this morning," she said. "They're having an evening meal. Ryder's daughter and her family won't be here till after 5:00."

"I wondered about her family. She has children?"

"Three girls. Elinor is beside herself. She said, 'A year ago I was an old maid librarian. Now I'm a wife, a mother, *and* a grandmother.'"

"Talk about 'happily ever after,'" I said. "Have you heard from Monty?"

"He and Charlotte are coming later for dessert. We miss you."

"I miss you, too," I said. "It's not the same here without you."

"Thanksgiving at the Magnolia Arms has never been the same two years in a row," Margaret said.

When I returned to the table, I sent Ivy Leigh to talk to Margaret and discovered the group had voted to delay dessert till later. The musicians carried their plates to the kitchen and invited Flossie and Winnie to their afternoon practice. The rest of us cleared the table and put away the leftovers. When the dishes were done, Chester invited Grace to go on a walk. Nestor transported a pumpkin pie to Ida Willingale's house for the annual dessert exchange. Grateful for a moment alone, I sat down in the kitchen. Morton stuck his head in the door.

"Your turn, Agnes," he said. "Oliver and Lorna are taking the rest of the day off."

"Now?" I asked. "I haven't been near a piano in two weeks."

"No time like the present," Morton said.

"I was waiting for Nestor to come back. I've hardly seen him since I've been here."

Morton's eyes twinkled. "There will be time for him tomorrow."

"All right. I'll go upstairs for my music."

"Already on the piano," Morton said. "Come on. No more excuses."

Feeling like a seven-year-old, I pattered across the hall, slid onto the piano bench, and leaned in to gawk at the thousands of notes scrawled on the pages in front of me.

"Where are Lorna and Oliver?" I asked.

"On the porch," Morton said.

I nodded at Flossie and Winnie on the sofa. "Are they going to stay?"

"No more stalling," Morton said.

I lifted my hands to the unsuspecting keys. Even Flossie, occupied with Fletcher's blue blanket, grimaced when I stumbled to the end of the first page. Winnie whispered to her and then approached the piano. She laid her hand on Morton's shoulder.

"I think I'll see if Ivy Leigh is off the phone," she said and left the parlor. She closed the door behind her.

I pushed through to an inglorious end and let my hands drop into my lap.

"How did you sit through that?" I asked Morton. "You must be in agony."

"I admire tenacity in anyone," he said. "Besides I owe you."

"Owe me? For what?"

"You know perfectly well," he said. "For Lorna. And for Winifred. These last few days have been the happiest of my life. Now ... let me help you."

As Morton and I lumbered through one painful measure after another, I began to be more at ease. His infectious love of music and inexhaustible patience awoke my confidence. After only an hour, my technique had improved.

He looked at his watch. "I'll leave you alone to practice. Lorna will be here in a few minutes to go over your festival piece."

"On your way to find Winnie?" I asked.

He pointed over his shoulder at Flossie dozing on the sofa. "Neither of us wants to exclude Flossie from our company. But I need a few minutes alone. I have something to say."

Perspiration glistened on his forehead; his hands trembled.

Lorna came into the parlor. "I hear quiet. I guess you're ready for me."

"She's a quick learner," Morton said, as he passed Lorna on his way to the door.

"Told you," Lorna said. "It's not fair. One person with so much talent."

"Talent?" I asked. "Are you joking?"

She stood by Morton's chair. "No. I'm not joking. You're a terrific teacher. You play the piano. You write. I've heard you also sing a little. You're a Renaissance woman."

Morton stood at the door. "Have you seen—?"

"In the kitchen," Lorna said. "She has your tea ready. China cups. A flower in her hair."

Flower in her hair? How many romantic interludes were going on this week?

"He's an amazing teacher," I said, after Morton left the room.

"Turns away students every semester," she said. "You have no idea how many people want to study with him. Now if you'll trade places with me, I'll play your festival piece."

As I slid into Morton's chair and Lorna took her rightful place at the piano, I thought I heard the piano whisper a sigh of relief.

Lorna removed Liebestraum and replaced it with a new selection.

"Do you like Tchaikovsky?" she asked, smoothing open the pages.

"He and Rachmaninov are my favorites."

She smiled. "I thought so. Deep brooding personalities are always drawn to each other."

"Brooding?" I asked.

"You love minor keys, don't you?"

"I do, but how … ?"

"Are you familiar with The Seasons?"

"You mean Four Seasons by Vivaldi?" I asked.

"No. Tchaikovsky. He wrote a series of twelve pieces, one for each month of the year."

"News to me," I said, "and I thought I was pretty cultured."

"For you," she said, "I've chosen Barcarolle, the June piece. If there is music that perfectly captures who you are, this is it."

Lorna had known me all of three months, and she knew *this*?

But as she began to play, I found myself swept along with the simple, elegant tune—sweet, sad, reflective, minor, easing into major, and back again, ending without flourish.

"Beautiful," Flossie mumbled, as she slid her knitting off her lap. "Could someone help me to my room? I'd like to freshen up before dessert."

Lorna stood. "Thanks for the reminder. I volunteered to set the table. Try not to get too inspired, Agnes. Dessert's in an hour." She left for the dining room.

Flossie pushed up from the sofa. I crossed the room and put my hand under her elbow to help her stand. We started down the hall.

"I'm sorry you got hurt," I said. "Kind of ruined your holiday."

"You'd think so, wouldn't you?" she said. "But, actually, it's been heartwarming to see how much everyone cares about me. By the way, have you called your mother today?"

"No," I said. "I should."

Flossie knew best.

My mother was delighted when I called.

"We've had a wonderful day," Mom said. "The boys are getting so big, and so is Janette."

"Full bloom of motherhood," I said.

"I've never seen Toby happier," she said. "They drove the Hamptons' car here." She lowered her voice. "It didn't even bother me when Toby took me for a ride."

Holding the receiver away from her, she asked if "anyone else wants to talk to Agnes" and one by one, everyone said hello, except Alfred David, who was napping in the guest room.

Happy, I hung up the phone and joined my friends in the dining room. After pie and polite conversation, we settled into that comfortable stupor that follows a satisfied appetite and full heart. The ten of us—a circle of friends who had known each other years or only hours—had found refuge in each other's company in that wonderful house. We allowed the rest of the day to unfold as it would. The men straggled off to the chessboard. Grace, exhausted from her all-night train ride, could stay awake no longer and said good night, as did Flossie.

Winnie, Lorna, and I stayed in the kitchen to help Ivy Leigh and discuss plans for the next day.

"We're going shopping in Raleigh, Agnes," Winnie said. "Want to join us?"

"Who's going?" I asked, curious, though I had no intention of joining them.

"Morton and I, Lorna and Oliver, Chester and Grace," Winnie said.

"No, thank you," I said. "I still haven't done any writing and—"

"Nestor said you'd say that," Winnie said.

"He knows me better than anyone," I said. "Is Flossie going with you?"

"I'm taking her out to lunch tomorrow," Ivy Leigh said. "She needs a little treat."

"Sounds good to me," I said. "I hope all of you have a wonderful day. I'm going to bed."

I climbed the stairs to the third floor. Thanksgiving, the day I had dreamed of, was over, and had been nothing like I'd expected. I had another 48 hours at the Magnolia Arms and then it was back to Brighton Park to dodge Dr. Sherwood, prepare for the festival, and practice with Ham, all while teaching and finishing my book. There was no way to do everything and do it well. I put on my pajamas and lay back on the bed, my heads folded behind my head. Two more days. I had to make the most of them.

When I heard footsteps on the stairs, I got up and opened the door. Ivy Leigh was jiggling the doorknob of the study.

"Sorry to wake you, Agnes," she said. "I forgot this door sticks."

"Did you need something?" I asked.

"No. I'm going to sleep up here tonight."

"Did you give Margaret's room to Lorna? Because if you did, I—"

She bowed her head. "No, the room's empty, but I can't sleep there again tonight."

"Why?"

"Because when I woke up this morning … for just a few seconds … I thought Marshall was there. It was our room before he died, and my mind played a trick on me. I can't—"

I put my arms around her. She laid her head on my shoulder and wept. It was the first time I had seen her cry.

"I'm sorry," I said. "I should've remembered. I would've traded rooms with you."

"No. I know how important your room is to you. I promised you could always have it."

"You can't sleep on that lumpy old sofa in the study. I'll get my stuff and move into Margaret's room. You take my room for tonight."

"Would you mind?" she asked.

"No," I said. "You've always said Margaret's room is the nicest one in the house."

I grabbed my manuscript and toothbrush and walked down to the second floor.

The next morning I had not yet thrown back the covers before there was a tap at the door. I opened it and found Ivy Leigh, tray in hand.

She whispered. "Coffee and blueberry breakfast bread. Now get to work."

I set the tray on the round table by the window, took my manuscript from the nightstand, and began to edit as I sipped coffee, smiling as I read Julia's account of Jameson's first Christmas. An hour later I heard Lorna and Grace chattering on their way to breakfast. I kept working. An hour after that I watched as Ivy Leigh's Buick, carrying six passengers, backed out of the driveway. Two hours later, I heard Ivy Leigh and Flossie getting into Nestor's truck. With the house empty except for Nestor and me, I slipped downstairs for lunch.

When I reached the first floor, I stood in the hall and called for Nestor.

"Nestor," I said. "Want to have a turkey sandwich?"

No answer.

I entered the empty kitchen and was taking inventory of the leftovers in the refrigerator, when I heard a voice behind me.

"Any pie left?" Nestor asked. "I had lunch an hour ago."

Hands full of plastic containers, I turned to him. "Why didn't you come get me? I would've eaten lunch with you. We haven't had much time to talk."

He took plates from the cupboard. "I didn't want to interrupt you. Besides that, I've been busy getting ready for tonight."

I set the leftovers on the table. "The private party? How many guests are coming?"

"Just two," he said.

"An anniversary?" I asked.

"No, not an anniversary. So … did you get any writing done this morning?"

"Yes. There's no way I'll finish by December, but I'm farther along than I was. It's just as well we didn't get Julia's things from Millie. I wouldn't have had time to look at them."

"Pickle?" he asked.

"Thanks. Are you doing anything special in the dining room?"

He nodded. "Yeah. Candles, flowers … music."

"Must be a close friend of Ivy Leigh if she's closing the restaurant for a party of two."

"Very good friend," Nestor said. "How's your family?"

Our conversation turned to ordinary matters for the remainder of lunch. Twenty minutes later Nestor said he had to get back to work and suggested I do the same.

The house was calm till the shoppers, more boisterous than when they left, came home at 3:00. Lorna tapped on my door.

"Did you get any work done today?" she asked.

"I did. It's amazing what you can do when ..."

"When there's no one to bother you?" she asked, laughing.

"I didn't say that. But if you're coming to ask about my festival piece, I ..."

"No worries, Agnes. Ivy Leigh needs to see you."

"Probably to help with *our* dinner," I said. "I suppose the hired help will have to eat in the kitchen tonight."

She shrugged her shoulders. "Ivy Leigh didn't say."

Planning to remain in Margaret's room a second night, I left my papers scattered on the table and went downstairs. Before I reached the first floor, I could smell a delectable aroma coming from the kitchen. Breathing deeply, I walked in.

"What in the world are you making?" I asked Ivy Leigh. "It smells wonderful."

"A recipe Muriel sent. Butterflied pork loins stuffed with porcini mushrooms, apples, blanched kale leaves, chopped onion and garlic, thyme and rosemary, cooked in butter and—"

I held up my hand. "I get the point. That's not on the menu for the normal people, is it?"

"That's what I want to talk to you about," she said.

"Pork loins stuffed with mushrooms?" I asked.

"No. As you know, Posey is my most experienced server, and she's not here."

I lifted a potato slice from a dish on the counter. "These are cute—look like dominoes."

"They're supposed to," Ivy Leigh said. "Will you pay attention?"

"Sorry. Posey's not here ... and?"

"And I wondered if you would serve tonight?"

"I assumed Nestor would do it," I said. "He's better at it than I am."

"Nestor worked all day setting up. I don't want to ask him to do anything else."

"Okay," I said, "but you know I spill things when I get nervous."

"It's a party of two, Agnes. You can handle it."

I started toward the hall. "I'll go upstairs and change."

"One more thing," Ivy Leigh said. "The uniform won't do. Do you have something a little more formal?"

"You want me to dress up to serve pork and potatoes?" I asked.

"Promised my friend we'd go all out," Ivy Leigh said.

"I brought the navy blue dress I wore to the dinner party at Charlotte's," I said.

"Perfect. Be back in an hour. I want to introduce you before dinner."

I couldn't help being flattered by Ivy Leigh's request. She didn't entrust her customers to just anyone.

Returning to my room, I took my dress from the closet. No ironing needed—this dress had not left the hanger since the miserable evening I had first worn it. The only thing that had stopped me from donating the dress to charity was the scarf Charlotte had given me. She was sure to ask if I had worn it. This night presented a golden opportunity to create a new memory. From now on, when I wore this dress, I could remember the role I had played in the romantic evening this mystery man had planned for the woman he loved.

I returned to the kitchen and presented myself to Ivy Leigh, also dressed for the occasion in a stylish black dress.

"You're dressed up, too?" I asked.

"I'm the hostess," she said.

"These people must be really special for all the trouble you're going to."

"They are," she said. "Ready to go in?"

She led me down the hall as if I did not know the way.

When we reached the dining room, she stood to one side as she opened the door and allowed me to enter first.

In the center of the room was a round table covered with a white tablecloth. China and crystal were set at two places. In the center of the table a clear glass vase held a pale yellow rose with wine-red edged petals. White taper candles flickered everywhere. A fire blazed in the fireplace. At one end of the serving table, lined with silver chafing dishes, was the cut glass vase I had seen in Posey's hands days before—holding red roses too numerous to count. From a record player in an unlit corner, Frank Sinatra sang "The Nearness of You."

Next to the round table stood Nestor in a dark blue suit.

He walked toward me and held out his hand.

"Will you join me?" he asked.

Barely breathing, I walked to the table. He seated me and then sat across from me.

Ivy Leigh stepped behind me. "Water?" she asked.

I looked up at her. "Yes … yes. Thank you."

She filled both our glasses and then took my plate.

"Surprised?" Nestor asked.

"I … am," I said and sipped my water.

"You look beautiful," he said.

"So do you … look … handsome, I mean. That's not Xander's wedding suit, is it?"

"No."

I looked over my shoulder at the serving table. "And that vase. It was for …"

"You," he said. "For the roses."

Ivy Leigh set my dinner in front of me and took Nestor's plate.

"I don't know what to say," I said. "I never imagined—"

"You can't imagine anyone would go to this much trouble for you?"

"No … I mean yes. I mean … What was the question?"

Unfolding his napkin, he placed it in his lap. "It's all right, Agnes. I knew you'd react exactly this way. So relax. You're with a friend. Enjoy your dinner."

After Ivy Leigh served Nestor, she left the dining room.

Grateful to have something to do while I regrouped, I stabbed a potato with my fork.

We ate in silence for several minutes. Strange … I'd never felt awkward with Nestor.

"Ivy Leigh has outdone herself," I said. "I've never eaten anything better."

"She's been as nervous about this evening as I have," he said.

"How … long have you been planning this?"

"Technically … about a year. Logistically … since Sefton broke up with you."

"A year?"

He put down his fork. "Xander was right. He told me you had no idea."

"About what?"

"That I fell in love with you … hopelessly … after I'd known you only a week."

Dazed, I took a roll from the basket on the table and asked for the butter.

"Why haven't you said anything before now?" I asked.

"I was going to tell you last November, the night before you and Margaret left. Remember? We thought we were losing the house, and we had Thanksgiving dinner early?"

"I remember," I said.

"I was so nervous that night I could hardly eat. I was going to tell you right after dinner. You remember what happened?"

"Sefton and Jameson showed up."

He nodded. "Jameson saved the house. But I lost you."

"I'm sorry, Nestor. I had no idea you—"

"I wasn't too worried at first, but before I knew it, you were carrying on long distance with Sefton, and all I could do was stand back and watch. If it hadn't been for Ivy Leigh …"

"She's known all along?"

"Margaret, too."

My head was spinning. "When you came with Monty … to Charlotte's house, was it because you wanted to see me?"

"Uh-huh."

"And when I had the flu … you …"

"You can't imagine how happy I was to have you all to myself even though you looked like death warmed over."

More to myself than to him, I said, "Winnie *said* it was because you loved me."

He moved his chair next to mine and took my hand in his.

"Remember the first night you came here for dinner?" he asked.

"Of course," I said. "I think about it all the time."

"Do you remember the story I told you when I drove you back to your motel?"

"Yes. You were working on your Ph.D. at Princeton and realized the world didn't need one more book on the French Revolution, and you got on a bus and came here."

"And what did you think of me when I told you that?" he asked.

"I admired you for having the courage to—"

"Pursue what would make me happy," he said. "See this rose on the table?"

"Beautiful," I said. "One of yours?"

"Yes. Another hybrid. I want to name it for you."

"The Agnes Quinn Rose," I said. "That's so—"

"No," he said. "The Agnes Carlyle Rose."

Chapter 13

I'll Be Seeing You

"Are … are you saying what I think you're saying?" I asked.

"What do think I'm saying?"

"You want to *marry* me?"

"*I do*," he said, grinning.

I leaned back in my chair. "We … we're not even *dating*."

He was unfazed. "You weren't dating Sefton either, and you would've married him in a New York second … if he'd had the good sense to ask."

"That … that was different. We were involved in a long distance relationship."

"*Wrong* distance relationship, if you ask me."

"We … we *called* each other," I said.

"We do, too," he said. "And who do you enjoy talking to more? Me? Or that stuffed shirt who never had time for you?"

"That's beside the point."

"No, it's not," he said.

"You … you're my best friend. Just because we love the same things and the same people and have the same quirky sense of humor, that doesn't mean …"

"We should spend the rest of our lives together in the house we both love?"

I propped my elbow on the table and rested my chin on my hand.

"Chester," I said.

"Chester?"

"He asked me if I learned anything from my experience with Xander. This is why."

"Uh-huh."

Leaning forward, I squeezed his shoulder. "And the working out. It wasn't so *Xander* would look good in his tux or to help Chester with his therapy."

"Yes, it was. We're all geeks, Agnes. We know we have limited appeal to women, and we all had a good reason to ramp up our game."

"Did *everyone* know you were going to propose tonight?"

"Everyone except maybe Ida Willingale."

I shook my head. "You'll have time for him tomorrow."

"What?"

"Morton. I told him I was waiting for you to come back from Ida's. That I hadn't had time to talk to you. He said I'd have 'time for you tomorrow' … I mean today … I mean …"

Nestor stood and returned his chair to its place. "Be back in a minute."

"Wait. What are you doing? You can't ask someone to marry you and then walk off."

"Sticking to the plan," he said.

"What plan?"

"Ivy Leigh told me you wouldn't know what to say. She said after I popped the question, I should walk away and give you time to think. So I'm going for dessert."

When he opened the door, I saw Grace and Lorna hovering in the hall. Hopping up and down, Grace clapped her hands, while Lorna smiled and gave a thumbs up.

No doubt the *rest* of them were waiting for a report in the kitchen; Flossie and Winnie hugging; Chester calling Xander and Posey; Morton and Oliver commending Nestor's courage; Ivy Leigh joking about sending them all to their rooms if they "couldn't be quiet."

And there I sat.

Center stage.

In a perfect setting.

In the starring role.

And I couldn't think of a single line of dialogue.

What kind of writer was I anyway?

Ivy Leigh, carrying a silver tray, returned with Nestor. He sat down as if nothing had happened. She served me a slice of yellow cake with vanilla ice cream and a sprig of mint.

I lifted the plate and inhaled. "Lemon buttermilk?"

"Muriel's suggestion," Ivy Leigh said.

"She's in on it, too?" I asked.

Ivy Leigh lingered behind Nestor as she set down his plate. Feeling her staring at me, I looked up. Only Ivy Leigh or Margaret could say so much with raised eyebrows.

I read her meaning: *Yes, I've known all along. We'll talk later. Don't mess this up.*

She left us alone.

Calmed by the familiar smell of my favorite dessert, I ate.

"So," Nestor said. "What's new?"

Mouth full, I looked up. The same old Nestor, my comfortable friend, had returned.

With the candles burning low, Sinatra silent, and the rose to be named for me still between us, I spent the rest of the evening pouring out my feelings about Kennesaw Fleming, Bentley McBain, the fine arts festival, the whistling competition, and Ryder's new family.

Nestor edged back from the table. "It's getting late. We should say good night."

"Only one more day," I said. "Saying goodbye never gets any easier."

"What would you like to do tomorrow?" he asked.

Ivy Leigh opened the door. "I hate to disturb you, but Millie Hubbard's on the phone."

Nestor and I glanced at each other and hopped up from the table. I could barely keep up as he sprinted toward Ivy Leigh's office.

He reached for the phone. "Hello? Yes ... Yes, ma'am ... I'm sorry to hear that ... Uh-huh ... Yes, I can do that ... I'll leave first thing in the morning. Thank you ... Goodbye."

"What is it?" I asked.

"Millie Hubbard is back. Her sister-in-law died, so she's home for the funeral. She's leaving Sunday, but said if I bring Julia's letter tomorrow, she'll let me look in the cedar chest."

"Tomorrow?" I threw my arms around him. "I thought there'd be no way we'd get the cedar chest till after Christmas ..."

And then it happened.

Nestor kissed me.

And to my astonishment ... it was as storybook perfect as the rest of the evening.

"Now," he said, "I should get some sleep. If I leave before dawn, I might be able to get there and back before your train leaves Sunday."

"I could go with you."

He shook his head. "The trip is too long. Traffic will be awful with people coming home after the holidays. If we were delayed, you'd miss your train. I have to go alone."

"Nestor, I …"

"Please don't say another word. This evening was as perfect as I could have hoped for. Let me believe … at least for tonight … Good night, Agnes."

We parted at the foot of the stairs. If our friends had been congregated in the kitchen as I had envisioned, they had long since dispersed. I tiptoed to my room. Hoping Lorna and Grace were already asleep, I eased my door open and pushed it closed. I sank into the same blue-flowered chair where I had been sitting when Margaret asked if me I'd ever been in love. When I answered, 'once or twice,' she had told me I would *know* when I experienced real love … that it was "frightening, exquisite in its own painful way."

The moment when I should have *known* I was in love had come and gone. And the man I had shared that scene with was nothing like I'd imagined.

I wasn't frightened.

I was confused.

When I heard a knock at the door, I kept quiet.

Ivy Leigh stepped in and walked across the room. She sat in Margaret's chair.

"How are you?" she asked.

"I don't know. How *should* I be?"

"Nestor's over the moon," she said. "I'm proud of you for not deflating him."

"Did you think I would?"

"It hasn't been that long since Sefton. I told Nestor he might be jumping the gun."

"How long have you known?"

"Since Jonas and Margaret's wedding," she said. "When we left to come home, he was so sad. I thought he missed Margaret. That's when he told me he loved you."

"I love him," I said.

"I know."

"But I've never thought of marrying him … not even once. Margaret said—"

"Stop right there," she said. "Margaret is my best friend, but you can't use her exalted notions about love as a measuring stick. She has no experience."

"No experience? She and Jonas are the happiest married couple I know."

"You didn't know me when I was married to Marshall, or you wouldn't say that."

I ducked my head. "Sorry. I didn't mean to—"

"Margaret fell in love with a handsome stranger who came to town and left her before they had a chance to know each other. She spent her life loving an *image* of Jonas, not him."

"I suppose you're right."

"Of course, I'm right. Have you asked her about love now that she's seen Jonas' hair when he wakes up, and they've shared grilled cheese sandwiches and raked the yard?"

"Can't say I have."

"She'd give you a very different answer now. She'd say love is 'comfortable,' and there's nothing better than talking over the day with someone who loves you exactly as you are."

I gazed out the window at the stars. "That's Nestor," I said.

She reached over and patted my knee. "Go to bed. Flossie and Winnie are leaving early, and you should come down and say goodbye."

Though I thought I would never be able to go to sleep, I drifted off within minutes and did not wake up till Ivy Leigh jiggled my arm as the sun was rising.

Slipping on my pink seersucker housecoat, I hurried downstairs.

My former roommates, suitcases at their feet, were waiting by the door.

Winnie, wrapped in Morton's skinny arms, was crying.

Flossie limped toward me. "It was good to see you again, Agnes."

When I hugged her, she whispered. "I'm going to lose Winnie. I'll be alone again."

"I'll call when I get home," I said.

When I approached Winnie, Morton released his grip.

"Goodbye, Winnie," I said.

She hugged me and collapsed into tears. "It's been a *wonderful* week." She stood back and held my shoulders. "When I think my search for Darlinda led me to you instead ..."

"We've had some good times," I said, unsure of how to respond.

"Tell our friends we said hello," she said. "And Mary Smith."

Chester and Grace came from the kitchen. Chester lifted Flossie's suitcase. Morton took Winnie's and the five of them were off to the train station.

Embracing the silence, I ambled to the kitchen and headed to the coffee pot.

"No piano," I said. "Are Lorna and Oliver taking another day off?"

Ivy Leigh set a slice of lemon buttermilk cake in front of me. "No. They left the same time Nestor did. Oliver's driving Lorna home."

"Wow," I said, cutting a bite of cake. "Is Grace catching the train, too?"

"No, she *said* she was going along to be moral support for Morton, but I think the real reason is she doesn't want to miss a moment with Chester. She's leaving the same time as you."

Great, I thought. Grace will talk my ear off all the way home.

Ivy Leigh and I were dawdling over coffee and the newspaper when Morton returned. Without a word to us, he retreated into the parlor and closed the door.

Mournful tunes drifted across the hall.

"I don't recognize those melodies," I said. "You think he's composing?"

She looked up from her crossword. "One of us should check on him."

"I'll go. Maybe if I ask for a lesson, it will distract him."

My last opportunity for solitude took a backseat to a friend in need.

Returning to my room, I got dressed and found my music under my most recent chapter. When I stepped into the parlor, Morton stopped playing.

"Such a long time till Christmas," he said, staring at the keys.

I joined him at the piano. "You're spending Christmas with Winnie?"

Head bowed, he nodded.

A tear dropped onto middle C.

"I'm happy for you, Morton. She's a lovely person."

He took a handkerchief from his pocket and wiped his nose. "It's no longer academic."

"What?"

"The anguish of the great composers. I never understood … till now … the sense of loss that tears a mortal wound in the soul. Music is the bleeding *and* the balm."

"Speaking of partings," I said, desperate to change the subject, "I thought I should have one more lesson. I'm getting nervous about the festival."

This wasn't exactly true, but I thought if he felt obligated to a fellow musician, he might disregard his pain for the sake of his art.

Standing, he gestured to the bench. I sat and flexed my fingers for effect.

Teacher and student, adrift in a tempest of churning emotions, we sailed into our practice with abandon.

I had never played so well.

After spending the morning alone, Chester and Grace, hand in hand, returned for lunch. The five of us ate turkey sandwiches and talked of absent friends.

Nestor called that evening.

"You'll love Millie," he said. "We spent hours going through the cedar chest. She's invited me to stay here tonight. Will you tell Ivy Leigh?"

"I will," I said.

"It's the first time I haven't taken you to the train station after one of your visits."

"I've had enough goodbyes for now," I said. "This will make things easier."

By "easier" I meant I was relieved I wouldn't have to stand on the train platform and figure out if I should hug my old friend goodbye or kiss the man who was in love with me.

The next morning, as we gathered in the foyer, Ivy Leigh handed me a brown paper bag.

"The rest of the cake," she said. "Don't eat it all on the train. Save some for tomorrow."

The three remaining guests climbed into Ivy Leigh's Buick. Morton and I sat silent in the back seat while Grace and Chester, side by side, whispered in the front. When we reached the station, Morton and I exited the car, carted our suitcases to the platform, and waited.

When the loud speaker announced Morton's train, he took my hands in his.

"Keep practicing," he said. "I'll come early for one last lesson before the festival."

Alternately miserable and buoyant, Chester and Grace approached arm in arm. Morton gave a final wave as he walked away.

Feeling out of place, I gave Chester a quick hug and got on the train. I settled in a seat by the window and glanced at the platform, vacant of anyone who hated to see me leave.

Grace waited till the last possible moment to board the train and then sank into the seat beside me. I was wrong about her talking my ear off. She didn't say a word for over an hour.

At last she asked, "What are you thinking?"

"About the last time I left. How Nestor hugged me goodbye, and I met Kennesaw Fleming on the platform and hid from him on the train and how Winnie filled me up with Russian tea."

"I was thinking about my trip here," she said. "How heartbroken I was."

"You're not heartbroken now, are you?"

She turned to face me. "No. But I do regret putting up with Kennesaw for so long. Do you regret that about Sefton?"

Wincing as if I had sunk my teeth into a lemon, I shook my head. Did she have the nerve to compare my year-long relationship with Sefton to her pretend courtship with Kennesaw?

If we hadn't been trapped on a train for several more hours, I would have launched into a litany of contrasts between her "relationship" and mine.

But I didn't have the strength to argue the point with her.

I shrugged my shoulders. "I don't know."

She leaned back in her seat and folded her arms. "I can't wait to see Kennesaw."

"Why?"

"So I can ignore him."

Jonas and Margaret met us at the station. We hurried to them like homesick children. Grace hugged Margaret, thanking her again and again for sending her to the Magnolia Arms. Jonas took me in his arms and held me.

"You okay, kiddo?" he asked.

"You know me. I never can quite figure out what's going on."

Grace chattered about Chester all the way home, which suited me fine. I had no desire to talk about Nestor, especially not in front of Grace. The only thing I would have liked to know was how Ryder's reunion with his daughter went, and I could find that out from Elinor tomorrow. For the first time in longer than I could remember, I was looking forward to going to sleep in my own apartment and doing something as normal as going to school.

Saturn gave me a perfunctory welcome. I tried to win back his favor with kitty treats, but it would be at least twenty-four hours before he forgave me for leaving him for almost a week.

Leaving my suitcase unpacked, I put on my favorite pajamas and was about to curl up in bed when the phone rang.

"That'll be Mom seeing if I'm home," I said to Saturn, and picked up the phone.

"Hello, Mom."

"It's not your mother," Sefton said. His tone was withering. "I've been trying to call you for days. *Where* have you been?"

"The Magnolia Arms," I said, puzzled. "On Thanksgiving break."

"I should've thought of that. I could've called you there."

"Why?" I asked.

"To find out what you said to Lorna."

"About what?" I asked.

"About *me*. I wrote to her after we met at the dinner party, but she said she wasn't interested. What *exactly* did you say to her?"

"I didn't say anything."

"Come on, Agnes. I know you were upset when we broke up, but that doesn't give you the right to disparage me to Lorna or anybody else. I thought I explained—"

"Hold on just a minute," I said. "I saw you staring at Lorna at the dinner party, and quite frankly, when you didn't meet me the next morning, I thought you met her."

"I wish," he said.

My voice rising, I pressed on.

"I saw your letter to Lorna in her mailbox at school. When I asked her about it, she said she wasn't interested in you and *never would be*, because—"

"I'm supposed to take *your* word for that?"

"*Because*," I said, speaking over him, "you're too much like the idiot boyfriend who dumped her in college. Anyway … you're too late. She's already dating someone else."

"I don't believe—"

"And for your information, Lorna was *with* me at the Magnolia Arms," I said.

"What was she doing there?"

"Making a comeback," I said as I hung up.

Apparently, so was I.

Grace was right. I *did* regret putting up with Sefton for so long.

Monday dawned clear and cold. I stopped by the Drifters' Rest for coffee and reported to Muriel on the success of the dinner, adding I had found the domino-shaped potatoes particularly charming. As I drove to school, I pictured Ivy Leigh and Chester at the kitchen table. Were Posey and Xander with them? Was Nestor? Were they getting back to normal or still missing those of us who had left? Was Winnie making wedding plans? Was Flossie finished with Fletcher's blanket? Would the "mortal wound" in Morton's soul stop bleeding long enough for him to make it through his lessons today?

My mind swirling, I entered my classroom to retreat into the safe, predictable world of lecturing on numbered points and illustrating with time-worn selections.

Putting on my teacher face, I stepped behind the lectern.

Announced the lecture was on the Shakespearean sonnet.

Wrote sample lines on the board. Divided syllables with diagonal marks. Accented the second syllable in each "foot"—counted off five feet per line.

Called it "iambic pentameter" and marked rhyme scheme. a-b-a-b. c-d-c-d. e-f-e-f. gg.

"Of course, when reading a sonnet," I said, "you don't accent the syllables or pause at the end of the line. You read according to the punctuation."

I had memorized my illustration, Sonnet 29, when a misty-eyed teenager, so I returned to the lectern, switched on my poet face, and intoned:

"When in disgrace with fortune and men's eyes, I all alone beweep my outcast state and trouble deaf heaven with my bootless cries and—"

My throat tightened. My eyes watered.

By the time I said, "… change my state with kings," my voice was barely audible.

One girl rifled through her purse for a handful of Kleenex and brought them to me.

"You okay, Miss Quinn?" Ray Spalding asked.

"I guess I didn't get enough sleep last night," I said. "I took a long trip and … I guess … that's enough for today. We'll start here on Wednesday."

The students filed out as if they were leaving a funeral.

I gathered my books and notes, stashed them in my book bag, and was on my way out the door when Kennesaw Fleming walked in.

"Agnes," he said, "I wonder if we could talk a minute. I want to … are you all right?"

"Hello, Mr. *Ellershaw*," I said. Stepping past him, I stood in the door with one foot in the hall. "You shaved your beard. Have you given up re-enacting?"

"No. I shaved because my sister wanted to take the first family photo we had taken in twenty-five years."

If he had come to defend his conduct, I could have lectured him.

But this simple pronouncement shut me up.

I had so often grieved over Ryder's absent children—the image of his family, reunited, reduced me to tears … again.

Dropping my book bag, I sat in a desk on the front row.

"I can't tell you how many times I've looked at that photo on Elinor's desk," I said.

"Dad took us back to the Drifters' Rest so we could sit in the same spot," John said.

Tears dripping down my face, I looked up. "Is your sister still here? I'd like to meet her."

"No, the girls had to go back to school."

Staring at the floor, I dabbed at my eyes with the Kleenex. "I can't imagine how happy Ryder must be." I looked up. "But *why* did you wait so long to find him?"

John sat next to me. "One of my earliest childhood memories was my mother telling me my father wanted nothing to do with me. That he had left *us*. I've resented him my whole life."

"So why are you here *now*?"

"My mother passed away in January. She told me the truth before she died—to clear her conscience, I guess. It took me a while to grasp the real story ... and then to get a plan in place."

"But when you found him, why didn't you just tell him ... tell us ... who you were?"

"I was afraid. I'd grown up believing my father wanted nothing to do with me. If I had showed up, told him I was his son, and he'd rejected me ..."

"That would have been worse than not knowing at all," I said.

"I wanted to watch him first. Find out who he was and what he'd been doing. Of course, you know the man I came to know was nothing like my mother had described."

"You used Grace," I said.

"I know." He hung his head. "And I'm sorry for that. I spoke to her first thing this morning in Elinor's office. She was surprisingly forgiving."

"She's like that," I said.

"I thanked her for understanding. And I want to thank you, Agnes."

"For what?"

"If Bentley hadn't coaxed the truth out of me, I would've kept up my disguise a lot longer. But I'm glad it's over. I've never had more peace. Friends?"

"We'll see," I said.

Struggling to regain my composure, I walked to my Advanced Grammar class. Surely I could lecture on future perfect continuous tense without being maudlin.

And what was the matter with me anyway?

Post-holiday letdown? The usual depression following a trip to the Magnolia Arms?

My Advanced Grammar students believed the lie I told them about my red nose and puffy eyes—"allergies"—and we strode into the orderly world of verb tenses.

After class, intending to barricade myself behind a mountain of work, I headed to my office. Jonas, Drifters' Rest bag and Thermos in hand, was waiting by my door.

"You're welcome," he said.

I pointed to the bag. "For the food?"

"Yes. *And* your friend Sharon was here when I arrived. When I told her we had an appointment, she left. Said for you to see Dr. Sherwood before you go home today."

I unlocked the door. "Thank you. I couldn't have taken a scene with her … not today."

"Margaret said you were free at eleven," he said. "I thought you might be hungry." He followed me in.

"Just like our old lunches in the math department office," I said.

"I miss having lunch with you," he said, handing me the bag and Thermos. "I do not miss the math department office." He brought a chair from the corner.

I deposited my book bag on the floor and spread our feast on my desk.

"You surprised me," I said. "I thought Margaret would check on me, but not you."

He opened the jar of spicy mustard. "Tired of getting my information second-hand."

There was no need to ask what was in the bag. I knew Jonas had ordered a chicken salad sandwich for me, and Muriel had fixed it exactly like I liked it.

"Did you enjoy Thanksgiving?" I asked.

"We did. Bentley kept staring at all of us like he couldn't believe where he was. Mr. Hampton insisted on inspecting the pergola. Ham was ill at ease—quiet all day."

"Missing his mother, I suppose."

"Maybe," Jonas said. "How about you?"

"Never had a Thanksgiving quite like it," I said. "Every day there was another surprise."

Jonas arranged pastrami on an onion bagel. "I told Megs she should've let you know Grace was coming."

"Somebody should've let me know a *proposal* was coming. Although, after I thought about it, just about everyone dropped hints. I didn't put it all together till later."

He nodded. "I told Nestor not to be disappointed if you didn't react the way he hoped."

I bit into a pickle. "Ivy Leigh said the same thing. Don't you have any faith in me at all?"

"It's not that," he said, spreading mustard on his sandwich. "Look Agnes, I could beat around the bush half the day to try to get to my point, but I'd rather come right out and say it."

"Go ahead," I said.

He laid his sandwich on the desk. "The fact of the matter is, I don't want you to end up like me and that's exactly what's going to happen if you don't change the way you think."

"End up like you? That's exactly what I *do* want. You're married to someone you adore. You live in a beautiful home. You're building again, like you've always dreamed of doing."

He pointed to his gray hair. "But how long did it take and how many years did I waste brooding? If you hadn't come along and shoved your way—"

"Shoved?"

"Okay, 'nudged' your way into my personal business," he said, grinning, "I'd still be *mourning* the woman I lost, instead of being married to her."

"What's your point?"

He leaned forward. "You're all dreams, Agnes. You *dream* about writing and you *dream* about marrying the ideal man, while your *real* life is playing out right in front of you."

"How can you say that?" I asked, teetering between being insulted and hurt.

"I can say it, because I was all dreams, too. And I'd still be dreaming if—"

"—I hadn't shoved my way into your life."

"The same way I'm 'nudging' into your life now," he said. "The only difference between me and you is, I dreamed of an impossible *past* and you're dreaming of an impossible *future*."

He reached into the bag, produced a small white box, and opened it. The incomparable aroma of Muriel's almond cookies floated up.

"Just what I need," I said, taking two. "So … you're saying I should give up writing?"

He cut his sandwich in half. "That's the *least* important decision you have to make."

I licked powdered sugar from my fingers. "You mean Nestor. What am I supposed to do? I don't want to hurt him … or lose him, but I'm going to have to give him an answer eventually."

He twisted open the Thermos and poured coffee into two cups.

"And that's a problem, because—?" he asked.

"Because … I don't love Nestor *that* way."

"What way is that?"

"Like you and Margaret. Love at first sight. Soul mates. Storybook romance."

He set a full cup on my desk.

"Would you like to hear the *whole* story about me and Margaret?"

"I know the whole story," I said, "right up to the happy ending when Margaret got off the train and fell into your arms."

"I mean *after* that," he said.

"You built your dream house, got married, and moved into it."

"After *that*," he said, "once the honeymoon was over, we realized we were strangers. We had a beginning and an end, but nothing in between— thirty years of living we'd never shared."

"I never thought about that."

"Not something we've told anyone. Well, Margaret has probably told—"

"Ivy Leigh," I said.

"Before we knew what had happened, Margaret was busy at school and I was occupied with the house, and we were farther apart than before we got back together."

"What did you do?"

"I asked her out on a date," he said, biting into his sandwich.

"You what?"

He swallowed. "Made reservations at a restaurant in Raleigh, bought a dozen roses, put on a suit, and left the house before she came home. Then I knocked on the door."

"How romantic," I said. "What did you say when she came to the door?"

"I said, 'Hello, my name is Jonas Grinstead. I'm new in town, and I'm looking for a place to stay. Are there any rooms available here?'"

"And she played along," I said.

"You know her well. She said, 'I'll have to ask the landlord.' I said I'd trade handyman chores for room and board." From then on, we started 'dating' and got to know each other."

"As the people you are now …"

"You need to forget Nestor is the 'gardener,'" he said. "You need to forget he's your 'best friend.' You need to start from the beginning and get to know him as a person."

"Do you realize this is the same advice you gave me about Toby—to forget I was his sister and think of myself as his friend?"

"It worked, didn't it?"

Maybe it was Muriel's magic touch with chicken salad. Maybe it was the almond cookies and coffee. Maybe it was an honest conversation with an old friend. Or all three.

But I felt as if the world, upside down, had righted itself.

"Where do I start?" I asked.

"You'll have to figure that out for yourself, but if you need advice, I'll be close by."

Jonas left me with the rest of the cookies and my thoughts.

He was right. I spent a ridiculous amount of time being disappointed with unrealized expectations—Thanksgiving being the most recent example. I had spent a week with the people I loved in the place I loved, attended a private concert by two gifted pianists, taken lessons with a teacher who was apparently legendary, but had come away exhausted and frustrated all because I couldn't sneak away to a stack of paper and a typewriter. The friends, however, who had shared the time with me, had gone away convinced they had experienced one of the most remarkable weeks of their lives.

I rifled through my book bag for my manuscript, as if to prove a point to myself.

"Even if I had spent every waking minute at the typewriter," I said aloud, "I still couldn't have finished writing—"

No sign of my manuscript. Had I packed it in my suitcase?

Turning my bag upside down, I emptied the contents on my desk.

My music fluttered to the floor. I stooped to pick up the pages.

Liebestraum. The whistling competition. As important to Ham as my book was to me.

I flipped through the pages and found my own piece, Barcarolle, behind them.

The festival. Weeks away. Appearing on the same stage with Lorna? I had to give a respectable performance.

At the very least, I did not want to disappoint Morton when he gave me my final lesson.

In a sudden burst of resolve, I tucked my music under my arm, grabbed my coat, locked my office, and headed to the maintenance office for the key to Rehearsal Hall.

Tapping on the door as I entered, I greeted Mr. Hampton.

"Hello, Agnes," he said, switching off his table saw. "What can I do for you?"

I held up my music. "I wondered if Ham would unlock Rehearsal Hall, so I can practice."

Removing his safety glasses, he walked to a pegboard and retrieved a numbered key.

"Here you go," he said. "Have a nice trip?"

"Yes," I said, holding the key on my open palm. "I'll bring this back when I finish."

"No need. No one goes in there but you and Miss Maron. Keep it as long as you like."

"Are you sure? Ham told Lorna he would have to let her in there whenever—"

"Ham wants an excuse to walk with her and listen while she practices." He folded my fingers over the key. "I know that secret is safe with you."

My heart folded in from the edges.

"You mean Ham is—?"

He lowered his voice. "Hopelessly in love, I'm afraid. And I didn't discourage him."

I sank down on a stool by the workbench. "Jonas said Ham was quiet during dinner. Was it because he missed Lorna?"

"Ham began dreaming about Thanksgiving last month. Wanted to invite Lorna to our house. Even thought of inviting the Grinsteads, so Lorna wouldn't feel uncomfortable."

"He must have been heartbroken when Lorna left," I said.

"I haven't seen him so low since the first holiday without his mother. He's better now that Lorna's back. He got a glimpse of her this morning."

I propped my elbow on the workbench and leaned my head on my hand. "I don't know how to say this, but Lorna … I'm pretty sure Lorna is in love with someone else."

Mr. Hampton brushed sawdust onto the floor. "Someone here?"

"No, another musician. He travels a lot. I don't think he'll show up here, not for—"

Mr. Hampton bowed his head. "My son is the finest man I know, but he'll never marry a woman like Lorna. Do you think I was wrong to let him believe it … for a while?"

"No," I said.

He patted my hand. "Thank you for that. Not a word to Ham, all right? Not yet."

"I'll take good care of the key," I said, turning to go. "I'm going to practice every day. At least *one* of Ham's dreams is going to come true, if it's the last thing I …"

Standing at the open door, I noticed a frame hung above the lintel. The message was faded. I took a step back, squinted my eyes, and read:

Do the duty that lies nearest thee. ~ Carlyle

"Counted cross stitch," Mr. Hampton said, answering my unasked question. "My wife Rosalind made it for my shop. When you're in maintenance, everyone thinks their request—"

"Should come first," I said.

He nodded. "I learned to do the urgent first; then take things in order."

"Carlyle?" I asked.

"Thomas. One of Rosalind's favorite poets." He put on his safety glasses. "Your young man noticed that sign the first time he visited here.

"Sefton?" I asked.

He shook his head. "Nestor."

"Nestor?" I asked. "When would he have—?"

"When he came for your dinner party."

Pointing up, I asked, "How long has that sign been there?"

"Years. You've never noticed before, because you're always in too much of a hurry. Nestor noticed right away. He said he couldn't have said it better himself."

"Carlyle," I said, laughing.

He winked and snapped on his table saw.

I started toward Rehearsal Hall. Eyes riveted to the sidewalk, I heard Sharon's high heels clicking before I saw her.

As usual, she was holding her clipboard. Was she never without it? Even asleep?

"Did Dr. Grinstead not give you my message?" she asked.

Mind occupied, heart throbbing with a dull ache, I blinked my eyes to bring her into focus. "Elspeth wants to see me before I leave. The day's only half over."

My pleasant tone and obliging response stunned her.

"Oh … well … I can save you the trip. She wanted you to have this by the end of the day."

She handed me a folded sheet of paper.

"What's this?" I asked.

"The program for the festival. Dr. Sherwood wants you to look it over and make corrections and improvements. She also wants you to write a paragraph about Lorna."

"Okay," I said. "When does she want it?"

Her eyes widened. "Just like that? You're not going to argue?"

I shook my head. "This is an important project. I'm happy to help."

"Oh … uh … well, thank you." She turned away and then looked back. "How's your mother, by the way?"

"Fine. Yours?"

For the first time in our lives, we parted on good terms.

The door to Rehearsal Hall creaked open. Comforted by the solitude of a familiar place, I walked down the aisle and up the steps to the stage. Pushing back the worn maroon velvet curtain, I turned on the spotlight and thought of all the musicians and actors who had endured the private anguish of the lines or notes they had forgotten here. Sitting at the piano, I opened Liebestraum and played, remembering Morton's advice, while I pictured Ham in an ill-fitting suit, hands at his sides, his clear tone and pure heart admired by all who would hear him.

I remained in Rehearsal Hall the rest of the afternoon—practicing and thinking.

By the time I walked back to my office and packed my book bag, it was almost 5:00. I stopped by the Drifters' Rest for supper and arrived home after dark.

My tardiness did nothing to endear me to Saturn.

After a long bath, I put on my pajamas and went to the phone.

I called Flossie to see if her foot was healing.

I called my mother to say I was looking forward to Christmas.

I called the Magnolia Arms to speak to Nestor.

Chester answered the phone. "He's not here, Agnes. He and Ivy Leigh have gone to look at some property."

"Property?"

"For the restaurant your friend Muriel is going to open. Did you see Grace today?"

"No," I said. "Too busy. Muriel's going to open a restaurant? I thought she was going to run the one at the Magnolia Arms."

"Ivy Leigh has decided to close it. Well, move it. She wants things to be simpler once she leaves and the new manager takes over."

My heart pounded. "I thought her trading places with Muriel was only temporary."

"I don't know," he said. "You'd have to ask her. Tell Grace I miss her."

"I will."

"And will you find out if they need any physics teachers at your school?"

"You're coming here?" I asked.

"Eventually," he said.

After we hung up, I leaned back and ran my hands through my hair.

I could not process one more piece of information today.

I picked up Saturn and turned on the television on my way to the sofa. I draped Flossie's magenta afghan across my lap and patted the space next to me. Saturn snuggled in and was soon purring.

The quiet at the end of the day—a perfect time to proofread.

It would be a simple matter to hop up, get the manuscript out of the suitcase, and …

But I didn't want to disturb Saturn. He had been alone every day for a week.

As if reading my mind, he nuzzled my hand. I scratched his head.

"Do the duty that lies nearest," I said, and stayed where I was.

Chapter 14

White Christmas

Saturn and I, well-content, slept on the sofa till a lustrous full moon, beaming though the living room window, woke me before dawn. Half-asleep, half-dreaming, I stood, wrapped the afghan around my shoulders, stepped out into the crisp morning air, and gazed up through the bare branches of the sweet gum tree that grew near the street. I couldn't remember the last time I had enjoyed such an unblemished moment. Shivering, I walked inside and turned on the coffee pot. The perfect weather for my favorite sweater, I thought, and headed to the unpacked suitcase.

I sorted through my folded clothes, searching for my royal blue cardigan, unpacking and piling things on the bed or dresser as I went. When I found my sweater in the middle of the stack, I lectured myself for not hanging it up the night before and turned on the iron. Then I returned to the suitcase for the rest of my clothes and my manuscript, which must be in there since it wasn't in my book bag. When I lifted out the last pair of jeans, I stood there, dumbfounded. The manuscript wasn't there—only an empty manila folder marked "Outline."

Sitting on the bed, I blinked my eyes like a survivor drawn up from a deep well.

I had made four trips to the Magnolia Arms and had *never* left anything behind.

Until now.

In an instant I remembered I'd left most of my work on the third floor when I'd traded rooms with Ivy Leigh. The rest, shoved aside when I searched for my music, was in Margaret's old room. After the week I'd had, was it any wonder I hadn't managed to pack everything?

Taking my sweater to the ironing board, I tested the temperature of the iron. The steam smoothed the wrinkles; my reflections straightened my thinking.

There was no point really—was there?—in working on the story before we sifted through the material Nestor brought back from Millie Hubbard.

Without the compulsion "to write" on my mind, I could concentrate on teaching ... and practicing the piano.

Once the fine arts festival was over, I would get back to work on the book ... the beginning of the story Sefton had left half-finished and turned over to me.

For now ... I was ...

Relieved.

At long last ... I had one less thing to worry about.

But I was still worried about Ham.

When I arrived at school, I headed straight to Lorna's classroom. Since several students were already in their seats, I stood at the door.

Her face brightened when she noticed me. She snatched her coat from the back of her chair and hurried over.

"Cold, isn't it? Already feels like Christmas. Didn't we have the best time?" she asked. "It's so hard to concentrate on work."

"That's what I want to talk to you about," I said. "The time we had, I mean."

Puzzled by my somber tone, she stepped into the hall.

When I told her about Ham, tears pooled in her beautiful blue eyes.

"I didn't mean to give him the wrong idea," she said. "Should I talk to him?"

"No. Don't say a word. And whatever you do, don't mention Oliver ... not yet."

"Margaret and Elinor know," she said. "Grace, too, of course."

"I'll talk to them. Ham has a small social circle, so we should be able to keep Oliver a secret for a while. So, are you and Oliver officially—?"

"I'm not sure what we are, but whatever it is, it's wonderful."

"Oliver doesn't remind you of Nolan?" I asked. "Temperamental artist and all that?"

For the first time since I'd known her, Lorna laughed—heartfelt, joyful, infectious.

"No," she said. "They're not in the same class. Oliver is more talented than Nolan could ever hope to be. And best of all, way more talented than me. And he knows it."

"And that's a good thing?" I asked.

A faraway look in her eye, she buttoned her coat. "Yes. Oliver will never be jealous or insecure, so he'll never resent me. In fact, he's determined to help me succeed."

"You're going back to the piano?"

She nodded. "I'll finish the year teaching, and then start where I left off."

"Does Morton know?"

She laughed again. "He said nothing has ever made him happier … except Winnie."

When I returned to my office after morning classes, I found a note under my door. Charlotte had invited me to dinner "to discuss an important matter."

After school, I hurried home to feed Saturn, change clothes, and get my winter coat out of the closet. The temperature had been dropping all day.

The phone rang as I was leaving.

Winnie was almost breathless when I answered.

"I'm glad I caught you," she said. "Flossie's at her cake decorating class."

"Is she all right?" I asked.

"She's fine. I wanted to talk to you in private. How's Mary Smith?"

I glanced at the peace lily in the corner. "Thriving," I said.

The lilt in her voice was like Lorna's. "Thriving … like me."

"I'm on my way out the door, Winnie. Can I call you back?"

"This will only take a minute. It's about Christmas. You've probably guessed Morton and I plan to spend it together."

I pressed the receiver between my right ear and shoulder as I aimed my left arm at my coat sleeve. "Yes."

"We had planned to go back to the Magnolia Arms, but when I called Ivy Leigh, she said the house would be closed this year."

My coat swung behind my back as I grabbed the receiver with my hand. "What?"

"Xander and Posey are going to her home. Chester is spending the holidays with Grace."

Inconceivable. The Magnolia Arms empty and cold and dark when there should be 'chestnuts roasting on the open fire' and sugar cookies baking in the kitchen? Even if I wasn't going to be there myself, I wanted an appropriate image to keep in mind.

"But what about Ivy Leigh … and Nestor?" I asked.

"Margaret has invited them to visit her and Jonas. Didn't you know?"

"No, I haven't talked to them since I got home."

"It's one thing to meet Morton at the Magnolia Arms. Flossie would have other people to talk to. But you know the old saying, 'Two's company; three's a—'"

"She wouldn't want to go, anyway," I said, "under those circumstances."

"I don't think so either, but I still can't find the courage to tell her my plans."

"Don't say anything … not yet," I said. "I'll call tomorrow and invite her here."

"I knew you'd say that," Winnie said. "Could I ask you one more question?"

I propped the receiver on my left shoulder and slipped my right arm into my coat.

"Yes, but then I have to go," I said. "I don't want to be late to Charlotte's."

"It might be a little premature, but I've been wondering about my new name … hypothetically. Parker-Potts has a nice ring to it, but Parker-Potts-Penrose … is that too much?"

Glad Winnie could not see the look on my face, I steadied my voice.

"Are you sure you're not getting a little ahead of yourself? You hardly know Morton."

"Just because I didn't expect love to show up doesn't mean I'm going to refuse it."

What did I know? Winnie had been married twice to men she loved so much she couldn't bear to part with their names.

"Then this might be a good time to make a clean break with the past," I said, "and be known simply as Winifred Penrose. I'm sure neither Vernon nor Arthur would mind."

"Maybe … but I do so love hyphenated names. And there is my novel to consider."

"Your novel?"

"*The Gladiola Murders* by Winifred Parker-Potts. Remember? I told you on the train. I've imagined the cover so often, I don't know if I could change my name willy-nilly."

Straightening my collar, I struggled to sound serious.

"Parker-Potts could be your pen name," I said.

I could almost hear her face breaking into a smile. "Of course. Like the Brontë sisters and Mary Ann Evans. Thank you, Agnes. You always know what to do."

For everyone except myself, I thought.

Picking up the red pen on the kitchen table, I added Flossie's name to my Christmas list and hurried to my truck.

When I arrived at Charlotte's house, the butler led me to the dining room where the table was set for two. A fire roared in the fireplace.

"Isn't Monty joining us?" I asked, as Charlotte took her place at the head of the table.

She spread the linen napkin in her lap. "A little subterfuge on my part. I asked Jonas and Margaret to invite him to their home, so I could talk to you alone."

"Monty's better, isn't he?"

Holding a crystal goblet with pinky finger raised, she sipped her water. "Yes, he's improving ... doing so well I'm going to surprise him with a trip to England."

"You're not eloping, are you?"

"Goodness, no," she said, so startled by my question her glass clinked against the edge of her plate as she set it down. "Whatever gave you that idea?"

"It seems like everyone I know is in love and getting married."

"Everyone?"

"Maybe that's an exaggeration. But you'd understand if you knew the whole story."

"The evening is young," she said. "And I do love your stories."

Beginning with Morton's unexpected arrival, I recounted the events of the previous week. In spite of my solemn tone, Charlotte laughed often, saying she "wished she could've seen that."

"And then on Friday," I said, "Nestor proposed."

She held her hand to heart. "What a relief. The night of the dinner party my heart *ached* for him as he watched you with that lawyer." She held out her hand. "May I see your ring?"

"I ... I didn't say yes."

She looked at me as if I'd confessed to stealing her silverware.

"You refused him?" she asked.

"No ... not exactly. I didn't answer at all."

"May I ask *why*?"

"I'm ... I'm not in love with him."

"Hmmm," she said, as if I'd confessed to believing the earth was flat.

"Not my fault. He *told* me not to say anything—that the 'evening had been perfect' and Ivy Leigh told him I wouldn't *know* what to say and he should let me think."

"A true gentleman," she said. "Just like my Exton."

She referred to her husband Exton Vale Wrayburn II, a wealthy, self-made man, whose formal portrait in the library had never once reminded me of Nestor.

"I've never thought of Nestor as a gentleman … exactly," I said.

"Then you have a faulty notion of what the word means. Come with me."

Leaving the dining room, I followed Charlotte past the staircase and the conservatory to a room I had never entered. She opened the double doors, turned on the light, and breathed in.

"After all these years," she said, "the room still has Exton's scent."

She walked to her husband's magnificent mahogany desk and standing behind his burgundy leather chair, rested her hands on the back. The wistful look in her eyes led me to believe she was reliving the memory of placing her hands on Exton's shoulders to remind him of dinner. I kept still until she motioned me to join her. When I stepped beside her, she pointed to the framed family photos lining the desk. Among them was a drawing of penciled stick figures with smiling faces—a man and little boy—with "Thanks—Love, Joe" scrawled underneath.

Since I knew Charlotte had one daughter and one son, Exton Vale Wrayburn III, I asked if Joe was a nephew.

"No. A lifelong friend. Exton was awarded many honors and commendations. He's received letters from senators, governors, corporation presidents. See any of them on display?"

I surveyed the room. "No."

She took the framed drawing from the desk and walked to the brown leather chairs by the window. Sitting down, she patted the arm of the other chair. I joined her.

"Like you and Nestor," she said, "Exton and I were friends. Our fathers became business partners when we were twelve, and our mothers decided we would be perfect for each other."

"Your marriage was arranged?"

"Not exactly, but both sets of parents saw the wisdom in the match. I resisted, out of childish rebellion, because, like you, I dreamed of romance with a white knight."

I was miffed at the 'childish' comparison. "Not a white knight exactly. I—"

She held up her hand. "I knew Exton loved me, but no matter how much my mother reasoned with me, I refused to see him except at the social events which threw us together."

Holding Joe's drawing with both hands, she gazed at it as she spoke.

"One snowy evening Exton arrived late at a formal dinner party at our home. He was shivering. His shoes and pants, up to the knees, were soaked. His face was red and chapped."

"I suppose his tardiness was frowned on," I said.

"Fourteen pairs of condescending eyes turned on him. He apologized without explaining, slid into his seat, and hunched over his soup, trying to warm himself."

"Had his car broken down?"

"No. He'd arrived on time, but when he got to our house, he found a little boy crying on the sidewalk. He was delivering his evening papers when his wagon lost a wheel."

"Joe."

She nodded. "Exton tried to fix the wheel, but when he couldn't, he walked the rest of Joe's route with him. The next day Joe came to our door with this note and told me the story."

"He thought Exton lived at your house," I said.

"He said he'd watched the 'nice man' come into our house and asked me to deliver the note. When I unfolded this paper and read it … I fell in love with Exton on the spot."

"That's a wonderful memory."

She turned to me. "Like you, I expected my heart to pound and my stomach to quiver when the man I loved looked into my eyes. But that's a pitiful excuse to marry someone."

I thought of my mother and Russ Wilcox.

"I've heard."

She turned Joe's drawing to face me.

"Any number of ordinary men can make your heart flutter on a moonlight stroll, but precious few will make your heart swell with pride as they help the 'Joe's' of this world."

"Do you know where Joe is now?" I asked.

"On the faculty of Harvard Business School. He credits Exton with his success."

"Is that why your husband kept the note all these years?"

She returned the photo to the desk. "No. He kept it because he said it was this note that drew my heart to him."

The door opened quietly as the butler entered.

"Excuse me, ma'am," he said. "Your son is on the phone and insists on speaking to you. Shall I have him call you back, or would you like to take the call now? He says it's urgent."

"I'll take the call in here. Thank you." Charlotte said.

She picked up the phone on Exton's desk.

"Hello, dear … No. I haven't changed my mind … I know we pay her well, but I refuse to ask her to give up her trip home, because you forgot to tell me you're all going to Aspen."

I'd never heard Charlotte sound stern.

"That won't be necessary," she said. "I've thought of a solution on my own. No, the house will not be empty. No need to worry. I'll call when my plan is finalized."

She hung up the phone.

"Is everything all right?" I asked.

"That will be up to you. Shall we have coffee and dessert in the library?"

We walked to the library and settled in the wingback chairs with cups and saucers on the end tables and dessert plates in our hands.

"Even though Exton is no longer here, I try to do things as he would," Charlotte said. "He always allowed our staff to spend the week of Christmas at home with their families."

"Very generous."

"I've never wavered from that tradition. My florist has the house decorated by the 5th of December, and my cook prepares plenty to eat for any family or friends who visit."

"Do you ever spend Christmas at your children's homes?"

She lowered her voice as if the room were full of people. "To tell you the truth, I don't much care for it. I love my daughter and daughter-in-law, but their celebrations are so formal."

More formal than this house? I thought. How is that possible?

"I don't travel much anymore," she said, "but on the rare occasions I do take a trip, one of my grandchildren will volunteer to stay here and take care of Primrose. She's a sensitive little bird and needs companionship. My children think I'm silly to dote on a canary the way I do."

"Not silly at all," I said. "I feel the same way about my cat."

"When my family found out I would be spending Christmas in England, they made plans to go skiing in Aspen. No one is available to come here."

Smiling, I asked, "Is Primrose the 'important matter' you want to discuss?"

"He is. I want to hire you to bird-sit. You won't lack for anything, and you can play the piano to your heart's content. I know you're practicing for the festival."

"In the first place, you wouldn't have to hire me," I said. "I'd love to stay, but I promised my parents I'd come home."

She leaned forward. "Would they consider coming here instead? There's plenty of room. You can invite anyone you wish and have Christmas dinner in my dining room."

Since my mother had met Charlotte on her first and only trip to see me and could not believe "such a cultured lady" would befriend me, I was sure she would leap at the opportunity. I dialed my parents' number, told my mother someone would like to speak to her, and handed the phone to Charlotte. After a polite greeting, she issued the invitation, responded to a few more questions from my mother, and returned the phone to me.

"What do you think, Mom?" I asked. "Would you like to spend Christmas here?"

Mom whispered as if Charlotte could overhear. "Can you find out if we can use her kitchen to cook dinner? I thought it would be rude to ask. I hardly know her."

"I'm sure it won't be a problem," I said.

"And I'll need the address so Aunt Minnie can forward the fruitcake there."

"Have her send it to my apartment," I said, mortified at the thought of the cardboard box decorated with candy cane stickers showing up on Charlotte's doorstep.

"I can't believe it," Mom said. "I never dreamed I'd get to see inside Charlotte's house."

"We'll invite some of my friends for Christmas dinner," I said, "if that's okay with you."

"Jonas?" Mom asked.

Mom had also met Jonas on her first visit. His charm had won her heart.

"Yes, and his wife Margaret," I said. "And a couple of friends from the Magnolia Arms."

"How nice. I've never met any of your friends from … what's the name of the town?"

"Dennisonville," I said. "There'll only be two of them. Ivy Leigh and Nestor."

"Ivy Leigh is the owner, right?" Mom asked.

"Yes."

"And Nestor. He's the gardener … I think you said?"

"Yes, and owns his own floral business—Plum Perfect Posies."

"I remember. You don't talk about him very often, but, of course, last year Sefton was here. It wouldn't have been right to talk about another man, even if you were only friends."

"No. I guess not."

"I've always wanted to ask a professional gardener about my daffodils," she said.

Charlotte and I spent the rest of the evening going over the arrangements.

"There's one more thing," I said. "May I bring my cat?"

"Yes," she said. "My daughter Alexandra always had a cat. He had an adjoining room."

I thought she was joking. I found out she wasn't.

When I arrived at home, I called the Magnolia Arms. Ivy Leigh answered.

"Do you have something to tell me?" I asked.

"Now don't get testy," she said. "I was going to tell you when I called to say we found your book in Margaret's room. Nestor couldn't believe you left it behind."

"Neither could I."

"I'm surprised *you* haven't called before now. I thought you'd be in a panic."

"I knew it would be safe with you."

"Safe with Nestor, you mean. He has the whole thing spread out on the floor in Monty's room. He's forbidden me to clean in there."

"Tell him to go upstairs," I said. "The rest of the book is in *my* room."

"Hold on. I'll get him. You can tell him yourself."

I took a deep breath and hoped he wouldn't bring up the proposal again. Not yet.

In a few minutes Nestor picked up the phone.

"Hello," he said. "How's school?"

"A little rough getting started again. But I'm getting back in the swing of things. Ivy Leigh said you found the manuscript."

"To tell you the truth, I'm glad you left it here. It's made it easier to piece everything together. I gotta hand it to Sefton. He was a mediocre writer, but he knows how to take notes."

"At least he had one good quality, even if he is a terrible judge of people."

"His loss … as the saying goes," Nestor said.

I didn't know if he meant me … or the book … and didn't ask.

"I've got good news for you," I said. "The rest of the manuscript is in my room."

"That doesn't sound like you." He paused. "Is it my fault?"

"I couldn't say."

The moment went unaddressed.

"Once I get things in order, I'll make a copy of everything and bring it when we come for Christmas," he said. "Think we'll have time to work when I get there? When do you go home?"

"We'll have plenty of time. Charlotte offered to let me stay at her house while she and Monty take a trip to England. My parents are coming here."

There was a long silence. I could picture him holding his hand over the receiver and whispering to Ivy Leigh, who, in turn shook her head and held her finger to her lips.

His voice was calm. "That's good news. I'm excited about … meeting your parents."

"Charlotte said we could have Christmas dinner here. I'll invite Margaret and Jonas tomorrow. And Ryder and Elinor. Bentley and the Hamptons. And Flossie."

"Flossie's coming back?"

The mention of Flossie eased us into our familiar way of talking about friends and work. The proposal never came up. We said good night.

The next day I called Flossie and told her about Charlotte's invitation.

"Charlotte wants me to stay in her room with the canary, so I was hoping you could come here and keep an eye on Saturn. You know jealous he can be."

We *both* knew what I was really saying, "I know you don't have anywhere else to go," but we left this unsaid, and she assured me she would love to come.

When I called Margaret about Christmas dinner, she told me Ryder and Elinor had been invited to spend the holidays at his daughter's home. Kennesaw … John … was going with them.

As requested, I informed Charlotte of the number of guests who would be needing rooms, as well as the names of the people invited for dinner. She sent out formal invitations.

As soon as the inevitable bluster and bustle of December overtook us, Grace and Lorna drafted me for a shopping trip to "buy presents for our boyfriends," a ritual I might have embraced in high school or college … even last year … but not now.

I offered a dozen different excuses, all refused.

"We hate to admit it," Grace said, "but at this point you've known both our boyfriends longer than we have."

The absurdity of this argument was unsupportable enough, but then Lorna had the nerve to ask what I'd "bought for Sefton last year."

When I replied "a Cross pen," they commended me for a brilliant idea.

"Oliver could use a nice pen to sign autographs on concert programs," Lorna said.

And Grace, hopeful Chester was joining the Brighton Park science faculty in the fall, said, "A pen is the perfect gift for a new teacher. Would Nestor like a Cross pen?"

"Somehow I doubt it," I said. "He usually has a pencil behind his ear."

"Even if all he does is leave the pen in a desk drawer, it's still a great gift," Lorna said.

"And we can have them engraved," Grace said.

When Lorna asked if we should use their initials or full names, Grace looked puzzled.

"I don't know Chester's middle name. Do you, Agnes?"

"As a matter of fact, I do," I said. "Xander used to make fun of it … Godfrey."

"Godfrey," Grace said, "It's so … noble."

"What's Nestor's middle name?" Lorna asked.

They were stunned to discover I didn't know. So was I.

In spite of nose diving temperatures and ceaseless office chatter about "the worst winter we've had in years," I moved through the remaining days of the semester in good spirits.

Without his beard and alias, John Ellershaw no longer seemed threatening. Grace, ever deeper in love, smiled all the time. Lorna practiced every day. Even Sharon and Elspeth were at peace with me after I revised the festival program and produced a glowing introduction about the "principal artist." I frequented Rehearsal Hall and pounded away at Liebestraum and Barcarolle till they were near perfect. Without a writing deadline to distract me, my teaching schedule didn't seem daunting. Infused with Christmas spirit, I devoted one class period to reading "A Christmas Carol." Big Tony Castarini accepted my invitation to sit in.

Nestor and I talked once a week—sometimes more. When discussing the Bridgers, we were the same familiar friends. But once the official collaborating was finished, an invisible door closed between us, isolating us in separate places. I hated to admit I was to blame for the quiet, unfamiliar melancholy in Nestor's voice. After every phone call I rehearsed the same scenario with the same outcome: If I said I loved him, and we tried and failed at a "relationship," I would lose my best friend. When I returned to the Magnolia Arms, nothing would be the same.

Almost as distressing was my growing awareness that Nestor was outdistancing me in his knowledge of Bridger family history. He seldom mentioned his past, so I often forgot he had once pursued a Ph.D. in history and was adept at organizing research and crafting it into a coherent, engaging story. Sometimes when he reviewed what he'd found among Millie's well-kept family archives—a photo of Julia and Jameson at Eliot's grave, a picture of the church steeple where Julia "donated the bell in Eliot's memory," the deed to the Bridger family property, even Julia's recipe for pound cake—I envied him.

Charlotte and Monty left on December 19th. Saturn and I drove over that night. The estate manager let me in, handed me an envelope marked "Room Assignments," and gave me his number in case of an emergency. Thanking me, he left. I toured the downstairs, finding Christmas trees, each decorated with a different theme, in every room except the kitchen, where the counters were lined with containers of cookies, candy, and gourmet coffee. Over the fireplace in the formal living room was a garland of holly and five red velvet stockings embroidered *Agnes, Stuart, Elizabeth, Flossie, and Saturn.*

Tucking the envelope under one arm, I picked up Saturn and walked upstairs. I stood in the wide hallway, opened the envelope, and found a diagram indicating which rooms were to be used. I entered Flossie's room. On the nightstand was a note explaining the door to the right opened into "Saturn's room." Beyond that door was a feline paradise, complete with bed, dishes, multi-tiered cat tower, and exercise wheel. I deposited Saturn and found Charlotte's room. My whole apartment would have fit inside with space left over. I tiptoed to the gilded bird cage and whispered to Primrose.

"If it weren't for you, little birdie," I said, "I'd be on a train all night. So thank you."

Flossie, happy to see me, but more reserved than usual, arrived the next morning. Claiming to be tired from her trip, she spent most of the morning knitting in the library. Over lunch I tried to start a casual conversation about the plans for the new baby, but she shared as little information as she would offer to a total stranger. When we finished eating, she went to her room. I practiced the piano and stared out at the garden, remembering the first time I had strolled there with Charlotte when she told me how she and Exton had met Jonas.

My parents arrived on the 21st. My mother, who usually greeted me with a barrage of questions, hardly acknowledged my presence as she walked through the downstairs, admiring the paintings, chandeliers, poinsettias, furniture, and windows.

"Everything is so elegant," she said, "and yet it's very warm and homey, isn't it?"

"That's because of Charlotte," I said.

With Saturn in her arms, Flossie walked downstairs.

"He started meowing when he heard your voice, Mrs. Quinn," Flossie said.

Saturn leaped from Flossie's arms and sauntered to my mother.

Mom picked up the cat and met Flossie at the foot of the stairs.

"You must be Flossie," she said. "And please, call me Betty."

I couldn't believe what I was hearing. After all the times my mother had referred to Flossie as "that woman who lives with me," she appeared to be delighted to meet her.

Maybe it was the surroundings which bred culture and civility in her.

Or a little taste of Peace on Earth, Good Will to Men.

My mother couldn't rest until she had taken a tour of the kitchen. Flossie, assuming the role of hostess, led the way.

Leaving them to explore the pantry and refrigerator, I went to look for my father, and was surprised to find him scanning the shelves in the library.

"I knew you'd like this room," I said. "Isn't it beautiful?"

He took a book from the shelf and peered at Exton Wrayburn's portrait on the wall. "You wouldn't think a man like Mr. ... what was his name?"

"Wrayburn."

"... Mr. Wrayburn would have Zane Gray on his shelf, but I suppose there's a little cowboy in all of us, no matter how much money we have."

"What book is that?" I asked.

"*Riders of the Purple Sage.* Can't remember how many times I've read it, but old books are like old friends. Sometimes you need to drop in on them again to see how they're doing."

He sank onto the leather sofa and opened the book.

It was strange to see to see my hard-working, middle-class father at ease in this luxurious setting and even stranger to hear him speak like a poet.

Nestor and Ivy Leigh arrived that night. Margaret called to discuss plans for the next day.

"Ivy Leigh and I are taking Elinor shopping tomorrow," Margaret said. "She needs a new coat for the trip and presents for her new granddaughters. Would you girls like to join us?"

My mother jumped at the chance. When Flossie tried to resist, my mother refused to allow her to stay home.

The following morning Jonas dropped off Margaret and Ivy Leigh at Charlotte's house. Then he borrowed my truck to take my dad to the Hamptons' home.

"Tourists would pay to see their workshop if they only knew," Jonas told him.

We picked up Elinor, and the harrowing ride began. I hadn't stopped to consider the key factor these five women had in common was *me*. Wedged between Flossie and my mother in the back seat, I cringed at every question about my childhood and winced at every embarrassing story my mother told. Elinor and Margaret shared the story of my disastrous first year at Brighton Park and then moved on to the day when I'd "practically tackled Elspeth Sherwood." Ivy Leigh told how I'd bested Oliver when we first met, and conned him into being in the talent show.

No matter what I tried, I could not steer their conversation away from me.

My mother leaned over me to speak to Flossie.

"How about you, Flossie? Any stories to tell about your old roommate?"

Flossie pursed her lips. "Well, there was the time she stood up for me to the rector's wife, and took me in when my son kicked me out, and came to take me home after I was kidnapped."

Everyone fell into an awkward silence—more uncomfortable than the teasing.

"So, Elinor, tell us about Ryder's daughter," I said. "What's she like?"

Elinor's story lasted the rest of the trip. On the return trip I insisted on driving.

At the end of the day we dropped off Elinor at home and drove to Jonas and Margaret's house. We were surprised to find Mr. Hampton's car in the driveway.

Nestor, as he had the night of the dinner party, met us at the door and bowed low.

"Welcome, ladies," he said. "Dinner is served."

"You must be Nestor," my mother said.

He took her hand. "I am. I understand you're having problems with your daffodils."

As they walked away, he glanced over his shoulder and winked at me.

Jonas took Margaret's shopping bags and pointed to the table, set for dinner.

"What's all this?" Margaret asked.

"Mr. Hampton's idea," he said. "He knew you'd all be tired and suggested we fix dinner. The steaks are on the grill."

"Steak?" Ivy Leigh asked.

The table was spread with macaroni and cheese, baked beans, and rolls. The men wasted no time in crediting Mr. Hampton and Ham with the preparations.

"When two men live alone," Mr. Hampton said, "they learn how to cook or do without."

I introduced the Hamptons and Bentley to my mother and Flossie.

We sat down with solid food and solid friends.

Jonas was at the head of the table with Margaret on his right and Ivy Leigh on his left. I loved seeing Margaret and Ivy Leigh across the table from each other again. There is no laughter as genuine as that shared by women who've been friends for decades. Jonas, supremely happy, spent most of the meal shaking his head at their silliness and smiling at me.

Nestor sat at the other end with me on his right and Bentley on his left. Flossie sat next to Bentley. The two were soon engaged in quiet conversation. When I heard Flossie say, "Warner," I wondered if she was asking Bentley about prison life.

My parents sat between Margaret and Flossie. My father was absorbed in his eating, but my mother was the life of the party. Quizzing each person in turn, she could not garner information fast enough. When she realized Mr. Hampton was the man who gave Toby the Thunderbird, she nearly came out of her chair.

"That makes perfect sense," she said. "I don't know why I didn't put it together sooner. I have to thank you, Mr. Hampton. You transformed my son's life."

"Call me Torbert," he said. "It wasn't my doing. He only needed a little perspective."

"And you, too ... Ham, isn't it?" my mother asked. "Toby told me all about you."

Ham looked up. "We like Toby. Hope he'll come back."

His voice was flat and lifeless. When the conversation shifted to the frigid weather and the storm expected on Christmas Eve, I leaned over and whispered to him.

"How are you, Ham? Did you have fun showing off the workshop to my dad?"

He looked at me as if I were tapping out Morse code.

"I'm sorry ... what?"

"The workshop? Did my dad ask a zillion questions about your tools?"

"He wasn't there very long. He and Nestor went for a drive in the Corvair. They were gone most of the afternoon."

"They were? I didn't know my dad was interested in—"

His eyes vacant and voice hollow, Ham turned to me. "Have you heard from ... I mean do you know where Lorna ... Miss Maron ... is? Did she go home for Christmas?"

Nestor looked up from his plate.

"She didn't tell me," I said, "but I assume she's at home."

I knew she was with Oliver.

He moved his uneaten food from one side of the plate to the other. "I didn't get a chance to see her before she left. Do you think she'll call you?"

"She might."

"If she does ... would you tell her we hired a piano tuner for the piano in Rehearsal Hall? It wasn't in the budget, so I offered to pay for it. My Christmas gift to her."

"Maybe Margaret knows how to reach her. I'll find out."

When dessert was offered, Ham and I both said no. We had lost our appetites.

At the end of the evening, my mother told everyone she felt as if she'd "known them all her life" and "it would be like having family over" when they came for Christmas dinner.

Ivy Leigh waged war with Mr. Hampton over who would clean the kitchen, insisting, "Those who cook shouldn't have to clean up," when the phone rang. Jonas left to answer it.

After Bentley and the Hamptons left, Margaret stood chatting with Flossie and my parents at the front door. I was lingering a few feet away when Nestor grabbed my hand and pulled me back toward the living room.

"I need to talk to you," he said.

"I know. I'm sorry we haven't had time. I've been so busy with—"

"It's not about me. It's about Ham. Is there anything we can do to help him?"

"What do you mean?"

"He's in love with Lorna, isn't he?"

"What makes you think he's in love?" I asked.

He rolled his eyes. "You're seriously asking *me* how I recognize the symptoms?"

"Sorry."

"I knew something was bothering him," Nestor said, "but didn't know what it was till he mentioned Lorna to you. Ham doesn't know about Oliver, does he?"

"No. Not yet."

Jonas returned from his office. "Is Ivy Leigh still in the kitchen?"

"I think so," I said. "Was the phone for her?"

He nodded. "It was the neighbor, Ida—?"

"Willingale," Nestor said. "She's taking care of the house. Is something wrong?"

"It's raining, and the temperature is dropping. Ida's afraid of an ice storm. Kept talking about the maple tree next door and saying conditions were 'just like they were in '73.'"

My father approached us. "The ladies are ready to go, Jonas. Are you still driving them back to Charlotte's house?"

"I'll get my keys," Jonas said. He turned to Nestor. "Will you give Ivy Leigh the message?"

Nestor sighed. "I will, but she's not going to like it. See you tomorrow, Agnes?"

"I'm taking Mom to the grocery store in the morning. After that?"

"I'll be there. Bye, Mr. Quinn," Nestor said. "It was nice talking to you."

They shook hands. Nestor left for the kitchen.

Dad put his arm around me. "All right if I ride in your truck with you?"

I held out the keys. "If you want to drive my truck, all you had to do was ask."

"I've driven enough for one day," Dad said. "I want to spend a little time with my favorite daughter."

We had not reached the end of the driveway before Dad cleared his throat.

"I had doubts about this trip, but I really enjoyed the day. You have good friends."

"Toby thought so, too."

His eyes were fixed on the road. "I was a proud dad today, Agnes. Every one of those men had nice things to say about you." He paused. "One of them asked if he could marry you."

My foot slipped off the accelerator.

"I … I was going to tell you and Mom when you got here, but—"

He held up his hand. "I'm not upset. I admire Nestor for asking my permission even if you haven't given him an answer. He's a step up from that guy you brought home last year."

"You never told me you didn't like Sefton."

Snow began to fall.

"Saw straight through him," Dad said. "But your mother liked him, so what could I say?"

I turned on the windshield wipers. "You like Nestor?"

"After five minutes. You need to tell your mother he proposed. She'll be hurt if she finds out from someone else, and there are a lot of people who know."

The next morning I invited my mother to breakfast at Bob's Pancake World. When we sat down, she looked at her watch.

"I want to leave for the store in 45 minutes," she said. "If it starts to snow before we get back, the groceries in the back of the truck will—"

"Dad thought of that. He found a tarp in the garage. I don't know why we need to go to the store anyway. Charlotte had the pantry and refrigerator stocked before she left."

Mom stirred cream into her coffee. "I know, but there are special things I use. And we still need to go by your apartment to see if Aunt Minnie's fruitcake arrived."

Promising to watch the time and check on the fruitcake, I ordered a scrambled egg.

Then I told my mother about Nestor's proposal.

She rested her elbows on the table and let her coffee go cold.

"He grew a rose and named it for you?" she asked. "That's the most romantic thing I ever heard. So … are you telling me you're engaged?"

"No. I haven't given him an answer yet. He took me off guard."

She took a sip of her cold coffee and grimaced. "Don't talk to me about being taken off guard by a proposal. First prize for that goes to me."

I signaled the server and asked for more coffee. "Which proposal? Russ? Or Dad?"

"Both, actually. But I meant when your dad proposed." She stared out the window. "I'd been crying in my room all day. Mama came to the door and told me to come downstairs."

"How soon was this after your ... separation ... from Russ?"

"The next day. Can you believe it? My father and Stuart were waiting for me in the living room. Papa said, 'I've come up with a solution to our problem, and Stuart here has agreed.'"

The server returned with hot coffee. Mom held the warm mug with both hands.

"Yikes," I said. "Did you want to fall through the floor?"

"I felt worse for Stuart. He had on the same suit he'd worn to the homecoming dance. Papa told me to sit down. Then he clapped Stuart on the back and left the room."

She looked down at the table, straightening the salt and pepper shakers as she spoke.

"Stuart knelt on one knee and took my hand. He said, 'I know I'm not your first choice, but I do love you. If you'll marry me, I'll take care of you and love your child like my own.'"

"Talk about a knight in shining armor."

"And I didn't see it till then, because he'd always been the 'boy who worked for my father.'" She looked at her watch. "Look at the time. Are you finished?"

"I ... I guess so," I said, startled at the abrupt change of subject.

Standing, she put on her coat. "The groceries aren't going to buy themselves."

"Is that all you have to say?"

She picked up her purse. "Even after all these years, I still don't like to talk about it. And besides that, I'm not really the best person to ask for relationship advice, am I?"

"But you've been married for over thirty years."

"To a man who loved me in spite of my faults and waited forever for me to love him back." She picked up the ticket the server had left on the table. "Can you leave the tip?"

There was no more talk about Dad or anything else. Mom was quiet on the ride to the store and then busied herself comparing prices and checking things off her list.

When we arrived at Charlotte's house, we saw Jonas' car in the driveway. I parked near the kitchen door, pulled the tarp off the groceries and lifted two bags from the back of my truck.

Nestor, tying a gray plaid scarf around his neck, bounded from the house. "Need some help?"

"We were just talking about you," Mom said.

He took the bags she was carrying and gave her a peck on the cheek. "Something good, I hope," he said.

"The Agnes Carlyle Rose," she said. "Can you send me a picture of it?"

"As soon as I get home," he said.

Holding a bag in both arms, I followed them into the kitchen.

"Can you two get the rest?" Mom asked. "I'm going to change shoes and get to work. Did Jonas come with you?"

"He's talking to your husband," Nestor said, and left through the back door.

I took off my coat and started unloading the bags. Nestor made two more trips outside.

"That's it," he said, shaking snow from his hair. "So now both your parents know. Did they say anything?"

I set a jar of marshmallow crème on the counter. "My dad said he never liked Sefton."

"Said that to me, too. What did your mom say?"

"She said your proposal was—"

Flossie came into the kitchen. "Need some help before I go?"

I turned around. "Go where?"

"Bentley invited me to spend the day with him. He got his driver's license back last week and wants to celebrate. Do I look all right? I can't do as well with my hair as Winnie can."

Dressed in black pants and a red pullover sweater, she had dabbed rouge on her cheeks and tried to style her hair.

"You look beautiful," Nestor said. "Where are you going?"

"He won't tell me," Flossie said. "We're going in Torbert's car, the 1949 Olds. Have you seen it?"

"I have," Nestor said. "It suits you."

"I hate to leave your mother with all the work, Agnes," Flossie said. "Will she mind?"

"Not at all. I'm sure Ivy Leigh will show up later today. Does Bentley remember how to drive in snow?"

"Didn't ask," she said. "I knitted him a new scarf last night. Green to match the car."

"Maybe you and Bentley should stay here," I said. "You could have lunch in the conservatory and watch the snow fall."

She shook her head. "Everyone in my life is being romanced except me. It's my turn."

"Don't worry," Nestor said, after she left. "Mr. Hampton won't give Bentley the keys if he's worried about their safety." He folded the last empty bag. "Ready to get to work?"

"Not much to do today. Mom will do most of her cooking tomorrow."

"Not dinner. Your book. I brought everything with me. Can we work in the library?"

"No. Dad's taken it over. There's a better place."

Nestor followed me to Exton's study.

We stood in the open door. Nestor gazed around the room.

"Sure it's okay for us to be in here?" he asked.

"I'm sure. Charlotte brought me in here before."

We walked to the chairs by the window.

He put two cardboard file boxes wrapped in brown paper on the floor.

"Wow," I said. "Looks like you were transporting state secrets."

"Not about to let anything happen to this cargo," he said. "Not after all the work I did. And I could never face Millie if I lost Julia's things."

He unwrapped the first box and pulled out a stack of paper an inch and a half thick. His eyes riveted on me, he laid the pages on the table between us. I pulled up my chair and beginning with "Chapter One," thumbed through page after page of pristine manuscript.

"When did you find time to do this?" I asked.

"Not much to do in the yard this time of year."

"You've done more work than Sefton and I put together."

"You don't give yourself enough credit," he said. "Once you look over it, you'll see."

"It's almost finished?"

"That's what we need to talk about," he said. "You'll have to decide on—"

There was a knock at the door.

"Agnes, are you in there?" my father asked. "Jonas needs to see Nestor."

Nestor walked to the door and opened it. My dad and Jonas came in.

"Sorry to interrupt," Jonas said. "Just got off the phone with Margaret. She said Ida has called four times since last night."

"Is the house all right?" Nestor asked.

"For now," Jonas said, "but Ivy Leigh is frantic. She insists on going home."

"She can't do that," Nestor said. "Not in this weather."

"That's what Margaret told her, but she won't listen."

Nestor closed his eyes. "I'll go."

"If you do," Jonas said, "you'll have to leave right away."

"Does your truck have snow tires, Agnes?" Nestor asked.

"Yes, but wouldn't the train be safer?" I asked.

"Maybe. But if a freight train gets stuck on the tracks somewhere, I could be stranded. Better to drive."

"I'll come with you," I said.

"No, you won't," Dad said. "Your mother would worry herself sick."

We walked to the front door. Mr. Hampton was waiting with Bentley, who was helping Flossie with her coat.

"I'm playing chauffeur for the afternoon," Mr. Hampton said. "Bentley's a little uneasy about the snow."

Bentley tied his new green scarf. "Haven't driven in it in years."

My mother, wiping her hands on her apron, came from the kitchen.

"Do we have company?" she asked.

Jonas explained Nestor was leaving for Dennisonville.

"How will you get there?" Mr. Hampton asked.

"Agnes is going to let me borrow her truck," Nestor said.

Mr. Hampton shook his head. "Take my truck. I put snow tires on it yesterday. My wife used to call it The Tank."

My mother put her arms around Nestor. "Please call us when you arrive."

"I will if the phone lines aren't down," he said. "Don't worry. I'm a good driver."

"Drive Nestor to my house, Jonas," Mr. Hampton said. "Ham can give you the keys to the truck."

"After I pack and say goodbye to Margaret and Ivy Leigh," Nestor said.

Flossie hugged Nestor. Bentley shook his hand.

"I'll wait for you in the car, Nestor," Jonas said.

My parents told Nestor goodbye.

Dad tugged on my mother's hand. "Is there any coffee, Betty?"

She took his hint, and they left for the kitchen.

Alone with Nestor, I felt small and childish. "Are you sure you have to go?"

"I'd be terrible company if I stayed, and Ivy Leigh would be a nervous wreck. At least I got to bring the book to you. Let me know what you think."

Putting my arms around him, I whispered. "Be careful."

He held me and then stepped back, took my face in both his hands, and kissed me ... for the second time.

Even better than the first in Ivy Leigh's office.

I helped him with his coat. "Wait. Let me get your Christmas present."

"Keep it till I come for the festival," he said.

"You're coming for the festival?"

"After all the practicing I had to listen to at Thanksgiving, I think I deserve to hear the finished product."

Shivering, I stood on the porch and watched as he and Jonas got in the car. They were halfway down the long circular drive when I ran after them, calling and waving.

Jonas stopped. Nestor got out. "What's wrong?"

"What's your middle name?" I asked.

"Remington. Why?"

I shrugged my shoulders. He laughed and got back in the car.

When I stepped back inside, Dad was waiting for me.

"Your mother sent me," he said. "She doesn't think you should be alone."

I followed him. We sat at the kitchen table with coffee, the comics, and the crossword puzzle, while my mother chopped and diced, stirred and flurried.

For a long time we said nothing. Then Mom placed her hands on the counter and gazed out the window as she spoke to my father.

"Do you think we'll get snowed in, Stuart?"

"Hard to say," Dad said. "But if we do, we have everything we need."

"Everything except our guests. I think they should come now, don't you?"

"Come now ... for Christmas?" I asked.

"Why not? If we get snowed in, Jonas and Margaret and Ivy Leigh will be alone over there, and we'll be alone here. We're all worried about Nestor. At least we could worry together."

"Bentley and the Hamptons could come, too," I said. "There's plenty of room."

Mom's face brightened. "Go call them. Tell them to pack some clothes and come on."

She turned back to the chopping board with renewed vigor.

When I talked to Margaret, I could hear the relief in her voice.

"A brilliant idea. It will give me and Ivy Leigh someone to stare at besides each other. As soon as we get Nestor on his way, we'll be over. I'm sure Jonas will agree."

When I called the Hamptons, Ham answered.

"Dad's not home yet," he said. "He's taken Bentley and Flossie to the Drifters' Rest."

I told him Nestor was leaving for the Magnolia Arms and invited him and his dad to join us at Charlotte's house.

"I'm sure Dad would love to come," he said.

"You'll come, too. Won't you?"

"Nestor will need someone to help him drive and take care of the house if anything happens. Where is he now?"

I explained his father's offer.

"Call and tell him I'll drive the truck to Jonas' house," Ham said. "We'll leave from there."

I had never heard Ham sound so confident and self-assured.

By mid-afternoon Jonas, Margaret, and Ivy Leigh arrived. The men retreated to the library. The women joined us in the kitchen. Ivy Leigh, sick with worry, said little, but Margaret shared the details Mom and I were eager to hear: Ham had arrived with the truck, and Margaret had prepared enough food to get them all the way to Dennisonville without stopping to eat.

"They were in great spirits," Margaret said, glancing at Ivy Leigh, who wasn't listening.

Mr. Hampton arrived with Bentley and Flossie, who was glowing ... not entirely from the cold. Mr. Hampton brought more food, board games, and a dart board.

After dinner, we congregated in the library. Jonas and Dad started a chess game. Bentley and Flossie sat side by side on the sofa, hardly aware of the rest of us, who were foolish enough to play Monopoly with Mr. Hampton. His cool-headed line of attack left us all bankrupt. After the game, my mother, as she had since I was nine, insisted I play the piano "for company." Everyone except Dad and Jonas, still locked in combat, moved to the conservatory. It was the wrong night for melancholy, so I played as many show tunes as I could remember.

Ivy Leigh nudged Margaret. "You're up, Megs. 'Hello, Dolly.'"

Margaret complied, singing as if she had practiced only yesterday, and then pulled Ivy Leigh from her wicker chair.

"Come on, Abby dear," she said, signaling Ivy Leigh to reprise their scene from "Arsenic and Old Lace," performed at the Magnolia Arms talent show last year.

Then Mr. Hampton shocked us all by offering to sing "Some Enchanted Evening" in a luxurious bass voice. He left us all in tears.

At 10:30 Dad came to the door. "Nestor just called. He and Ham are halfway there and doing fine. They said we should stop worrying."

Suddenly exhausted, we all went to bed.

Peeking under the cover on Primrose's cage, I whispered good night. Then I lay awake, thinking of the people sheltered under one roof, safe from the cold and snow. In this time and place, this poignant merging of my different worlds, only Margaret and Jonas seemed the same. Mr. Hampton, rough-hewn, was a singer. My frugal parents were at ease, reveling in luxury. Ivy Leigh, never ruffled, was anxious and distracted. Shy, awkward Ham had refused to stay behind when a friend needed help. Flossie and Bentley, cast aside so often in life, had found solace in each other.

I closed my eyes and prayed for Nestor and Ham and the house on Belmont Drive.

The next morning my mother tapped on my door.

"Wake up, Agnes. The snow has stopped, and Flossie made waffles."

The last to arrive at the dining room table, I sat next to Jonas.

"Is there any news?" I asked.

"I watched the morning report," Mr. Hampton said. "Plenty of stories about how the weather is affecting the big cities, but nothing about Dennisonville or any other small town."

We ate well and asked for seconds. Flossie stayed in the kitchen, producing plate after plate of her perfect golden waffles. Bentley, white towel over his arm, scurried back and forth, refilling cups and offering syrup or jam.

Jonas leaned over and whispered to me. "Margaret and I have come up with a way to keep Ivy Leigh occupied this morning. Will you follow my lead?"

I nodded.

Jonas pushed back from the table and suggested a snowman building contest.

"Count me out," Ivy Leigh said. "I'm not up to—"

"I'm in," Margaret said. "Let's make it a couples' contest."

"I like that idea," my mother said. "Stuart used to build snow forts with Toby."

"Haven't built a snowman in years," Bentley said.

Ivy Leigh stood and laid her napkin on the table. "As I said, that lets me out. I'm not part of a couple."

"Excuse me," Mr. Hampton said. "I have no partner."

"Agnes," Ivy Leigh said.

Margaret zeroed in on me with a diminutive shake of her head.

"I promised Nestor I'd work on the book today," I said. "I'll stay inside and listen for the phone. When you're finished, I'll be the judge."

"Remember who paid half your college tuition," Dad said.

"Mrs. Ransom," Mr. Hampton said. "We have a contest to win."

The couples paired off and planned their strategies. I brought *Briarwood Manor* from the study and read in the conservatory as the "grownups" waged creative war in the backyard. Twice ferrying hot chocolate back and forth, I was warmed to hear Ivy Leigh giggling. At noon the judging commenced. Despite my mother's insistence that their snowman was a perfect likeness of Zero Mostel and Jonas' had rendered a remarkable reproduction of the Sphinx, I awarded second prize to Bentley's duck-billed platypus and first prize to Mr. Hampton's "The Thinker."

"I would've made the pedestal more to scale if only I'd had more time," he said.

Once the hilarity was over, however, Ivy Leigh camped by the phone, dialing the Magnolia Arms again and again. No answer.

Over dinner my mother quizzed my friends about their most memorable Christmas.

On Christmas Eve I read "A Christmas Carol" in the library, while we waited for the phone call that never came.

Christmas Day dawned. Zero Mostel stared through the window as we exchanged gifts. When I saw Ivy Leigh slip out of the room, I walked behind her. She was dialing the phone in the kitchen again.

"Still can't get through?" I asked.

"I can't stand this much longer," she said. "We don't even know if they got there."

I laid my hand on her shoulder. "Wouldn't we have heard if they didn't?"

She hung up the phone. "I don't know, but if we don't hear something by noon, I'm going to call the—"

The phone rang. Ivy Leigh grabbed it. Her face melted into a smile.

"Merry Christmas to you, too. Are you all right … you're where?" She spoke to me. "They had to drive to Kirkwood till they found a phone that would work. Go get Torbert."

I hurried from the kitchen with the news that Nestor and Ham were safe.

By the time Mr. Hampton and I returned, Ivy Leigh was in tears.

"What about the kitchen? My room? No. Don't worry about me. I'm fine. I know you'll take care of things. I'll be home as soon as I can. Thank you, Nestor."

She handed me the phone and sank onto a chair. Mr. Hampton sat next to her.

"Nestor?" I asked. "Are you all right?"

"Yes, we're fine. Just tired."

"And the house?"

"Ida was right. The maple tree fell. But it could've been worse. It just grazed the front of house. Half the porch is gone. The foyer is a mess. The study … and your room."

"*My* room?"

"It's a good thing the house was empty. No one was hurt. And remember. Ham is here. He can fix anything. Did you open your Christmas present yet?"

My room. The third floor room with the arched window that looked out on the street. My bed with the white chenille spread. Jonas' roll top desk. His typewriter. The creak in the floor.

"Agnes," Nestor said. "Did you open your Christmas present?"

"No. I didn't see one. You mean a present from you?"

"I hid it behind the tree … seemed like a good idea at the time. But now … well, that's a little too much dramatic irony, isn't it? We have to get back. I'll let Ham talk to his dad."

Handing Mr. Hampton the phone, I returned to the living room and stepped behind the Christmas tree, where I found a small box wrapped in red foil paper. Inside was a handwritten poem in a narrow wooden frame.

You came into my life as does the spring,

Thawing icy soil so it could breathe.
Your quiet ways have warmed my wintry heart,
Whose fallow ground awoke to stir and seethe.
Like a garden, dormant in the cold,
My soul, so long enclosed, was sadly mute.
You only spoke and tender seeds made bold
To crack the frigid soil and dare to root.
Too long I'd dwelt secure with bound'ries walled.
The entrance, through disuse, had rusted closed.
My life, restrained, had slowed and all but stalled,
Till you arrived, asked entrance and reposed.
 Believe, my love, the words I feebly sing.
 I love you as the fair earth loves the spring.
  December 1977
  NC

My dad walked in. "Did I leave my glasses in here?"

Clutching the sonnet to my heart, I glanced around the room.

"Here they are," I said. "On the arm of the sofa."

Dad picked them up and hugged me. "Merry Christmas."

"Merry Christmas," I said.

He stepped back and pointed to the frame.

"What's that?" he asked.

"A note from the gardener."

"Charlotte's?"

"No. Mine."

Chapter 15

Stage Door

We gathered around the table as if nothing had happened, chatting as we passed bowls and platters, and complimented my mother.

As soon as the last dish was washed and put away, Ivy Leigh, determined to pack and take the first train home, asked Jonas and Margaret to take her back to their house.

While Mr. Hampton thanked my mother for her hospitality, Bentley whispered to me.

"Could I stay awhile?" he asked. "You could take me home after Flossie leaves."

I agreed.

After my parents, travelling south to warmer temperatures, left the following morning, I found a card on my pillow. Inside was a check for $100 and a note thanking me for a wonderful Christmas and instructions to buy a new dress for my "piano recital."

Ivy Leigh and Flossie, going north, had to wait one more day for improved conditions.

Bentley rode with me and Margaret to take them to the train station.

Ivy Leigh fixed her eyes on her approaching train. "Don't be concerned if you don't hear from me. There'll be a lot to do when I get home. I'll fill you in when I come back on the 7th."

"You and Muriel are going ahead with your plans?" I asked. "I thought—"

"I'm more convinced than ever that coming here is the right thing to do."

"What about Muriel?" I asked. "Wasn't she going to move into the Magnolia Arms?"

"She can stay at Ida's house till the repairs are done."

I asked Ivy Leigh to hug Nestor for me, and we said goodbye.

As we waited for Flossie's train, she thanked me for inviting her for the holidays.

"I *knew* you didn't need 'help' with the cat," she said. "You didn't want me to be alone and now"—she glanced at Bentley—"I'm not."

"She's coming back for Valentine's Day," Bentley said. "Can she stay with you?"

"Of course. It'll be like old times."

Flossie straightened Bentley's coat collar. "I'm knitting a new red scarf."

Saturn and I went back to my apartment on the morning of the 28th. When Charlotte and Monty returned that night, she called to share the thank-you note my mother left in the library.

"*Best Christmas we ever had,*" Charlotte read. "*Wish we could come back and bring our son and his family. Love, as ever, your friend, Betty.*"

"Sorry," I said. "My mother can get a little … exuberant."

"Not at all. Cook said the kitchen was in perfect order—better than when my own family visits. No reason we can't plan this again. Primrose was quite cheerful."

Christmas was over.

Aunt Minnie's fruitcake was in my freezer.

Everyone was home … except Ham.

Alone at last, I brought Nestor's manuscript into my living room and sat on the sofa. Like an art connoisseur, I lifted the stack of paper, turning it sideways, judging its weight, admiring its height. I had never held a nearly finished book in my hands. Expecting to begin with Eliot and Julia Bridger's wedding, as Sefton and I had planned, I was surprised Nestor had started the story with Eliot's father, Sidlow, a shadowy figure I'd encountered only twice in my research. Leaving the manuscript on the end table, I went to my bedroom for the box of Julia's mementos.

Sitting on the floor, I removed the brown wrapping paper from the box. On top of the contents were two pages in Nestor's handwriting: an "Annotated Index" and a letter to me.

Agnes, I still regret we couldn't go to Millie Hubbard's house together. Since then I've been in a quandary about how much to tell you about what was in the cedar chest. You've devoted so much of the last year to researching the Bridgers—I wanted you to experience the same joy of discovery I did when I held Julia's "life" in my hands, especially her prized possession—Eliot's journal. So many times I wanted to read it to you over the phone, but didn't. I wanted you to meet Eliot like I did … one page at a time.

The manuscript forgotten, I lifted out the journal and began to read.

Eliot's entries began in 1887, when, "as a matter of conscience," he turned his back on the family business, an empire made wealthy by exploiting its workers. As the eldest son of Sidlow Bridger, an infamous "robber baron," Eliot was expected to follow in his father's footsteps. But when Sidlow continued to ignore Eliot's pleas for better wages and conditions for their laborers, Eliot "took to the open road." Travelling east from Chicago, he looked for work. Unaccustomed to physical labor, he was often more trouble than he was worth to the farmers or shopkeepers who paid him a daily wage.

Eliot's story read like a novel. He was a brilliant writer with a keen eye for detail and empathy for the human condition. In addition to notations on the books he was reading—Twain's novels, Emerson's essays, and Robert Browning's poems—Eliot commented on the daily perils of his journey and the historic events he witnessed. He credited the "kindness of strangers" for his survival during the Great Blizzard of '88 and chronicled the devastating Johnstown Flood the following year. At last, exhausted from "living hand to mouth," he wandered onto a West Virginia farm where he met Julia Lane.

"I knew I was home," he wrote.

Sitting cross-legged by the bed, lying on the floor, propped up on pillows, sprawled on the sofa, hunched over the kitchen table, I spent the rest of the day with Eliot Bridger.

No wonder Julia loved him.

When I finished reading, I tried to call the Magnolia Arms. No answer. The phone lines must still down, I thought.

So I wrote Nestor a letter, thanking him for the sonnet and for letting me discover Eliot Bridger for myself.

"No one but you," I wrote, "would have known me well enough to think how much it would mean to me."

On the first day of classes, Elinor announced her retirement. She and Ryder were moving to Harrisonburg, Virginia, where his daughter Caroline and her family lived.

John Ellershaw was going with them.

The historical re-enactors' club would be a thing of the past.

Grace returned with an engagement ring. Lorna did not.

Ham remained at the Magnolia Arms till January 7th and came back with Ivy Leigh. She and Muriel had three days together at the Drifters' Rest before Muriel left for Dennisonville.

I stopped by for breakfast on Ivy Leigh's first day as manager.

So did Margaret and Jonas, Ryder and Elinor, Grace, Lorna, and Mr. Hampton.

We all wanted to ask about the Magnolia Arms.

"Ham is a miracle worker," she said. "Not only did he repair all the damage, but he fixed some cracks and drips I've been putting up with for years. Wait till you see your room, Agnes."

Two and a half weeks after the ice storm knocked out the phone lines, service was restored to Dennisonville. Nestor called that night.

"I got your letter," he said. "You liked the sonnet?"

"Yes. I had no idea you were a poet. Anything else you haven't told me?"

He laughed. "I used to have a dog named Ezra."

"Is that the dog in the photo on your desk? The one of you and your dad?"

"Yes, that's Ezra, but that's not my dad. It's my uncle. He raised me."

"Your ... uncle? I thought—"

"You asked if there was anything else I haven't told you. That's not a fact about me that fits easily into conversation."

"What happened to your parents?" I asked.

"When I was two, my mother died giving birth to twin girls who lived only a few days. My dad couldn't cope with losing my mother and having to raise me on his own. He took off."

My heart broke half in two. "I don't know what to say, Nestor. I'm sorry. I'm sorry that happened. And I'm even sorrier I never asked—"

"Don't cry. Not many people know. I don't bring it up very often. And we haven't had all that much time together. A few weeks last fall, a few weeks last summer."

"And most of the time we were together, I was yakking about Sefton," I said.

"That's not what I was going to say. But we have time now. What do you want to know?"

Nestor and I started talking and asking each other questions. Not about our friends. Or about the Magnolia Arms or gardening or English classes or the weather.

About ourselves.

We talked about our childhood hopes and heartaches, adolescent foolishness and failures, bitter regrets yet to be forgotten, and impossible dreams yet to be realized.

We talked every night for two weeks until rehearsals for the Fine Arts Festival began.

"I don't see why we have to rehearse," I said. "It's all individual numbers. Not a play."

"Ham said there are a few set changes for the actors," Nestor said. "He volunteered for the stage crew, so he could be near Lorna."

"I haven't seen him much since he got back. Do you talk to him often?"

He laughed. "Not as often as I talk to you. But while he was here, he began to trust me enough that he confided in me about Lorna. Has anyone told him about Oliver yet?"

"Not yet. Lorna doesn't want to hurt him. She's going to talk to him after the festival. She's got enough on her mind already."

"What if Oliver comes for the festival?" Nestor asked. "To surprise her."

"He's on a concert tour. Won't be home till February."

On the night of the first rehearsal, I entered the rear of the auditorium and walked past Stella Wagner and Liam Harding running lines for their scene from "A Tree Grows in Brooklyn." At center stage Violet Pate played vocal exercises on the piano for Wanetta Haverford and her singers, Jane Frewen and Peg Bellingham. Jane and Peg "oohed" and "ahhed" up and down the scales as Violet played.

Althea Creighton, upstage of them, shouted at some poor stagehand struggling to adjust the lights. Rosie Creswell, still in her team shirt, sat on the first seat of the front row. Grim-faced, she clutched her clarinet case. Somewhere in the dark Arley Mayhew was warming up on his bassoon.

I chose a seat near the wall and sat back, surprised at the unexpected flutter in my stomach. The sights and smells of the cavernous auditorium—nervous chatter, shouted instructions, studious faces—awoke in me the prickly realization I had not performed for a large audience in years. And *then* I wasn't playing the piano. I was acting and could have ad-libbed if needed. Wrong notes are harder to disguise than fumbled words. What was I doing here? The only reason I had agreed to participate was to be moral support for Lorna, but now she no longer needed it.

"Miss Quinn. Are you all right?"

Ham stood next to me in the aisle.

"Yes … I'm fine," I said. "I was just going over my piece in my head. I haven't seen you much since school started. Where have you been?"

"In the shop. Helping Dad catch up on the work he got behind on when I was gone."

"Ivy Leigh said you worked miracles at the Magnolia Arms."

He hung his head. "I wouldn't say that exactly. It was an honor to work on such a beautiful house. And to be in the same place where Lorna … I mean where my friends …"

I pretended not to hear. "After this festival is over, we need to start practicing for the whistling competition. It's coming up soon, isn't it?"

Althea Creighton, hands on hips, called from the stage. "Ham!"

"Gotta go," Ham said. "Time to get to work."

Althea, like a wagon train scout looking for watering holes, scanned the empty rows.

"Is Lorna here yet? I want to ask if she likes where the piano is."

"Not yet." I glanced at my watch. "She still has five minutes."

"Musicians," Althea muttered, and went in search of another stagehand to instruct.

Ivan Brenner pointed up the aisle with his violin bow. "There's Lorna. Hey, Lorna, Althea wants to know if you like where the piano is."

Lorna arrived at my row and called to Althea. "Yes, it's fine. Thank you."

Hugh Galbraith, sporting a black cowboy hat, hopped down from the stage and strode toward us.

"Would you like to warm up, Lorna?" he asked. "Otherwise, we'll start the rehearsal."

Lorna sank down beside me. "I practiced before I came."

"Very good," Hugh said. "I'm hoping to talk Althea into rehearsing our scene one more time before we perform. It's been a long time since I acted."

I raised my eyebrows. "I thought you were doing 'Gunga Din.'"

"Althea thought it was too high brow for our audience. She talked me into doing the tack room scene from *The Rainmaker*. I hope we can pull it off."

Assuming his role, he planted his feet wide and spread his arms. "I needed a name that had the whole sky in it and the power of a man. Star … buck. Now there's a name, and it's mine."

"And Althea is Lizzie Curry?" I asked. "Perfect casting."

"She was made for the part," he said.

He tipped his hat and leaped onto the stage in one bound.

"That'll be something worth seeing," I said. "They're a little old for those roles."

"Uh-huh," Lorna said. "Just what we need. Another love scene."

"What's wrong? Did you and Oliver have a fight?"

"No. I had a fight with Nolan."

"Nolan? You talked to him?"

"Can you believe it? A few days before I'm going back on stage, and *he* has to call."

"How did he know where you were?" I asked.

"Dr. Penrose."

"Dr. Penrose? Didn't he know better than to tell him that?"

She shook her head. "I never told him Nolan was the reason for my panic attacks."

"What did Nolan want?"

"Said he'd made a terrible mistake and wants me back. He's coming to the festival."

"May I have your attention?" Althea said from downstage center. "Welcome to the first rehearsal of the first annual Brighton Park Community College Fine Arts Festival."

Polite applause rippled across the stage.

Settling her glasses on top of her head, Althea continued.

"Stella is going to pass out the program to you. Tonight's run-through is to work on scene changes, entrances and exits, and to get an accurate time."

Lorna reached for my hand. "Why did Nolan have to call? Why *now*?"

"Men like that always want the last word. If you were still a mess, he wouldn't have bothered, but he can't stand to think you've gotten over him and moved on."

"Places, everyone," Althea said. "Lights."

The house lights went down. The spotlight came up. Lorna walked to the piano.

Sitting down, she bowed her head. Then she lifted her hands to the keyboard.

I held my breath.

Lorna played the opening measures of Chopin's Polonaise (Opus 53, according to the program). This was the same piece she had opened with when she and Oliver gave their concert at the Magnolia Arms. I was no virtuoso, but I had heard Lorna play often enough to know she was in trouble. Thousands of perfect notes were there; her passion and grace were not. Tearing along at a breakneck pace, she pushed through as if this were the last piece she would play before the building, already burning, collapsed on us all. Dazzled, the other performers applauded when she finished.

I hurried backstage and found her trembling.

Ham was offering her a glass of water.

"What will I do if Nolan shows up here?" Lorna asked. "I'll never be able to go on if he's in the audience."

"Who's Nolan?" Ham asked.

"Someone Lorna knows," I said. "From college."

We could hear Ivan Brenner on stage playing Meditation from Thaïs on his violin.

Lorna leaned against the wall. "I have to leave. I can't do this tonight."

Althea Creighton appeared behind Ham and tapped him on the shoulder. "Excuse me, Ham. Mr. Davenport—you know, the stage manager?—needs you … if you're not *too busy*."

Ham walked away as Althea shouted for Truitt Spenlow, our orchestra conductor, next on the program with his oboe.

Taking Lorna's hand, I led her to the kitchen table where Liam and Stella would sit for their scene from "A Tree Grows in Brooklyn."

"Now, listen to me," I said. "You've come a long way since you showed up here with your chin drooping and your eyes staring at the ground. You've become a good teacher and—"

"I know. That's all the more reason to—"

"And you've made friends and even found love … real love." At least I thought that's what she and Oliver had. "You can't back out now. There's more at stake than just you. Dr. Penrose. All these teachers involved in this program. Everyone who's helped you … like Ham." This was a low blow, but I hoped it would be the jolt she needed. Who could disappoint Ham?

She sighed. "You're right. I let Nolan get the best of me once before, and it nearly ruined my life. I can't let him do it again."

"No, you can't."

Jane Frewen, Brighton Park's premier soprano, was only a few feet away loosening her lips and disciplining her diaphragm. I kept talking, parroting every inspirational saying I knew. I was on the verge of saying, "Win one for the Gipper," when Althea called my name.

My stomach lurched. I grabbed Lorna by the arm. "I don't remember a single note."

"Go on," Lorna said. "Once you sit down, it will all come back to you."

I stood. "You're not heading out the back door while I'm on stage, are you?"

"No. If I don't face this now, I never will."

I walked the hundred miles to the piano bench and sat down. Closing my eyes, I imagined myself back at the Magnolia Arms, practicing with Morton.

Once I heard his voice in my head, I ordered myself to concentrate … and started playing.

The applause for my piece wasn't as deafening as for Lorna's, but when I left the stage, Wanetta Haverford touched my arm as she passed by on her way to accompany Jane Frewen.

"You're a fine musician," she said.

"Thank you," I said. "I've been practicing. Even took some private lessons."

"Next year you can help me with the accompanying."

Jane Frewen swept in, adjusted her posture, and placed her hand on the piano.

Wanetta played the introduction to O mio babbino caro. Jane's voice soared up and rained down, drenching us, slaking our thirst for a beauty beyond ourselves, lifting us up and out of the gray world of hallways and sidewalks, quieting our unspoken yearning for a glimpse of the sublime.

Lorna was transfixed. Embraced in the serene moment, she leaned forward with her hands held over her lips.

When Jane finished, there was no applause … only stunned silence.

"What is someone like her doing at a community college?" Lorna asked.

"I don't know," I said, "but people ask the same thing about you."

Lorna returned to the piano for the Rachmaninov Prelude in G Minor.

Flawless. Splendid. Breathtaking.

My barrage of words had not swayed Lorna.

Jane Frewen's voice had called to her—soul to soul—and summoned her to greatness.

Or healed her.

"Thank you, Lorna," Althea said. "Curtain."

The curtain closed. The stage crew, silent as the shoemaker's elves, entered from stage right and left, carrying flats—wooden frames covered with muslin. After they edged the piano upstage, they positioned the painted scenery in front, transforming the concert stage into a tenement kitchen in Brooklyn.

Ham walked to where we were sitting.

"Sorry," he said. "We need this table for the next scene."

Lorna and I returned to the audience.

Rosie Creswell stepped in front of the curtain and proceeded to downstage center as Wanetta took her place at an upright piano on the floor and played an introduction.

I wouldn't want to be in Rosie's athletic shoes. Following Jane *and* Lorna.

But Rosie was unfazed. Steady nerves from all those close games, I thought. She played beautifully and sauntered off the stage as though her team had just won the national championship.

The curtain opened and Liam and Stella transported us to New York, the land of unfulfilled promise and impossible hopes. What were these two doing teaching philosophy? The curtain closed again. Arley Mayhew took Rosie's place and performed the Weber Concerto for bassoon. Who could have guessed a skinny guy blowing on something that looked like a stovepipe could leave us breathless?

As Arley walked off, the curtain drew back to reveal the tack room of the Curry farm. Althea, transformed in every way into Lizzie Curry, brought a patchwork quilt to Starbuck and wept over her plainness and failed dreams. Lorna and I sat wide-eyed in the dark theatre and forgot where we were.

Again the curtain closed. Peg Bellingham, respected grand dame of the history department, following in Rosie and Arley's footsteps, took center stage. Squaring her shoulders, she drew herself up to her full height and nodded at Wanetta. Then she filled the room and our hearts with her rich alto voice: *When you walk through a storm, hold your head up high, and don't be afraid of the dark.*

I had to remind myself to breathe.

Lorna slipped backstage as Peg made her exit. When the curtain opened for the last time, Lorna was already seated. She made brilliant work of Chopin's Fantasie Impromptu No. 66 (I glanced at the program) and took a final bow.

Althea, applauding as she returned to the stage, said, "You should plan an encore, Lorna." She then turned to the rest of us. "Splendid work, everyone. Meet again next Tuesday."

Thanks to the excitement the festival generated, January, usually interminable, sped by.

After an advertising agency, hired by Lorna's father, peppered our hallways with glossy full-color posters of "Miss Maron" seated at a Steinway grand in front of a full orchestra, students and teachers alike began to speculate about why she had abandoned her musical career.

Rumors ran the gamut from the "tragic death of her fiancé in a car accident" to a "bout of pneumonia that impaired her hearing"—each story more fantastic than the one before, and none of them as poignant as the truth.

Other than the volleyball team, who knew Coach Creswell had played the clarinet in high school, everyone was buzzing about Rosie's being included on the list of performers.

A few teachers, who had not heard the undersized Arley Mayhew play, made jokes about the audience being able to "tell the difference between Peewee and his bassoon."

Those who had heard Peg Bellingham sing "How Great Thou Art" at First Baptist Church assured everyone else they "had never heard anything like her."

Even I fielded questions from students once they discovered I was on the program.

But no one wondered why Ham stood gazing at the festival poster outside the maintenance office or why one day the poster mysteriously disappeared.

With a recommendation from Margaret, Ivy Leigh presented herself to Dr. Sherwood and offered to cater a reception following the performance. Elspeth referred Ivy Leigh to Dr. Maron, who added shrimp and caviar to the menu and sent a check to cover her expenses.

Once Nestor, still busy with renovations at the Magnolia Arms, settled into his new role as manager, he called less often, but I never mistook his silence for indifference.

When he was able to call, he had plenty of news.

Muriel had christened her new restaurant "Mollie's," a combination of her own name and her sister Dolley's. The loyal clientele of the Magnolia Arms dining room made a speedy transition to the new location and praised the additional parking.

Posey and Xander went back and forth between Mollie's and the Magnolia Arms, helping as much as they could before leaving on February 1st for their wedding.

"I guess you'll have to fend for yourself till you find a new cook," I said.

"We already have one," Nestor said.

An unexpected pang of jealousy shot through me. A stranger taking over our kitchen?

"Where did you find her?" I asked.

"I didn't find *her* exactly. She came with the new guest."

"I thought you weren't taking in guests till the remodeling was finished. Didn't you say there was still work to do on Ivy Leigh's room and mine?"

"It's not Ivy Leigh's room anymore. It's Millie Hubbard's."

"*The* Millie Hubbard?" I asked.

"She called and said she and her housekeeper were tired of trying to take care of her 'big old house' by themselves, especially in the winter."

"So Millie's housekeeper came with her?"

"Not a housekeeper exactly. She's more like a combination housekeeper, cook, and caregiver," Nestor said. "Pinetta Fraleigh."

"Pinetta?" I asked, pronouncing a short 'i.'

"No. Pine—etta. It suits her. 50's. Tall. Thin. Wears a white blouse every day. Only lemon in her tea. She asked for my room so she could be near the kitchen and near Millie."

"Is she a good cook?"

"Not as good as Ivy Leigh, but then who is? This has worked out well, actually. Pinetta and Millie will stay at the house while Chester and I come for the festival."

"I'm glad you're both coming. We're going to need all the help we can get."

I gave Nestor a quick update on Nolan's phone call and the effect on Lorna.

"Don't worry," Nestor said. "Between me and Jonas and Chester, we can keep this Nolan guy from trying anything. Will Ryder be at the festival, too?"

"I'm sure he will. Elinor never misses a school activity."

"Is Oliver coming?"

"No. He's on tour."

"That solves one problem," Nestor said. "Ham couldn't take seeing the two of them together."

Margaret, thinking ahead as usual, asked Charlotte if Morton Penrose could stay at her house when he arrived for the festival. That decision led to Lorna's being invited as well.

"What better place could there be," Charlotte asked, "for Lorna to put the finishing touches on her pieces?"

Prompted by Dr. Maron, Elspeth offered Lorna time off to prepare for the festival, but she refused. After teaching her classes every day, she slipped away to Charlotte's house every afternoon.

I was glad for Ham's sake Lorna kept to her routine. It was hard enough for him to give up their daily walks to Rehearsal Hall without her disappearing from his life entirely.

Morton did not forget his promise to me. The night before the festival he invited me to Charlotte's for one final lesson.

Once he assured me I had made "impressive progress" since Thanksgiving, I was ready.

On the morning of the festival, Grace and I were at the train station before dawn. Chester, first off the train, nearly tripped and fell as he ran toward Grace. Nestor and I, old hands at reunions, hugged each other and tended to the luggage. Then I drove everyone to the Drifters' Rest where Ivy Leigh had breakfast waiting.

She cried when she saw Nestor. It was the longest they had been apart since Nestor had arrived at the Magnolia Arms four years before.

After 45 minutes, Chester and Grace called a taxi and left to spend the day alone.

Ivy Leigh stood at our table. "I hate to rush you, but I have a big reception to host tonight." She hugged us both. "Your next stop is Margaret's. Lunch is on her."

I sensed a conspiracy.

Did our friends want to see Nestor or keep me distracted from my nerves?

We spent the morning with Margaret and Jonas … rather I spent the morning with Margaret, while Nestor and Jonas "talked shop" about the renovations to the Magnolia Arms.

"So," Margaret said, as she chopped celery for the salad, "how are you?"

"I'll be glad when tonight is over. Have you talked to Lorna? I haven't seen her."

She shook her head. "Charlotte's been keeping me informed. She said Lorna has been polite, but reserved."

"She'd be fine if Nolan hadn't called."

"If Nolan shows up, he had better hope he doesn't run into Jonas. He's looking for a good excuse to escort Nolan from the auditorium."

"Nestor would be right behind him," I said. "I told Althea if anyone shows up backstage claiming to be an old friend of Lorna's, he's not to be allowed in … no matter what his story is."

"Not even Nolan could get past The Dragon Lady," Margaret said.

The four of us had a peaceful lunch, talking about our friends and our memories.

When he finished, Nestor laid his napkin by his plate. "May I borrow your car, Jonas? I told Ham I'd be in town this weekend. We have a few chores to do."

"Of course," Jonas said. "I'll get the keys."

Nestor leaned over and kissed me on the cheek. "You should rest this afternoon."

"I'm going to stay here till time for my hair appointment."

"Hair appointment? That's a first."

"Althea's orders," I said. "If she said 'formal attire' once, she said it—"

"Good thing I brought a suit," he said, smiling.

"That will be a first, too," I said, remembering Sefton's sulking over wearing a tie.

Margaret suggested I nap in my room, but I did not want to be alone with my thoughts. So I stretched out on their sofa for an hour and left early enough to stop by Charlotte's house on the way to my hair appointment. Hopefully, one more successful run-through with Morton would subdue the horde of butterflies in my stomach. As I entered the foyer, I could hear Lorna playing. She sounded even better than at our last rehearsal. Why wouldn't she—alone in that beautiful room with her teacher at her side and no threat of uninvited visitors?

Charlotte put her arm through mine. "Come upstairs, dear. Primrose will want to say hello, and I have a little something for you."

As I was greeting Primrose, Charlotte opened a box on her dressing table.

"Sit here on the corner of the bed," she said, and stepped behind me.

Around my neck she clasped a diamond pendant suspended from a double strand of pearls.

"These were a gift from Exton," she said. "You and he would've been great friends."

I reached up to touch them. "I can't wear these."

Ignoring my objection, she reached for a hand mirror on her nightstand, held it up to me, and stepped back to admire the effect.

"No more arguing. Lorna told me your dress was black, which will set these off nicely. Now hurry down for your rehearsal."

Primrose chirped as I left the room.

Tapping on the door of the conservatory, I walked in. Morton and Lorna were seated by the window, deep in thought and conversation.

"And here's our other pianist," Morton said. He pronounced the word "pyanist" as two syllables rather than three.

I sat on the bench. "I wouldn't exactly refer to myself as a pianist."

"Nonsense," Morton said. "I wish the audience could hear you play Liebestraum, too."

"I told you before, Agnes, without you backstage with me I wouldn't go on," Lorna said. "It's more important now than when I first asked you."

"And I'll tell you what you told me," I said. "Once you sit down at the piano, everything will come back to you."

That night, in my new black dress with my hair swept up like a beauty queen and Charlotte's pearls and diamond pendant around my neck, I arrived backstage.

Althea, already in costume in a pale blue shirtwaist dress, her hair slicked back into a tight bun, apprised me. "I'm glad someone took me seriously about the word 'formal.'"

Hugh Galbraith whistled.

A faraway look in his eye, Ivan Brenner added I was a dead ringer for a Russian violinist he once knew.

But none of these opinions warmed my heart like Ham's compliment.

"That's a pretty dress, Miss Quinn. With your hair like that, you look a lot like my mom."

But once Lorna arrived, no one gave me a second thought.

Her dress, purchased with her father's oversight, I assumed, was a shimmering silver gray. At her graceful throat was a teardrop sapphire, diamond encrusted, on a white gold chain … a similar loan from Charlotte. Unlike the rest of the ordinary mortals in the cast, Lorna seemed to float rather than walk in. Her lustrous auburn hair was pulled back at the sides and hung in soft waves at her shoulders. Her pale blue eyes, fragile, anguished, darted around the stage, gazed up at the lights overhead, and came to rest on the piano. I could not allow her time to reflect.

Taking her elbow, I led her to the piano. "Sit down. Close your eyes and imagine you're in the parlor at the Magnolia Arms. Worked for me."

She did as I said … and played.

Ham and I watched from opposite sides of the stage, each of us wishing our friend well, willing her to succeed, hoping this would be the night her broken spirit, strengthened by our love, would take flight and carry the audience with her.

Althea called us to attention to issue her final instructions and deliver the traditional "you've all worked hard … now go out there and enjoy yourselves" speech.

"I've waited a long time for an opportunity like this," she said, "and I'd like to thank—"

Unable to continue, she turned away, fanning herself with a fluttering hand.

"Stand not upon the order of your going," Hugh Galbraith said. "Now go."

Lady Macbeth was not, perhaps, the best Shakespearean character to quote, I thought.

Nevertheless, we took our places.

The roar of the audience softened, silenced, as the curtain went up.

Watching from the wings, I held my breath, knowing our friends in the audience were doing the same.

Lorna executed a perfect chord.

And fumbled on the next passage.

She rested her hands on the keyboard.

Her head drooped.

Her shoulders slumped.

Closing my eyes, I willed her to remember the Magnolia Arms.

And remembered myself.

Without thinking I strode across the stage, shouting as I walked toward her.

"No. No. No," I said. "You've started with the wrong piece."

Plopping down on her right … I began playing "Chopsticks."

Halting at first, she moved her fingers. With increasing momentum, she rippled across the keyboard, improvising, whispering to me to "follow her lead" as her right hand edged toward mine, and she nudged me off the bench. Taking her cue, I stood, shrugged my shoulders and rolled my eyes at the audience, then walked behind her to sit on her left. She kept playing. I pounded out chords. When she whispered, "lean back," I complied. Playing octaves with both hands, she charged from one end of the piano to the other, standing as her fingers sounded the highest notes.

Leaping up, the audience went wild, laughing, cheering, and shouting "bravo" with enough force to produce a seismic reading.

Beaming, Lorna motioned for me to bow.

Standing next to her, I grasped her hand and we bowed together.

"Don't make me come out here again," I said and exited.

Althea was waiting for me backstage.

"Clever, but you might've given me a little warning. I nearly had a heart attack."

"We wanted to surprise you," I said.

Even Althea believed we had planned the whole thing.

Lorna began again.

Her triumph set the tone for the entire evening.

From Truitt Spenlow to Rosie Creswell, the New York tenement to the Kansas farm, Jane's aria to Peg's Broadway tune, every one of us—including me—exceeded expectation.

By the time Lorna returned for her final number, the whole cast was giddy.

Already organized for our curtain call, we huddled in groups behind the curtain on either side of the stage to enjoy the Chopin Fantasie-Impromptu.

Enraptured, the audience rose to their feet before they heard the final notes.

Her hand to her heart, Lorna bowed again and again.

Althea, next to me, extended her right arm to hold back our group and held up her left hand to signal the performers lined up on the opposite side of the stage to remain in place.

Lorna was going to play an encore. She stepped forward and spoke in a strong voice.

"There are so many people who made this evening possible and"—arms outstretched, she looked from one side of the stage to the other—"I wish I could dedicate an encore to each of them. But there is one person without whose help I could not have succeeded."

Peeking from behind the curtain, I tried to find Morton, so I could watch his reaction.

Lorna continued. "When I first decided to go back to the piano, I needed somewhere to practice. This gentleman not only found the perfect place, but escorted me there every day."

My heart began to pound. I grabbed Rosie's arm to steady myself.

Lorna turned to stage left where Ham was watching from the darkness.

"I'd like to dedicate this piece to my good friend, Mr. Talmadge Hampton."

Lorna returned to the piano and played the song Ham had requested after our first trip to Rehearsal Hall.

His mother's favorite—"Widmung."

Lorna, at one with the piano, was taking the final steps of her journey back to a mended heart. No one stirred. Each of us was lost, suspended, in the once-in-a-lifetime moment. My memories of Lorna on the first day of school, at dinner with Flossie and Winnie, riding horses at Sloan's Canyon, Thanksgiving at the Magnolia Arms, unfolded, replayed, underscored by the music. Somewhere in the audience Morton Penrose was weeping. Lorna's parents were holding hands. Margaret was smiling at Jonas. Nestor was preparing to grab Nolan's arm if he made one move toward the stage after the performance.

I peered around Althea's head to get a peek at Ham on the other side of the stage.

He had changed from his work clothes into a suit and held a dozen red roses in his arms.

The final notes of Lorna Maron's encore ended the first annual Brighton Park Community College Fine Arts Festival.

Again the audience rose, the cheering and applause even louder than before.

Lorna bowed and beckoned the cast to join her.

We trooped forward.

Taking our places, we joined hands, raised our arms, and bowed as one.

Tireless, the audience went on clapping and shouting.

With the spotlight in my eyes, I could not see past the first five rows, but a few things became clear in the light spilling over from the stage.

Dr. Morton Penrose was blowing kisses with both hands.

Beside him, Dr. and Mrs. Maron were applauding.

And two men, one in the right aisle and one in the left, were coming toward the stage.

One of them had to be Nolan. He had decided to make a grandstand play.

Prepared to do whatever was needed to prevent Lorna's success from being sullied, I let go of Althea's and Rosie's hands and inched forward.

Shielding my eyes from the spotlight, I glanced from one aisle to the other, straining to make out faces, when I heard Lorna gasp behind me.

Before I could turn and grab her, she stepped out of line to meet the man making his way up the right aisle.

Oliver Martin Farrell, a dozen roses in his arms, was almost at the steps.

I looked to the left aisle.

Nestor Carlyle, a bouquet of roses cradled in his right arm, stepped into the light.

Still preoccupied, I noticed he was straightening his tie as he approached.

Or so I thought.

Peering at him, I leaned forward and saw he was tilting his head to the right.

He came closer. He wasn't straightening his tie. He was pointing.

I whirled around just in time.

Ham, still clutching his roses, stared, disbelieving, as Oliver Martin Farrell placed a gorgeous bouquet in Lorna's arms and kissed her on the cheek.

Without a word between us, I understood what Nestor wanted me to do.

Smiling, I walked toward Ham and took the flowers from him.

Mouth open in amazement, he blinked at me like a man, half-drowned, trying to cling to a life preserver as wave after wave crashed over his head.

"Thank you, Ham," I said. "They're lovely."

With one last glance at Lorna, he turned and walked away.

Nestor stepped onto the stage as Oliver stepped down.

I bit my lip, at a loss about what to do next.

Nestor winked as he passed by. He walked straight to the startled Althea and laid his bouquet in her arms.

"Who ... who are you?" she asked.

"The florist" he said. "A gift from your grateful cast."

He kissed her hand. She blushed.

Applause erupted again.

Nestor turned to go, reaching out and squeezing my hand as he walked by.

"I'll make it up to you," he said. "There'll be other roses."

In one grand gesture, an inspired plan thought up and carried out on the spot, Nestor had spared Ham from embarrassing himself, prevented Lorna from being haunted by the pain on Ham's face, and provided Althea with a sublime moment she would never forget.

He had even saved our cast from the disgrace of failing to present our director with flowers—a fine point of theatrical protocol we had overlooked.

I watched Nestor as he descended the steps and walked back up the aisle.

Before he had returned to his seat ... I knew.

I was in love with Nestor Carlyle.

At the reception I gained even more notoriety. Not only was I renowned for my clever performance of "Chopsticks"—"you were so convincing we *honestly* thought Miss Maron had forgotten her music"—and my own piece—"we didn't know you knew how to play the piano"—but also for being on the arm of the mysterious stranger who had "stolen the show" when he kissed Althea's hand and for my comfortable familiarity with the new owner of the Drifters' Rest—"how do you know Mrs. Ransom?"—whose grace and excellent food had delighted everyone present.

Balancing a plateful of almond cookies, I edged through Lorna's admirers.

"Any sign of Nolan?" I whispered.

Smiling as she autographed a program, she whispered back.

"No. I should've known he was lying."

Elspeth, resplendent in a deep purple tea-length gown, found me in the crowd. She held out a business card. "My brother-in-law, Daniel Ogden, the publisher, is expecting your call."

Morton clasped my hands in his. All he could say was, "Agnes. Agnes."

Dr. Maron shook my hand. Mrs. Maron kissed my cheek.

But the one who had unlocked the door of Rehearsal Hall and watched over Lorna as she practiced and regained her confidence was missing from the jubilant crowd.

Somewhere Ham was passing his dark hour alone.

After the groundbreaking ceremony for the new Maron-Sherwood Concert Center ten days later, Althea lost no time petitioning the administration to reserve a date on the school calendar for the *second* annual Brighton Park Community College Fine Arts Festival.

Everyone was disappointed, but not surprised, when they learned Lorna Maron planned to leave at the end of the semester to resume her music career.

And marry Oliver Martin Farrell.

Ham submitted his two-week notice and left for Dennisonville to become the handyman at the Magnolia Arms.

Not even the whistling competition could tempt him to stay.

When Nestor asked if Ham could move into my third floor room, I did not object. I wouldn't need it anymore.

Nestor had proposed again on the weekend we attended Xander and Posey's wedding. We were getting married in August.

Three babies were born in March.

Mr. and Mrs. Buck Sloan welcomed Geneva Gilbey Sloan and vowed she would be on a horse by the time she was two.

Mr. and Mrs. Toby Quinn welcomed Elizabeth Agnes Quinn, a petite little redhead they called Liza for short.

Mr. and Mrs. Warner Bingham, in separate prisons, became the parents of Fletcher Quinn Bingham. Grandmothers Flossie and Winnie took him home to a fully equipped nursery.

Winnie was true to her word. She remained with Flossie till Fletcher was four months old, and then proudly assumed the title of Mrs. Winifred Penrose in an elegant June wedding.

Chester and Grace married in July. The Brighton Park science faculty welcomed Chester.

Grace was awarded the well-deserved position of Head Librarian.

Bentley resigned as the chief dishwasher at the Drifters' Rest. He thanked Ivy Leigh for the opportunities she and Muriel had given him, but he needed to think of the future. A larger salary and benefits were essential to a man about to take on a family. Bentley replaced Ham in the maintenance department.

The Sloans took care of Fletcher while Mr. and Mrs. Bentley McBain went on their honeymoon. When they returned, the new family moved into my old apartment and put their names on a waiting list for a two-bedroom apartment.

At the end of the six-month trial period for the trading places of Ivy Leigh and Muriel, each decided she would remain where she was. Muriel was already legendary in Dennisonville, and Ivy Leigh "refused to part with her best friend Margaret again."

Margaret confided to me their friendship was not the only reason.

"All I can tell you is that Ivy Leigh told me Torbert Hampton 'is no Marshall Ransom,' but he's a very close second."

The day I found out Muriel was staying in Dennisonville, I asked her to cater my wedding reception.

On August 20, 1978, holding a bouquet of Agnes Carlyle Roses, I followed my matron of honor, Margaret Grinstead, down the stairs of the Magnolia Arms. My father waited for me at the bottom step. We walked to the dining room where the wedding guests had gathered. Only two of our friends were missing. Considerate of Ham's feelings, Oliver and Lorna Farrell had sent their regrets. Under an ivy-covered arch in front of the fireplace, Nestor waited with Jonas, his best man.

In the room where we had first met and Nestor had first professed his love, we were married.

The reception was a joyous jumbling of old friends and new. My mother and Flossie cooed over Fletcher and Liza and then traded babies to coo some more. Mr. Hampton was delighted to see Toby again and meet his family. Millie Hubbard and Charlotte chatted as if they had known each other all their lives. Pinetta Fraleigh, as starched as Nestor had described, served as Muriel's assistant, keeping trays piled with hors d'oeuvres and giving orders to Ham, who was outfitted in Nestor's old waiter uniform.

When I thought my heart was so full it could not hold one more fragment of happiness, Jonas called the crowd to attention and announced Mr. Montague St. James.

Monty played "The Anniversary Waltz" on his accordion as Nestor took me in his arms.

Instead of throwing my bouquet, I untied the ribbon around my flowers and presented a rose to my mother, another to Margaret, to Ivy Leigh, Charlotte, Flossie, and Winnie.

"You see," Winnie said, "I told you so."

"Told me what?"

"A year ago, when we met on the train, and you leaned over me to wave goodbye to Nestor, I *said* you were in love with the gardener."

And she was right.

Julia's Letter to Millie

Dear Millie,

I hope this letter finds you well and happy. I was thrilled about the news of your first child and hope he or she will bring you as much joy as Jameson has brought to me.

As for me, I am a little nervous about marrying Leo and becoming the mother of another son and daughter, but hope in time we can all become one family. Olympia and Bentley, poor dears, have been without a mother longer than Jameson has been without a father.

I know you and our other sisters have reservations about my marrying Leo, but be assured I am positive this is the right course of action for me and my son.

I've been hesitant to tell you (or anyone) Leo wants me to leave my past life behind. I hope you will not think ill of him for this. He insists Jameson and I bring as few of our personal belongings into their home as possible.

I do not mind leaving behind my furniture, but I cannot part with the cedar chest Eliot made for me. For this reason I am entrusting it and its contents to you. Someday I will be gone, and I want Jameson to have the mementos—humble though they are—his father and I deemed precious.

I leave this in your care, dear sister, because you are the youngest and have the fewest possessions of your own. Also, because you've never thought me romantic and foolish as Hettie, Jane, and Dora often do.

Please keep this safe. And when the time comes, see it safely delivered to Jameson.

Ever your loving eldest sister,

Julia

Julia's Letter to Bentley

My dearest Bentley,

I hope this letter finds you well. I am not at all familiar with what life must be like inside a prison, but I hope you have at least found a friend and are able to spend your days reading good books. Do you ever get to spend anytime outside?

I wish I had good news to share with you, but unfortunately we are not doing well at present. Your father and Jameson had an awful row, and Jameson has been banned from visiting me. Since I am in the hospital at present, I have no way to contact him. In fact, I do not even know where he is.

Your father refuses to talk to me about him, and I need not tell you your sister Olympia cares little for me or my son.

I fear I may not leave the hospital, and this is why I am appealing to you. I have no one to turn to but you, dear boy, and I pray you will take my request to heart.

When I married your father, I entrusted care of a cedar chest to my youngest sister, Millie Hubbard. She is newly married and has recently moved to Greenwood Road in Jacksonville. I have no idea if she will still be there when you are released. But I wanted you to know where she is, so you can tell Jameson where to find her.

Please think of me kindly.

Your loving stepmother,

Julia Bridger McBain

Chapter Titles

Paying Homage to Classic Films

Strangers on a Train. 1951. Agnes meets two strangers on her train from Dennisonville, but unlike the strangers' encounter in the classic Alfred Hitchcock thriller, murder does not result.

Guess Who's Coming to Dinner. 1967. Starring the incomparable Spencer Tracy and Katherine Hepburn. In this chapter multiple dinners are involved.

It Happened One Night. 1934. Frank Capra film starring Clark Gable and Claudette Colbert. The first film to win all five major Academy Awards: Best Picture, Director, Actor, Actress, and Screenplay. In this chapter the runaway is not a bride.

Grand Hotel. 1932. Academy Award winner for Best Picture. With all her unexpected visitors, Agnes can echo Dr. Otternschlag's famous line, "*Grand Hotel … always the same. People come, people go. Nothing ever happens,*" when exactly the opposite is true. There is also an "Agnes" in the film.

Random Harvest. 1942. Based on the novel by James Hilton, also author of *Lost Horizon*. Toby, Agnes' brother, is not shell-shocked like "Smithy" (Ronald Colman), but he doesn't really know who he is. There is also a "Margaret" in the film.

The Lost Weekend. 1945. Best Picture. Best Director. Best Actor Ray Milland. None of Agnes' friends or family is an alcoholic, but both Agnes and her roommates experience their own facing of reality during their weekend trips.

And Then There Were None. 1945. Based on Agatha Christie's novel. Perfect title for the transitions taking place in Agnes' life, but no one on a remote island is murdered.

A Song to Remember. 1945. The life of Frédéric Chopin. Songs play a crucial role in this story. As does Chopin's music.

Great Expectations. 1946. If ever there were a character with her own array of "great expectations," it is Agnes Quinn. This is also a nod to the key role the book played in *Trevorode the Defender.*

Shadow of a Doubt. 1943. Another Alfred Hitchcock film. Mysterious Uncle Charlie (Joseph Cotten) arrives and adds some excitement and mystery to his niece "Charlie's" life. While her family remains unaware, she deduces he is a murderer. Kennesaw Fleming is no murderer, but mysterious nonetheless. "Charlie" is a nickname for Charlotte.

Lost Horizon. 1937. Frank Capra. A plane carrying Robert Conway (Ronald Colman) and four other passengers is hijacked and crashes in the Himalayas. They are rescued and escorted to Shangri-La. Another story of the quest for a sense of belonging out there somewhere.

Holiday Inn. 1943. Academy Award for best original song, "White Christmas." Bing Crosby. Fred Astaire. An inn. And musical numbers. Agnes feels as though she's landed in Holiday Inn when she arrives at the Magnolia Arms for Thanksgiving. "How many pianists does one house need?"

I'll Be Seeing You. 1944. Ginger Rogers and Joseph Cotten as wounded souls, each with a secret, who meet each other on a train. They spend a few idyllic days together at Christmas before their painful parting. The song "I'll Be Seeing You" was made famous by this film.

White Christmas. 1954. Bing Crosby and Danny Kaye. Another story about an inn. In this film the problem is there's *no* snow, rather than too much. The song "White Christmas" is featured here, too, also sung by Bing Crosby in *Holiday Inn.*

Stage Door. 1937. Several aspiring actresses living in the same boarding school. Also starring Katherine Hepburn and Ginger Rogers. In this story an actress named Kay has enjoyed initial success, but no roles since. Like Lorna, she dreams of a comeback.

Addendum: Until the author formulated this list with all its particulars, she did not realize there are:

Two films by Alfred Hitchcock: *Strangers on a Train. Shadow of a Doubt.*

Two films by Frank Capra: *It Happened One Night. Lost Horizon.*

Two films starring Ronald Colman: *Random Harvest. Lost Horizon.*

Two films starring Katherine Hepburn: *Guess Who's Coming to Dinner. Stage Door.*

Two films starring Joseph Cotten: *Shadow of a Doubt. I'll be Seeing You.*

Two films starring Ginger Rogers: *I'll Be Seeing You. Stage Door.*

Two films starring Bing Crosby singing White Christmas: *Holiday Inn. White Christmas.*

Two films of stories by James Hilton: *Lost Horizon. Random Harvest.*

Three films made in 1945: *Lost Weekend. And Then There Were None. A Song to Remembe*r.